A
SOFT BREATH
of
WIND

A SOFT BREATH *of* WIND

ROSEANNA M. WHITE

WhiteFire

This is a work of fiction. All characters and events portrayed in this novel are either fictitious or used fictitiously.

A SOFT BREATH OF WIND

Cover design by Roseanna White Designs
Cover images from Shutterstock.com

WhiteFire Publishing
13607 Bedford Rd NE
Cumberland, MD 21502

ISBN: 978-1-939023-45-2 (print)
            978-1-939023-46-9 (digital)

To the ladies of the Mount Hope Christian Center's Refresh book club.
If it weren't for that Skype call we shared
after you guys read A Stray Drop of Blood,
I may not have been inspired to write this.
Thank you a million times over for sharing with me
how God worked in your lives as you read my book.

And to every reader who e-mailed me about Stray Drop, *too.*
This one's for you guys!

one

HER SISTER WAS THE MOST BEAUTIFUL WOMAN IN THE WORLD. Zipporah handed the bridal veil to their mother and then scooted back, out of the way. Anna sat before the polished bronze mirror, smiling as their mother draped the translucent white cloth over her face.

Samuel would be tongue-tied when he spotted his bride, Zipporah was sure. He would look at Anna in that way he did, with his heart in his eyes, that patient love on his face. They would stand together before all of Rome's nobles—Anna, the just-freed slave and Samuel, the adopted-Asinius—and they would be the most beautiful couple ever to pledge their lives to each other.

Ima adjusted the fabric, but her smile grew strained. "Are you certain you are ready, Anna? They will judge you. You must know they will."

"Ima." Anna turned on the wooden stool and gripped their mother's fingers. "Samuel was a slave once too, and now he is a joint-heir with Abigail and Titus's other children. Why should they judge him for marrying me?"

They would not, when they beheld her beauty. How could they? They would whisper, perhaps, but one could not help the whispers.

Still...it sounded so strange to hear Anna call them *Abigail and Titus*, with no "mistress" or "master" before their names. How much stranger would it be if she began calling them Father and Mother, as Samuel did?

Zipporah backed up another step and reached behind her for the cool stone of the wall. Her sliding fingers moved into empty space. The window. She turned and pulled open the lattice just enough to see out without showing the world what lay within. Flowers' perfume teased her nose. The sun streamed down, warm and steady and...so very bright. It seemed brighter than usual.

Perhaps even the heavens would celebrate with Anna and Samuel this day.

Zipporah closed her eyes, drew in a long breath, and sent a prayer for them winging upward. They would be happy. They *must* be happy. Anna had never wanted anything but to be Samuel's wife, and he had never loved anyone but her. *Please, Lord God. Please bless them. Bless their day. Bless their union.*

A laugh brought Zipporah's eyes open again and made her throat close off. The bridegroom was exiting the wedding tent, the sun gleaming off his golden curls and garnering the eye of many a guest. But it was not Samuel, beautiful as any statue of Apollo in Rome, who made her stomach go tight. It was not Samuel who laughed, but the eldest of his younger brothers.

Her fingers knotted through the lattice. Benjamin. She pulled back a bit, behind the shadow of the shutter. If he saw her, he would pretend he did not.

Look the other way. Ignore her very existence, as he had done for months. And it would slice as it always did.

Her fault. She knew it, but what was she to do? She did not mean to look at him so that the whole world knew her heart. She did not mean to make things so awkward every time they were in the same room. She did not mean for anyone to tease *him* because of *her* affections.

They did. She knew they did, though she had never heard the exact words. Well could she imagine them though—the other young men in their late teens or early twenties jabbing an elbow into his side and saying, *Are you ever going to take pity on ugly little Zipporah?*

Samuel glanced her way. He probably hoped for a glimpse of Anna, but no disappointment clouded his features when he spotted Zipporah instead. He grinned at her and kept on walking. Just an hour ago he had drawn her into a hug and said how glad he was to be gaining her as a sister. He had clapped a hand to Mark's shoulder and said how another brother was always welcome.

Zipporah could agree with that. Even as she called herself a fool for wishing he became her brother through *her* marriage someday, not just Anna's.

But Benjamin Visibullis would never want Zipporah. Even were her face as perfect as her sister's...even if her figure someday developed into more than a stick...even were she born free and wealthy like the noble women flocking the villa's grounds today, *still* he would not want her. He was too good to put stock in superficial things. Too good to judge on social station or status. He just...did not like her so well, despite all the dreams they shared of the wide world beyond the villa of Tutelos. Of spreading the good news of salvation to the nations. *He* may go someday, but not with her by his side as she wished every night.

They disappeared around the corner of the house, and Zipporah closed her eyes again. *Father God, please take this desire from me. I beg you. Fill me instead with your Spirit.* A tingle swept up her spine. She had prayed it this morning too, had prayed it every day for months. She was thirteen, nearly the age when a woman was expected to marry and start a family. But she did not want to be promised to some man who would not even want her, who would wish she were her sister instead. She wanted to *go*, to spread her wings and fly the world over. To be like Paul or Timothy or Silas, preaching and teaching and making disciples.

Perhaps if she cut off her hair and wore the dress of a man. She pressed her lips against a giggle. Anna and Ima would be horrified at her even thinking such a thing. Though she could probably pass as a boy. She could stow away on one of Master Titus's ships and...and...

No.

She drew back from the window, pulling the lattice closed with her. The Lord did not often speak so clearly to her. Why he had to now, when she was only daydreaming...but she shoved those stray thoughts down, away, and drew in a long breath. *I will not, Lord. I promise. I only want purpose. I want to serve you. But I would never run away. Just show me how to serve, please. Show me what you have for me. Show me...please, Lord, show me yourself.*

She had prayed those words this morning too, as the brethren were gathered for morning prayers. Her eyes had been squeezed shut, her face tilted upward.

Then her father had put a hand on her shoulder. Perhaps he spoke in his prayer language, words she could not understand—or perhaps her ears had been too filled with the strange, crystalline song to know what he spoke. But she had felt it, that rush of wind the others had spoken of. That lick of fire through her middle.

She had felt the Spirit before when the church gathered, but always as a pressure, a lifting. Like she was just one member on a boat bobbing along on a sea, swelling when the others swelled, dropping when the others dropped.

This, though, had been different. Summer's sun compared to a candle's flame. A whirlwind compared to the gentlest breeze. The force of it had brought her to her knees and, when that had not been enough, down still more until her face pressed against the cool mosaic tiles.

The song had filled her. She had never heard the like, could name no instrument that sounded so sweet, nor could human voice ever raise such glorious strains. It had filled her, consumed her, seemed to lift her up higher the more she pressed herself to the floor. Hands splayed against the tiles, all else had ceased to exist.

But then she had risen, and the world had all come rushing back. It was her sister's wedding day, and too many tasks awaited for her to dwell, to bask in whatever it had been. Even so. The lamps looked brighter. The sun shone as it never had. Her ears perked up, waiting for another wisp of that song.

Her mother smiled into the mirror at Anna's reflection. "There. Perfect."

Perfect. Zipporah smiled too. In another hour, her sister would be Anna Asinius, wife to a man who would love her all his days. Who would look at her with complete adoration, as his little brother would never do to Zipporah. She knew it. Knew it as certainly as she knew the sun would rise the next morning. Benjamin Visibullis would never want her. She knew it.

It just hit harder today than usual.

You are enough for me, Lord. More words she had said before. But never before had the memory of that song still filled her. Never before had her spirit still felt so strong from the breath of his wind. Never before had she meant them so fully.

A knock sounded on the door, and Zipporah scurried to open it. She expected to find Mistress Abigail on the other side, as she had promised to return shortly.

And indeed, there she stood, nearly as beautiful as Anna. Today Rome would remember why Benjamin's father had risked his future to marry Mistress Abigail, though she had been but a slave. Today Rome would remember why, after Jason Visibullis's death, Titus Asinius had fallen in love with her and married her despite his father's ire.

The mistress smiled and reached out to tuck away the curl that was always falling onto Zipporah's cheek.

Zipporah opened the door wider, noting her father was there too, behind their mistress. "I think she is almost ready."

"Good." But Mistress Abigail took Zipporah's arm and pulled her out into the hall rather than stepping into the room. "But before the wedding begins, we need you for a moment, Zipporah."

They needed *her*? Zipporah lifted her brows, aiming the question at her abba. "Does Sarah need something?"

Mistress Abigail laughed. "She has made a mess of herself chasing the younger children around, but that is a hopeless cause. No, little one, we need to talk to you. Come."

Talk to *her*? Though both the mistress and her father smiled, still her pulse kicked up. Never in her thirteen years could she recall a time when she had been summoned for a conversation, unless it were when she had found herself in a bit of trouble thanks to her escapades with the other children. But never alone.

Abba slid an arm around her shoulders. "It is nothing to fear, Zip."

"Indeed." The mistress patted her arm and drew her along, down the hall of family bed chambers and toward a door that led outside. "Your sister's wedding has just reminded us that we have yet to discuss *your* future with you."

"Oh." Her stomach clenched so suddenly, she nearly doubled over. Would they arrange *her* marriage now, to some other slave who would curl his lip at the thought of her? Or assign her a permanent task, like serving Sarah—not that Zipporah would mind that. Sarah was her dearest friend, but...

The mistress's fingers ran a soothing line over her forearm. "You and your siblings are among the few people born slaves here at Tutelos. Many others have accepted our offers of freedom. But your parents did not."

Zipporah glanced at the silver ring in her father's ear, the one he had worn since he was little more than a boy, when he had chosen to serve the Visibullis house for life.

Abba leaned over and pressed a kiss to the top of her head as they stepped out into the sunlight. "Your mother and I both chose to serve, chose to bind ourselves for life to this family we love like our own. Mark has chosen to serve Benjamin all his days. Anna, though...Anna will tread a very different path."

The knots in her stomach eased, though now her throat went tight. This, then, was their intention. They would offer freedom to her today, as they did all their slaves at some point or another. She could choose to bind herself to the Visibullis house with Benjamin as her master, or perhaps to Master Titus's household—separate, though they lived here together on Benjamin's estate. Master Titus had raised Benjamin as his own son but had always preserved the legacy of Master Jason—his friend and the father Benjamin had never known.

Zipporah could choose to be given papers testifying to her freedom but serve here still, in exchange for room and board, as many others had done.

Or she could be *free*. Free to go wherever she willed.

No. The word came clearly again, and behind it, above it, she caught an echo of that song. *You are needed here.*

Needed? Looking over at Mistress Abigail's serene smile, Zipporah forced a swallow down her tight throat. She had never really been needed, not yet. She kept Sarah company, yes, and brushed her hair, helped her straighten her room. She lent a hand in the kitchen or the house when another hand was asked. But *needed*?

Yes, Lord. I want to be needed. I want to serve you wholly, fully. Use me however you wish...wherever you wish.

Movement caught her eye. Or rather, a quickly moving light, like the dance of sunshine on glass. She turned her head to follow it but saw nothing. At least, she did not *think* she saw anything. Just the sun glowing through the water of her eyes.

Was it not?

"Have you put the question to her?"

Zipporah started and faced forward again at the voice, *his* voice. Benjamin had joined them in that moment she looked away, and now he stood closer to her than he had in months. Wearing a strained smile, he still managed to avoid her gaze.

Oh Lord, help me. I beg you, please.

"We were just about to." Mistress Abigail smiled at her son and then transferred it to Zipporah. "You have a choice to make, little one. When we purchase slaves at the urging of the Spirit or to fill a need, we always make it clear we view it as purchasing their freedom. If they do not want to serve here, they may go where they will. If they choose to stay, we welcome them to the flock. Some have chosen to remain slaves, like your parents, and so when children are born to them, we wait until they are of age and then let them decide what they will do."

Of age. Was she of age? Sometimes, when she dreamed of making a life with Benjamin, she felt as old as any of the other young women now wives. Other times...times like these...she wished she could hide behind her ima's skirts like she had done a few short years ago.

"You are younger than your siblings were when the decision was put before them," her father said, his arm still around her. "But with Anna marrying Samuel today, becoming a mistress, it seemed cruel to leave you forced to serve."

She shook her head and refused to let her gaze wander back to Benjamin, even though she wanted to soak up the image of him. "I am never forced to serve, Abba. It is my joy to do my part."

The mistress's fingers twined through hers. "And you are a bit young to be striking out on your own, we know that. But you can have your freedom, Zipporah. Benjamin has the document ready."

Zipporah's eyes would not obey her command not to look, not now when Benjamin pulled out a rolled parchment from his toga. She *had* to look at the document, at the strong hand that held it out. And then she could not help but follow his muscled arm up to his handsome face.

But he did not offer her the charming smile he gave everyone else he met, just that same tight, distant one he always gave her lately. Gone, it seemed, were the days where they could laugh together. Where they could wonder together what lay beyond the walls of Tutelos, beyond Rome, in those lands they read about in the letters from other churches. Gone was their friendship.

She had ruined it by wanting more. And now he would no doubt be relieved if she took that rolled parchment. If she were no longer his in any sense of the word.

Take it. The words slid into her ear, nearly sounding like the Spirit had. But they did not resonate as they should. A chill clawed at her. *Take it and leave. Go see the world. Go. Go and be free.*

Her arm lifted, her fingers reached out. Then a shadow caught her eye. She jerked her head to the right, trying to see what had cast it, but there was nothing that could have. No clouds in the sky to have whispered before the sun. Just a shadow crouching behind her. Like a...like a man. But not.

She eased closer to her father. As alluring as the world sounded, she did not want to see it alone. And had the Lord not just minutes ago told her to stay here, that she was needed? She let her arm drift back to her side and shook her head. "I will stay here. With my family." *With you,* she thought but did not dare to add as she glanced up at her handsome young master.

Benjamin held the scroll out farther, nodded. "Of course. But you can still do that and be free. If you choose to bind yourself to my house, Zip, choose it of your own volition, you will be agreeing to be bound by my authority and my will. Do you understand that?"

Like a wife, promising to obey her husband. Not that they all *did*, but a home would not be at peace if two wills were always clashing—and their home, Tutelos, where so many Christians and Jews sought refuge, needed peace above all. She folded her arms across her middle lest she be tempted to reach out again. "I understand."

For just a moment, old affection paired with challenge in his eyes, as it had used to do. "You will have to give up arguing with me."

"I do not argue with you!" The moment the words escaped, she clamped her lips together, even as their parents laughed.

Benjamin eased a step closer, making him only three steps away. The scroll he held out was inches from her. "Stay. But be free, Zip."

But she did not want to be free, not of him. If all the claim she would ever have on him was that he was her master...and really, what was the point? She shook her head. "I am a girl, Ben. I am under my father's authority even if I take that parchment, and he is under yours."

And she could trust him, just as she trusted her parents and his. She could trust him to make wise decisions that she would not chafe under. Trust him to go where the Lord willed.

Go. Take it and go. Adventure awaits. The world is at your fingertips. Take it and go discover what it has for you.

The shadow seemed to move—no, *did* move. She saw it slide onto her shoulder, and it moved with her when she shrugged. Unease scrabbled its way into fear. What *was* it?

Then a flash, bright and shimmering, and the song leapt through her mind. Gone before she could grasp its words, if there were any. Gone.

As was the shadow.

What had it been? Shadow and light...oily whisper and crystal song. As if... as if...

"Here." Benjamin tapped her arm with the rolled parchment.

He had drawn even closer. Her throat went dry, and all she could manage was a shake of her head.

Benjamin sighed. "Must you always be so stubborn?"

"I am not stubborn." And *now* she found her tongue?

His lips twitched into the beginnings of a smile. "You are arguing with me again."

"Because you will it, Master." From somewhere inside came the strength to grin, as if it were a year ago and she had not yet begun to dream of being more than his slave, his sister's friend. As if they could still tease and talk.

His mother laughed and patted his arm that held the offended document. "It seems she has made her decision, my son. For now, at least. Perhaps we will revisit it in a few years' time, hmm?"

Benjamin sighed again and put the scroll back into the folds of his toga. "Do you think she will be any less stubborn at sixteen or eighteen? Because thus far it has compounded with age."

The mistress winked at her. "It is all a matter of what she has decided is right. Is it not so, little one?"

How could anyone help but smile in the face of Mistress Abigail? "And of what the Lord wants of me."

"*For* you." The challenge rekindled in Benjamin's eyes.

"*Of* me. I am meant to serve him, not be served *by* him." It was what they themselves had taught her, so why did they all stare at her so?

Abba shook his head and urged her back around, toward the villa's door. "Sometimes, my darling girl, I think your faith is greater than any of ours."

She chuckled, though her father did not. "You are being silly, Abba. I only believe what you have taught."

He patted her shoulder as he led her back inside. "Exactly."

Two

"YOU, GIRL. REFRESH MY WINE."

Zipporah paused, though her feet had been aimed toward the tent's exit, and turned toward the deep Roman voice. She was not dressed to serve, not today. The mistress had provided soft linen for her and the rest of her family, not the coarser stuff that would not be ruined by spilled wine or food or the mud of the vineyards, if she were carrying water out to the workers. Today, she was supposed to be merely the sister of the bride.

Apparently, though, she still looked like the servant she had just an hour ago decided to remain.

Anna, her face glowing with joy, put a hand on Zipporah's shoulder and turned her brilliant smile on the guest. "My sister does not serve today, Lord."

"Sister?" The noble's incredulousness came off him in waves. He all but sneered at Zipporah, his gaze sweeping from her uninspiring face down her shapeless figure. "Forgive me, Lady Asinius. She bears little resemblance to you. Though I confess, now that I see *you* I understand young Samuel's determination to wed you."

Zipporah left Anna to accept or parry the flattery and tried to convince herself it was amusing.

A familiar hand touched her back as she slipped out of the tent. Samuel did not try to halt her, just walked with her, looking down at her with that warm understanding he always offered. Though *how* he understood what it felt like to be plain when he had always been the most beautiful man in Rome, she could not fathom.

"Do not let him bother you, little sparrow. He is an oaf."

"He is the fifth person today to be shocked to learn I am the sister of the bride they all agree is as fair as Venus." She shrugged. "I suspect Anna wearies of defending me."

He rubbed a soothing circle on her back. "There is nothing to defend. You may not look like Anna, but you are you, and you are beautiful."

A breath of laughter slipped out. "Just because you are now my brother does not mean you must lie to me."

He smiled, but his gaze drifted back toward the tent, where Anna beckoned for him to rejoin her. "I have no need to lie. All my sisters are beautiful, everyone knows it. *All* of them."

"Samuel." She gave him a friendly shove. He had only two sisters, but she would not argue with him counting her among them. She might have argued more about the obvious falsehood of her sharing their beauty, but now was not the time. "Go back to your bride before she grows irritated with your absence."

"Anna? Irritated?" He grinned and tugged on her braid. "Sarah was running over by the fountain a moment ago. Go find her and play."

She lifted her chin. "I am too old to play."

Laughter danced in his eyes. "And yet I suspect you will suffer it."

A grin stole over her lips. "Only for Sarah's sake."

He took a step toward the tent, but backward, so that he still faced Zipporah. "Tell her to be careful. I would just as soon not have to tend any scrapes or bruises today if she falls."

She waved him on, back into the throng of laughing, gossiping guests. Her own feet she pointed toward the fountain, but she took only a step before she halted again. A zephyr stirred, snatching up the curls that escaped her braid and grabbing at her skirt. A gentle wind like any other, except that with it came another flash of golden light. Her eyes were quick enough to follow it this time. Through the air, across the land, over the road and toward the gate.

A plume of dust signaled a late-arriving guest. That explained why she spotted her father and Master Titus walking that direction. What it did not, *could* not explain was why she saw that streak of light stop and take form. Why she saw a shadow looming, darkening, until it too looked more like a crouching man-beast than some trick of light and cloud.

Her feet were running, though she did not recall giving herself the command. She had to reach Abba and the master before they reached the gate and that...that *thing*.

No, not just a thing. Her soul recognized it the closer she got, the feeling she had often experienced pairing with what her eyes now told her. The enemy. A dark one, a demon. She had felt this sticky unease many a time on the streets of Rome. She had felt it again just an hour ago, when that voice had told her to go away from all she knew. Now panic nipped at her, and she ran all the faster.

"No! Abba!"

He was already all but at the gate, he and the master. And just outside it hunkered that inky black shadow-creature, where a man ought to have sat in the litter. Where a man *did* sit, twisted somehow through the shadow.

Her father turned, as did Master Titus, frowns on both their faces.

Zipporah pumped her legs harder. "Do not let them in!"

She saw their frowns, but only for a moment. Her gaze locked upon the man in the chaise.

Did she know the face? No. At least, she thought not. But she could scarcely even see it. It was as if...as if his face were but a mask, thin as the bridal veil Anna wore. She could see eyes, nose, mouth, chin—but those features, usually solid, shifted. And her eyes pierced straight through to the beast behind it.

Black as night. Ugly as sin. Seething as a tempest.

The creature hissed, spat something she could not hear, and then the mask-lips moved. "Is there a problem, Titus?"

Her feet pounded over the final stretch. "Do not let them in! Lord, hear me! They are the enemy—they are out to destroy us!"

Titus stepped toward her, hands out, palms down. "Zipporah, be calm. What is it? What is the matter?"

She flew a step past him, beside her father, would have gone another step still, but a flash of light came down. Halting, blinking, she followed it up. Up still more into a bare outline of a face that shimmered and gleamed, yet seemed no more substantial than a mote of dust dancing in sunlight.

Remain inside. The warning came as a whisper in her ear, deep as the sea and as echoing as a canyon. Quiet as the gentlest breeze.

Her breath hitched.

"Zipporah?" Abba put his hand on her shoulder, but he did not look toward the shimmer. "What is it?"

She forced her gaze back to the creature. "You cannot let this man inside our walls, Abba. The demon within him is gnashing his teeth, too eager to pass through the gates."

Titus sucked in a gasp. Abba's hand slipped away. "Demon?"

The creature hissed, and the man laughed. "Is this how the slaves all behave here, Titus Asinius? Claiming the land is *theirs*? Daring to speak against your invited guest?"

"Andrew?" Titus spoke in a murmur to her father, but his tone said much. Most of it a question.

Abba's gaze felt heavy on her face. "She has always had good instincts, Lord. And would never dare speak against anyone unless she felt something very powerful."

Felt? Perhaps in the past she had *felt* the peace from the being of light, *felt* the oily shadow of the evil ones. But this was so much more than feeling. Her fingers curled into her palm. "Please, Master. Please. For the sake of the flock."

Silence pulsed, unbroken by anything but the singing of the flaming swords held before the gate and the hiss of the creature behind the man.

The mask snarled. "Titus, this behavior is appalling. If one of my slaves ever acted thus, I would deliver her to the arenas—and if her father defended her, he would find himself a eunuch by night's end."

Titus rested a hand momentarily on her shoulder and then stepped past her, putting himself between her and his guest. He looked about to take another step, beyond the beam of light, but halted. Did he see it? Sense that the protection ended there? "My apologies, Antonius."

The man-mask turned in a smug smile while the creature chortled. "I will not hold it against you—though I expect you will at least make the girl serve me as recompense for her behavior."

The way he looked at her as he said that—Zipporah's stomach churned. She had seen men aplenty look at Anna so, any time they went into Rome. Hence why her sister was seldom allowed outside the villa walls—Mistress Abigail said beauty must be protected.

But Zipporah had never needed that kind of protection, and she knew well it was not the man lusting after her shapeless figure now.

It was the beast inside him, wanting to devour.

"No." Titus held up a hand when Antonius climbed down from the chaise. "I was not apologizing for Zipporah. I was apologizing for having to refuse you entrance after first inviting you. I know it is a slight you will not soon forgive. But I must trust my people."

The black figure lashed, screamed, lifted the man's arms like puppets. Would he come at Master Titus? Would he dare advance to the sentinels?

But they stayed where they were, those columns of light, they did nothing, *nothing* to force the enemy back. How could they just stand there? Why did they not take the offensive?

The shadow-hand reached inside the man's toga, red eyes flashing when the angels' two blades of light crossed in front of him.

She watched Titus's muscles coil, ready to move. But not backward, farther behind the protective guardians, *forward.* "Master, no! Stay within the gates!"

She meant only to grab his arm, pull him back. But somehow, when he moved in response to her plea, she overstepped.

As she passed through the light, the singing filled her. One glorious, frozen eternity of the most beautiful sound she had ever heard.

Then the wind rushed past.

Come back! Hurry!

She heard the cry, but before her feet could obey, the shadow loomed. Pounced.

Her own cry came out a strangled gasp as the man's hand closed around her throat with demon talons. Helpless against the strength so much greater than her own, she could only kick at him. The next moment the world tilted, and the earth struck at her back.

Looking up, she could see those flaming swords above her, over her chest, repulsing man and beast from lunging at her stomach. But it came again, even as her father and Titus leapt at it. The sun's dimmer light caught on the metal slashing toward her face.

She could only close her eyes and whisper, "Jesus."

Samuel Asinius pulled the needle through the last bit of torn flesh, tied the wisp of silk, and snipped it free. Only then did he let himself look away from the ugly gash running from temple to chin and to the eyes of his new little sister.

When they carried her in, interrupting the wedding feast with their shouts and panic, she had been unconscious. A mercy. She had awakened while he stitched her face, and though they had offered her wine and a few herbs to dull the pain, stubborn little Zipporah had refused and just focused her gaze behind them all, on the low ceiling of the chamber she had always shared with Anna.

"There." He smiled and stroked one of the few unmarked pieces of flesh on her face. Poor girl. She was fortunate, so fortunate Father and Andrew had been only a step away. One more slash, better aimed, and she may be in the bosom of Abraham. "All finished, little sparrow."

On the other side of him, Miriam blinked back tears and held fast to her daughter's hand. "Will it scar, do you think?"

Need she ask? He let his breath out slowly and shifted his gaze from the silent girl to her mother, and then over his shoulder to where Anna stood awkwardly in the doorway, her face perfect as her sister's would never be. He dredged up a smile for them all. "Barring a miracle. But the scar will fade over time, and being on the side of her face as it is, I daresay it will scarcely be noticeable. She can cover it easily. And praise Jehovah he missed her eye. You are *certain* you can see clearly?"

Zipporah attempted a smile, though only a hint of it shone through the bruises and dried blood they had yet to scrub completely away. "Quite certain. And the scar is no matter, Ima. I have no beauty to lose anyway."

"Oh, my sweet little bird. You have always been beautiful. And you shall be so still." Miriam raised the girl's hands and kissed her fingers, bathing them with her tears.

Samuel felt movement behind him and shifted instinctively to welcome Anna to his side. How very white her wedding garment looked, how pristine and unmarred in its embroidered splendor. He glanced again at her sister, whose linen tunic was stained scarlet with her own life.

"Anna." Now Zipporah's meager smile faded, and her eyes finally pooled with the tears she had yet to shed over her pain. She reached out her free hand. "I am so sorry. I ruined your day."

With a trickle of laughter, Anna bent to her knees at her sister's side and clasped her fingers. She, too, kissed the girl's knuckles. "Yes, why did you not choose a more convenient time to be attacked?" When she closed her eyes and held Zipporah's hand to her cheek, Samuel's breath caught. He had seen her every day of her life, knew her better than he knew his own mind, but how long would it take to really believe she was his wife?

"I was so afraid," Anna whispered. "When I saw Abba carrying you in, I thought...I thought you had been stolen from us. I could not bear that, Zip. You must be more cautious."

A throat cleared from the hallway, and Samuel looked away from the women knowing well who would be waiting outside. Anyone else would come in, check on their injured friend. Only Benjamin, too aware of Zipporah's infatuation, would stay away to keep from giving her false hope. With a nod to his bride to say he would return directly, Samuel rose and stepped through the doorway even as her brother Mark slid into the room.

Sure enough, Benjamin stood in the shadows of the corridor, his brow furrowed in concern. "How is she?"

"You could go in and see for yourself."

"Sam."

"She would think nothing of it." But Samuel knew, even as he said it, that Benjamin would shake his head.

"Just tell me."

Samuel drew in a long breath and would have reached up to pinch his nose had his hands not still been in dire need of washing from his work upon her face. "The slash is deep. I did my best, but it will scar. Her eyes will be black by morning, she has bruising on her throat but seems to have no trouble breathing or speaking, praise the Lord. She is awake and no doubt in agony, but of course, this is Zipporah."

"Stubborn little thing." Benjamin drew in a deep breath and glanced again at the open door. "Father and Andrew will be here in a moment. Is she well enough for questions?"

"No. But I doubt that would stop her from answering them." Their footsteps sounded from down the hall even now, but Samuel focused instead upon the ones from within. Anna reappeared in the doorway, her expression what he had expected it to be. Sorrow and concern, joy that her sister would survive, a bit of sickness from the sights and smells.

But there was another gleam too, one he hesitated to name as she reached for him but then stopped upon spotting his hands.

As the older men neared, Andrew's pace increased to a near-run. He paused outside long enough to embrace his elder daughter and plant a kiss upon her head and then hurried through the door.

Father hung back, no doubt to give the family inside a morsel of privacy. He loosed a long breath and leaned into the wall. "Is she awake?"

"Yes, but she said nothing of what happened." Though Samuel dare not touch his bride, he eased a step closer to her. "It was Antonius Merillius? Why would he attack her?" He had never particularly liked the wealthy merchant, but he had not thought him the kind to come at a slave girl for no reason.

"She accused him of having a demon."

Anna sucked in a gasp, covering her lips with elegant fingers. "Why would she say such a thing?"

"Because it was true. I have encountered this occasionally over the years— when he came at her, it was not Antonius's expression upon his face." Father clenched his strong jaw, shook his head. "The way she spoke—I must talk with her. Do you think she is well enough, or should I wait until tomorrow?"

"Now, she says." Andrew spoke from the doorway, motioning to the lot of them. "But Miriam wisely counsels us to be quick."

"Wait for me!"

Samuel turned at his mother's voice, reaching out an arm to welcome her to the group. She carried the clean bandages he had sent her for a few minutes earlier. As she was already bloodied from her ministrations, he hesitated not to put his hand upon the small of her back.

The tiny chamber nearly burst with all the people pressed around Zipporah's pallet. It gave Benjamin a legitimate reason to hover in the threshold, to be sure. And Samuel rather hoped the rest of his siblings waited before coming back. Zipporah may be strong and stubborn, but having that many people towering over her...

"How did you know?" Father had crouched down beside her, and his voice was low, solemn. "You came running—it was no coincidence that brought you to the gate. You knew he was coming. How?"

"Did you feel something amiss?" Miriam smoothed the hair from her youngest's brow. "You have always been so sensitive, especially these past years since you began studying the Scriptures."

"Did the Spirit prompt you to come to us?" Andrew this time.

"Let her answer." Mark must have been grinning, given his tone. And the tickling finger he ran over his sister's bare foot.

Samuel marked not her smile, but rather the degree it reached before the pain flared in her eyes when the action pulled upon her wound.

Zipporah cleared her throat. And winced, making him think she began to feel the bruises inflicted there too. "It was not...not a feeling. I..." She paused and accepted the sip of water Miriam offered her. "The wind blew. And I glimpsed the light, so I turned, and...and they were there. The angels, guarding the villa. Stationed around the walls, just as we pray every day they will do. And then I saw the dark one."

"*Saw* it? With your eyes?" Anna's incredulity pulsed through the room, a perfect match to the way she had folded her arm over her chest.

Why had he not washed his hands before stepping out to see Benjamin? Samuel wanted—needed—to touch a hand to her shoulder, to remind her without words that the spirits within them could sense what lay beyond. Lessons she often forgot.

Lessons her little sister must have taken to heart. Samuel eased a bit closer, careful to tuck his soiled hand into the folds of his toga. "What did they look like? Light, you say?"

He had his own images, his own impressions. But an angel...he had never seen one, not clothed in heavenly brilliance. How terrifying it must have been.

She looked upward now, not in recollection, but focused. Focused upon the corner of her chamber. "Light, yes. Shimmering like a mote caught in sunlight. Even more fearsome in demeanor than Master Titus."

A trill of shared laughter released some of the tension. Still, Samuel could sense the doubt too. From Anna, but not only. They all, it seemed, wanted to reserve judgment. He shifted to better see his new sister's mottled face. Did she see them still?

She met his gaze, looking so much older with her bruises and blood. Yet so much the child with the shimmer of uncertainty in her eyes when she glanced at the others in the room. "I...I do not understand why they would not leave the walls to fight off the enemy. Why the protection ends at the gate."

"We have only so much authority on this earth." Father sighed and reached for Mother's hand. "We pray it around ourselves and what is ours, but the evil surrounding us is so great...perhaps the heavenly forces, much like a legion, have to concentrate their efforts. And perhaps they must obey orders just as we do."

The explanation seemed to do little to settle her thoughts, given her knit brow. "I did not mean to step beyond the gate. I only meant to keep you inside, Lord, but I...I am sorry. My carelessness ruined what should have been a day of rejoicing. Will you forgive me, Anna?"

"There is nothing to forgive." Yet behind Anna's words, behind her smile, Samuel saw the weariness. "Who is to say what would have happened had this...*creature* entered Tutelos? You may have saved us all."

A murmur of agreement came from the others. Samuel edged his way around them until he reached the basin of water still waiting. "You have been given a precious gift indeed, little sister. We have been praying that someone among us would receive discernment beyond which we have thus far seen, someone to tell us what spirit is within each stranger who comes to our gates."

"No." Miriam's quick objection brought his gaze up and around and to her frantic eyes. "No, she is only a child. She cannot be burdened so. Perhaps it was only today. Because of how urgent the need."

Perhaps. But the twitch of Zipporah's lip said she hoped her mother was wrong. Samuel at once hoped they were both right. Such a gift—it would change so much at Tutelos, if they all listened to her. Provide such protection.

And yet Miriam was right. What an immense burden for a girl of thirteen.

But Jehovah knew best where to send each portion of his Spirit. Perhaps... perhaps it required the faith of a child to see beyond the veil, to the world the rest of them too often forgot to remember.

"We should let Zipporah rest. Time will tell how this gift rests upon her." Mother sank to the floor beside Father and leaned down to press a gentle kiss to the girl's forehead. "Thank you for your sacrifice for us all today, sweet Zipporah."

Zipporah opened her mouth but emitted only an "I..." before a fit of coughing overtook her.

Her throat—Samuel would pray it was only bruised, that after a few days' rest she would feel the injury no more. Heaven knew she procured enough today that would never go away. "Everyone out." As the closest thing Tutelos had to a physician, Samuel shooed the crowd through the door and heard no arguments. Everyone but Miriam filed back into the hall and to their duties.

There were guests here still, after all. And Father would have to see to the return of Antonius's body to Rome. If Samuel unraveled the jumbled exclamations correctly when they rushed in with Zipporah, the man had turned his blade upon his own stomach when Father and Andrew flung him off the girl.

The girl who once again stared at the corner as if seeing something no one else could. Samuel promised to check on her in the morning, reminded Miriam to fetch him if he was needed in the meantime, and stepped out into the corridor.

Anna waited for him, that weary look in her eyes again. "You invite interruption on your own wedding night. Only you, Samuel Asinius."

He chuckled and pulled her close, bent low so he could capture her lips with his. Heat swept through him. Yes, he prayed no knock would sound upon their door tonight. "Your mother would only come if it were an emergency." He held her tighter still, let his hands run the length of her sides. "I am sorry violence visited us this day."

Anna sighed and pulled away, weaving her fingers through his and tugging him toward the hall that would lead to his chamber. *Their* chamber. "We are all sorry. Do you..." Her feet did not pause, but her tongue did as she looked over her shoulder at him, her perfect face pinched. "Do you really think she saw such things? Perhaps the blow to her head—"

"The blow came after she accused him. No, beloved, I think your sister saw exactly what she said she did."

Her rich, dark locks swayed when she shook her head. "Demons. Angels. I would just as soon focus on the world I can see. And I sincerely hope..." She stopped, let him bump into her, walked her fingers up his chest as she gave him a spiced smile. "...that tonight at least you will do the same."

His lips pulled up. "That, beloved, will not be a problem."

three

BENJAMIN STARED AT NEREUS, CERTAIN HE MUST HAVE MISHEARD his friend. "Pardon?"

"You heard me." To punctuate, Nereus gave him a shove in the shoulder, just hard enough to cross the line from friendly to threatening. "Stay away from my sister."

"I *have* been away from her." Benjamin blinked, unsure when he had even last seen Nereus Rufus's sister. A month ago, perhaps? He sent his gaze out over the vineyards, scarcely seeing the servants checking the grapes. Yes, a month ago. Decima had been at the home of the Aristobulus family when Benjamin had visited Livius. They had spoken at length, it was true. Though why that would earn him such a reaction so many weeks later he could not discern.

He looked back to his seething friend. "My apologies if I overstepped the bounds of our friendship, Nereus. I have spoken with you often about the faith, I did not think you would mind me sharing the same with your sister when she asked." Not that he would have refused to explain the Way to a curious mind, a seeking heart, even if Nereus *had* disapproved.

"The *faith*?" Nereus spun away, his cape swirling in a flash of blue. "As if that were your sole intent in speaking with her."

Benjamin sighed. "You think I...?"

"She has spoken of nothing but 'Benjamin this' and 'Benjamin that' for a month." Nereus faced him again, drawing in a long breath that did little to ease the muscles gone taut in his neck. "We have been friends for nigh unto two decades, you know I harbor no ill will toward you because of these arcane beliefs of yours. But our father would never permit her to marry a Hebrew. Especially one whose mother was once a slave."

A smile teased Benjamin's mouth, though he bit it back. How fortunate, then, that he had no intentions of pursuing Decima, pretty as she may be. "And *my* father would never permit me to wed one who did not share my 'arcane beliefs.' So rest easy, my friend. Your sister is safe from me."

Rather than looking appeased, Nereus pursed his lips.

A cool wind blew the scent of rain past Benjamin's nose. Hopefully the workers would finish getting the harvest in before the storms came. So many families, now, relied on what his land could produce. On the protection offered by his walls. So many called Tutelos home. He looked out over the sprawling fields from his favorite perch atop a knoll and breathed a silent prayer for all those toiling. Once he sent off his friend, he would don his work clothes and join them.

Assuming his friend ever so much as budged. "Is there something else?"

"Have you really not seen her? Not arranged a meeting or—"

"Nereus."

"The way she talked, I thought..." Nereus trailed off with a shake of his head. "And now I have come and insulted you."

A breath of laughter puffed from Benjamin's lips. "I am Hebrew. My mother was a slave before my father married her. These are facts, not insults."

"Still. I—" The way he cleared his throat and shifted from foot to foot brought the grin back to Benjamin's mouth. He need not turn to know who must be trekking his way. Nereus's "Good day, Lady Asinius" only confirmed it.

"I thought I saw you come in, Nereus. How do you fare today?"

"Well. Thank you."

Benjamin welcomed his mother to the knoll with a fresh grin. Given her pink cheeks, she had been out for some time already in the crisp air. "I thought you went into Rome with the girls."

Mother waved that off. "Not with rain on the horizon and the fields ripe for harvest. But I sent Phillip with them. Nereus, will you join us for dinner this evening?"

"I am engaged elsewhere, but thank you." His friend's smile went warm. "I ought to return now, in fact. Will I see you next week as planned, Benjamin?"

"Indeed. Safe travels back into the city, my friend." He reached out to clasp Nereus's wrist and then lifted a hand in farewell as the young man headed back to the horse he had left grazing at the bottom of the knoll.

Mother eased close to his side. "He looked upset when I spotted him. Is something amiss?"

Benjamin chuckled. "Nay. He merely thought me interested in his sister, which did not meet with his approval."

Tucking her hand into the crook of his elbow, Mother sighed and turned them toward the villa. "Given your laugh, I assume this is no disappointment on your part. But I fail to see why anyone would object to—"

"Ima." He covered her hand for a moment, knowing the touch, combined with the name for her he had rarely used since childhood, would reassure. "We all know the prejudice against us, but it bothers me not. Especially since I have no interest in marrying a Roman lady, unless she is a follower of the Way."

His mother arrowed a sharp look up at him. "And have you set your eye upon a young lady from among the brethren?"

The groan refused to be stifled. "I am only twenty. I know I need an heir, but I have many years ahead of me."

"I do not mean to push." Though no one the world over was half so good at it. "But you speak so often of traveling, and with the dangers of such things..."

She wanted him wed, with a babe or two to name heir, before he went anywhere. He knew that. Still, the call of distant lands sang through his veins.

He wanted to see the places their visitors spoke of. Ephesus and Corinth and Angolia and Jerusalem—places where other believers in Christ had unified and started churches. "But what if the wife the Lord has for me is waiting in some other land?"

An argument Samuel had suggested to him just the night before. Benjamin's best bet, his brother had suggested, at convincing their stubborn matron to send him off with a blessing.

Rhetoric she obviously saw straight through, given the arch of her brow. "Promise me another year here, at the least, before you go gallivanting off in search of adventure."

A thrill coursed through him. A year was not so long, especially given the planning he ought to do. The course he ought to set. The correspondents he ought to alert. "You have my word."

Rumbling wagon wheels underscored the thrill. His sisters Ester and Sarah returning from Rome, no doubt, with the ever-vigilant Phillip to guard them—and likely a gaggle of the maidservants too, whomever could be spared. They were always eager to pass an afternoon in the markets.

A year ago, he would have rushed for the crowd of females in search of Zipporah. No one else understood half so well his desire to travel, no one else would rejoice with him so much at this bit of promise. But that gleam still lit her eyes whenever she looked at him, so he would squelch his instinct. Better to avoid her until the infatuation passed and spare her embarrassment.

"Oh, not again."

His mother's tone—a combination of frustration and panic—inspired Benjamin to at least look toward the wagon now halted before the villa. When he saw the bloodied figure Phillip lifted down, he knew not whether to sigh or scream.

Zipporah must have done it again.

Mother ran over the distance between them, Benjamin only a step behind. "What happened?" Her *this time* remained implied.

Phillip had to unclench his jaw before he could answer his mistress. "She was two stalls away when he came at her. I got to her as quickly as I could."

"She does not blame you, Phillip." Zipporah's voice was strong, praise Jehovah, though one eye was swollen shut, her nose had a laceration with smeared blood around it, and red stained her stomach too, around a rip in her tunic. She squirmed, obviously wanting to be put on her feet, but Phillip held her tight.

Benjamin's gaze fastened on the lower wound. "Were you stabbed?"

His mother's breath hissed between her teeth.

Zipporah lowered her head. Perhaps accusation had laced his concern. "A nick is all, Master. I am sorry."

Phillip grunted. "Samuel can be the judge of whether it is only a nick."

"Take her in, please." Mother reached out to touch Zipporah's arm as they passed. "We expect a full explanation, little one. You cannot keep returning bloodied from the markets."

Zipporah turned her face toward Phillip's chest. "I am sorry, Mistress." Gone was the strength in her voice. It wavered now, though Benjamin could not remember when last he saw her cry.

Nor could he remember when last she returned from Rome without some new bruise or scrape, at the least. Certainly not since Anna and Samuel's wedding six months ago.

His mother looked to Ester, the elder of his two little sisters, who in turn looked around in search of something. Or rather, someone. After a few hours away, she would be eager to get her arms back around her small son.

"Ester, did you see what happened?"

"No, I was looking at the most delightful display of toys." She climbed carefully from the wagon, one hand on the growing mound of her second child. "Do you know if Aaron is awake yet? Is he with Zachariah?"

"I have been in the fields, I am not certain."

Sarah hopped down and gripped Mother's arm. "Do not be angry with her, Ima. She did nothing wrong."

"I am not angry." Smiling in proof, their mother smoothed an escaped tendril back under Sarah's head covering. "But this cannot keep happening. We will let her father and Benjamin decide what is to be done."

Him? In moments like these, Benjamin wished Father were master of Tutelos, that he had not been slowly handing over all control these past few years. He hooked an arm around Sarah's shoulders and led her toward the door as three of the vintner's daughters scurried out of the wagon and back toward the smaller outbuildings the field workers called home. "How bad is it?" he asked in a murmur, once their mother had stridden ahead to catch up with Phillip.

Sarah sighed and leaned into him. "I think her nose is broken, but that is the worst of it. Truly, the knife barely touched her."

"This time."

Another sigh. They stepped into the atrium, and Benjamin saw Mother already dashing around, calling for Father and Andrew and Miriam and asking where Samuel could be found.

Sarah gripped Benjamin's hand. "They do not understand how it is for her. I know they want the best for her, I know they fear for her safety, but how is she to remain true to the Spirit and bite her tongue too?"

Benjamin only shook his head and followed the others toward the peristylium. He spotted Samuel and Anna in the courtyard as soon as they entered, half a step apart but with arms still about each other. He bit back a grin and mentally composed a few teases for later.

Upon spotting Phillip and his burden, however, the couple's arms fell away. Anna rushed forward, hand to her mouth. "Zipporah!"

The girl wiggled again, and this time Phillip put her gently on her feet. "I am all right, Anna. Just another attack."

Just another attack. What world did she live in, that she thought that deserved a "just"?

Anna framed her sister's face, tilted it, and touched a hand to the injured side. She must have been satisfied, since her expression moved from concern to irritation. "As always, your timing is impeccable."

Silence pulsed for a moment, then Zipporah whimpered and threw her arms around Anna. "You were telling him! I am so sorry, I am the worst sister in history. I—"

"Enough." The look on Anna's face was comical—utter horror when Zipporah pressed against her, no doubt at the thought of blood transferring to her pristine white stola, and then resignation and amusement following quickly on its heels. She laughed a little as she wrapped her arms around the girl too. "I am no less with child because you interrupted. We can rejoice in an hour as surely as we could now."

With child? Benjamin lifted his brows at Samuel, a corner of his mouth tugging up. His brother grinned like an idiot for half a beat and then stepped forward. A hand on his wife's shoulder and another on Zipporah's was sufficient to ease them apart. "Come sit, little sparrow. Let me see what I can do for you today."

Mother received Anna into an embrace with a happy laugh, but Benjamin, after releasing Sarah to join the crush of femininity, drifted toward Samuel and Zipporah. Deliberately staying behind the couch upon which his brother urged the girl to sit, he waggled his brows at Samuel.

Samuel spared him a half-smile but then focused on Zipporah. He probed at her nose—gently, but enough to earn a wince. "Broken, I think. It is too swollen for me to tell if it is still aligned properly."

"Probably not. A crooked nose to match my scar." Resignation may have saturated the words, her shoulders may have slumped, but Benjamin heard none of the pouting he half expected. She touched the wound on her abdomen. "This is only a scratch, I promise you. You need not stitch it."

The truth? A bid for modesty? Benjamin knew not, but Samuel, after a long look into her eyes and a quick peek at the rip and whatever he could see beyond it, nodded. "Clean it well with wine, make sure no fabric is stuck within the wound. If it grows hot in the next day or two—"

"I will let you know at once so you can smear your acorn paste on it. Thank you, Samuel."

"I did nothing."

"This time."

Samuel chuckled. Perhaps his mood was still soaring from the news of his impending fatherhood, because otherwise Benjamin could not fathom why the man would laugh about Zipporah's continued run-ins with the rabble of Rome.

And given the matching thunder in their fathers' brows when they stormed in a second later, no one else saw cause for amusement either.

"Zipporah."

She rose, head bowed. "Abba. Master Titus."

Andrew went directly to her and tipped up her chin. From where he stood

Benjamin could not see her face, only her father's. And in Andrew's familiar brown eyes he found an increasingly familiar pain, one that compounded each time Zipporah came home injured. "Tell me."

Benjamin slid a few feet forward so he could see them both in profile.

"There was a child." She paused as her mother rushed into the room, swallowed. "A little boy, perhaps seven or eight. He had red hair, freckles across his nose." Her good eye slid shut.

Benjamin tried to swallow, but his mouth had gone dry. A red-haired boy—slave or free? Redheads were prized commodities in slaves. Though he hoped, prayed she went a different direction with her story.

Miriam slid to a halt beside her husband. "A child did this to you?"

"No." A smile flitted over her mouth like sunshine through the clouds, there one second and gone the next. "I turned a second before he came around the corner. He was running, glancing over his shoulder, obviously trying to escape someone. My first thought was that he was a thief—but they...I..." She shook her head and looked down again. "He had such a desperate innocence about him. And the man who came tearing around the corner after him—the boy ran straight toward me, hid behind me."

"You were protecting a child." Andrew drew in a breath and nodded. "From whom? Who chased him?"

"His master." Her words lowered to a whisper. "Were the boy just a slave, the man just a master, I would have said nothing to the darkness in him. But I could hear the creature hissing what they would do to the child when they got him home."

Benjamin's stomach went tight, roiled. He shot a glance at Samuel—whose hands had curled into fists—then at his parents.

Mother stepped away from Anna and Sarah, gripped Father's hand. "And he attacked you for coming between him and the boy?"

Zipporah's gaze sought the ground again. "We...exchanged a few words."

Mother's eyes slid closed. "Zipporah."

"You rebuked him." Andrew shook his head and half-turned away. "A grown man, presumably a citizen, and you in the dress of a slave. He could have killed you, and what could we have done but demand your price from him?"

Zipporah pressed her quivering lips together and curled her hands into her tunic. "What was I to do, Abba? Say nothing and let him take that poor, frightened child home to be abused?"

"And did you stop him?" Though his hands were splayed before him, Andrew's tone said clearly that they were tied. That *all* their hands were tied. "Did your provocation, your injury, achieve anything? Or did he haul the boy off anyway after he had dealt with you?"

She dipped her head still more. "I could not say nothing."

"You *must* say nothing. You must learn, my daughter, that we cannot right every wrong. We cannot save every victim. We cannot defeat every enemy simply because they are there!"

"But how do we defeat *any* if we never try?"

Father stepped forward. He wore, as always, the toga of nobility, but they all knew he still trained every morning like a soldier, and trained all the able-bodied men with him. Proof that one could be ready for battle but still live in peace. "We choose our fights through prayer, little one, and the urging of the Lord. You heard the enemy—but did you hear the Spirit? Did he tell you to speak to this man?"

Bottom lip between her teeth, Zipporah shrugged.

Andrew settled his hands on her shoulders. "And that, Zipporah, is the problem. You have an amazing faith, an amazing gift, but still so much to learn. Until you do, until you have proven you have temperance and wisdom to match your vision...I have no choice. You will not leave the villa, not even to go to market."

How well Benjamin understood the horror that cloaked her face, the agony such a pronouncement would bring. How well he understood her longing to go out and explore, to spread her wings like the sparrow after which she was named. If Father had ever given *him* such a command, it would have felt akin to shackles.

Tears streaking down her cheeks and wetting the dried blood, she fell into her father's chest. "Abba, *no*. Please. I will behave, I will be silent, I will do whatever you tell me."

"I am sorry." Looking nearly as agonized as she, Andrew held her close. "I am sorry, little one. But you are too precious. The pushes and shoves, the scraped knees and bruised arms I could suffer. But this? You invite too much danger, and I cannot bear the thought of losing you. It is for your good. For the good of us all. You must stay within the protection of Tutelos's walls."

For one second, her gaze came up and caught on Benjamin's. He could speak, undo the command. Andrew, strange as it sometimes felt, answered ultimately to him. A few words, and he could give her back what freedom she had chosen. But did he dare interfere in a father's handling of his child?

No hope of rescue, no unwanted interest shone amid the tears in her eyes. Just one soul crying toward another she knew would understand her. Of their own volition, Benjamin's feet moved him a step closer. But by then she had already disentangled herself from her father's arms and run from the room.

She left silence in her wake. It stretched, hummed, and was finally shattered when Samuel huffed out a breath. "Would any of you really have done differently, had you known what she knew? I certainly hope not."

Andrew closed his eyes. "I know how this strikes you, Samuel. Had Master Jason not come along when he did, bought you and saved you, you could have suffered the same fate as this boy. But Zipporah is only a girl. A slave. She has no power against such a man."

Again Benjamin's stomach turned, as it always did when talk turned to how Samuel had come to join their house and eventually become adopted. Though he now bore Father's surname, Samuel would never forget from what he had been saved, even if he had not understood it fully at the time.

Samuel shook his head at Andrew's reasoning. "So we protect her. We teach her. We do not imprison her."

"She is protected here. We can teach her here. And when she has proven herself capable of seeing an enemy without feeling the need to put her life at risk by engaging him, she can roam about freely again." Andrew looked to his wife...and then to Benjamin. "Unless you disagree?"

Benjamin clenched his teeth until the muscle in his jaw jumped. For Zipporah, he wanted to argue, wanted to plant his foot and declare it too cruel. But if it were Ester or Sarah, he never would have argued with their father. He moved his gaze back toward his older brother. "She is his daughter, Samuel. Can you fault him for wanting to keep her safe?"

The turn of Samuel's mouth was more sorrow than smile. "No more than I can fault a person for wanting to keep a songbird in a cage. But it makes me feel no less sorry for the bird." With that, Samuel strode for the exit, pausing only long enough to kiss Anna's cheek and whisper something into her ear. A question, perhaps, because it was with the motion of her head toward the door that he took the last steps through it.

Benjamin sighed and raked a hand over his hair. The dictate would not last long, surely. A few weeks, a month or two at the outside, and Andrew would hand her freedom back to her. And as prisons went, Tutelos was a fine one. She only left the walls rarely anyway.

Still. Part of him wanted to go after her, assure her he understood. He could not, not without giving her the wrong idea, but hopefully Samuel would catch her and let her know she had a champion.

Benjamin moved to Anna's side and pressed a brotherly kiss to the top of her head. "Congratulations, Anna. You and Sam will make excellent parents."

"Thank you." Her eyes followed Samuel's form as he disappeared from sight. "Not exactly how I planned to celebrate, but I suppose I ought to get used to such interruptions. They seem to be my lot."

Given the resigned amusement in her eyes, he chuckled. "Did he go after her?"

"Can Samuel see a hurt creature and *not* seek to soothe?" She shook her head and touched a hand to her stomach. Her gaze went soft. "I cannot wait to see him with his own child. And perhaps, with my sister confined to the villa, we will be able to enjoy those first moments without another emergency calling him away."

Perhaps. But Benjamin would not have placed any stakes on it.

ZIPPORAH FOCUSED ON ANNA'S GLAZED EYES, ON HOLDING THE hand now lying limp in her smaller fingers. "Anna. Anna, look at me."

Instead, her sister's beautiful eyes stared at the nothingness of the middle of her bed chamber. Nothingness, emptiness—no flashing light, no slithering darkness.

So why, *why* was the whole world threatening to unravel? "Anna?"

The midwife, her face streaked with sweat and creased with worry, patted Anna's knee. "Try again, Mistress. Another push, I feel the muscles coiling. You can do it."

But the woman's fearful eyes flitted to Ima and Abigail. Silent words passed between them, words Zipporah knew not yet feared she understood. *Jehovah, where are you? Why are your angels not here, lending their strength? Help my sister, Lord God! Please.*

"Zipporah." Her mother's hands touched her hair, her shoulder. "Go ask them to pray more, more specifically. Tell them the babe will not come. And tell...tell Samuel to get here quickly. Please, daughter. Go, hurry."

No. No, no, no. She did not want to leave Anna's side, did not want to let go the fingers she had held now for so many long hours.

Anna groaned, her muscles contracted. Weakly, far too weakly. Sweat glistened on her brow in the lamplight, slicked the hair usually so lustrous. Her face had gone pale, with smudges of shadow under her eyes.

"Zipporah?"

She set Anna's fingers upon the bed and rose. Her legs were numb. Or perhaps her heart. Something. She could feel nothing in her limbs as she strode and then ran from the room, could feel nothing at all but the painful, fearful beating of her own heart.

Anna could not die. She could not. If she did, the sun would surely fall from the heavens. The stars would cease to shine.

She turned the corner, some remote, barely functioning part of her mind directing her to the peristylium, where surely the families waited in prayer. Only, she made it no farther than that first turn before she ran into the lot of them, kneeling on the floor.

Light shone here. Some days she scarcely saw it anymore, so accustomed had her eyes grown to the flashes and glimmers, to the shadows that flew about. Like cricket songs or a steady breeze, her senses no longer noted the normal, unless she focused upon it. Now she needed it, sought it. Begged it to shed hope upon her.

"Samuel."

He sprang to his feet, face a careful blank slate. "Has she...?"

"No." Zipporah looked past him, to the others. Her abba, her brother Mark, Benjamin and Ester and Sarah. Even the younger Asinius sons, Cleopas and Jason, were here, back from their schooling, praying beside Master Titus and Phillip. The steward, Jacob, knelt with his family too. "The babe will not come. Anna grows so weak. Please, pray strength into her. Pray the babe...pray...just pray he is born quickly."

Samuel's nostrils flared as he took a step toward her. "I am coming with you."

"Yes. Come." She could manage no more words, needed none. Her feet turned her back to where her heart led, Samuel at her side.

Twelve hours ago, the screams had seemed deafening—but oh, how she wished to hear them again now. To hear something, anything that said Anna still fought, still labored.

The moment they entered the room, Samuel halted. Zipporah slid past him, glancing at his face. Hating what she saw. Terrible recognition, the kind that drew tears to his gold-flecked green eyes and a quiver to his lip. After that one beat of hesitation, he flew to his wife's side and sat beside her, taking the hand Zipporah had so recently held and stroking his free fingers along the edge of her face. "Anna, beloved. I am here. Speak to me."

Zipporah eased backward a step. From her place at Anna's side she had seen only the changes in her sister's face, the looks upon the countenances of Ima, Mistress Abigail, and the midwife. From here, she could see the mound of bloodied towels that made her wonder how Anna could yet live with so much of her life upon the floor.

Jehovah God! But she had no other words, could not even form those with her lips.

Anna's head rolled toward Samuel. "Save...baby."

Zipporah squeezed her eyes shut, unwilling to see what agony would cross Samuel's face at that command. How many times these last six months had she and Anna spoken of the coming child? Of Anna's fear that this very thing would happen, that something would go wrong? Of how ceaselessly she prayed that the babe was a boy, an heir for her husband—necessary, because if she were to die, they all knew Samuel would mourn her forever.

"I cannot..." The midwife's frustrated cry brought Zipporah's eyes open again, though she wished she had kept them closed when she saw the woman draw her blood-stained arm from her sister.

"Zip?"

Her gaze flew to Anna, half-sure she had imagined the breath of a word. Her sister's eyes were now focused out the window, on the spot of the wall nearest them, where that ever-present column of light stood sentinel. Did she see him? Zipporah came forward a step. Anna's head lolled back to the middle, their gazes caught.

Recognition, wonder lit Anna's eyes. And something else, something...apologetic. Then it was gone. Just like that, her eyes went from gleaming to empty, her legs sagged.

"No!"

Was the scream hers? Samuel's? Ima's, Abigail's, the midwife's? Zipporah did not know, could hear nothing over the rushing in her ears, could feel nothing but the terrible rending of her heart. She found herself at the bedside without giving her feet a command to take her there. "Anna! Anna!" She fell upon her sister's chest. Still warm. Surely still alive. Surely, surely the earth would have trembled and opened in mourning had she passed from it.

Weeping invaded her hearing, Samuel's arm bumping her as he, too, draped himself over Anna's torso. He murmured what must be a prayer, so desperate were its tones, but the words were neither Greek nor Latin nor Hebrew.

And then they were. He was praying for healing, praying the Lord would give her back. Commanding her to open her eyes and rise.

Yes. Yes, God could do that. They could pray it. Had Christ not raised countless people from the dead? And had he not promised his followers they would perform these signs and more? Anna was not lost. Not yet. They could...they could...

A flurry at the bottom of the bed shattered her thought.

"What are you doing?" Ima, eyes wide, face stricken, stared with horror at the knife the midwife now held.

The woman shook her head, mouth set. "I am sorry. Leave the room if you must, but it is Roman law. She is gone, and I must do anything I can to save the child. I must—"

No! Zipporah's heart screamed it again, her vision blurred. They could not—that woman must not—they could still save her. She could be raised. They could...she could...

A sob choked Zipporah, lifted her. She stumbled up, around the women, her strong-willed feet taking on a mind of their own again. Eyes blurred with the storm of tears, she stumbled her way out of the room. Then her feet gained surety in the familiar halls, flying down them, through them, along them, heedless of who she might have passed. She erupted from the rear door and pounded her way out into the warm night.

There was only one place her body knew to go, one place that offered sanctuary since childhood. The ilex tree that grew at the westward wall, its sprawling branches stretching out over the hedgerow's stones. As a child she had crawled up its trunk, onto the twisted, reaching limbs, and scooted her way over the shoulder-high wall for a forbidden frolic in the stream on the other side.

Perhaps she would do the same now. Climb up, over, drop down on the other side. Escape this place. Run away.

She was in the tree, her feet upon the sturdy branch, hands gripping the one above her, before she noticed the gleaming white arm blocking her way.

A shudder shook her as she followed it to the beautiful, terrible face of the warrior standing sentinel on the stones. He gleamed like the morning, yet she saw the night through him. Saw in his face—was it possible? Did angels feel pain?

The sob that started at Anna's bedside heaved its way out now. "Why did you do nothing? Why did you not save her?"

The warrior shook his alabaster head. *It was not in my power.*

Not in his power? How? How could anything be outside the power of God's warriors? With a wild shake of her head, Zipporah took three more steps along the branch. The stones were directly under her now, freedom only a leap away.

Do not. Look.

She did not want to look, did not want to see the shadows lurking, waiting to pounce. Yet her ears found so easily the soft padding, the near-silent crunch of paws on undergrowth. Her eyes latched at once upon the animal, a deeper shadow in the night. Moonlight caught on its vicious teeth as it snarled. Oily hatred gleamed from its eyes.

A wolf. Terrifying enough in itself—more so given the creature hissing from within.

Zipporah forced a swallow. "What does it matter anymore? Perhaps I should let it devour me."

The warrior said nothing. Perhaps he recognized the childish petulance in her tone as surely as she did, perhaps he saw how firmly rooted to the branch her feet had become. Whatever the cause, the heavenly figure turned to face the night, putting his back to her, his flaming sword no doubt making it clear to the wolf-demon that it would not be permitted to leap upon the wall.

Keening pierced the night, faded and distant, but her heart must have been straining to hear it. Her own cry heaved, her knees went weak, and Zipporah took one step back on the branch and sank down to it. Resting her forehead on her raised knees, she let the tears come and time slip away.

At some point she heard footfalls, fast and heavy, and ragged breathing. Too tired even to fear they would come her way, she sat and listened. They grew nearer, then flew by. Ragged breathing, half-sob, gusted by.

Samuel. She squeezed her eyes shut for a moment. He would run the perimeter of Tutelos, a blur of speed and desperation, as he always did when upset or anxious. But when the guardian shifted a minute later, sword flashing and face toward the gate, she realized he must have left, must be running the road to Rome. Not since his grandmother died five years ago had her brother done such a thing.

"Lord God, protect him, I beg you. Surround him and keep him safe."

She half expected the warrior beside her to fly off. Instead, he paced the wall, chose a new spot twenty feet away. Repositioning—she had seen them do it before when one of their numbers darted away from the walls.

The wolf on the other side of them lowered to the ground.

It was enough. She let her eyes go unfocused, let the night wrap around her. Perhaps she slept for a few minutes now and then, but if so, it never lasted. The pain always hit anew, brought a new twist to her heart, a new cry to her lips.

Anna was gone. Beauty was gone. "My sister." Her voice had gone hoarse through the tears. "Jehovah, why did you take my sister, who everyone loved? Why did you not take me instead, if you needed one of my family in Paradise?"

She heard it before she felt it, the whistle of wind over hills and trees. It brought the dawn with it, the first brush of light in the east, no more than a pearl-gray sheen that made the darkness ease away. And when it reached her, when it whipped the ilex leaves into a frenzy and sent her hair tangling about her, the impression settled in her wrung-out heart.

Her time would come. Jehovah would lift her from this world too, when her service here was complete. Visions of violence filled her mind, all the stories they had heard of the martyred brethren. Men cut in half, crucified, tortured, stoned. She shuddered at a stronger blast of wind. Of course that was what awaited her. Had she not already proven herself a mark for such things? One of these days, there would be no one to rescue her, and the enemy would succeed in sending her home.

She forced a swallow and watched the pearl gray lighten, brighten to a rose. How fortunate no one loved her as they did Anna. She would be missed, be mourned, but not like that. Her passing would send no one running out into the wilderness in uncontrollable grief, would set up no keening that rang through the seven hills of Rome.

"There you are."

Fresh tears surged, but now she had to blink them away, had to swallow them down. Why, why did the Lord have to send proof that no such love existed for her? She rested her forehead on her knees, wrapped her arms around her head. Why would he lead Benjamin here?

But of course Benjamin knew this place already—he had been the one to show it to her when she was a mite.

"Go away." She winced even as she said it. Untraditionally as the family may treat them, she was still but a servant. "Master. I will...I will be in to attend Mistress Sarah soon."

"Do not speak so. You know that is not why I am here."

Did she? How *could* she know why he was here, when he had scarcely exchanged a word with her in over a year? She heard him hoist himself up to the branch beside hers, the one he had always taken. The one he had not touched, so far as she knew, for so very long. He had better things to do these days. People to charm, dreams to chase. No time to climb into the ilex as he had so often in the past, to walk that branch until he could drop down on the wall to—

"No! Master, do not sit there." She lurched forward, hand flying out as if to snatch him back, even as the wolf sprang to its feet and snarled.

Benjamin froze, feet upon the wall, and looked over his shoulder at the scrawny beast. "It cannot jump this high."

"Perhaps not under its power alone. But that one hosts a demon." And the master of Tutelos, the protector of every Christian for a hundred miles, was no doubt too tempting a target for it to pass up.

He hesitated so long, she wondered if he disbelieved her. If, because she had given up speaking of it except when she *must*, he thought the gift had left her. But then he stepped back onto his branch and settled across from her. "Your mother needs you. You must return soon."

Zipporah nodded. Her ima would indeed need the comfort of a daughter's arms around her as she mourned Anna. And Zipporah's soul longed for the comfort of an embrace too. Soon. She darted a glance at Benjamin. "The baby?"

His silence spoke before his lips did. "Stillborn. They did all they could. Samuel—" He broke off, shook his head, but Zipporah needed not his words to tell her that her brother would have used every lesson he had ever learned at the hand of the physicians to try to revive his wife and babe.

She turned her face away. All Anna had wanted was to deliver her husband an heir. She would have given herself freely, gladly for the sake of her babe. But to give her life, only for the child to go with her to the bosom of Abraham?

Why, God? Why? Zipporah drew in a shuddering breath when no answer came. "Did you see Samuel before he ran?"

"Briefly." Weariness mingled with grief in his voice. "He will not recover easily from this."

Of course he would not. How could he, how could anyone? Surely all the world would mourn their beautiful Anna. "Has he returned?"

"No. I daresay he will not until evening."

She nodded against her knee, turned her face his way. And almost wished she had not. He sat on the branch easily, comfortably, dawn washing him in the palest gold as he looked beyond the wall. Her heart squeezed as she took in his strong jaw, his darkest hair, the planes and angles that equaled masculine perfection. How could she not wish that he would love her as his brother did her sister? Even half as much—a quarter. Just a sliver of such affection from him would sustain her through the decades.

Or however long she had left to serve him and the Way.

"Do you always see them?"

She had to follow his gaze to the pacing wolf to realize what he meant. A sigh gusted forth. She ought to be glad, she supposed, he was asking her *something*. Showing an interest at all. Sometimes she wondered if the congregation even believed her. "I suppose. Though I hardly notice them most of the time."

Now he looked at her, his eyes incredulous. "How can that be?"

The breath of laughter felt mournful on her lips. "They are just *there*. Like the villa in the distance that I could never make out but you always could. You do not think of it often, do you? Unless there is a reason to. Unless you focus on it. You know it is there, we all know you can see farther than the rest of us, but..." She shrugged. "It simply does not matter until it does."

Benjamin hummed, studied her for another moment, and then looked toward the brightening horizon. "Sometimes...I was here when the baptism of fire and the Spirit first came upon Mother and Father, you know. Just a babe in her arms, but I think—maybe that is why the faith has always been so important to me, even through the uncertainty of growing up. Perhaps it lit something in me that day."

Lit something to make him shine, make him so very *good* that she could not help but love him. "It makes sense." She looked to the horizon too and wondered what he could see in the distance that she could not. What he *would* see when he struck out to visit the other churches in five short months, that she never would. "Mark has spoken of nothing but the coming travels. I keep threatening him that I will cut off all my hair and don the clothes of a boy and come with him."

A foolish thing to say, probably, given that they all knew it was the *him* before her now she would be following, not her older brother.

But Benjamin only grinned, for once, and made no move to jump down and leave as he usually did. "I would not put it past you." He met her gaze again, his smile fading. "I am sorry you have been trapped here at the villa. I know I could have overruled him, but I did not want to interfere in family matters. And I thought surely your father would have relented by now."

Had he? "I wonder if he ever will. Especially...now. Anna is gone. Mark will be leaving with you." She shook her head.

"He will. Comforting as these walls are, we cannot stay within them forever. The good news will never spread if we huddle together in safety."

And so he would go, taking Mark with him. Anna was—Sarah would no doubt marry soon...and here Zipporah would stay. She reached for a twig growing on the side of the branch, toyed with its green leaf. Was that all life was? A series of farewells?

Her chest went tight. She had already bid farewell to Benjamin, it seemed, even though he had never been more than a few miles from her. So foolish, in the face of a loss that could never be undone. She could not get her sister back, not until she too crossed the great divide. But why had she pushed away her friend with this love she knew he would never requite?

The first rays of the sun peeked over the horizon, shooting crimson and purple into the sky. Another day, when it felt the sun should have stopped spinning about the earth. New light in a world that felt so dark. Her eyes moved to the wall, sought and found each of the shimmering columns. Her fingers curled around the leaf, cupping it, hiding it.

If she could learn to live with this vision, learn not to respond to every flash of light and every wisp of darkness, if she could somehow master her tongue as her father demanded, then surely she could master this too, this unrequested affection. She could secret it away, like a leaf in a palm.

A deep breath, a silent prayer for strength, and she looked over at Benjamin again. "Master?"

Just like that, wariness entered his gaze again, as if he knew what thoughts she tried to shove away.

Zipporah swallowed. "You need not avoid me anymore. I know that you... that is, I do not—we all go through such phases as we grow." The lucky ones, like Anna and Samuel, never left them, never had to. But her? She forced a smile. "You ought to know, having made a complete fool of yourself with Leah not so many years ago. But I assure you, Master, it has passed."

Would he shake his head and jump down, walk away? Call her on her lie? Nay, praise be to Jehovah. He laughed and, miraculously, transferred himself to her branch. Sat close and even bumped his shoulder into hers, as if they were both still children. "I only meant to spare you embarrassment—a kindness our steward's granddaughter certainly did not show me as a boy of fifteen."

Because he expected it, she grinned. Because the grin felt so wrong right now, she let it fade quickly. "I know. And I appreciate that." *Lord, forgive the falsehoods.* "But it is necessary no longer."

He nodded and sighed. "Good. I have missed your friendship, Zipporah. No one else ever understands my yearning to see the world as you do. You have always been like another sister to me."

Sister. The word bludgeoned her like a club, seeming to hit her heart from two directions at once—that he thought of her as one, but more...*Anna.* A sob rose, and try as she might, she could not push it down again.

Benjamin sucked in a quick breath. "What a fool I am. I am so sorry, Zip, I ought to be knocked upside the head for speaking so thoughtlessly. Come here." As he had when she was a girl, as she had dreamed these eighteen months he would do again, he wrapped his arms around her and pulled her to his side. Rested his head atop hers. "I am sorry. So sorry. We will all miss her."

"I know." How could an embrace at once warm her and make her cold with hopelessness? She held tight to the leaf that had pulled off in her hand. It was dead now, though it would not look it yet. Separated from the stem, from the tree. It would shrivel and dry up and turn to earth.

She had to wonder how long until she did the same.

Four years later

JERUSALEM GLEAMED GOLD AND ALABASTER IN THE EVENING SUN. Samuel paused at the corner they had been told to turn at, but he was in no hurry to reach their inn. Perhaps he ought to be, after the trek from Joppa, but echoes strummed through his memory, luring him onward.

"Familiar?" Benjamin paused at his side, a grin on his mouth.

Though he shrugged, Samuel smiled too. "It has been too long. Everything looks familiar, and nothing does. I was only six when I left. And yet...and yet I feel like if I turn quickly enough, I will catch a glimpse of your father striding toward us. Or some other face long since faded."

Mark, a step behind Benjamin, turned in a circle. "Our parents have spoken of the city so much, I feel I *should* know it."

Benjamin chuckled. "My feelings exactly."

And Samuel was glad to be here, he was. He drew in a breath of warm, dry air...and wondered why he felt the need to convince himself. All the other places they had gone, with only one short trip to Rome between, had spurred him ever onward. Strange how looking out over the city of his birth made him realize how ready he was to go *home*. For good.

"Here." Mark reached for the bags slung over their shoulders. "Go explore the markets as I see you want to do. I will make certain our rooms are ready."

"Thank you." Samuel handed his friend the bag as Benjamin did, and then watched him stride down the street. He was the only one of their trio dressed in traditional Hebrew fashion, so he received no undue notice as he went.

Samuel, however, felt wary eyes on him and Benjamin as they headed onward toward the din of the markets. "Perhaps we should have exchanged toga for mantle."

Benjamin snorted a laugh. "As if it would have mattered. We have Roman hair, a Roman accent, apparently. And if we are to believe Phoebe, we carry ourselves like Roman soldiers."

"Father's fault. When we go home, we should lay the blame squarely at his feet." But Samuel smiled, even if the citizens of Jewry *did* go to the other side of the street to avoid them.

"Are you ready?"

His brother's voice came softly, gently, making it clear he spoke not of the markets but of Rome. For after their two weeks in Jerusalem to celebrate Passover and visit briefly with the brethren here, they would walk back to Joppa and sail for home.

Samuel sucked in a slow breath. Her image no longer battered him every time he closed his eyes. He could think her name without the agony and guilt. Somewhere over the years, through the travels, his purpose in coming had been met.

He had not forgotten—but he had continued. Life, as Mother had promised him it would when she all but ordered him to travel with Benjamin, had gone on. Sometimes he marveled that it could, but other times he looked up at the heavens and felt that whisper of peace.

The Lord had taken Anna home. The Lord had left Samuel here. His part was to find the purpose in that.

"Yes," he said in answer to his brother. "I am ready. I miss everyone, and I want to make it home in time for Jason's wedding. Although..." He angled a grin at Benjamin. "*You* have yet to find a wife, so perhaps we ought to prolong our travels until you do."

With a groan, Benjamin headed for a stall that looked to offer novelties. He usually picked up the most bizarre item he could find for Jason and Cleopas. Then Benjamin would send them home with a letter exaggerating the item's history so greatly that their younger brothers no doubt roared with laughter. "I can hear Mother now. 'You have visited nearly every Christian home the world over—do you honestly mean to tell me that nowhere in the world could you find a worthy bride?'"

His high-pitched imitation of their mother brought another tickle of laughter to Samuel's throat. "And yet she, who defied the world and married Father for love, will understand why you wait for the same."

Lopsided grin in place, Benjamin touched a finger to a pendant hanging from a rod, sending it swaying. "She can chide me as much as she pleases, if it means we will be home again. For all my longing to *go*, I never thought I would be so anxious to return."

"Mm." Samuel leaned into the stall, trying to ignore the hungry way the proprietor eyed their clothing. *Rich Roman dogs*, he would think, and was no doubt devising ways even now to unburden them of some of their coin. Samuel's gaze wandered over the offerings and settled on a pointy white object with a black leather band going through it. He tapped it with a finger. "What is this, my friend?"

The man smiled, revealing yellowed teeth, and picked up the necklace. "Shark's tooth, Lord. From the Mediterranean, rare indeed. This is from the greatest of the beasts."

"Rare, is it? Strange, then, that I have seen them in every port at which we have stopped." None so big, though—hence his question.

"And if you prepare to travel back to Rome, Lord, you ought to have it. A... talisman, let us say, to protect you against the rages of Neptune."

Samuel turned a cynical gaze on the vendor. "And why do you assume I serve the Roman gods? I am as Jewish as you. And Jehovah cares nothing for talismans." But still he picked up the necklace. "I will give you a lepton."

The man looked affronted. "You will give me a drachma."

"Ha! An entire day's wages for the tooth of an old fish? Try again."

Benjamin shook his head. "Why are you even inquiring? Neither Jason nor Cleopas would wear that."

"True enough." Though they had not been who he had in mind for the gift, he had learned how to haggle at the hands of Mother, a true master. He put the necklace down.

The vendor's eyes widened. "An assarius!"

"A dilepton."

The man sighed. "I paid more than that for it. I must have at least two dileptons for it or my children will go hungry."

Looking at the man's paunch, Samuel sincerely doubted that. But it was a fair price. He drew out two of the small bronze coins from his change purse and dropped them into the man's hand. Then picked up his prize.

And found Benjamin staring at him with incredulity. "Why in the world did you buy that?"

"For Zipporah." He held it up, marveling again at the size of the thing. Though he would do well not to think too much of the shark it must have come from before sailing for home. "In a pinch, she can use it to fend off the wild dogs and vagabonds."

At that, Benjamin laughed again. "You would do better to get her a dagger, brother. Or have that armor made for her."

His lips twitched. He had threatened as much when they were last home and he saw the new scars she had collected in his two-year absence. Apparently even keeping her confined to the villa did not equal safety for his wife's sister, though she swore the lot of them were from harmless-enough scrapes with animals...and the occasional tussle at the gate. "You really think she ought to carry around a blade for someone to turn on her?"

Benjamin winced and sidled to the next stall. "You do have a point. She should have trained at our sides under Father." He ran a finger along a necklace of Egyptian beads that looked much like one their mother frequently wore—the first gift Benjamin's father had given her.

Samuel could hardly resist a tease. "Will you get the beads for her, Ben, instead? I can imagine no greater protection than your promise."

As expected, his brother's answer was a playful shove.

Samuel laughed. "Come now. You found no wife elsewhere. Perhaps because love awaits you at home."

"Do not make such jests. Besides, she long ago put aside her infatuation."

Not from what Samuel had seen on their visit home. True, it had been another two years since then...but if the first two had not been sufficient to remove Benjamin from her heart, why ought Samuel assume these last had been?

But she had greatly improved in her ability to hide her feelings. A necessity, but it kindled sorrow in his chest. That she needed to...and that she had walls enough inside to accomplish it. "One never knows what might happen when we go home, though, hmm?"

Benjamin rolled his eyes. "She is eighteen. Andrew has surely betrothed her to someone by now."

"You think their letters would not have mentioned that?"

"Sam." Benjamin turned toward another section of the market. "She has always been a sister to me. I could never..." Trailing off, he frowned.

"What?" Samuel turned, though he could see nothing to warrant his brother's attention. The only stalls before them offered baskets and wool. "You have fallen in love with a bolt of fabric?"

Benjamin slapped his arm this time. "No, you blockhead. That vendor there behind the cloth, the young man. Does he not look familiar to you?"

"Should he?" Samuel looked the fellow over, but nothing stirred. The boy could be no more than eighteen or nineteen, with a head of fair curls that, he granted, stood out against the dark hair of all those around him.

"Blockhead," Benjamin said again with a grin. "He is the very image of you. Or how you looked ten years ago, anyway."

"Nonsense." And yet he looked again. Tried to compare the boy to the reflection he occasionally glimpsed in Mother's mirror. "Does he?"

"The very image. Could he be a relative? Have you cousins?"

Had he? Samuel could only shake his head. That world—the one where he had relatives by blood—he had long ago forsaken, when it first forsook him. "I cannot remember. Perhaps...I think I...I have some vague memory of an uncle. Or maybe of mention of him." He cared to probe no deeper. Trying to remember faces or words would only bring to mind that year he refused to consider. The one after his father had died, when his mother had struggled to keep food on the table. Failing eventually, which was when she took to the streets.

Not to sell herself though—nay, to sell *him*.

No, best not to dwell on those days.

Benjamin strode in the boy's direction. Samuel leapt after him, grabbed him by the arm. "What are you doing?"

His brother looked at him as though he had gone mad. "I am going to talk to him. Introduce ourselves. He could be a relation—would that not be a blessing?"

Would it? "I have what family I need. Let us leave it at that and go to the inn."

Benjamin's gaze probed. "Sam. You said you had forgiven her."

And he thought he had. But it was easy to say when he was across the sea from all thoughts of the woman who had birthed him, who had betrayed him. When faced with the possibility of someone who might know her, though... Samuel closed his eyes and drew in a breath that did little to steady him. Perhaps he had *not* forgiven, not really. Perhaps he had merely pushed it aside all these years, buried it under the love for Abigail, whom he deemed his true mother, for Titus his father, for the collection of siblings with which they had blessed him.

Perhaps this was the Lord's way of shining a light upon a dark sliver of his soul, so that it might finally be washed clean. A splinter finally removed after decades of festering. Perhaps that was why the Spirit had led them to Jerusalem for this Passover. "All right. Let us ask him."

Nodding his approval, Benjamin smiled and led the way. Samuel could only wish for the confidence evident in his brother's stride and whisper a prayer with each step.

All too soon, they stopped before the booth. Fine wool lined it, some beautifully dyed, other bolts of pure white. Baskets of yarn sat upon the table, raw wool behind the vendor, woven lengths in the bolts, some thick and warm, others thin and smooth. The young man did not even look up from the scroll he was reading, not until Benjamin cleared his throat.

Then look up he did, revealing a set of smoky green eyes that flickered more with irritation than a desire to please, irritation that deepened to near contempt upon spotting Benjamin's toga. "Do you need something, Roman?"

Samuel nearly turned. If this *was* a relative, did he really need an acquaintance with him?

Then the young man's eyes drifted to him, widened. He rose to his feet, his scroll falling to the ground. "What...who...who are you?"

Samuel's lips forgot how to form words.

His brother did not. "You see it too then. A marked resemblance between you." Benjamin motioned between Samuel and the stranger. "When I noted it, we had to come introduce ourselves and see if perhaps there is some relation."

The boy still stared. "You are the image of my father. Though he was no Roman."

"Nor am I by birth. I was born in this very city." A fact which Rome would have held against him, had he not been adopted by Father. A fact which, in turn, Jewry would never forgive. But he had long ago resigned himself to that. "Did your father perchance have a brother?"

"Yes, but my uncle had no sons. Perhaps a cousin though." Curiosity displaced the contempt in the boy's eyes, and he went so far as to smile. "Come, my mother will know."

Exchanging a glance with Benjamin, Samuel hesitated only a moment before stepping around the booth and following the young man to a doorway farther along the alley. Through it he glimpsed more of the wool, and a brilliant tapestry in scarlet and blue.

"Mother!" the boy called as they entered. "I have a guest for you to meet." He turned once inside the room, grinning now. "I am Jonathan Bar-Jonah."

Jonah—was that his uncle's name? It had been too long. Samuel could not even recall his own parents' names. They had been simply Abba and Ima, his whole world. But he summoned up a smile. "It is good to make your acquaintance, Jonathan. I am—"

"Samuel!" The shattering of pottery punctuated his name, coming from the far side of the room.

Every fiber of his being froze. He may not know her name, but the voice plucked at strings of memory. And her face, as she stood there staring at him aghast, brought a torrent of them pouring down.

He may not know her name, but he knew her. His fingers curled into his palm.

The woman reached out a hand into the chasm of empty space between them, a combination of horror and longing on her face that would have struck him as beautiful had it been upon anyone else's. "Samuel. It is I. Do you not know me?"

Benjamin shifted closer. "Sam?"

He forced a swallow, deliberately relaxed his hand, and otherwise prayed that he could imitate Father's Stoic facade, though he had rarely had cause to try it. "I know you."

But he did not remember her name—and would *not* call her Mother.

"Mother?" Confusion laced Jonathan's tone. "Who is this man? Is he a relation?"

The woman came a step forward, haltingly. "He is...he is my firstborn son."

"*What?*" The boy sounded nowhere near pleased at being presented with a brother. He stepped away from Samuel, the thunder in his brow aimed solely at the woman. "You had no son by my uncle—it is why my father married you!"

Her face shifted, but not in a way that kindled sympathy. From horror and longing it flicked to irritation with her son. The one she had chosen to keep.

The dry laugh that came from Samuel's throat felt foreign. "I daresay she could hardly admit to the man come to redeem her that she had sold his brother's son to the first Roman who happened by."

"Samuel." Benjamin shifted closer still. Warning saturated his tone. Not, Samuel was sure, because his brother feared the response of these people.

Nay, his brother would warn him because he would sense the darkness creeping over Samuel's spirit.

His eyes slid shut. *Abba Jehovah, forgive me. Help me. Help me to forgive her, for I cannot do it on my own.*

Jonathan had hissed something at his mother, though Samuel caught not what. She slid a bit closer as Samuel opened his eyes again, wariness lighting hers. "Please, my son. I was desperate. You would have starved had I kept you."

"There are fates worse than death." And how was she to know that he had been spared them, that Jason Visibullis was a man of honorable intentions instead of perverse ones?

"There is nothing worse than death. And here you stand, tall and so very handsome, living proof that in my desperation I saved your life." She tried a smile, splayed her hands. "Returned to me, as I always prayed you would do."

Really? She expected Samuel to believe that, while married to the uncle who wed her to give his brother a son, she would have welcomed his return?

More likely she would have denied him entirely, were they not speaking of this second husband in the past tense.

But that thought, too, rang with bitterness. Samuel drew in a deep breath and struggled to push it aside.

"You sold your son to a *Roman*." Jonathan spat upon the floor. Then spun on them, his gaze piercing, not Samuel, but Benjamin. "And who are you, then? His master?"

Benjamin snorted a laugh. "He has no master."

The woman had edged closer still—now only ten feet separated them, little enough that Samuel had to quell the urge to increase the distance. She, too, looked at Benjamin for a long moment, then back to Samuel. "Then he must be your...your lover?"

"*That* is your first thought?" He could not look at his brother—Benjamin would be holding back another laugh, which did not begin to fit Samuel's mood. He passed a hand over his hair. "Of course that is your first thought. You thought you were selling me as a catamite, and what boy ever really escapes such a lifestyle? No, woman. Despite your best efforts, I received no such abuse when I left your house. This is the son of the man to whom you sold me."

"Benjamin Visibullis." Yes, a smile lit his brother's voice. "My abba was Jason Visibullis. He would have adopted Samuel had he not been killed in the uprising led by Barabbas twenty-five years ago. But my mother called him son despite her husband's death, and when she remarried, her new husband *did* adopt him, and raised us both as sons along with the children they had together."

Samuel turned to Jonathan and held out a hand to clasp. On his finger was the ring Jason had, in his last moments, instructed Father to give him. But this other brother of his could not know that. "Samuel Asinius."

Apparently Benjamin deemed the name not enough. "Joint-heir to one of the most affluent businessmen in all the empire, as well as all said businessman inherited from his father, who was a consul. His own master, to be sure."

Jonathan, expression stunned, clasped his wrist briefly. "I...welcome you to my home. Brother."

"Then it all turned out." The woman reached out again, though she apparently thought better of it and quickly tucked her hand back against her middle. Her attempt at a smile wavered. "You lived a good life. You were safe and happy. All I prayed for."

A whisper moved through him. About that much, she was right. Samuel had lived a better life than she could have given. A life of love and provision. He had trod the path the Lord had mapped out for him, not just despite her decisions, but because of them. Perhaps for that he owed her thanks.

All he could manage just now was a question. "What is your name?"

Was that pain that flitted over her face, or frustration? "You do not...? It has been a long time, I suppose, and you never had cause to call me by it as a child. I am Martha."

Samuel nodded and looked back to her son. "I thank you both for speaking with me and answering our questions. But the hour grows late." And escape beckoned.

"No!" She nearly leapt at him. Perhaps she knew Samuel's mind, that he intended to walk away and avoid this part of the city for the rest of his stay. "Please, my son. Stay, dine with us."

He wanted to turn and run. Instead, he merely shook his head. "We are expected."

She reached out, with both hands this time, and she did not pull them back in. "But I want to know of your life. Where you live now, if you have a family of your own."

"I live just outside Rome at the Visibullis villa, called Tutelos. My wife and son both died in childbirth. We are only in Jerusalem for Passover." Samuel shot a glance to Benjamin, a silent plea for help.

His brother, eyes narrowed, was looking beyond Martha to the curtain-covered exit of the room. No help there.

Samuel shook his head. "I am sorry. We really must be going."

"Would you return?" Had it been Martha's question, he would have answered with an unequivocal *no*. But it was Jonathan who asked, genuine desire in his jade eyes. "Please, brother."

Brother. Samuel had three of them by adoption, another by marriage. Two with him in Jerusalem even now, and missives from the others no doubt awaiting him at the inn. He had a father, a mother, sisters back in Rome. Family enough to keep anyone.

But this man-child before him had, it seemed, only Martha. And something inside Samuel insisted that a woman who would sell one son when times got rough had not been the most loving of mothers to her next one. Perhaps he was wrong, and she had poured affection upon Jonathan to make up for past failings.

Samuel found that unlikely though. Anyone who put herself above a child as young as he had been, anyone who loved herself so much more than her son, would not likely change. Not unless the Father called her to repentance.

So for Jonathan, Samuel drew in another breath and nodded. "Tomorrow."

May the Lord give him the strength to survive it.

Six

BENJAMIN SHIFTED, HALF HIS ATTENTION ON THE CONVERSATION... and half on the curtain. The fluttering had drawn his eye, but what he glimpsed beyond it kept him riveted. Or rather, who.

A girl, without question. When she darted away, he caught the outline of curves and long golden curls. Golden curls far too like Samuel's and Jonathan's for Benjamin to come to any other conclusion—another sibling for his brother. She was obviously listening, so why did she not come out?

"For the evening meal, then," their young host was saying. "Your...brother is welcome too, of course."

Benjamin dragged his gaze from the now-still curtain and summoned up a smile for Jonathan. "I thank you."

Samuel nodded. "We have another companion traveling with us as well, my late wife's brother."

"He is also welcome."

Martha frowned, though not, it seemed, over the invitation. "Your wife. Was she...Roman?"

"Hebrew. Though," he added, shoulders back and face unpassable, "by mere coincidence. Her heritage would not have mattered to me so long as she shared my faith."

Benjamin pressed his lips together against a smile Samuel would not appreciate. His brother, the gentlest, most sensitive soul he knew, had never in all his memory looked so set on *not* winning the approval of someone. Benjamin cleared his throat. "Her name was Anna, and she was hailed as the greatest beauty in Italy. Minstrels sang songs of her."

Samuel shot him a glare. "My brother exaggerates. Not her beauty, but her fame."

Benjamin's grin sneaked out. "The minstrel may have been our youngest brother, and his songs may have been laughable, but it is still fact."

Mention of Cleopas brought a softening to Samuel's green-gold eyes. "I suppose it is, at that. Though her beauty was as incidental as her heritage—it never mattered to me."

Martha clasped her hands together. "I would have liked to meet her."

Benjamin nearly snorted. Anna—whose last words had been a command to save her child no matter the cost to herself—would not have wanted to meet *her,* this woman who had traded her firstborn for her own comfort.

"We must go." To prove it, Samuel pivoted toward the exit, sparing only a nod for Jonathan.

Benjamin followed with one last glance toward the curtain. Back through the door into the sunshine slanting down and burnishing the city, past the stall, down the street. "Sam?"

His brother slowed but did not halt. "Not yet, Ben. I know not how I am or what I feel. I must let it all settle."

"Of course." Benjamin could not even imagine how his brother's thoughts must be churning right now. Sidestepping a pack of children playing with marbles at the corner, he looked over his shoulder at the innocuous booth of wool.

And froze. "Samuel. Wait."

She held him captive, just by standing there in the doorway he had passed through moments ago. Perhaps, having grown up with Anna and his own renowned sisters and mother, beauty ought not to have fazed him. But their faces he had seen every day. The woman who watched him now—her image struck him, rendered him immobile.

Perhaps in part because of her familiarity. He knew those fair golden curls, yes, and some of the features. Without question, she was a relative of Samuel's as surely as Jonathan was. But where beauty took masculine form in the men, it was purely feminine in her. Her face was perfection, the kind that sculptors in Rome would use as a model for Venus. Delicately arched brows, defined cheekbones, chiseled lips. Graceful neck, sloped shoulders, her belted tunic showing slender curves.

He had never in his life seen a woman so lovely.

Samuel drew even with him again, glanced where he stared, shrugged. "Perhaps tomorrow they will introduce us. I daresay they were still too hesitant—and surprised—to want to call forth the daughter of the house to meet two strangers."

Strangers. Yes, but not for long. Surely tomorrow Benjamin would learn the name that went with the face. Perhaps he would get to speak with her.

"Ben—really?" No amusement colored his brother's tone, which managed to steal Benjamin's attention. He looked over and found Samuel shaking his head. "Now of all times you decide to be rendered stupid by a pretty face?"

"Sorry." He turned back toward their destination. "Though you must grant it is an *exceptionally* pretty face."

Samuel pinched the bridge of his nose. "I need to think. To pray. If you have had enough of staring, could we go?"

He had to smile. Samuel was so rarely in a foul mood, Benjamin had not the heart to begrudge him it when it came. "Of course. My apologies."

But he stole just one more glimpse. When her lips curled at the corners in the beginnings of a shy smile, his stomach went tight. It took all his willpower to shake himself free of her gaze and catch up with Samuel.

"I am glad we head home after Passover," Samuel muttered as they turned back onto the street housing their inn. "I could use the wisdom of our parents."

"I daresay the wisdom of our Father in heaven will suffice, once you have had time to seek it." Benjamin clapped a hand to his brother's shoulder. "Rest tonight. Pray. Focus on the blessing of finding that which was so long lost."

Samuel's only response was to raise his hand and uncurl his fingers from around the shark's tooth. It was a wonder he had not deformed the thing—given the impression in his palm, he must have clung to it like a lifeline. "I never thought...I never thought to see her again. I never thought to pray for her. She had simply ceased to exist for me."

Benjamin shook his head and moved sideways to avoid colliding with another distracted passerby. "You were a child, Sam. You coped as best you could—and in a way in keeping with who you have always been. You loved. When your own mother refused you, you focused your love upon the one who protected and welcomed you."

The wound was apparently still there, though, a scar if not a festering. Shadows lurked again in his eyes, shadows Benjamin had thought were finally banished after Anna's death. He sighed. "Something good awaits you in this, my brother. You have only to find it."

Samuel flipped the tooth around in his hand, ran a thumb along the smooth edge. "I know. I apparently still need healing when it comes to this, and to forgive. I thought I had, but..." He shook his head and slid the tooth into his change purse. Smiled, though it looked forced. "I suppose it is like Zipporah's nose—day to day, one can ignore the old injury. But it throbs in the face of a storm."

Poor Zipporah. Benjamin chuckled. "Let the rains cleanse you, and I daresay it shall heal up better than her nose did. The Lord is a better physician than you."

Samuel laughed at the dig, even gave Benjamin's arm a playful shove. In the next moment a shout of greeting from Mark directed them toward the inn.

Benjamin looked around him again before following Samuel inside. He had lived only a few days in this city before his mother took him to Rome to claim the Visibullis estates, he had no vague memories of it. But it was good they had come. To see the place where their Savior had been crucified and risen again, to meet up with some who had known him. To share the Passover with other Jews who followed the Way.

A glimpse of gold caught his eye, though he lost sight of it again before he could see what it was. Long curls, perhaps, framing a face and figure of perfection? A grin tugged at the corner of his mouth. Probably not. But a man could hope.

Dara watched the two disappear into the inn, the younger man with one more look over his shoulder in her direction. Though her breath quickened, she did not reveal herself again, nor did she smile.

Another brother. She had never suspected, never thought to question how many children her mother had birthed. Though heaven only knew why Dara had ever assumed anything Martha said to be true.

But a brother—a brother with a brother who was not hers, one who sent a wave of recognition through her. "Benjamin Visibullis." She tested the name on her tongue and found it sweet, as sweet as his image was to her eyes.

Her destiny had arrived.

Spinning away from the inn, she darted back down the avenue with its familiar faces. Most of those faces ignored her, just as she had trained them to do. A few greeted her with a smile or a quick "good day," if she had given them a favorable word in the past. A very few turned away from her. Self-righteous fools, they, judging what they could not understand.

The strangers were always easy to spot. They were the ones who stared.

Tutelos. She knew the name but could not remember what the master had said about it. She must go to him, tell him of this strange new wonder that had charged into her life.

Their booth still sat unattended in the street. Usually no great concern, as Jerusalem had learned long ago that if they stole from her, she would be knocking upon their door within the hour. Though Jonathan too often used it as a crutch, an excuse for laziness. And what would her brother do when she left his house, when his business no longer affected her?

Her lips turned up. Perhaps then she would make him pay like everyone else for her vision.

Dara rushed into the house, far from surprised to find Martha and Jonathan hissing at one another, right where their guests had left them. Ignoring them, she headed back to her room, where the loom stretched through most of the space, awkward and large but too vital to be put anywhere else. When the visions clouded her eyes, when the images chased away sleep, she needed the loom to make sense of it all.

With a few brisk movements, she whipped her everyday covering from her hair, untied the woven belt from her waist, and slipped off the tunic she wore around the house. Not that she had never showed up at the master's house in her everyday garments, but not today. Not when she came to tell him their future waited. Nay, for such a momentous visit she donned the finest creation of her hands, the one so soft it flowed over her curves like water.

On her wall she had a mirror, polished to a shine. That she used to straighten the fabric, to fasten the belt, to arrange her curls just so. She added a head covering, one thin as a wisp that did little to hide her hair, and then hurried back through the curtain.

Jonathan turned away from their matron with disgust upon his face. "Say what you will, woman, it does not change facts. You sold your son to a Roman dog."

A breath of laughter puffed from Dara's lips. She could not help it. "You sound surprised, brother. Though I cannot think why you would be."

At her voice, Martha turned her way, eyes sparking as she took her in. "Where do you think you are going? We must prepare the meal—"

"Prepare your own meal." She strode toward them, intending to pass by without another glance. "I am going to my *master*."

Her mother grabbed her by the arm and drew her to a halt. "You say it as if you regret my decision. As if you did not lord your *master* over us all, as if you do not revel in all he has made you. You ought to thank me, and so should Samuel."

Dara gripped Martha's wrist until her fingers loosened and then shoved the offending hand away. "Just because our lives turned out well despite your selfishness does not make you right in the things you did." She shook her head and glanced toward the spot where he had stood, this brother of hers she had never seen. He was as beautiful as the rest of them, even handsomer than Jonathan. And she remembered well the features Jonathan had boasted as a child, so delicate and perfect that they had to keep him indoors lest one of the perverse Greeks in the city steal him away. "You thought you were selling your firstborn son as a catamite—a plaything for some disgusting old man. Tell me, mother, did you think you were making me a whore?"

Martha turned away, the pulse in her neck the only sign by which to gauge her reaction.

Dara arrowed her gaze into Jonathan. "Well, now we know. Now we know why she protected you and not me. She has that much conscience left, it seems, that she could not bear to consign a second son to the fate to which she thought she delivered the first."

As if Jonathan had ever wondered. With a shake of her head, Dara strode past them. "I would suggest you tend your wares, my brother. There are many strangers in Jerusalem for Passover who do not realize we are the last ones from whom they should steal."

Not waiting to see if Jonathan obeyed or not, she sped back out the door and into the evening sun.

The master lived on the other side of the city, in the rich section among the others of his station. She remembered trembling the first time she had put her sandaled foot onto the street, a child of nine with no idea why she must follow him that day, why he had put coins into her mother's hand. At the time, he had seemed old.

Perhaps he had aged in reverse, for seven years later his features looked young to her eyes, and his smile fueled her through the days. Seven years later, she had traversed the path to his house so often, from every point in the city, that her feet knew all the routes by rote. The quickest, the safest, the shortest.

Today she opted for speed, even though it took her through a section of town any reputable woman would avoid. She had no fear of the harlots though, nor of the men who frequented them. If a man were too blinded by lust to note the white head covering that no whore would ever wear, the modest garments that declared her station, he would snap from his haze when she tossed a powder of burning herbs into his eyes and plunged a dagger into his stomach.

The last to try to put his hands on her had lived only long enough to tell the tale. With a small smile, she touched a finger to the hilt of the dagger concealed in her belt. The master had given it to her. Its blade was an elongated pyramid, the shape specifically designed to inflict a wound that would not heal properly.

The poison she dipped it in killed within a quarter-hour.

Dara glanced at the angle of the sun and increased her pace. Night would come soon, and she must not ever enter the master's house in the night, lest his neighbors see and judge. She knew not what they thought of her frequent visits as it was. Sometimes, yes, she carried a basket with her so they would think she came to sell something. But just as often she showed up as she would now, with nothing in her hands.

No matter, though. The master could take care of any gossiping tongues. He could—

"Mistress! Mistress, stop, I beg you!"

Stop she did, though with a scowl when she saw that she was even now in the heart of Jerusalem's seediest district. Already women had draped themselves in their doorways, displaying the wares for the hungry wolves that prowled the streets under the guise of men. Her eyes latched onto the wretch stumbling to her knees a few feet away. "What do you want?"

The girl's hand shook as she reached out, a denarius glinting in the fading rays of the sun. "Please. Please, my sisters tell me you have the second sight. I need—I must know. I must know what I should do."

Dara did not move. Rather, she studied the bent figure, the down-turned face, the shaking arm. The girl could be no more than fifteen, just a year or so younger than Dara. She had no lines in her skin to attest to her hard life, no hunch. She was pretty. Pretty enough that she would be a popular choice for the men slinking by.

Dara's hand snaked out, made a cuff around the slender wrist, and tugged the girl to her feet. Sometimes the visions came on their own. But when she needed one upon command, touch helped.

The girl rose with wide eyes, as if Dara were more serpent than woman, ready to devour her whole. "Mistress?"

"Silence."

"Do you need me to tell you what—"

"I said *silence*, wretch." Holding her wrist was not enough, or perhaps the irritation with her was too great. No flashes, no whispers. With a low sigh, she took the coin from the harlot's fingers so she could force her palm open, flat, and splay hers out against it. Sometimes she did this for theatrics, when patrons thought they needed a show along with their futures. Mostly, it was for Dara's sake. Closing her eyes, she emptied her mind and filled her lungs, let the woman's warmth seep into her. Palm to palm, fingers to fingers.

Focused on nothing more, nothing less, the light flashed behind her eyelids. Visions that had confused her endlessly when first they began, pictures too quick to latch onto. But the master had trained her patiently, taught her to unravel truth from possibility, one future from another.

Though all, in this case, were equally hateful. She took a step away, breaking contact, and opened her eyes. "Despicable creature. You think this man will raise you up and save you? Go to him, become his concubine, and you will be dead within the fortnight. Stay as you are, and you will die of disease within the half-year."

She spun away, but the creature grabbed her by the arm, lighting fury in Dara's veins.

"Wait! You cannot—that is no help at all! Die or die? From violence or disease? That is no choice."

"I cannot give you choices, woman. I can only tell you what will happen if you choose the ones already set before you. If you want to live, then return to your husband and spend many long years with his bruises upon your flesh."

Tears gathered in the girl's eyes, though such things had ceased to ignite any compassion years ago. What did people expect when they asked to see the future? Tragedy filled life as much as joy, often more. The next crisis was never more than a few years around the bend. Was it *her* fault that people sometimes came to her when it was already upon them?

"Please." The girl's voice squeaked, broke. "What if...what if I go to the Temple and buy a sin offering? Ask forgiveness and return to my husband repentant? Will he forgive me?"

Dara peeled the fingers from her arm. "Your sacrifices are wormwood to Jehovah, and your husband knows not how to forgive. Perhaps you should have come to me a year ago, before you decided the streets were better than your home."

With a shake of her head, Dara ignored the next sobbing plea from the harlot and strode onward. She must hurry.

No other distractions hindered her path, thankfully, and sunlight still bathed the city as she hurried onto the master's street. Many of the people milling about she knew, knew parts of their lives they may wish she did not. Many did not understand that if they asked her to peek into their inmost for one particular answer, the entirety of their lives flooded her. Though how they could expect her to speak on the one without knowing the all, she could hardly guess.

She had no need to knock at his door, no more than she had to hail one of the many servants to ask direction. No, these cool stone hallways were more familiar to her than her own. She knew the feel of them under her feet, the smell of his costly lamp oil burning to keep out the encroaching night. The sound of his meal being prepared, the murmur of the servants.

Familiar, yet naught but background chatter. She headed for the courtyard, knowing that this time of day he would be in the shade of the portico on a chaise, a chalice of wine beside him and a scroll within his hands.

Yes, there he rested. Dara paused on the threshold to drink in the sight of him. Just yesterday she had last seen him, but it was not enough. If he would but allow it, she would move her things entirely from her mother's house and into his, hardly caring what Jewry would say.

But the master cared. The master protected her reputation and her virtue equally—murmuring time and again into her ear that they must not...they could not...that she had a greater purpose than becoming his lover, even if they both wanted it so badly.

She loved him the more after every refusal of all she offered. And clung to the promise that, someday, she would fully be his.

She watched him stretch out his arm to reach for the wine, muscles extending and contracting and making want well up inside her. How handsome he was with his strong features, the two streaks of silver at his temples amidst the darkest brown, the full, thick beard. How her heart galloped when he looked up and spotted her, love kindling in his hazel eyes.

"Dara." Smiling, he put aside the scroll and held his hand out to her. "What brings you here, beloved?"

She went to him, pulling her head covering off as she sank onto the chaise. "My day has been eventful." She stretched herself out alongside him, slid an arm onto his side. Breathed in the scent of incense. He must have just returned from the Temple. "I have another brother."

His hand, in the middle of its first stroke over her hair, paused. "A brother."

"By my uncle, my mother's first husband. Martha apparently sold him to a Roman before my father found her and married her."

"That woman..." Disgust filled his tone, and apparently it reached all the way to his heart, for he tangled his fingers in Dara's curls and pressed her closer, captured her lips with his. A move he so rarely allowed, one she gave herself fully to, holding him close and trailing her fingers over his back. Perhaps today he would forget himself. Forget anything but his desire for her and...

No, she knew, even as his lips broke from hers and moved over her jaw, that he would not. He would indulge just enough to make *her* forget, and then he would pull away. Send her home and call for his concubine.

"Praise Jehovah I could save you from her schemes," he murmured into her ear. He shook his head and kissed her again.

Dara pressed tighter to him. She dared not think of her mother's schemes. The master may want her *now*, but he had never looked on her so when she was a child. May still not, had she not a year ago brazenly slid onto his chaise much like she just did. Captured *his* mouth before he could protest and pressed her body to his to show him she was no longer the slip of a girl he had first led home.

Other men, she knew all too well, would not have respected her age nor her innocence.

He kissed her once more, loosened her hair, stroked through it as he so loved to do. "This brother?"

"He too was apparently fortunate in who bought him. The woman's second husband adopted my brother legally. He is Roman. An heir, it seems, to much wealth."

"Interesting." Calculation sharpened the haze of desire in his eyes, and his hand's stroke went from purposeful to absentminded. "Though I wonder why you never saw it. Some things, I suppose, are kept from us until we need them. What kind of man is he?"

She shrugged. "He did not come here looking for his mother, merely stumbled upon us. His shock was strong. But that is not all."

"No?" He smiled, brows arched.

She slid her arm back to his chest so she could smooth her fingers over his beard. Her brother and his brother were clean-shaven, in the Roman fashion. So very unlike her strong Jewish master. "He came with the son of the man who bought him, whom he calls brother. Benjamin Visibullis, master of Tutelos. I have heard you mention it."

His arms tensed around her, his face turned to granite. "Tutelos. Your brother's brother owns *Tutelos*?"

By his face, his posture, she would not have known if the knowledge pleased or infuriated him. But by his eyes she knew it was excitement that rendered him as stone. "Yes."

He remained still for another moment, then laughed and kissed her again, fast and hard. "I knew it. I knew you would prove the key to our cause. Do you know what it is, beloved? This Tutelos?"

The key? Such pleasure welled up that she had no name for it, no measure of it. Thus far she had helped so little in the great cause, nothing but a few false words spoken to the zealots to lead them astray. "No, Master. I only recognized the name because I overheard you speaking of it once."

"It is one of their strongholds. The place where the Jews congregated when they were expelled from Rome—many of them were then sucked into the cult of Christianity. They call themselves a *church*, as if they are anything but a gathering of sacrilegious sinners. Letting Greek and Jew dine together, work together, marry one another." Even his snarl was handsome. "They make a mockery of all that is sacred, and Jehovah demands we scourge them from the earth, remove them from the tribes of Israel."

Dara curled her fingers into his tunic. "But the estate is owned by this Benjamin. So if we could gain control of *him*..."

"Then we could undo them from the inside." He sat, pulling her up with him, and then rose to his feet so he could pace. Dara smiled at his deliberate steps, the way his fingers curled and uncurled as thoughts raced through his hazel eyes. "We have tried to infiltrate them so many times to no avail. The enemy is strong there—a few times, many years past, we managed to get people into the villa, but too often they were won over or forced out. And recently."

He spun, facing Dara with a flashing gaze. "Recently none have even gotten past their gates. They have a...a witch among them who always alerts her masters of who we are."

A witch? Something deep, deep within Dara shrank. She had nothing to fear, she knew that. The power within her came from Jehovah and was surely greater than anything the adversary could throw against her.

But a *witch*—there was a reason Jehovah had ordered them all tossed from the camp of Israel.

"Dara. My precious, beautiful Dara." The master sat beside her again and took her hands. His eyes gleamed with such flame it was a wonder his gaze did not burn her. "How well do you love me?"

"Must you ask?" And yet the fact that he would—but she knew why. Of course she did. Had he not been preparing her for this for the last seven years? She summoned a smile and gripped his fingers. "You know I love you more than life. You are my all."

"Is my cause your cause?"

"Yes." A trill sounded inside her. Excitement that things were finally to happen. It drowned out any voice of fear from the child still locked inside, under the layers of woman. "Yes, you know it is. I will do anything to aid in wiping out the followers of the Nazarene."

He lifted a hand and stroked her cheek. "Even if your brother is one of them?"

A low breath of laughter slipped from her throat as she leaned into his touch. "You think I have any bond with the man just because we share Martha's blood? He is nothing to me."

"And *his* brother, Benjamin Visibullis. What did you feel when you saw him?"

She closed her eyes, savoring her master's touch and letting the feeling sweep through her again. The jubilation when she heard his voice, the instant knowledge that the man at whom she peeked from behind the curtain was her destiny. He was the one through whom she would change the world...and finally gain the full love of the master. "That he is the one for whom I have been waiting."

"Good. Good." Yet he sounded as sorrowful as he did joyous, which brought her eyes open again, to fasten upon his face. Was that strain upon it for her? Before she could study it enough to decide, it faded, vanished, leaving nothing but the confidence she knew so well and loved so much. "According to the last information I received about the master of Tutelos, he is yet unwed. That will make it easier for you. You must act now, fair one, before he departs Jerusalem after Passover. You must leave with him—as his wife."

Yes. Yes, she could do that. She could bind herself to the handsome young man who had made desire pull tight in her belly. She could catch his eye, ply her wiles, convince him to wed her. She could go with him across the Mediterranean, to the enemy's stronghold, and do her master's work within Tutelos.

No. No, she could not! "But Master, if I wed him..." Marriage allowed no easy escape for a woman. She could not just pick up and come home and be with *him* when she had done her duty. How could she?

The master chuckled and pressed his lips briefly to hers. "You think one man will come between us? Nay. Serve me in this, beloved, and we will soon have all we yearn for. To whom do you belong?"

The anxiety stilled. Certainty washed through her. "You."

"That is right. I bought you, paid the price for you. You belong to me, and I do not relinquish my rights to you. I will not be the one giving you in marriage, it will be your brother—but has he the right in the eyes of God to do that anymore?"

"No." Praise to the Lord, he was right. She could marry this young man, but it would mean nothing before Jehovah, because her master was her true husband. He could demand her back, demand her body at any time. She nodded and leaned into him. "Forgive my doubt, Lord. I will do anything you ask. Go anywhere you send me."

"I know." He eased her back again, this time laying her flat and settling on his side, pressed to her. He trailed his fingers down her neck, down her torso, igniting a flash of want. "You will have to pretend to be one of them. A Christian. You know enough of their lies to pretend to it, do you not?"

Did she? "I...think so."

"You need not worry about the details too much—they will forgive you any mistakes if you claim you have been forced to practice in secret." He traced her ear with his nose. "It is the only way he will marry you. Though even then, you must be willing to...convince him. Not just to take you with them, but to take you with him as his wife. That is critical. Do you understand?"

She stretched into his touch, willing it to continue. "Yes."

"Because you will have no authority there if you show up merely as his brother's sister. They would deny you entrance and send you straight back to Israel."

"I understand."

"Good." He kissed her, long and deep, pressing her into the cushion of the chaise with enough energy to promise the reward for her obedience. "And then, my love," he whispered against her lips. "After you are his, you can finally be mine."

She caught his mouth again. Jehovah had been smiling on her indeed the day this man pressed coins into her mother's palm.

seven

"WITCH! SHE IS A WITCH, I TELL YOU! TURN HER OVER TO ME SO THE authorities can deal with her!"

Zipporah sent her eyes heavenward and sighed. "Good day to you too, Virgil. Back again, I see."

The beggar leveled a gnarled finger at her, one that shook with more than weakness and hunger. He stood a good ten paces from the gates, staggering back and forth upon the road but getting no closer.

No, he had learned his lesson the last time, apparently. He would not try to pass through the gates again.

The steward sighed right along with her, his eyes tracking the bony old man. "I thought we cast the devils out of him again last month."

"It is a different one."

Jacob's brows rose. "That makes how many now?"

"Five." Zipporah shook her head and settled her hands upon her hips. When first the beggar had shown up with that shadow within him, she had felt pity. But at this point...pity accomplished nothing. Offering him peace in his troubled mind worked only until he invited another spirit into him. It seemed that the cleaner they made his soul, the more happily did an enemy move in, sometimes bringing a dark brother with it. "At least this time it is but one. A weak one."

Jacob pressed his lips together and passed a hand over his iron-gray hair. "Much as I hate to simply ignore him..."

"It is the only real option. Virgil welcomes them. So until he is ready to fill his heart with salvation and the Holy Spirit in place of these *unholy* ones, we can accomplish nothing."

A flutter, a coo. Zipporah turned from the gate and spotted familiar wings flapping her way. A smile tugged at her lips as she held out a finger for her dove to land upon. "There you are, Columba."

The bird settled with a flutter of feathers onto her finger, cooing another greeting.

The beggar outside the gates took up a new hiss. "See? She has a familiar! A witch, I tell you, a witch."

Jacob chuckled. "Yes, a one-legged dove she rescued. Terrifying. Be on your way, Virgil. You are welcome to some of the food in the basket there as you go."

Stroking a hand over the soft gray feathers of her bird, Zipporah looked past the staggering old man and to the plume of dust coming their way upon the road from Rome. Expected, hence why she and Jacob were at the gate when the delightful Virgil stumbled by. But larger than it should be from one cart. "Master Titus has brought company."

"Indeed." Jacob raised a hand to shield his eyes from the bright mid-morning sun. "A fair number of them from the looks of it. Will you run and tell the women to prepare for them after making sure they bring no unwanted guests, Zip?"

"Of course." She squinted into the distance and wished for Benjamin's unsurpassed eyesight. "They seem to be moving slowly. I can run now and be back before they reach the gates."

"Hurry, then."

With a nod, she tapped her finger onto her shoulder so Columba could hop onto it and took off at an easy run. Her feet knew well the road from gate to villa, each turn and undulation. Her eyes knew each row of grapes in the vineyard, each elm supporting the vines, each olive tree in the grove, each field planted with crops to see them through the year. Sometimes it felt as though she must know every blade of grass and bud of wildflower within the gates.

Her gaze tracked to the wall, beyond it. Passover was only days away. They would be home soon, unless they met with delay. Four long years coming to an end. And as always when they sprang to mind—which was often—she prayed for them. Mark, Samuel, Benjamin. The missing pieces to their little world here at Tutelos.

As always when they sprang to mind, her heart wrung out a new ache. Who would have thought that she could miss them so much, for so long?

Familiar faces went about their daily business as she sped by, most of them greeting her with a nod or a smile, but none trying to slow her. No one ever did—they assumed that if she ran, it was for a purpose.

Her feet took her around the back of the massive villa, toward the kitchens from which the scent of the midday meal wafted. There she smiled at finding all the women she needed at once. Her mother, the aging Dinah who still reigned supreme in here, and Mistress Abigail too.

Dinah greeted her with an exaggerated sigh. "What have I told you about bringing that creature into my kitchen, Zipporah?"

Zipporah grinned and palmed a berry. "I cannot recall. That I must do so at least once a day, was it not?"

Dinah pointed a finger at her, but her eyes crinkled in a suppressed smile. "I saw you take that berry. You had best not feed it to him in here, I will not tolerate bird droppings."

"Because you are as wise as you are kind." She took another berry, this one for herself. "It looks as though Master Titus is returning with company."

Dinah had paused mid-reach to return a bundle of root vegetables to their basket but now plopped them back onto the counter. "Have you a guess as to how many?"

"I could not see, but I will be sure someone provides the details, and if they need rooms." That she directed to Ima.

Mistress Abigail dried off her hands and motioned Zipporah to join her. "I will greet them and see what needs done. Perhaps it is Aristobulus's house, deciding to take Passover with us after all."

"That would be lovely, Mistress. Though even if they do not, the villa is bursting for the feast."

The mistress laughed, full and rich. "Is that your way of inviting me not to wish more work upon us?"

Zipporah grinned. "I have no reason to complain of housework." Rarely did she get through a task without being called to the gate. And when not out there, then she was most often with Sarah. No, hers was not a hard life. Rather, it was one that left her too much leisure to think of all the ways she could be more useful. "I finished cleaning the mosaics in the atrium before Jacob called me out, though."

In answer, Abigail patted her arm. A familiar touch, warm and motherly and as much a part of her life as her own mother's embrace. "You know well your presence at the gate is more important than the cleaning. Just as you know we all trust you to do what you must, when you must." Smiling, the lady smoothed away a lock of Zipporah's hair—the very one Ima always pulled free to cover her scar—and stroked Columba's head.

A laughing shriek echoed through the corridors, another sound as normal as the wind in the trees. Sarah came careening around the corner, though she slowed to a more sedate pace upon spotting them. "Ima, Zip, tell me you have come to rescue me. If I have to listen to another of Cleopas's songs, I shall split a side from laughing."

Abigail arched one delicate black brow. "Did you finish with your assigned chamber?"

"Yes."

"Then consider yourself rescued." The mistress welcomed her youngest to the group with a flourish.

Zipporah offered her arm, knowing her friend would link hers through it within seconds. "Your father is on his way back, and it appears he has guests."

"Oh?" Did Sarah's cheeks flush more, or did the light from the windows merely better show the one already there from her laughter? "I wonder who it is."

Zipporah bumped their shoulders together. "Probably Nereus, back for another intense discussion on the Savior in hopes of winning your hand."

Whether or not it had before, her flush certainly deepened now. "He will need to do more than have a few discussions, as I have told him before. But he cannot come to faith for my sake."

Abigail laughed. "When Benjamin realizes he is pursuing you, after Nereus's reaction when he thought your brother was interested in Decima..."

"Justice to make any poet delight. Though if he *does* come to faith—well, that is up to Father, and I begin to think he will never approve a marriage."

"He would have years ago, my sweet, had you looked on any of the men who approached him with favor." As they stepped out into the warm sunshine, Abigail moved to her daughter's side and took her other arm. "Though it is true we are in no hurry for you to leave home."

Zipporah acknowledged the out of doors by offering the berry to her dove. Columba took it and flew off, no doubt to enjoy his repast without the shrieking and laughing of the humans. Zipporah watched him wing away, unhindered in flight by the missing leg. A lesson she had better learn herself. Her dearest friend would marry sooner or later and likely go elsewhere to live, as Ester had last year, leaving Zipporah with their brothers and parents. Relegated only to what visits Sarah could manage and what letters they could send.

How could one feel so lonely in the place that had always been home, surrounded by friends and family?

Sarah's gaze was on the gate and the mass of people nearing it. "Perhaps the boys changed their minds, Mother, and have come home for Passover instead of going to Jerusalem."

Zipporah's heart lurched at the suggestion, even as she told herself it would not be so. Too often over the years she had wished, had dreamed Benjamin would come home unexpectedly...but no. Their one visit had been well planned and had sped by so quickly she had scarcely gotten to speak two words to him. Every minute, it seemed, some new person had to be introduced, some new task undertaken. Had Samuel not spent hours with her reminiscing of Anna, she could have convinced herself the entire month had not really happened at all.

Abigail squinted into the bright light. "Whoever it is, they seem to have an entire household of servants with them."

And wagons and chaises and horses and donkeys and...and one figure leaping down and running toward the gate. Zipporah's eyes went wide. "It is Menelaus!"

Sarah must have recognized him in the same moment, because they took off together even before Zipporah finished her shout. Abigail laughed behind them and picked up her pace as well.

"Menelaus!" Sarah, obviously far from thoughts of potential husbands, looked younger than her sixteen years as she waved her arms wildly, as they had done each and every time he came back after one of his trips to spread the Gospel.

Zipporah laughed. "It is all I can do not to shout 'What did you bring us?' at him."

Sarah's laughter joined hers, adding a melody to the rhythm of their feet that surely would have inspired a new epic in Cleopas. They reached the gate as Menelaus did.

He held his arms wide. "My daisies, waving their arms in the breeze."

Another laugh. Somehow, Menelaus always brought mirth with him, no matter how dark the day may have seemed. They both leapt into his arms, making him stagger backward. No longer could he lift them both at once and spin them around, but he made up for it with a squeeze that threatened to crack a few ribs.

"Let me see you." He set them away, eyes agleam, and made a show of measuring them against him. "Sarah, you have grown another foot."

She giggled. "Nay, I still have only the two. Nor have I grown any taller since I was twelve, which was three visits ago."

"And her wit is still as sharp as her mother's, I see. And my sparrow." He took Zipporah's hand, spun her around once until her tunic twirled about her legs. "Have you learned to fly yet?"

She halted with a grin. "Of course I have. Shall I show you how?"

He barked out a laugh himself. "I knew you would put our year apart to good use. Did you know I saw your brothers?"

"Did you?" Sarah clapped her hands together and bounced, sending her curtain of dark hair swaying. "Where? When? How are they?"

"At Thessalonica, before I sailed for Rome and they for Judea. They are well. Although..." He made a quick bow between them as Abigail came up. "I do regret to inform you, Lady Asinius, that your son has *still* not found himself a bride. Or had not those few months ago, at any rate."

The mistress stretched out her hands for her old friend as she chuckled. "Somehow, I am not surprised. And what of you, Menelaus Cassicus, who are far older than my son? Have *you* yet found a wife to keep you in your old age?"

He took Abigail's fingers in his and grinned. "As a matter of fact."

Zipporah could only stare at him for a long moment with Sarah and Abigail, sure he would burst out with another laugh in another moment. Instead, his grin turned to a warm smile and he stood to the side, extending one of his hands behind him, toward the caravan pulling to a halt.

"Oh." Sarah gripped Zipporah's arm and tried to jerk it from its socket. "Oh, he did! He really did! There is hope for the rest of us yet!"

Zipporah rescued her arm with a smile, her eyes on the woman who stepped shyly forward. She was probably around the mistress's age, with the kind of soft beauty that seemed to find some people through a life lived in faith. And oh, the Spirit within her. Shining like a lamp, dazzling and brilliant.

Zipporah pressed a hand to her mouth. Their old friend had found a fine wife indeed.

"Menelaus!" The mistress stepped forward to reach a welcoming hand toward the newcomer.

"This is Priscilla." Menelaus tugged her closer. "The reason I stayed so long in Macedonia."

Abigail no doubt sensed her sweet spirit too. Rather than being content with clasping her hand, she drew the woman into an embrace and whispered something into her ear that brought tears to the woman's eyes and a smile to her lips.

With a happy squeal, Sarah rushed forward, too, and threw her arms around them both. Zipporah breathed a laugh and wrapped her arms around her middle. And then thought to look at the rest of the assembly when she felt many heavy gazes in their direction.

The master sat astride his favorite horse, boyish grin in place as he watched his wife welcome his friend's new bride. No doubt they had talked the whole way from the port in Ostia. Abba held the reins to their supply wagon, but his attention was on the rest of the travelers.

Zipporah frowned. They were not with Menelaus and Priscilla, certainly. Their Greek friend always traveled light, and though he occasionally brought a guest with him, never more than one or two at a time. This group, however, consisted of no fewer than twenty people, and many of them shifted from foot to foot as if impatient for the reunion to finish.

And an interesting collection they were. One she recognized—an old Roman friend of Master Titus, though he had never come to the villa for a visit. She had seen him a few times in Rome, back before she was forbidden from leaving the walls. What was his name? It began with an L, she thought. Lu-something.

He looked less than happy to be here now...yet she saw a spark of light within him. A kindling, ready to be nurtured. Beside him on his chaise was a woman dressed in elegance and wealth, with a patient expression that said she was willing to listen. Willing to learn. But had not yet heard anything to convince her to turn her heart over to Jehovah.

The other chaise carried only a trio of little girls, two of whom were fast asleep. The oldest, eyes open and innocent, could be no more than seven. The children of the master's friend? Reasonable, but only until she saw another man stretch up to exchange a word with the girl and saw "Father" upon her lips in response.

Another nobleman, then. His toga bespoke as much, though Zipporah had failed to note it behind the slaves among whom he walked. He patted his daughter's knee and then strode toward Titus. More than a spark in this one. He was a believer already.

Jacob slid to her side. "Any cause for concern, Zipporah?"

She scanned the group again, being sure to look at each slave, each child, each beast. "None. Except that that man"—she hooked a thumb toward Menelaus—"seems unnaturally happy, even for him."

Titus must have overheard, for he dismounted with a laugh aimed her way. "And he comes bearing gifts from the boys, and some mysterious present for us all that he refuses to divulge until we have assembled. So no disappearing this afternoon, Zipporah."

The stranger stopped beside the master, his gaze narrowed upon her. Zipporah felt heat sting her cheeks. Her dress marked her as a servant, so what must this man think about her master's warning?

Perfect—not even through the gates yet, and already their newest brother would think her a lazy slave wont to run off and hide from her duties. He would not understand that the master and mistress had years ago granted her those hot afternoon hours to pray wherever she pleased.

Yet the corners of his lips pulled up. "This is she, then? The legendary Zipporah who can see beyond the veil?"

Legendary? Her gaze flew to the ground, and she slid closer to the safety of Jacob's side. She knew not how this stranger had heard of her, but it could not bode well.

Her father, though, smiled as he clicked up the donkey pulling the wagon. "Master Urbanus and his family traveled with Menelaus and Priscilla from Corinth on. Our friend has filled our guests' ears with many stories of our family here, my daughter."

Not so terrible then. She looked up, though nearly wished she had not when the other Roman appeared before her too, scowling at Master Titus. "Well you got me here, the both of you. Now what do you expect of me?"

The mistress released Priscilla with a grin and slid to her husband's side. Titus welcomed her with an arm about her shoulders. "Beloved, you remember Lucius, do you not?"

"As if I could forget him. Welcome to our home, Lucius. And this is your wife behind you?"

"Fabia." Lucius waved a hand toward Urbanus. "And this tyrant is Urbanus, my late sister's second husband. Their daughters are there behind him—Gratiana, Hadriana, and Juliana."

The mistress's expression went sorrowful. "We had not heard about Septima, Lucius. Our condolences. They had moved to Corinth?"

"As I had. But what happens when we arrive? Not a month or two there, and the tyrant orders us back to Rome for reasons he claims came to him in a vision."

Urbanus rolled his eyes toward the heavens. "Through prayer, my brother."

"He would uproot my family, his *own* family to chase a *prayer* halfway around the known world."

Jacob leaned down to Zipporah. "Are you *certain* this one is safe?"

A chuckle tickled her throat. "He is closer to believing than his wife."

Abigail sent a smile toward Fabia and motioned to the slaves bearing the litters. "Come, my friends, follow me. I will see you all settled. You too, Priscilla. Sarah, will you run ahead and tell Miriam how many rooms we need?"

Her friend took off with a nod, and the caravan moved forward again. Zipporah, left with no assigned task, stepped out of the way to let them by, smiling at the little girl who stared at her scar. The little one grinned back.

Though why she had left herself the sole female among the collection of men... She should catch up with the mistress or Sarah. Or perhaps wait for them all to pass and help secure the gate.

Though the continuing argument between the men held her feet rooted.

"Because," Urbanus was saying, "you will not listen to me. You will not listen to the brethren in Corinth, yet you still seek. You have questions, and perhaps here you will hear the answers to them."

"So the Christians here have some mystical knowledge that your *brethren* in Corinth do not?"

Titus laughed and clapped a hand to his old friend's shoulder. "What we have here, Lucius, is isolation. At Tutelos, you can close out the world for a few weeks and focus on things of the Spirit. You can ask your questions of anyone you see, master or servant or guest, and they will either be able to answer or to tell you who can. Or, if the questions have no answers, pray with you."

Urbanus's eyes gleamed, though his brother's scowl did not lessen. "Is it true that John Mark is with you? That he is writing an account of Jesus's life?"

"It is, based on what Simon Peter told him when they ministered together. He has been reading it to us as he writes it, though he has been taking his time, making sure every word is what the Spirit whispers in his ear."

Zipporah sent her gaze to the far side of the villa, where the light shone the brightest from the guardians. They had been praying a continuous hedge of protection around their visitor, lest a dark one swoop from the sky long enough to whisper in his ear instead.

Lucius growled a low Latin curse and set his gaze on Zipporah. "Fine then. Tell me, slave. Why, if this God of yours is greater than all mine, can he not speak to me wherever I am?"

Urbanus pinched his nose. "Must we revisit this now? You know well he can. But—"

"But," Lucius's words went from Greek to Latin, "you still felt the need to drag me back here so that I could ask questions of some ugly slave. Will she have the answers no one else does?"

"Lucius." The master's tone went hard as stone and cold as ice.

He would defend her, Zipporah knew it well. Who among the masters and parents had not at some point? And at first, when the enemy's words spilled from lips with no enemy controlling them, she had needed the champion to hush them, to assure her she was not ugly.

It was an arrow she had learned to deflect. With a touch upon the master's arm to let him know she needed not his defense this time, she inclined her head and summoned a smile for this man who needed a war for his soul. In Latin, she answered, "You are welcome to ask me any questions burning within you, Lord. But if you prefer a fairer face to deliver your answers, you will find no shortage of them at Tutelos."

He at least had the decency to flush. "Forgive me. I thought her Hebrew— but I forgot how you educate your slaves, Titus."

So he would apologize, not for the insult, but for her understanding of it. Ah yes, she could see why the mistress had greeted him with that dry note in her voice.

"Oaf." Urbanus pushed past his brother and inclined his head to Zipporah, as if she were Titus's daughter rather than his servant. "Allow me to properly beg forgiveness on his part. My brother says many things he does not mean and which bear no resemblance to the truth."

She had no need to force the smile for this one. "Rest easy, Lord. I am not offended. It is no great secret that Jehovah, in his infinite wisdom, saw fit not to burden me with beauty."

Lucius screwed his face up as if he questioned her sanity along with her face. "Titus, your slave is daft."

"Am I?" Since no one made move to do so, she extended a hand to invite them all to follow her to the house. "My sister was the greatest beauty Rome had seen in a generation."

"So I heard."

Of course he had. Who the world over had not heard the tales of Anna's fairness? Zipporah smiled, though it felt small now. The images of her sister had faded so over the years. "Did you hear, too, Lord, how that put her in danger? How she could not walk along the byways of your city without some patrician trying to seize her and make her his own? How Master Titus's son had to cut short their betrothal and wed her quickly to keep her safe?"

Shaking her head, she did not look behind her to see if Lucius understood her point. "With great beauty comes great danger. And given that I, in my homeliness, find plenty of that *without* inspiring lust in every passerby, I can only therefore assume that had I my sister's face as well, I would have been doomed to death or worse by now."

"She does not *want* to be beautiful?" Lucius's laugh held no amusement. "Whatever left her scarred must have addled her brains as well."

Zipporah closed her eyes and let her feet remember their own way for a few steps. *Give me strength, Jehovah.*

Titus rebuked his friend, but she paid no attention to the words he chose. She may not have even opened her eyes so soon had she not heard footfalls coming up beside her and felt someone blocking the sun from her face. Jacob, no doubt, ready to offer a kind word if she needed one. Blinking her eyes open and up to assure him she did not, her tongue tied in knots when she saw Urbanus at her side rather than the steward.

He studied her much like Samuel was wont to do, searching for injuries. His smile shone with the light of heaven. "He is a fool," he said softly. "I pray you can ignore him."

"You need not worry, Lord. He is fighting the pull of the Spirit—it is enough to make any man short-tempered."

The one beside her chuckled. "Perhaps he has been fighting the pull all his life, then, for his tempers have never been what one would call steady."

Smiling in return, Zipporah measured the distance between them and the rest of the party. Sarah was dashing even then into the villa, her mother and the female guests not far behind.

Urbanus's gaze had caught on the side of her face. Perhaps she should have pulled the long curl back from behind her ear before she greeted them. "May I ask what happened? Feel free to decline, of course, if—"

"I do not mind." To prove it, she renewed her smile. The scar had faded, as

Samuel had promised it would, but it would never disappear. "I was attacked on the day my spiritual eyes were opened, when I confronted a demon."

The Roman's eyes went wide. "A...a demon did this to you?"

"Through the hand of a man and the knife he carried, yes. Much like this," she added, tapping a finger to the bump upon her nose, "was from the fist of another."

Sympathetic horror filled their guest's eyes. "How terrible."

"No. Another kindness of my God." She grinned up at him. "Now I have an excuse for the lack of beauty."

He laughed, yet his eyes flashed pain. "Your good humor is refreshing. And yet I wonder that your parents and masters allow you to disparage yourself so."

"It is truth, not disparagement. And I assure you." She sidestepped a rut in the road and, when she heard the familiar flutter, held out an arm for Columba to land upon. "It is only about my face I offer such honesty. When it comes to my hair and figure, my vanity brings many a favorable lie to my lips."

He watched her carefully as she transferred the dove to her shoulder, no doubt searching for some hint as to whether she jested. At length he shook his head. "On the journey here, Menelaus and I spoke much about the idea of the church being a body—something the apostle wrote in his letter to us, and about which he spoke several times while he visited us. Menelaus brought you up because he said you were the eyes."

The eyes. She would have given that designation to a prophet, not to herself. Though she supposed she saw more than most did. Even if she would have preferred to be the feet, carrying the Gospel out into the world like he did. Like Benjamin. "An interesting analogy."

"And an apt one. Yet I get the distinct feeling that for all you see that we cannot, there remain some things about which your vision is cloudy."

Only some? She laughed and stroked a finger down Columba's feather. "Of that I have no doubt."

"Perhaps we can learn from each other."

Simple words, spoken with no artifice and much sincerity—an invitation to friendship. An instant acceptance that at once warmed her and, for some reason, made her that much more aware of how lonely she was so often.

She glanced over, up, and noted that his eyes were gray, like the mist off the Tiber on a cool morning. "Perhaps we can."

eight

ZIPPORAH SAT CLOSE TO SARAH ON THE FLOOR, AS CLOSE AS THEY could get to the trunk that Menelaus stood guard over. He, always happiest when all eyes were upon him, wore a grin as he doled out the gifts from the boys. A bolt of silk for Mistress Abigail, a manuscript for Master Titus. He handed to Jason a twisted horn with a note claiming it was from a unicorn and then drew out a length of worked leather.

"For Zipporah," Menelaus said, presenting it with a flourish but holding on to the scrap of parchment attached to it.

She stood to accept it with lifted brows. "Samuel, I assume?" It was too costly a gift to have come from Mark. And heaven knew Benjamin would never send her anything so...well, *anything*.

"Indeed. And he writes, 'As Ben, Mark, and I talked with Paul of Tarsus in Macedonia, we discussed the idea of spiritual armor. You, little sparrow, no doubt have that already, but I still maintain you could use some traditional as well. I have yet to find a breastplate to suit you, but perhaps if you gird your waist with this, it will at least protect you from the wildlife.'"

Everyone laughed, Zipporah with them. She fastened the wide belt around her middle and cocked a hip, her hand upon it, to show it off. Her friends and family hooted and clapped.

Rather than sit, she took the bag of nuts produced next and doled them out to everyone in the room. At the back of the chamber, she reached the newcomer and one of his daughters—Hadriana, was it not? Lucius and his wife had not joined the gathering, but she was glad to see Urbanus and his girls had.

He smiled and nodded at the leather, studded with metal. Question gleamed in his eyes. "A lovely gift. You and Samuel must be close."

It had not occurred to her that he would not understand. Or that pain, dull but there, would strike again. "He was married to my sister. Though she has been gone these four years, he is my brother still."

Understanding and apology lit his eyes. "Ah. I think I may have known that and am sorry to have forgotten. Though I confess I do not understand why you would need armor to protect you from wildlife."

She smiled. "You have already noted the largest of my injuries, wrought by man." She touched the side of her face, then a few places on her arms that he probably had not noticed, but which also sported thin scars in various degrees of fading. "The smaller ones are the result of animals driven over our gates by the dark ones. Mostly birds, frightened from their flight so that they come swooping at me."

Hadriana took the nut from the shell after her father cracked it for her and popped it into her mouth. "I like birdies."

"As do I." Grinning, Zipporah tapped her on the nose and slipped her another nut with a wink. "I have a pet birdie now, a dove that was injured in just such a tumble from the sky. I have named him Columba. I imagine you know what that means."

Hadriana nodded, her curls bobbing. "Dove in Latin," she answered in their usual Greek.

"Quite right. And did you notice that my brother, in his note, called me 'sparrow'? That is what my name means in Hebrew."

"My name is from a town." The little one grinned. "May I meet Columba?"

"You certainly may. He will come back for a few berries after we eat dinner—you can help me feed him, and your sisters too if they would like." She reached out to brush a thumb over Hadriana's cheek, smiled once more, and then moved on.

When she reached the front of the chamber again, Sarah was whipping a veil around her head with dramatic flair. She flounced out of the circle, spinning to a seat on the floor farther away from the crate, making room for the others.

Zipporah handed the remaining nuts to Mistress Abigail and joined her friend. She fingered the veil with a grin. "Lovely. Benjamin is quite right—it will be a perfect bridal veil when the day comes."

Sarah whipped it off her own head and onto Zipporah's with a giggle. "Or for you, when he finally comes home and realizes he has loved you all along."

"Ha." She heard her own cynicism in her imitation of a laugh.

"Well, one never knows, Zip."

"Yes, one does. *Every*one does. So please hush before the entire congregation hears your teasing."

"Oh, no one is paying any attention to us." As if in proof, Sarah glanced about the room, even turning around.

She halted so abruptly that she must have, in fact, seen someone who watched them. Zipporah did not care to glance back to discover who, though given Sarah's angle, it was probably Urbanus. Better or worse than one of their own?

She slipped off the veil and folded it into a neat square that she pressed into Sarah's hands.

At the crate, new laughter sprang up over an object she could not make out. Mistress Abigail shook her head. "Where do they find such things?"

Menelaus's grin went mischievous. "You ought to chide them for going out in search of them when they ought to be searching for a wife for Benjamin. Although I suppose there is hope. He might return home to find a bride awaiting him here all along. Eh, Zipporah?"

It pinched, punched, but she had long ago learned how to hide it. Zipporah shook her head and rested her arms on her raised knees. "Careful, Menelaus, or I will have to tell your lovely new wife the tale of you and that ferocious *bear.*"

The threat earned another round of laughter, one that Menelaus shared in. He held up his hands. "All right, all right, I surrender. No more teasing. Now, anyway. Time for the final gift, one for the entire assembly." He reached, not into the crate this time, but into the folds of his garment, and pulled out a thick scroll. "A letter from the apostle Paul, to you, the church of Rome."

A hush fell upon them as he handed the scroll to Titus. His host accepted it with eyes agleam and looked around him. "John Mark, you are the most in practice for reading aloud. Would you do the honors?"

The man stroked his graying beard and eyed the scroll with a smile. "I can begin, anyway. Though it looks as if the meal may come before the end of this letter."

"No matter. We can always reconvene to finish it."

John Mark nodded his agreement and took the seat his host offered him. Breaking the seal, he cleared his throat and then unrolled the scroll a forearm's width. "'Paul, a servant of Jesus Christ, called to be an apostle, separated unto the gospel of God (which he had promised afore by his prophets in the holy scriptures), concerning his Son Jesus Christ our Lord, who was made of the seed of David according to the flesh; and declared to be the Son of God with power, according to the spirit of holiness, by the resurrection from the dead: by whom we have received grace and apostleship, for obedience to the faith among all nations, for his name: among whom are you also the called of Jesus Christ.'" He paused, looked out over the group, and smiled. "'To all that be in Rome, beloved of God, called to be saints: grace to you and peace from God our Father, and the Lord Jesus Christ!'"

A cheer went up, complete with whistles and applause. Zipporah smiled along with the others. And tried to smother the ache in her chest from the reminder of all she would never have.

He should have stayed home. Samuel paused on the street corner and wished, not for the inn behind him, but for *home.* For familiar rolling hills, for lines of grape vines, for sun streaming through an impluvium. For the bottles and pots with all his medicines, his favorite needles, his scrolls and scrolls of notes and lines of familiar hands and feet in need of tending.

He never should have left. Why had he ever felt he should? He had been running away, pure and simple. Running from memories of the wife he could not save. Running around the world when the road to Rome had not proven long enough.

And look where it had gotten him.

Benjamin nudged his shoulder. "Are we going to stand here all day?"

"I am seriously considering it."

On the other side of him, Mark laughed. "Come, Sam. You agreed this is Jehovah's hand. Perhaps so you can forgive. Perhaps so you can learn something you need to know. Perhaps so you can reach them with the good news."

Theories that sounded grand and noble in the safety of his rented room. And which crumbled to dust now that he stood staring down the avenue that would deliver him back into her hands. "I..." He closed his eyes and drew in a long breath. The air was dry, warm, scented with a thousand spices and fragrances from the markets, and clanging always with the din of voices raised to hock their wares. Were any of them the same vendors who had sold oranges and dates and figs to Mother when she was but a servant in the Visibullis house? The same vendors who had slipped him an almond or an apple with a wink?

Had any of them been standing by while his mother called out, "Boy for sale!"?

Only through your strength, Abba Father. Not by my own can I do this, so if it is your will, fill me now. He opened his eyes and let out the breath that tasted of long-forgotten memories. "One meal. Neither of you will volunteer more if they ask, not unless I feel the Lord saying we ought. Are we agreed?"

Benjamin's hand gripped his shoulder. "Of course we are agreed. This is your journey now, my brother—we are but your servants in it."

One more deep breath, one more prayer, and Samuel strode forward. Boldly, lest he turn tail and run.

He spotted Jonathan packing up the bolts and skeins of wool at his booth. When the younger man caught sight of him, the look on his face combined pleasure with strain. "You came," was his chosen greeting when they neared. "I feared you would change your mind."

"Nearly." A hundred times. But he summoned a smile, weak as it may appear. "May I ask you something before we go in, Jonathan?"

"Of course." He put the last ball of yarn into a bag.

"Was she...is she a good mother to you?"

Jonathan's hands paused, the deep breath he sucked in saying it was not as easy a question as Samuel wished it were. His eyes flashed with weary lightning. "She tried, I suppose. As best she knew how."

Not exactly reassuring.

"Dara would say she was a better mother to me than to her."

Samuel felt Benjamin come to alert beside him and knew not whether to chuckle or roll his eyes. So he said only, "Dara?"

"Our sister. Come, I will introduce you." Jonathan slung the bag of yarn over his shoulder.

Samuel motioned Benjamin and Mark forward to help, though he need not have bothered. They were already shouldering the other bags and crates, as did Samuel.

The action seemed to mystify Jonathan. "I thank you. Though you need not—"

"It is our pleasure to help." Benjamin grinned in proof. Was it as obvious to the younger man as it was to Samuel *why* he was so eager?

No, that was unfair. Ben and Mark may have jested *ad nauseum* about the beauty awaiting their eyes today, but they were always happy to help anyone, any time. Regardless of whether they had just been promised an introduction to a pretty girl.

Samuel followed Jonathan back into the shaded interior of Martha's home and into a small chamber at the rear where other bolts and skeins were stored already. They deposited their load and backed out again.

His shoulders went tense, tight. Something skittered up his spine. When he pivoted, he saw that two women now stood but a few feet from him. Martha and a younger, fairer woman that must be Dara. She had the same golden curls that their father's family passed down, the same finely carved features.

But her gray-green eyes were the same shape and size as Martha's. Perhaps that was why he fought the urge to take a step backward when he looked at her. He knew not what else it could be—her smile was naught but sweetness and light.

Jonathan slid into the role of host, though it fit awkwardly upon his shoulders. "Allow me to make introductions. My—*our* sister, Dara. Dara, you can certainly guess which one is our brother, Samuel Asinius." His tongue turned to a hiss on the Roman surname. "Beside him is his brother by adoption, Benjamin... forgive me, I forget your surname."

"Visibullis. And you have not yet met our companion. This is Mark Bar-Andrew, the brother of Samuel's late wife."

Mark inclined his head, his eyes sparking much as Benjamin's were as he regarded the beautiful young lady. "And servant to Benjamin."

Martha had been motioning toward the water for them to wash their feet but halted at that. "Servant. Was your wife, as well, my son?"

The title grated, but Samuel kept his smile in place as they all shed their sandals. "She was. Though master and slave toil alike at Tutelos."

Martha pressed her lips together as they washed and then motioned them toward the table. "Forgive me my surprise. But you were raised a Roman—"

"And we all know they are better at crushing than working." Jonathan motioned Samuel to the seat nearest the head, the place of honor.

Why did he have to fight the urge to refuse it? Mother—his true mother, Abigail—would shake her head at him. He took the seat. "My mother was a slave herself, here in Jerusalem. Benjamin's father released her from her bonds when he married her. And her second husband, my father Titus..." His smile felt more natural now, as he considered the man. One who trained every morning as he had when a soldier. Who toiled every day as a man determined to see his businesses succeed. Who studied every night as a priest. "He has been grafted into Jehovah's family."

Martha frowned as she indicated seats for the others. Benjamin beside Samuel, Mark across from him on the other side of Jonathan. A slight that could hardly go unnoticed, that she placed the Hebrew slave higher than the Roman master.

Benjamin would laugh over it. And would not mind it a bit, since he sat across from Dara, who peeked at him demurely from beneath lowered lashes.

"Your father is a proselyte?"

"Not...exactly. He has made no official conversion to Judaism, but he studies the Law and seeks the Lord with all his heart."

Thunder possessed Jonathan's brows. "I cannot fathom it. My brother, raised by Roman d—"

Interrupt himself as he may, Samuel had no trouble finishing his word. *Dogs.* "Perhaps you should withhold judgment when you have never even met my father."

Lightning flashed in the boy's eyes. "I do not need to meet him. He is one of the oppressors, and I cannot understand how you can become one of them. Look at you, in Roman dress, with Roman hair. Are you not ashamed?"

"Jonathan." It was Dara who chided him, her eyes flashing too, though not in quite the same way. "Is this how you speak to our guests?"

Martha slid a tray of bread and apple clay onto the table but said nothing.

Jonathan folded his arms over his chest. "Some issues must be discussed at the outset if we are to establish any kind of relationship. Do you not agree? Brother?"

How could the word sound so right from the lips of Benjamin and Mark, from strangers in the churches, yet so wrong from lips actually related to him? *By your strength, Lord.* Samuel took the time for a deep breath. "I am sorry you are offended by how I was raised, Jonathan." As if the choice had been his. He shot a look to Martha. "But I have discovered that no matter how I dress, one side will take offense. Am I ashamed? No. Because I know that the oppression of Rome is beyond my influence—but the oppression of hatred on my soul is something I need not accept. If I have freedom from my sins, it hardly matters who rules the land on which I tread."

Martha's platter of fruit hit the table with a clatter. Disgust churned in her gaze. "Are you a Zealot?"

Benjamin laughed. "No, though the Zealots laid much of the groundwork for us. We are Christians, followers of Jesus the Messiah."

Martha froze. Dara studied the table. Jonathan stared at Samuel and Benjamin and Mark with incredulity.

Samuel sighed. It was going to be a long evening.

nine

BY THE TIME THE TRIO OF MEN COULD DECENTLY MAKE THEIR EXcuses and leave—something Dara could tell they wanted to do from the moment they stepped inside her mother's house—darkness cloaked the city.

Playing the part of demure daughter and sister had been no great challenge as they ate. Darting supposedly furtive glances at Benjamin Visibullis had been no great hardship, either. A more handsome young man she could not recall seeing. Perhaps she preferred the mature Hebrew look of the master, but she could be grateful that her fate lay with one so fair and not some paunchy old man.

And he sent as many furtive glances her way as she did his. She indulged in a smile as they disappeared into the night, as he looked over his shoulder one more time. Her brother had paid her little heed, the one they called Mark had kept his attention focused mostly on his lord, but Benjamin obviously took note of the care she had put into her appearance that eve.

She grabbed her head covering now, positioned it over her curls, and darted out the back door. Her mother called an irritated question after her, but Dara ignored the hiss. Where she went ceased to be any business of Martha's the day she took coins from the master's hand. Dara must move quickly, to intercept them before they reached the corner. They would frown on her following them to their inn and no doubt would be appalled if they opted for entertainment tonight and she followed toward the harlots.

As her feet found the familiar stones and packed earth of the alley behind their house, Dara whispered a prayer to Jehovah for the right words, the right manner, to come upon her. Then she ran toward the street, relieved to see their increasingly familiar silhouettes against the lamplight spilling from windows.

"Samuel!" Though her voice carried urgency, she kept it low.

But he heard her and paused, turned, question knotting his golden brow. "Dara?"

She emerged into a circle of the dim light, clutching her head covering as if uncertain. "Forgive me for seeking you in such a fashion. But I dared not speak up in my brother's house."

Moonlight gilded the curiosity in his gaze. "What is it of which you wish to speak?"

Her fingers tightened around the delicate cloth. "I..." Could she say it? Yes. She must. Her smile wavered, but surely that was to be expected. "I too am a believer. In Jesus." The name felt strange on her lips, distasteful. *Jesus.* A pretender, a rabble-rouser, a deceiver. The master had told her the tales of the man, of his gruesome death, and of course she had heard of the followers who spread lies about him rising from the grave.

Idiots, every one of them, to believe something so foolish.

She glanced at each of the men in turn and then at the ground. "I am afraid I am unschooled in the faith—I have not dared to seek out other believers. If Jonathan or Mother found out...but your coming is surely of God."

Her brother said nothing, merely studied her in the low light. The shadows obscured his thoughts, though she could only assume no warmth surged through him at her words, given his lack of reaction.

Benjamin, however, laughed and clapped a hand to Samuel's shoulder. "What did I tell you? There was a reason we stumbled across Jonathan yesterday. A sister in faith as well as blood."

"A praise indeed." Yet her brother's voice was even, distinctly lacking in joy. "How did you come to the faith, sister, if you have not met with other believers?"

She pulled out her slow smile while she scrabbled for an answer. The words whispered into her mind. "I heard a sermon a few months ago, when we were in the country checking on our flocks. The truth of the message of Jesus spoke to my heart, and I confessed my belief to a few of the others there. But when I went back to our tent, Jonathan and Martha mocked them—I knew I must keep my change secret for a while. I have been praying, though, to be put into the path of other Christians."

"And here we are, in your path." Benjamin's smile was warmth and charm and pulled taut a familiar ache in her belly—the one usually only stirred by the master. Yes, she could imagine herself in his arms. She could already feel how his lips would press to hers.

But his wife? So soon? And *Rome*? She dipped her head, knowing darkness and modesty would cover any hesitation on her part. "Praise the Lord. I have so many questions. Please, Lords, might I meet with you on the morrow, away from Mother and Jonathan?"

"Of course," Benjamin said without hesitation. "We will be at—"

"*Minime!*" Samuel's hushed interruption was too rapid a Latin for her to follow anything beyond the strong refusal. But there was no missing the tension in his face now, the caution on Mark's, and the way Benjamin's expression settled from exuberance to acceptance.

Whatever her brother's objection, it won the others over. Her fingers tangled in her veil. If they refused to see her again, what then? Would she have to resort to following them around like a dog?

Samuel turned to the third man. "Mark?"

The servant shrugged and answered in Greek. "I am not my sister. All I can say is to use caution but not hinder the Spirit."

Samuel nodded and turned to her with a weary smile. "I am sorry. It is not our place to disclose where the believers gather—there are those who seek to harm them, and too many already have been martyred. We will meet with you, but at a place of your choosing, not among the brethren."

He did not trust her. Prudent but frustrating. She injected hope into her smile. "I understand. Perhaps by the time you depart Jerusalem, you will be convinced enough of my sincerity to introduce me to someone who might continue to teach me the ways of Messiah. But until then, if I can but have a few hours of your time, I will count myself blessed beyond measure."

Benjamin eased half a step closer, though still a respectable distance away. "Name the time and place, and we shall be there."

Dara smiled. Perhaps this would not be so difficult a task after all.

Zipporah stretched out along her favorite branch of the ilex tree, her gaze seeking the gray-pink sky through the leaves above her. For the last two days, with the bustle of Menelaus and the Roman families arriving, with reading the letter from Paul, with needing to do more than the usual serving and assisting in preparation for Passover, she had found no time to sneak away and pray.

She knew well the Lord heard her just as clearly when her words came from within her small chamber. But she heard his answers best out here, in his creation. So she had risen earlier than usual to be assured that another day would not pass without the quiet of her sanctuary.

The breath she drew in tasted of damp earth and green, the bark of her branch was rough and welcome under her sandaled feet. One arm she stretched above her head to anchor her, the other settled at her stomach, where her fingers traced the metal finishings on the leather belt. The gift brought a soft smile to her lips. Samuel always remembered her in his letters, in his packages. Never had a crate of gifts arrived without something in there either from him or Mark, sometimes both.

Sweet of him. Yet every time he sent something, especially something as expensive as this, it made her all the more aware of how little she meant to Benjamin in comparison. He never even mentioned her in his letters, unless it were in a list of everyone to whom he sent his greetings. Say as he would that she was like a sister to him, she was not even that. She *was* a sister to Mark, truly like one to Samuel. To Benjamin she was...nothing. Just nothing.

Abba God... She focused on the last visible star, one that twinkled and winked out of sight when a leaf blew into her vision, back again in the next second. Soon to fade in the face of the rising sun. *How long will it hurt? How many more years must I wrestle with this silly infatuation? I know he does not love me. Will never love me. I know that I am yours, and that is all that matters. And for months at a time, I am happy with my lot. Content with the brethren, happy to serve those I love so completely. Then we will hear from them again, and it all comes rushing back. Every time. It is like I am thirteen again, all my progress lost.*

Somewhere in the distance, a dog howled. Zipporah's eyes slid closed. Sometimes she thought it would be nice to indulge in something so vocal, so obvious, so bold. Just to toss back her head and cry out to the world. Let her hopes and frustrations fly into the night. But as it would accomplish nothing that her silent howling did not, she always opted for the quiet approach.

The better to hear the whisper of her God. This morning it sounded like a breeze to her ear, but like a question to her heart. *Would you choose not to love?*

She opened her eyes again, traced the largest metal stud with her fingertip. "I would choose not to love *him*," she whispered back. "Not like this."

Did God laugh? It sounded like it as the leaves stirred above her in a gentle gust. *My daughter. Can you not trust me to use this to my glory? Do you not trust me to care for my sparrows?*

Her lips curved up. "You know I do. Imperfectly, without doubt. But I do."

Pray for him.

Simple little words, yet with them came a crushing tide within her, one that rose so quickly, crashed so fully that it forced the breath from her lungs. *Danger*. Not a word this time so much as an impression, a clutching feeling of dread that tied her stomach into knots. Such a warning, after being told to pray for Benjamin—fear clutched her with its talons. Had they made it to Israel, or had their ship met with hazards? Had they come up against an enemy? Fallen ill?

Four years of not knowing should have made her accustomed to this, to responding to the call to pray without knowing why or for what. Sometimes the Lord would give her a hint, but more often than not she or another here would merely hear the command. And so they would fall to their knees and beseech the Lord on behalf of their missing members.

No more direction came now as she lifted him up to the heavens and prayed protection around him, but the shining warrior on the wall nodded his encouragement to her choice of words. Surely his counterparts in Israel, or wherever Benjamin was, were being dispatched.

A reality that still baffled her. She had asked so many questions these last five years, had done all she could to understand the rules God adhered to in this realm beyond the veil, but some of it still perplexed her. The best explanation she had received for how the warriors responded, but rarely before they asked, had come from Titus after much thought and prayer.

"The world belongs to the evil one," he had said, pointing to the beloved Scriptures he had purchased for Abigail before they even married, well before Zipporah was born. "Dominion over it has been given to him and his. Through Christ we can take it back—but as any soldier knows, that requires action. We cannot just sit around without a word, without a fight, and expect Satan to flee. We must come out against him—and our only way of doing that is through prayer. So we pray, and heaven responds. But we must not grow weary in it— we see in Daniel that though the Lord dispatched a messenger at Daniel's first prayer, he was waylaid by demons in the heavens, and it took him weeks to reach Babylon. Still, the Lord answered him, as he answers us when we pray."

And how amazing was it that they could mobilize an army of angels with their pleas? As the first edge of the sun peeked over the eastern horizon, a blaze of red-gold against the gray-green, Zipporah felt familiar words of praise well up. The psalm spilled from her lips to the melody she had known since birth. "I will exalt you, my God, O King, and I will bless your name forever and ever."

How many times had her mother and Abigail and Dinah sung this song as they went about their work? Too many to count. "Great is the Lord, and greatly to be praised; and his greatness is unsearchable."

She sang quietly but happily, knowing that by the time she finished, the sun would be fully above the horizon, and it would be time to head back inside to assist Sarah with her morning preparations. Knowing that wherever Benjamin and Samuel and Mark were, they were in the Lord's capable hand.

And, praise to him, they would soon be coming home. Before the seas turned stormy again in winter, they would be back. "My mouth shall speak the praise of the Lord: and let all flesh bless his holy name forever and ever."

"Amen."

The unfamiliar voice jerked Zipporah upright, though her alarm stilled when she recognized Urbanus standing just outside the reach of the ilex tree, a smile upon his face and apology in his eyes. "Forgive me for interrupting—I was merely walking and praying, and your song pulled me in. I have not heard that psalm yet, I do not think, but it spoke to me this morning. 'He will fulfill the desire of them that fear him.'" His eyes focused on the rainbow of colors streaking the clouds around the sun. "I pray he truly does hear my cry."

How well she knew that feeling. Smiling, she hopped down from her branch. "It is one of my favorites. Though I did not realize you spoke Hebrew."

"Pardon?" He spun back toward her, eyes narrowed. "You sang in Greek."

"No. I sang in Hebrew." But obviously this man had needed to hear the words of the psalmist this morning, if the Lord opened his ears. Her smile grew. "Are you headed back toward the villa? We could walk together if so."

"Yes, certainly." Though his brow had not smoothed. "I have been hoping for a chance to speak with you more. I am still amazed by this gift you have."

A chuckle tickled her throat. "As I am, whenever I pause to consider it. I cannot fathom why the Lord chose my eyes to open. Perhaps because it required the faith of a child to see beyond the expected, and I was no more than one when he touched me so."

"I daresay it is more than how old you were." He sighed and turned his feet toward the villa. "I have yet to see in myself these gifts Paul spoke of."

Another slip of a laugh sneaked out. "Says the man who just heard in Greek a song sung in Hebrew."

He granted that with a tilt of his head, but no light entered his eyes. "But Paul said we are each given in measure to our faith. I fear that may leave me with but a sliver of the Spirit."

She shook her head, her long curls brushing against the backs of her arms with the movement. "Why do you doubt yourself so, Lord? I see the flame of the Spirit within you, and it is bright and strong."

The furrow dug itself deeper. "You can see that too? The Spirit within us?"

"It took much prayer and training of my own rebellious spirit to be able to do so, but yes." She fell in beside him, brushing the tree's dirt from her tunic.

At last a small smile touched his mouth. "You—rebellious? I cannot believe it."

She had no choice but to laugh...and glance at the wall she had not crossed beyond in four and a half years. "How is your brother settling in? I did not see him yesterday."

His smile faded again. "He has always been given to the sway of his moods. Since we arrived, they have been stormy. I pray I have not hindered the working of the Spirit by forcing him with me."

"I cannot think so. The spark I saw within him can be nothing but the Spirit's whispering in his heart. Give him time."

That seemed to ease him—his countenance relaxed, and his smile bloomed full when Columba's coo sounded a second before the bird winged into sight and then settled on her shoulder. She greeted the dove with a coo in return and stroked his pearly breast.

He nodded toward the bird. "Thank you again for introducing the girls to your pet. They spoke of little else yesterday."

"They are welcome to feed him any time. Your daughters are precious, and so beautiful."

"They are, yes." Yet shadows flitted through his eyes. Did he wish for a son? No, it was not that. "They all have the looks of their mother."

Ah, there it was, that cause for sorrow. She ought to have known. "Your wife must have been a lovely woman too, then. How...how long has it been?"

"She died birthing Juliana." He hooked a hand behind his neck and rubbed, presumably at where the tension rode. His gaze was set on the distance, though she doubted he saw the lines of the villa emerging from the mist. "I had come to faith two years beforehand, but Septima—she called me a fool, mocked me. I heard so many stories of entire households coming to Christ, but not mine. She would not trust me."

"I am sorry." Were she Abigail or Ima or Dinah, she would have touched a hand to his arm to give comfort. Were she Titus or Abba or Jacob, she would have known what words to say. Why did she always fumble when talking to someone she knew not well, when she could see them so clearly from a distance? "I can only imagine the difficulty of not sharing something so deep with your spouse."

"Indeed. I have sworn to the Lord that I will not remarry unless I can find a woman who will serve him beside me." He let his hand slide back down to his side.

"I imagine that looks to be a daunting task." Zipporah smiled. "But fear not—if he can find a helpmeet for Menelaus, he surely has one set aside for you."

That earned her a laugh, praise to Jehovah. The bunching in his shoulders eased. "I know he can, and perhaps he shall choose to. In the meantime, I will focus on my daughters, on learning more about the faith here in Rome, and be grateful for this chance to make new friends."

Not knowing what else to say, Zipporah smiled again and let the silence of the morning return. It wrapped comfortably around her as they covered the last of the distance to the villa.

At least until a familiar laugh spilled through the window of Sarah's chamber, bright as the sun ascending through the heavens. "Zipporah, is that you out there?" A moment later Sarah swung over the windowsill, her hair still loose around her shoulders and the flush of sleep on her cheeks. In her hand she held a scroll. "You must come read this play that Benjamin sent, it is—oh!" Having actually bothered to look up by then, she spotted Urbanus and immediately dropped her gaze and backed up against the wall. "Good morning, Lord."

Zipporah glanced at her companion in time to see the flash of appreciation in his eyes, quickly shuttered. She could certainly not blame him for finding Sarah an enchanting sight—nor for getting a quick reign on himself to keep from embarrassing her. "Good morning, Lady. I stumbled across your maidservant during my walk. I hope I did not startle you too badly."

Sarah's smile lit the morning as surely as her laugh had. She lifted her gaze. "Only a bit."

Urbanus smiled in reply. "I had better hasten back inside before my daughters awake. Good day to you, Lady Sarah. Zipporah."

They echoed his wishes and held their places until he turned the corner. At which point Sarah giggled and grabbed Zipporah by the arm, pulling her back to and through the window. "Oh gracious, how embarrassing—climbing through windows in front of him." Yet, being Sarah, she laughed again rather than flushing with the supposed shame. "Ah well. He is a handsome one, is he not?"

"Is he?" Zipporah looked back to the window, as if to see him again. "He did not strike me particularly so, though certainly I found no objections to his appearance."

Sarah rolled her eyes and plopped onto her down-filled mattress. "Silly Zipporah—you cannot even see anyone but Benjamin."

"Not true. I see other men all the time." Indulging in a smile, she fetched Sarah's brush and settled behind her. "It is just that none other can compare. Can I help that your brothers are all so handsome that gazing upon them every day is like staring too long at the sun? Can I help that all others dim in comparison?"

Sarah laughed again. "Do not let Jason hear you say so—he already thinks himself a rival to Adonis."

"No doubt because Deborah tells him regularly that he is." She stroked the brush through her friend's hair. "I hope Benjamin and Samuel and Mark make it home in time for the wedding."

"Oh yes," Sarah said on another laugh, "*that* is why you wish them home soon."

Zipporah gave a little tug on a lock of Sarah's deep brown hair and hoped the smile on her face would cover the ache in her heart. "And of course I miss my brother."

"Mm." Sarah spun around, taking Zipporah's hands in hers. "Zip—he will see. He will see your worth, he will see all you do for the brethren here, he will see what an amazing woman you have become. He will see that you are all he could wish for in a wife."

A chill skittered up her spine. "Will he?"

"Yes." And yet, even as she said it, she frowned.

The chill turned to a shudder. Perhaps Sarah was right, but a terrible certainty snaked through Zipporah's heart—he may indeed see...but it would be too late.

She dared not think why.

ten

BENJAMIN RECLINED ON A CUSHION IN THE UPPER ROOM AND laughed. "No, Dara. Having the Holy Spirit within you is not at all the same as being possessed by a demon."

Dara sat across from him, a soft smile on her face and a golden curl between her fingers. They had still not introduced her to the other brethren, but they had mentioned her, and one had volunteered this room for them to teach her and answer her questions. To ask her their own. They had met three times now.

And each time, his stomach went tighter when he saw her. The fault of the dreams, no doubt. He had obviously had dreams of women before, ones where the longings he kept a rein on in waking hours broke free. He knew well they were normal, and that while the Lord may hold him accountable for what thoughts he dwelled on, he would not count it a sin for what thoughts pounced upon him unawares.

But these...these dreams continued night after night and seemed to burn his eyes with their images. Even now, discussing the Spirit with her, they flashed before him. His mouth on her neck. His hands on her body. Her body bared before him, arching toward him, her lips begging him to make her his. He shook it away, but the impression lingered. Never in his life had he felt so helpless against the longings of his flesh.

"I pray you, Benjamin," she said, his name like a song on her lips, "how is it different?"

He glanced to Samuel and Mark. While the younger listened attentively, Samuel brooded into his plate of figs and grapes and pomegranate seeds. He had not said a word to his sister today, had not answered a single question. They would have to have a little talk when Dara left them.

Benjamin cleared his throat. "Well, when possessed by a demon, the demon controls a person. Forces him to do things he would not normally do. The Spirit never forces. The Spirit is a whisper in our hearts, a certainty and peace, a guide, a comforter. He advises our hearts and minds but never forces his will upon us. We are always free to choose which path we take, what actions we perform. Our wills remain our own."

"Ah." Her smile bloomed full. "That makes sense now. How did you become so wise in these things?"

Did Samuel just roll his eyes? Benjamin cleared his throat and focused his gaze on her face. Her perfect, breathtaking face. "Any wisdom I may have is from growing up in the Word, with godly parents to teach me."

Storm clouds raced through her eyes. "Well, that is something I cannot hope to aspire to. My father was a good man, but Mother..." She shook her head and looked to Samuel. "I know not how you could ever forgive her, brother, even if our Christ did teach us that we must."

At least he looked up from his pomegranate seeds, even if his gaze was more cool than warm. "It is a struggle, I confess. One I thought long ago settled, until I saw her again."

Dara's gaze sought the ground, and her fingers loosed the lock of hair. "She does not speak of it to me, but I know she must be sorry for what she did."

"Must she?" Samuel shook his head and pushed his plate away. "She did not sound so to me. And I daresay when my uncle came to redeem her, she was gladder than ever that she had rid herself of me."

Mark clasped a hand to Samuel's shoulder. "Yet we all know forgiveness cannot depend on the repentance of the offender."

"Hence the struggle." Samuel attempted a smile that faded when he looked back to his sister. "I have very few memories of life before Benjamin's father bought me, and I daresay my mind forsook them on purpose. But I hope you and Jonathan have had a good life."

Something flashed through her face, so quickly Benjamin would have missed it had he not been watching her closely. A bolt of pain, quickly covered by a smile. "We have gotten on well enough. Though Mother was always lax with Jonathan—out of guilt for her dealings with her other son, I now think. She never required anything of him, and now look at him. He cannot be bothered with responsibility. Hence why we must hire a shepherd for our flocks. Not to mention why I am sixteen yet without a betrothed husband."

A wave of relief washed over Benjamin. She certainly had never mentioned a husband, but he had wondered. After all, most young Jewish women were married or at least promised to a man by fourteen. In Rome, wealthy daughters were usually betrothed by twelve, though they remained in their parents' house until they were old enough to bear children. He had not wanted to consider, though, that he lusted so after another man's wife. Bad enough that he lusted so at all.

Father, help me. But maybe it was not so terrible that he felt drawn to her. Perhaps her brother had been remiss in his duties as head of the house for this reason. Perhaps...perhaps she was meant for *him*.

"I had better get home." Dara stood, her finely woven garment managing to show her curves without compromising her modesty. "Thank you all so much for meeting with me again. How much longer will you be in Jerusalem?"

The men all rose too. "Another week." Samuel looked at Benjamin as he said it, but certainly not to seek his opinion on the pronouncement. Challenge glinted in his eyes, as if he were thinking, *Try to say otherwise. I dare you.*

Benjamin grinned. "Six days, actually, and then we set out for Joppa once again. And from there, Rome."

Dara's smile faded to a frown. "So short a time. I had not wanted to ruin our meeting by saying so, but...my mother asked me to find you and try to convince you to dine with us again. Would you consider it?"

The muscle in Samuel's jaw pulsed as the silence stretched. At last he cleared his throat. "I know not, Dara. I will have to pray about it."

"Then...may I get your answer at our next meeting? In two days' time?"

How could her brother possibly say no when she looked at them like that, with such hope and longing? Samuel surely could not deny her the chance to soak in as much learning about the Savior as she could before they left.

Surely not—though he looked none too happy about it as he nodded his consent. Yes, they would be having a discussion in a few minutes. But for now, Dara. Benjamin smiled. "I will walk you down, my friend."

"I thank you." She turned her smile on him, all sweetness and gratitude and—dare he hope it?—a deeper appreciation.

Six days, wherein he could hope to see her no more than three more times. Was it enough? Enough to warrant speaking to her brother? Could he possibly be sure? He would pray about it. Though when he had tried over the last few days, her image kept crowding out his thoughts. His prayers turned to daydreams.

He pulled open the door and let her precede him through it, out onto the rooftop landing and down the outer stairs.

"I do hope you can convince him." She paused halfway down, turning to look up into Benjamin's eyes. "It pains me to realize he would just as soon never see any of us again. I understand his feelings toward our mother, but have I done anything wrong?"

"Of course not." And what was wrong with Samuel, that he had made this lovely young woman have to ask such a question? Benjamin lowered to her stair, then one more, so that their eyes were more on a level. "I beg you to have patience with him. This has all been a terrible shock, and he is struggling to regain his footing."

Her smile sad, she averted her face. "My patience has very little bearing on the situation. You will soon be gone, headed back to Rome, and my thoughts on it will matter not at all."

"They matter."

She met his gaze again with a lifted brow. "To my brother?"

Benjamin tried to swallow, but it caught in his throat. "To his brother, anyway." Without quite realizing his own intent, he lifted his hand to brush at the golden curls spilling from under her head covering.

Danger. The word whispered into his heart—a wise warning, given the jolt of longing that surged through him at the contact. What was he doing? He had no claim on this woman, no relationship to allow him to make such a move. Perhaps he could touch the hair of his own sisters, of his female friends at Tutelos whom he had known all his life, but Dara? They had only met four times now. He could not...should not...

All logic vanished when she stilled his hand's retreat, leaned into his fingers for one brief, glorious moment, and then blushed and retreated from his touch, eyes downcast. "I am so sorry. You must think me—"

"No. But you must think *me*—"

"No." She darted a glance at him again, a smile curling up to meet the flush in her cheeks.

"Dara." His rebellious fingers moved again, threading through her hair until they could touch the silken skin of her cheek. Yearning hit him like an earthquake. "I have never...never felt so drawn to anyone before. I..."

Her fingers settled on his arm, anchoring him there so that he could not even consider pulling away. Her lids half-shuttered the smoky green of her eyes. "Nor have I. I know it is foolish, that you will soon be gone, but..."

But. But she felt the same pull. The very one that acted on him now, as irresistible as a lodestone. Before he could think of a reason not to, he leaned over, down an inch, and caught her mouth with his. If he had intentions, if he could apply thought to this at all, he would have said he meant to merely touch her lips and retreat. A taste, a tease...too much a temptation. Instead of pulling away, he dove deeper, pulled her closer, and kissed her until the blood roared through his head.

Her arms came around him, just as they did in his dreams. Her lips met his touch for touch, seeking for seeking. A sigh of pleasure sounded in her throat.

Stop!

He knew the voice, and it was that of Wisdom. But it was mostly his strong desire to ignore it that brought logic back to his brain. He pulled away with a ragged breath, trying to turn his thoughts to prayer but managing only to turn them slightly away from the images in his dreams. An improvement, at least.

He closed his eyes and drew in a deep draught of air. "I am sorry. I have no right to embrace you so."

Her fingers curled into his toga. "As I am. Or I should be. Although..."

A chuckle slipped out as he opened his eyes to behold the conflict in hers. It was enough, somehow, to know her confusion matched his own. It gave him the strength to feather one more kiss over her lips and then pull away. "I will be praying. About Samuel and the situation there, and about...this."

She nodded and loosed his toga, drew in a huffing breath obviously meant to bolster her. "As will I. I suppose in the meantime, I had better hasten home."

"Indeed." He moved to the far edge of the stair so she could slip past him. And clenched his hands into the folds of his toga to keep from reaching for her again when she did. "Farewell, Dara."

Her smile shone warm and secret. "Farewell, Benjamin."

He could only stand there, leaning into the wall of the house, while she turned and disappeared into an adjoining alleyway. He stood there still half a minute later when footsteps sounded behind him and Samuel and Mark slid past him as well. Apparently they were going too. Benjamin's feet followed without needing instruction from his mind, thankfully.

Mark held up for him at the base of the steps and greeted him with an elbow in the side. "You ought to see the look on your face, Ben. I thought I would never see the day when a woman rendered you so addled. Eh, Sam?"

Samuel looked over his shoulder at him, his eyes far from amused. "Hmm. Though I wonder why, of all the women the world over, he has to be so addled by *her*. Any other, my brother, and I would rejoice for you. But Dara?" He shook his head.

Benjamin ran a hand over his hair. Was that flash of white at the end of the alley Dara turning? It must be. "What has she done to make you dislike her so, brother? She is your sister. She is of the faith."

"Something feels wrong." Samuel strode through the alley, fast enough to show he would rather run. "I mean, the Spirit being like a demon?"

The question made him chuckle again. "So she is unschooled. That is hardly something to hold against her. Have we not heard any number of strange questions from the brethren these years?"

"From those converted from paganism, yes. And legalistic questions from the Jews. But a *demon*? Is that really something anyone would ask if they had experienced the indwelling of the Spirit firsthand? And even if he has not come fully upon her, a believer still ought to know better."

Benjamin breathed an unamused laugh. "So because her questions are not any you would ever ask, you disbelieve her very faith? Perhaps instead *you* ought to ask yourself a question. Like, perhaps, if you dislike her so because she reminds you of her mother in some way."

That must have hit a nerve. Samuel flinched and turned the same way at the corner that Dara had gone. "She does, at that. Not on the surface, but when I look into her eyes. And yes, Ben, that terrifies me. Because the eyes reveal the soul. And if her soul is like her mother's, then you ought to dub her a siren, plug your ears against her song, and steer far clear of her."

Benjamin turned to Mark, hands up in a plea for help. "Speak reason, my friend."

But Mark pursed his lips in thought instead of immediately jumping to his defense. "It is possible Samuel is blinded by his bias against Martha. But then, it is equally possible *you* are biased by Dara's very lovely face." He shrugged. "Either way, it is foolish to let this come between you. We leave in six days, and the question then will not be about her sincerity, but rather about Samuel's healing."

"I have no intention of letting *anything* come between us." Benjamin followed Samuel onto the wide avenue bustling with Jews in all manner of dress, proof that the city burst with visitors for Passover. Still, he had no trouble spotting Dara a good ways down, moving with speed and purpose. His gut clenched. "But I do not know if I can leave her in six days, feeling as I do. What if she is the woman the Lord intends to be my wife?"

Samuel came to an abrupt halt and spun on him. Yet it was not anger in his eyes. It was pain. Which inspired an entirely different twist in Benjamin's stomach. His brother shook his head. "You want to delay our return? We would risk missing Jason's wedding."

"Of course not."

"What then?" The pain increased. "You cannot be considering wedding her so quickly. You scarcely know her."

A valid point, though a thousand examples from the Scripture sprang to mind of men who spotted a woman they desired, made them wives within days, and went on to produce the offspring whose stories they all knew by heart. But times had certainly changed. And the stories never told of the difficulties that must arise in daily life for such couples.

Benjamin sighed. "Of course not. But I may...perhaps...I could speak with Jonathan. Arrange a betrothal, and then come back for her. Become better acquainted then."

That did nothing to ease the worry in Samuel's eyes. "A betrothal is as binding as marriage itself, you know that. You must be very certain before you do such a thing. Have you prayed about this?"

"Of course I have." Why did it feel like a lie on his tongue? He *had* prayed. Or had tried to pray. And certainly he would make a more valiant effort before changing the entire course of his life over a woman he hardly knew.

A sudden gust of wind sent the women around them clutching at head coverings, and for just a moment, the fog lifted from his mind.

Was he seriously considering a betrothal? To a woman he had seen four times over the course of a single week? He must be going mad.

Mark cleared his throat. "If we are following her, we had better hurry. She is turning again."

"We are following her?" Even as he asked it, Benjamin moved forward with Samuel and Mark. The elder's hum eased some of the strain within him. He may not yet like this sister he had discovered, but he still wanted to make sure she got safely home. Wise, given the throngs on the streets, the many men in town who were no doubt just as stunned by her beauty as Benjamin was.

They hurried along the busy thoroughfare, turning again where she had turned. And coming to a halt together when, at the far end of the street, a man stepped from the shadows. Benjamin's muscles coiled, ready to spring to her rescue.

But she greeted the man with obvious recognition and stepped to his side. Instant dislike for the fellow unfurled in his chest. The man was obviously Jewish—and wealthy. Probably around forty years of age, with streaks of silver at his temples.

Who in thunder was he?

Whatever the answer, he whispered something into her ear, she laughed a response, and then he stepped away. Still, he touched a hand to her back as he did so. And though Benjamin could only see her in profile, she beamed a smile at him before hurrying on.

A friend of her late father's, perhaps? One who kept an eye on the family? That must be it, or something like it.

Samuel pivoted and started walking back the way they had come. Benjamin and Mark jogged to catch up. "Wait. I thought we were watching her home."

Samuel waved a hand. "She joined a group of women, did you not see? She will be fine from there." But his brows were knit into a question.

A feeling Benjamin knew all too well.

eleven

ZIPPORAH STEPPED OUT OF THE KITCHEN, THE HEAVY-LADEN FOOD basket on her hip. The sunshine nearly blinded her, and she had to lift a hand to shield her eyes. Laughter drifted to her ears from the gaggle of children darting around Sarah just beyond the garden in a lively game of chase. Her friend scooped up one of Urbanus's daughters amidst what looked to be a storm of giggles.

As Columba fluttered onto her shoulder, Zipporah strode toward the house under construction over the hill. Though apparently she ought to have done so twenty minutes earlier—the men who had been working on the dwelling for Urbanus and Lucius's families were making their way toward the house, Urbanus in the lead. His gaze was locked on where Sarah played with his children, and he looked none too happy as he watched them.

Zipporah altered her course a bit until she stopped before him, though he did not notice her. "Now that is a ferocious scowl. What thoughts could possibly be plaguing my lord so as he watches his daughters?"

Urbanus shook himself and produced a smile as most of the other workers passed them by. Shadows flitted through his eyes. "Memories, nothing more."

She hefted her basket to a better rest against her hip. "I was bringing you all lunch, but I see I was not quick enough." She smiled and shifted to watch Sarah with his daughters. "Your girls have joined Sarah's adoring throng, I see. She spends most days outside with the children."

He did not look back their way—his hand curled tight against his leg. "And you do not spend your days out here with her?"

"Sometimes." Interesting. She knew she had not mistaken the look of appreciation in his eyes whenever his gaze meandered Sarah's way. Why did he seem so displeased by it? Zipporah palmed a berry and held it up to her shoulder for the dove, who cooed his thanks. "But I have not the way with them she has—if you get close enough to listen, you will hear that as she plays, she teaches. The children all have better handles on the stories from the Scriptures than their parents. And often far deeper understanding of how Jesus fulfilled every promise. Not to mention their letters and mathematics."

His gaze had wandered their way again, though he huffed out a breath that hinted at displeasure with himself. Sarah rose with Juliana on her hip, pulling Hadriana up with her other hand. She cast a gaze over her shoulder and frowned. Something in her stance shifted.

Zipporah followed her friend's gaze and spotted Nereus striding toward her.

Urbanus must have too. "Children do not seem to be the only ones in her adoring throng."

"One of Benjamin's friends, who cannot understand why her faith forbids her from giving him her heart." Zipporah stroked her bird's neck and smiled at her father, who was coming up behind Urbanus, even as she took a step away to make room for Sarah and Urbanus's two youngest.

Abba stopped at Urbanus's side, between him and Zipporah. He leaned over to give her a smile and a kiss upon her temple and then greeted the fast-approaching Sarah with a grin. "More students, I see."

Sarah tickled Juliana's belly and then smoothed a lock of Hadriana's wind-tousled hair as she came to a halt in the space Zipporah had made for her. "Much to my delight. How comes the house?"

Before Urbanus could answer, Abba said, "Very nicely—the carpenter says you have an affinity for such work, Lord."

Urbanus inclined his head in thanks and held out his arms for one of his girls. Juliana reached for him first—her sister was too busy making cooing noises at Columba. "I never knew it could be so satisfying to work with my hands. Perhaps next I shall venture into the vineyards."

As he spoke, Hadriana was clamoring for Sarah to pick her up. He opened his mouth, no doubt to issue a gentle scolding, but Sarah beat him to it, saying with a smile, "Easy. You have only to ask." After a polite request, she lifted the girl, who strained toward the bird.

Zipporah could hardly blame the creature for taking to wing.

Hadriana apparently could, though. Her face fell, and her lip protruded. "Oh, no! Zipporah, you ought to keep him in a cage."

She smiled, gently but with no agreement as she watched Columba fly into the trees beyond the villa walls. "He will be back, Hadri."

The mite looked unconvinced. "But what if he gets hurt again?"

Zipporah tapped a finger to the tip of the girl's nose. "It is a risk we all run every moment of every day. But I will not put a cage around a wild animal—he was born to soar wherever he pleases."

Sarah hugged Hadriana tight. "And she has faith that the Lord knows how much she loves her bird, and that he will bring him safely home. Where there is faith, there is no need to be so unfair as to hold someone captive."

Abba stiffened. "Some things, Mistress, are worth more than a beast of the field, though. And sometimes faith dictates wisdom above fairness." Without another word, her father stalked off.

Zipporah sighed.

Urbanus frowned. "Have I missed something?"

"Only Sarah overreacting to a very old subject for the countless time." Smiling at her friend, Zipporah shifted her basket again and nodded toward the villa. "Shall we?"

Urbanus arched a brow at Sarah, though, who apparently decided to chat. "Her father has not permitted her to leave the villa walls since the attack that broke her nose over four years ago. Though he knows well she longs for nothing so much as to carry the Gospel to the world."

"*Longed.* That dream has grown old and is an impossibility for me in any case. I am needed here." Zipporah turned her feet toward the house too. "Master Titus has intercepted Nereus for you, Sarah. You had better gather your flock, they will all be hungry."

Though Zipporah strode ahead of them, she did not move quickly enough. She could still hear her best friend say, "Were I my brother, with the authority to do so, I would override Andrew and open the door to her cage."

"It may not matter if you did, Lady. A bird so long held captive often knows not what to do with freedom. Especially if its wings have been clipped."

"Not Zipporah."

Zipporah squeezed her eyes shut and hurried ahead, out of earshot. She appreciated her friend's defense...but could not be sure which of them was right. Could not be sure what she would do with her freedom, if ever Abba granted it to her.

twelve

NEVER IN HIS LIFE HAD SAMUEL LESS WANTED TO ENTER A HOUSE. Never before had dread curled so heavily in his chest as when he crossed the threshold of Martha's home again. He rubbed at it, the heel of his palm over his heart, and wondered if it was real or imagined. If it was the Spirit whispering a warning or just his own churning emotions making him want to run like a hart for the hills.

Abba God, is that you? Help me, please. Help me to glorify you through this somehow. Help me to stay focused on you and what you can work in their lives rather than on the old hurts. Help me to forgive.

Yet the dread only compounded when he took another step inside. If only Zipporah were here—she could tell him if there were any spiritual cause for distress, or if it was all within his own mind. But if it were his own mind, he would have felt just as strongly when Benjamin pestered him about accepting the invitation, would he not have?

He shot a glance at his brother laughing and smiling at Dara, who had emerged to greet them. Her mother was nowhere in sight yet, thankfully, but Jonathan lounged on a couch at the far end of the room, looking only slightly happier than Samuel felt.

Some reunion this had turned out to be. He longed for his own room at Tutelos, where he could measure out some chamomile and brew a tea to calm his nerves. Though he doubted even that would help right now.

His eyes sought and found Mark, who had entered last. Mark seemed to be the balance in this situation, the one affected neither by desire for the daughter nor bitterness toward the mother. If this dread were of the Lord, surely he would feel it too. In Latin, he asked softly, "What do you think, my friend? I have a bad feeling here tonight."

Mark did not smile. "I worry for Benjamin. His desire clouds his judgment, and I fear he will regret it if he acts on this attraction."

Samuel shifted, put his back to the room. Though seeing freedom through the open doorway only made him want it that much more. "Did you tell *him* this?"

"I did." Mark sighed. "He said *he* feared he would regret it if he did not."

Samuel pinched the bridge of his nose. Benjamin had never been held in the sway of lust before. He had surely felt pangs of it, as they all did, but always his focus had been on serving the Lord above his own flesh. Always he had kept a tight rein on his baser instincts. What did it mean that Dara made him forget that? That she was the one meant to be his wife...or something else entirely?

Samuel could not trust her. Perhaps that was wrong of him. Perhaps, as Benjamin said, he was only carrying over to the daughter his dislike for the mother.

Or maybe she was every bit as conniving as Martha.

It seemed too much a risk to take, by his calculation. Benjamin would not agree, but then, Benjamin did not carry the emotional scars wrought by this family's treachery. Without question, though, there were innumerable concerns left unanswered. For instance, Samuel was not certain why the Spirit had pressed him so strongly to follow Dara the other afternoon, to see her with that man Benjamin was so sure was a family friend, but he wondered.

He wondered. A sixteen-year-old woman, unwed—possible. But one as beautiful as Dara? Highly unlikely. Even if Jonathan were as irresponsible as she claimed, if he were too lazy to seek out a husband for her, it would not have stopped men from coming to *him*. And if he were so unwilling to be bothered, would he not have handed her over to the first man to ask?

Something felt wrong about it all, but pray as Samuel might for answers as to what, no clarity came. Just the ever-increasing certainty that Benjamin must be the one to see whatever the truth was, or it would do no good.

"Samuel, my son." Martha stepped into the doorway from the street, a basket of fruit and grains upon her arm and a wide smile upon her lips. "I scarcely believed it when Dara said you accepted our invitation. I hope you enjoyed a pleasant Passover."

He forced a lie of a smile. "Yes, thank you." Visiting with the brethren during the celebration had been a blessing—though part of him wished they had not come at all, that they had instead sailed straight home for Rome. Bypassed this entire situation.

Martha cast her face downward as she entered the house, sliding by him. "I had hoped...prayed you might join us for the feast. But of course you already had other obligations."

All his strength was required to stifle a groan. "We did, yes. Planned out for over a year."

"Of course." Her smile wavered. From genuine emotion, though, or some attempt to play upon his? She made a show of straightening, drawing in a deep breath, and then brightened the smile and nodded toward where Dara and Benjamin stood at the far end of the room, looking deep in conversation. "Your brother seems quite taken with my daughter."

And no doubt she had sense enough to know that was why Samuel had come back to this house, and for no other reason. "I imagine she is well used to the attention. I was frankly shocked when she mentioned in passing the other day that she has never been betrothed."

There, a falter in her gait, a hitch in her quick smile. But why? "I admit I have never pushed Jonathan on the issue, nor sought a match for her myself.

It is such a comfort to have her here with me, and she is happy with her loom. She weaves the finest cloth in all Israel. Perhaps in all the empire."

Monetary, then, her reasoning? Samuel would not put it past her to keep a daughter at home to profit from her, as surely as she would sell a son for the same reason. He looked to Mark, thinking perhaps he would have an opinion reflected in his eyes, but his friend still watched Benjamin.

"Come." Martha motioned him farther inside. "Sit, rest. You leave again soon, do you not?"

"Two days." Not soon enough. He took a step toward one of the low couches, opposite where she seemed to be headed after putting her basket down.

"Such a short stay after such a long journey!" Martha shook her head, even clucked her tongue. "I would have thought you would stay several months, given how long you must have traveled to get here."

A valid point, and one that had distressed them when they first planned this last stop. Now, though, he was so very glad time had not permitted more. "And yet it is just as long to get back, and we have many reasons to hurry. One of our younger brothers will be getting married this summer."

Martha settled opposite him, her smile looking forced. "Tell me of this family of yours, please. You have many...brothers?"

Samuel looked to Benjamin, who often piped in when such questions came up, but this particular brother paid no attention to his conversation just now. He laughed over something or another with Dara. Samuel nodded. "There is Benjamin, of course, who was born while we were still in Jerusalem. Then Mother married Titus in Rome, and they adopted me. Next came my sister Ester, who now has three children of her own, then Jason, who is the one getting married this summer. Cleopas is our resident poet, and the baby of the family is Sarah. She is about the same age as Dara."

And oh, how he looked forward to seeing them all again. Teasing his other brothers, seeing how Sarah had grown up in the two years since their visit. How good it would be to return to what was familiar. To see what new scars Zipporah had managed to attain even within the protected walls of Tutelos, to meet the new visitors who had taken up residence with them.

"And your wife. What was she like?"

He could smile now at the mention of her, and he knew when he went home, the memories of her there would be more comfort than pain. He would not see her in every hallway, on every path and think, *If I had only said something to her right then* or *Was that pain on her face that day? If I had done something in that moment, would they have lived?*

"Anna was..." How to describe her to one who had never met her? Again, usually Benjamin or Mark took over the discussion here. For many years, he supposed, they did it to spare him the pain of thinking of her so pointedly. But tonight, he was apparently on his own in the conversation. "Beautiful, as Ben said before. I am afraid her life revolved around that for several years, when she could not leave the villa without garnering unwanted attention. Our parents feared what fate may befall her if she remained a slave."

Martha's hands, previously occupied with a skein of wool, went still. "So she was not only a servant, but an actual slave."

He lifted his brows. "Why would that distress you? For that matter, why would it surprise you? Was I not sold to be one too?"

A scarlet flush took the place of the paleness in her cheeks.

Samuel shook his head. "Benjamin freed her before our betrothal."

Jonathan sent him a sideways glance that looked far too mocking. "I suppose you had loved each other all your lives."

"I had, yes, though I fancied it as a sister for most of that time." Until their parents approached him with the idea of a wedding. Until they said someone must protect her, and there was no one else they trusted to do so. Until Anna confessed that if she must marry, she would want it to be to him.

Sometimes he still wondered if he had made her happy, or if she would have preferred to wait for a husband who was not called off at all hours to bandage a wound or soothe an aching spirit. Sometimes he still wondered if she had loved him *for* those things that made him who he was...or despite them.

Sometimes he wondered if their parents regretted entrusting her to him.

"How long were you married?" Martha's fingers resumed whatever work they were doing with the wool.

"Only a year." Not nearly long enough to work through the excitements and the disappointments, to adjust to the changes in their relationship and form a new, stronger one. To reconcile hope and reality. They ought to have had so much longer. *She* ought to have had so much longer. She ought to have had the chance to hold their babe, nurse him, watch him grow. But the one time she had needed Samuel's healing touch, he could do nothing. Nor could he even obey her last demand to save their son.

Agony that had finally faded from knife-piercing to dull ache.

"Well." Martha put the wool aside and stood. "You are a young man yet, handsome and apparently quite well-off. I am certain you will have no trouble finding another wife."

And of course *now* Mark decided to pay attention, given the ticking in his jaw at that pronouncement. His friend had long ago urged him to look for another helpmeet whenever he felt ready, but coming from Martha's lips it sounded as though Anna ought not to matter at all.

Dara's laughter rang through the room, drawing all attention her way. She fingered the filmy veil that had slid from her hair to her shoulders, a blush in her cheeks. "I promise you, I did. I will show you my work later, if you would like. I take great comfort in my loom."

"I would love to see it." Benjamin's voice was what it always was, friendly and warm...and yet more. In it Samuel so clearly heard the desire, the attraction, the edge of desperation. His brother was fast running out of time to decide whether to act on those feelings and speak to Jonathan or go home and see if they faded or grew stronger.

Samuel curled his fingers into his toga and prayed with all his might that Benjamin opted for the wait-and-see approach.

Dara gave Benjamin a too-warm smile and turned away in either modesty or a skillful imitation of it. "I had better help Mother bring out the meal. Please, make yourselves comfortable. There is water ready for your washing."

Samuel moved with the others, but his mind was not on the ritual cleansing nor on the scents of fresh bread and spiced meat that soon wafted their way. With every step he took, every move of his arms, he felt the strangest sensation of weight. As if something were pressing down on the room, making the air heavier.

Jehovah, my Father. I know not what is going on, but please. Please protect us.

Zipporah dropped the bowl, sending raisins scattering over the mosaic. Everyone looked at her, but she hardly cared. Hardly noticed. Her gaze remained latched upon the window, and upon the flashes of light still streaking into the sky.

"Zipporah?" Sarah touched her hand, worry in her tone. "What is it?"

"Something is happening." She rushed to the window, craned to look around at the wall, but it was useless. She could see only one portion of it from here, which told her nothing. Nothing except that only one guardian stood where normally there were two.

She must get outside. Perhaps question the guardians remaining, if they would answer her. Spinning around, she nearly slammed into the mistress, who steadied her with a gentle hand on her shoulder.

Abigail's brows were drawn. "It is Benjamin, I think. I feel the strongest need to pray for him."

His mother's word was all it took to put an end to dinner. Titus stood first, came to his wife, and took her by the hand. "Then pray we shall. Everyone to where they feel they must go, but remain in groups of two or three at least. We will all stand together, but best to form unbreakable cords at every turn."

Wise, even if she would have preferred to be alone. But given that Sarah leapt up and wove their arms together, she had no real reason to complain. Praying with her dearest friend, who knew her inmost secrets anyway, would be no hardship. "Might we—?"

"Go to the ilex tree? Of course." Sarah pulled her toward the exit, her usually cheerful face covered in a mask of worry. "I feel taut as a bow. My spirit pulled tight just before you dropped the bowl, and I too heard my brother's name in my heart. What do you suppose it is, Zip?"

Zipporah could only shake her head. Then, since Sarah would act as guide and her feet knew well the path to her favorite retreat, she closed her eyes. Breathed out her everyday thoughts and breathed in the crisp wind of the Spirit. A physical danger? A storm at sea, robbers on the road? No. No, it was... "A decision, I think. A decision is before him that could change our whole world."

Sarah sucked in a gasp. "That is almost more terrifying. He has always made wise decisions, with a temperance beyond his years. What could possibly change that now?"

"I know not." But it made sense that it would be the stronger need for the church here. If something were to happen to him physically—may Jehovah forbid it—then he had the will in place to protect Tutelos and put it in the care of Titus. But so long as he lived, it was his, and all them with it, and so they all must abide by his decisions.

A shudder coursed through her and brought her eyes open again. They were cresting a knoll, and from its top she could see the wall.

It brought her feet to a halt. The guardians were only a few less in number, but they had concentrated on the wall where it met the ilex tree. Where, from the sides and above, dark forms swooped and screeched, talons flashing.

Of course. Why would the enemy work only on Benjamin, when they could attack them here too, and try to keep them from praying for him? She dropped to her knees and pulled Sarah down with her. "Here is good. A battle is raging, my friend. Fiercer than I have seen before. We must pray for heavenly reinforcements for us here as well as for your brother."

Another shudder, another squeezing of her eyes closed. *Benjamin. Benjamin, what are you doing?* But he would not hear the cry of her heart. He never did when he was right beside her, so how would he now? Only the Lord would, and only the Lord had the power to answer it. But oh, the terror within her.

Because if it were a decision for which they must pray, then their own power was limited indeed. Choice was the one thing God would not interfere with, she knew. He could calm a sea, he could still a storm, he could blind and paralyze attackers. But if one of his children chose freely the wrong way...then heaven help them all.

The wine had an interesting flavor, more herbal than he would have expected. And stronger, it seemed. After one cup, Benjamin's head went hazy as the vineyards on a foggy morn. He only sipped at the second cup Dara filled for him, but even so. Even so, he...he...

Or maybe it was not the wine at all. Maybe he was not even here. Maybe he was dreaming—that made sense. How often had he dreamed this, dreamed he was in her house again, his brother and friend beside him? And as in the dreams, their voices went distant and tinny, like so many clanging cymbals over a far-off hill. As in the dreams, his vision narrowed, until she was all he could see.

Dara. Beautiful, sweet Dara who smiled a secret smile into his heart and lit fires all through him. Was this to be the last time they saw each other? Would he then sail home and she stay here and that be that? Could he stand it if it were?

She looked at him from half-closed eyes, the gray-green practically glowing, pulling him in. A siren, Samuel had called her. But no. If she were any creature from the *Odyssey*, she would be Charybdis, the mighty whirlpool, her tug too great to be denied once he was in her current. He could even hear the rushing of the waters in his ears, drowning out those clashing cymbals of voices.

And clashing they were. He caught the words *Rome* and *tyranny*, and the name *Christians* spat like a curse from their host. That part of himself forever bound to his brother felt Samuel tense, felt the timbre of a reply with its anger held in close check. But he saw no reason to get involved. Samuel could defend what ought to be defended and leave the blame young Caesar deserved squarely at his feet. Samuel could handle it. Samuel could handle everything. Samuel could *always* handle everything, always knew just what to say, just what to do.

Sometimes it got annoying.

No. Benjamin was rarely annoyed by Samuel. Where had that come from? It was good he had a brother so capable, one who had always looked out for him. It was good he had family who cared so much. It was good...it was good he was here now. It was good that Dara had stood, had come around to his side. And oh, was it ever good that she touched a hand to his shoulder.

Hunger consumed him, though he was fairly certain, through the haze, that he had eaten.

"Come with me, beloved. I will show you my loom."

Her voice was honey, her touch fire, her words a promise. He rose, grateful that she held him by the elbow to steady him, otherwise he might have toppled over backward.

What had been in that wine? No one else seemed affected.

Their loss. The world had taken on a glow in the fog, like the first rays of sun to break through it. Beautiful. Nearly as beautiful as the woman leading him toward the back of the house and the curtain he had first glimpsed her behind.

But when he tried to pass beyond it, it was as though he walked into a wall of solid stone. He had no choice but to halt, and Dara halted with him. Glaring for a moment at the wall, as if she saw it as clearly as he felt it. Then she smiled.

She had the most beautiful smile. He could gaze at her all day long. All night long. At least until gazing ceased to be enough. Then he would have to kiss her. To pull her close. He would hear that sound of pleasure in her throat, feel her body press to his in invitation, in need.

Danger. He heard the word in his ear, in his heart, and the haze burned away. *Go no farther.*

He drew in a breath that made him queasy. He was just under the curtain, on the verge of the threshold. So that he could see that the loom resided in what was obviously Dara's chamber. Her bed was in the corner, an assortment of decidedly feminine items in the room. Pots that no doubt held balms and perfumes, perhaps cosmetics; wisps of delicate fabrics like she wore over her head; a few strands of beads more colorful than valuable.

Go back. Get your brothers. Leave this place. Flee!

The command struck a chord, made something akin to fear rise up within him.

But then Dara stepped in front of him, her smile brightest sunshine and her hand outstretched. "It is all right, Benjamin. Come. Come with me."

Go! Turn and run!

But that was ridiculous. Why would he run from Dara? She was Samuel's sister. A believer. And so very beautiful. She was everything he could want. Everything he *did* want. He could not bear the thought of leaving her, neither tonight nor in two days. He could not. He would see her loom, as she obviously so desired, and then he would speak to Jonathan and Martha.

He slid his hand into hers, and the stone crumbled around him. Her smile went warm, perhaps even smug. "Come, my love. Come with me."

Yes, go with her. A silent voice. The whisper of the Spirit? Maybe...though it did not resonate as it usually did. Benjamin took a single step, and the haze came back. Delicious and consuming. And then it was so easy to take another, and another. Why not? It was only a dream. Nothing but a dream, and what did it matter what one did in a dream?

Dara led him to the loom, but rather than turning to the fabric underway, she turned to him and wrapped her arms about his waist. Tilted up her face. Benjamin's stomach went tight as he slid his arms around her too. She felt so perfect in his embrace. Lit a million fires through him. Left him helpless. He dipped his head, claimed her lips.

She pressed against him, ran her hands up his back. Were he awake, he may have wondered at her boldness, but of course dream-Dara would know what she was doing. Just as dream-Benjamin had no reason not to follow his instinct to run his hands over her in return.

No reason not to indulge. No reason to wake himself up. No reason at all.

Thirteen

DARA PRESSED CLOSE, CLOSER STILL TO BENJAMIN, LET HIS HANDS wander to places he would no doubt never have let them had she not put those herbs into his wine. She had not wanted to, but what choice did she have? He would not do more than kiss her otherwise, she was sure. They had conversed enough that she was certain his will was iron, his dedication to his principles complete.

But there was always a way around them. Always. Now, with his inhibitions lowered, he was at the mercy of his desire for her, and she...and she...

No! She broke away, a cry swelling up inside. Why was she doing this? She did not want to seduce him. She did not want to marry him. She did not know this man, did not want her future forever tied to his.

Child. The master's voice echoed in her head now, and it was not the warm greeting he sometimes chose. It was an accusation. Was she still the nine-year-old he had led home that first time? Untrained, unskilled, nothing more than any other girl?

Benjamin blinked, though his eyes still did not focus. "What is the matter, beloved?"

No, she was not that child anymore. She would do whatever she could to serve the cause. To serve the master. If she had to be Benjamin's to ever be his, then so be it. She curved her lips into a simmering half-smile and took Benjamin by the hand. Led him toward her bed in the corner. Perhaps a shudder worked through her, perhaps she could still hear the crying child inside, but she pushed it away.

"Nothing is the matter, my love. Come. Make me yours. Show me how you love me."

"Dara." He let her pull him down, then gathered her tight to him and kissed her long and deeply. "Dara. You will be my wife."

"Yes, Benjamin." She tugged with shaking hands at his toga, at the tunic beneath it. "I am your wife. I love you as you love me."

He opened his mouth to reply, but she pressed a finger to his lips and smiled again. They had no time for conversation. The effects of the herbs would wear off soon. Kneeling beside him, she drew in a breath that tasted of tears and pulled her own tunic over her head.

Samuel sighed, though the long breath in and out did nothing to quell the rising disquiet within him. Being in this place was a chafing upon his spirit, a decided feeling of wrong. Their blood may be half in common, but could it be any clearer that he was not one of them? No matter what he said, Jonathan sneered and mocked.

And Martha merely sat by, fiddling with her wool and staring at Samuel.

At last, he stood, which cut Mark off mid-argument, though he had been making a fine case for Christianity. "Excuse me. The hour grows late, and we must get back to our inn." Though Samuel frowned when he looked around and realized that Benjamin was not in the far corner of the room as he had supposed. He could have sworn he had felt two presences behind him, otherwise he would have gone after his brother long ago. It was not good for him to be alone so long with Dara. "Where is Benjamin?"

Jonathan rose too, though he waved away Samuel's concern. "No doubt letting Dara boast about her cloth. Come, through here."

Samuel followed, but with every step his stomach twisted more. He shot a glance at Mark, whose eyes were dark with panic. He sensed it too, then. Somehow, that did nothing to make him feel better just now.

Martha joined their little group, saying something that Samuel paid no attention to. Something that turned to a scream when she pushed through the curtain. Jonathan, rushing after her, opted for a curse.

Samuel stopped just outside the curtain and closed his eyes. He need not join them to have a good idea of what they must be seeing. The on-going shouts provided all the narration he needed.

"Dara, how could you?"

"Dara? You blame your daughter, when it is obviously the Roman dog who is at fault? Cur! You will not get away with defiling my sister!"

Mark pushed by at a half-run. "Benjamin?"

Samuel pinched at his nose, but the ache behind his eyes would not go away. What had his brother done? And why, why had he done it? If it was as it sounded, then it meant Benjamin had turned his back on what he had always held dear. Was Dara's pull on him so strong? So overwhelming?

When Jonathan proclaimed, "I will have you stoned for this!" Samuel decided it was time to join them.

Pivoting through the curtain, he saw what he had expected. Dara frantically tugging on her clothing, Benjamin with a hand to his bowed head, his chest still bare. Mark knelt at his side, the frown in his brow saying there was something more than the obvious wrong.

Martha wept. Jonathan fumed.

Samuel prayed for calm. "You know the Law as well as I, Jonathan. A man is not stoned for taking an unwed woman to his bed." He caught Dara's gaze, held it. "Or from being taken to hers."

The flush in her cheeks may have said shame or modesty to another, but to him it looked like guilt.

Jonathan spun on him, sparks spewing from his eyes. "How dare you! It is obvious your *brother* forced himself on my sister."

Samuel did not so much as blink. "Odd—I did not hear her cry out, though she surely knew help was only a few feet away if she wanted it."

Red stained Jonathan's cheeks and neck. "Are you impugning my sister's honor?"

"She has done that herself. Look at her." Samuel leveled a finger her way and obeyed his own command. His heart twisted within him at what he saw. "She was not forced, she was not coerced. She at the least went willingly, and quite possibly used trickery to lure my brother in. Do you not see the smugness in her eyes?"

Just like her mother. Caring only for her own gains. Though how she thought to profit by disgracing herself... His breath caught. Marriage. She was forcing Benjamin to marry her. She would gain access then to all that was his. His money, his houses, his lands.

"Benjamin." Samuel's voice came out no more than a whisper. "What have you done?"

His brother looked up at him with cloudy, confused eyes, inspiring a frown in Samuel's brows to match Mark's. "I do not know," he murmured. "It was only a dream."

What had she done to him? Samuel's fingers curled to his palm. "Mark, please help my brother dress."

Martha bustled over to her daughter, gripped her arm with what must have been too much strength, given the girl's wince, and pulled her toward the curtain. "And you will stay away from him." The woman's voice shook, and it sounded more like fear than anger. Strange. As they walked by him, he heard her hiss, "Fool! What have you done? Why would you betray your lord like this?"

A fine question indeed. If she were devout in her faith, as she had done her best to convince them, then why would she do this?

Once the women were out, Jonathan spat another vile curse at Benjamin, who raised his head with a wince. "Forgive me." His voice still sounded strange, like he spoke from within the grip of slumber. He cleared his throat, shook his head, pressed a hand to his temple. "Please, I did not realize...I feel so strange. Foggy. I thought it all a dream."

Jonathan looked far from appeased. "So defiling my sister in a dream is acceptable to you? Nay—drunkenness will be no excuse for what you have done! I ought to kill you now."

Taking in the boy's spindly limbs, his muscles untrained and soft from sitting all day behind his booth, Samuel indulged in a bark of laughter. "You could try. Though I invite you to see reason. Look at him, he is obviously not himself, and he had only one chalice of wine."

"You think to make excuses because he cannot hold his alcohol?" He apparently had a choice word for that too, and his face transformed to something hideous when he snarled. Was that how Samuel looked in anger?

Perhaps, but he could not recall ever being in such a rage.

Benjamin stood up, shakily, while Mark draped his toga. "Please, argue not. I will marry her."

"You will not!" Samuel and Jonathan shouted it at the same time. Looked at each other, then back to Benjamin.

"No sister of mine will marry a Roman."

Benjamin's head shake was slower this time. "What choice have you, Jonathan? I am sorry, I did not realize what I was doing, but...it is done. The Law is clear—I *must* wed her. More, I want to. I planned to speak with you—"

"No." It hit Samuel like a foot in his gut. He stepped forward, hand outstretched, begging his brother to see, now, that this situation was far from right, far from what Dara would have it appear to be. "Think this through, Benjamin. She did this. Somehow or another, she orchestrated this, and why? To achieve this very thing. To force you to marry her. Perhaps she seeks your wealth, I know not, but you cannot give in."

Benjamin's eyes had begun to clear. "I have no choice, brother. Honor and the Law dictate a single course."

With a growl, Jonathan spat at Benjamin's feet and pivoted toward the curtain. "Dara, if you marry this dog, you cease to be my sister!"

There must be a way out, some way, some path of escape. A girl who would do this was surely no innocent. If they could prove it, could prove she had played the harlot...yet even as he thought it, his eyes fell on the rumbled bed and the red stain upon it. All the evidence her family would need of her virginity before this night.

His throat felt dry and swollen when he tried to swallow. "Come, Benjamin. We will discuss this at the inn once your head has cleared."

Jonathan spun again, his fury aimed now at Samuel. "You think I will let you walk away, to disappear in the morning and leave my sister disgraced, perhaps even carrying his whelp? We will find an answer to this now!"

His spirit cried out at the thought. He could stay here no longer, but neither could he abandon his muddled brother to them. Lifting a hand to try to rub away some of the pressure in his head, his gaze caught on his fingers. He reached for the signet he had worn since he was a boy too young to keep it anywhere but on a chain around his neck. *Jason, forgive me—but it is for your son.* He pulled it off, held it out. "I will leave you with a pledge. We will return in the morning, I promise you."

Acting as though it were a rodent waiting to bite him, Jonathan lifted a hand slowly. Once he had the ring, he bit the gold, examined the jewel. And smirked. "Fair enough. This is certainly worth more than my harlot of a sister anyway."

Benjamin lunged, though he likely would have toppled over had Mark not steadied him. "Do not speak so of her!"

Jonathan, smirk curling into a sneer, batted aside the curtain. "She has proven herself no better than one."

Samuel rushed, then, to his brother and supported him on the side opposite

Mark while Jonathan disappeared. "Come. We will get you back to the inn so your head can clear."

Benjamin swayed as they led him toward the outer room. "I feel so strange. You drank the same wine—was it overly strong?"

"No, it was cheap and weak." Tight anger laced Mark's words as he held the curtain aside. "This is the working of something other than wine, though I know not what. You have been tricked, Ben. Manipulated."

"I..." Did he lose his train of thought or forget he had been speaking? Hard to say, as his gaze went to the corner of the main room, where Dara sat beside a lecturing Martha, her arms crossed over her chest in defiance. "Dara."

She made as if to leap up, but her mother held her down, and Jonathan stepped between her and them, face stony again. "We will settle this in the morning."

Benjamin did not acknowledge the young man, merely craned his head as they moved onward, no doubt trying to get a glimpse of her.

Lord, help us. Samuel helped Mark propel Benjamin out the door and into the night. None of them spoke until they had turned the corner, at which point Samuel met Mark's gaze over Ben's bowed head. "Are we in agreement? We leave here at daybreak and get him away from this."

Mark jerked his head in a nod, jaw pulsing from what must be the clenching of his teeth.

Benjamin pulled away. Less wobbly than he had been, but not what one would call steady. "Why would you say such a thing? I cannot leave. Cannot abandon her after what I did. Why would you make me a liar, and a dishonorable one at that?"

"Ben, wake up." Mark shook his shoulder to punctuate the command. "This is not as simple as getting carried away with your passion and making a foolish decision that you must pay for. This is not natural, whatever stupor you are in. You are not to blame, and you ought not to be held accountable."

"But I love her. I *want* to marry her." He took a step, unaided, and gave his head a hard shake. Pressed a hand to his temple. "And you gave them my father's ring, Sam."

For the thousandth time, Samuel wondered if he should have given the ring to Benjamin long ago. But it was all he had of the man who rescued him from a future worse than death. Who delivered him to Abigail, his true mother. "And who is to say he did not give it to me for such a time as this? Your father would understand and approve of using it to free you from such a fate."

"My father—" He took a step toward Samuel, nearly steady, and poked a finger at him. "—understood what it was to love a woman so deeply one could not help oneself. To love her so much he could not leave her in a shameful state, no matter the opinions of his friends on his choosing to wed her."

"Your father did not love our mother so deeply after a mere fortnight's acquaintance! And unlike his friends', *my* disapproval has nothing to do with something as inconsequential as her social station. Dara cannot be trusted!"

Benjamin met his vehemence with a slow blink. In the moonlight, his eyes looked clearer but now pained. "I am going to the inn, where I will sleep this off. In the morning, I am returning to them."

The pronouncement felt like a death sentence to Samuel's soul. "Do not. Please do not."

His brother, rather than answering, pivoted and headed for the inn. No longer wobbly, though his step remained slow.

Samuel met Mark's gaze again. "Bind him, gag him, and haul him out of here by force?"

It at least earned him a weak grin. "Tempting. But perhaps we ought instead to pray the Lord speaks to him as he sleeps, so that he sees the best course himself in the morning."

Samuel had never considered his faith lacking. But at that moment, he had nothing but doubt that the Lord's voice would make it through whatever haze—be it lust or wine or something else—that clouded his brother's mind.

Zipporah toyed with the cool grass under her fingers, her gaze traveling the celestials alight in the heavens above her. The battle around the wall had quieted a few minutes ago, and the very moment the dark ones had retreated, Sarah had fallen silent beside her and drawn in a deep, tired-sounding breath. Zipporah had flopped onto her back.

The urgency had lifted from her spirit. Yet no peace had taken its place. "He made the wrong decision."

Sarah had stretched out too, their heads near and their bodies at a forty-five degree angle. She reached out to pat Zipporah's arm. "Maybe not. We could be wrong in thinking that was what we prayed for. Or perhaps he merely deferred it, if it were a decision."

Optimistic thought, which was just like her dearest friend. Sarah always focused on the rainbow, no matter the storm clouds behind it. Zipporah closed her eyes against the star-studded canopy above her. "Perhaps the others have more insight. We should rejoin them."

"Mm." But Sarah made no move, and neither did Zipporah. The night air was sweet and warm, and it felt too good to just lie here for a moment now that the hand of the Spirit had lifted. To rest, even if the true rest she longed for evaded her.

Even if her heart felt as though the twist in it were permanent. As if...as if she had lost him. Forever. Which was absurd, given that she had never had him to begin with. He had never loved her, she had always known he never would. And yet...and yet obviously she had hoped. Because now she felt stripped of it.

Alone.

Exposed.

Raw.

Tears tickled her eyes, and she dared not wipe them away, lest her friend see and question them. How would she explain to Sarah that it all felt empty now, those reservoirs of dreams? *She* felt empty, or at least that part of her heart did that had always belonged to Benjamin.

He will see, Sarah had promised one short week ago. Yet now, lying here under the cloudless night sky, with the enemy so recently laying siege to their walls, Zipporah felt certain her friend was wrong. He would never see. He had chosen tonight not to see.

Ridiculous. She flung her arm over her eyes to cover the brine without drawing attention to it. Ridiculous to think tonight, whatever it had been, had anything to do with her. What was she to him, that whatever attack he had been under would have any link to her?

Nothing. She was nothing.

From under her arm she caught a streak of light, one that inspired her to sit up again, hands now bracing her against the ground.

The warrior loomed tall against the inky sky, a brilliant column of purest white...who then crouched down before her. Still taller than any man would be in such a position, fiercer in stature and countenance, but he obviously made an attempt not to intimidate.

A friend, this mighty angel, the same one who had stopped her from leaping over the wall and into the wolf's fangs four years ago. He studied her now with an expression of such deep sorrow that she nearly let loose the sob that gathered.

Gird yourselves for war, he said, his voice a silent whisper in her ear. *Tonight was but a foretaste.*

A shudder overtook her as the messenger flew off again.

"Zipporah?" Sarah sat up too, eyes scanning the darkness but never hesitating where the lights glimmered. "What is it?"

Zipporah pushed to her feet. "More battles on the horizon. We must rejoin the others."

Sarah had no sooner stood than her name came to them on the breeze, spoken in a young voice. Zipporah could not tell which of the flock of children skipped their way until she was upon them. Hadriana, with her father a few steps behind.

Urbanus greeted them with an inclination of his head while Sarah scooped up his daughter. "The lady has sent me to gather all those at prayer outside, to come back to the peristylium. You two are the last of us."

"We were just coming." Sarah punctuated it with a kiss upon the girl's forehead.

Did she feel the weight of Urbanus's gaze on her as she did that, feel the way his eyes swept down her in admiration before he forced them back up to her perfect face? But then he turned—slowly enough not to look abrupt, but tension in the way his fingers curled to his palm.

So very curious. Why did this good, godly man who obviously wanted a wife and helpmeet turn so decidedly from the woman he felt drawn to, when she was all he could look for? And did he, in his determination to do so, miss the way Sarah studied him from beneath her lashes?

Zipporah did not miss it, nor the moonlit hope in her demeanor. Her friend had, at long last, found a suitable man on whom to fasten her hopes. A believer, a man of strength and dedication, one who was pleasing to her eye, of a good family too, who could give her the kind of life she deserved—though Sarah would never claim such things were important.

Her sight did not extend to such things, but her heart still swelled at the thought of her dearest friend finding happiness and a family of her own. Perhaps, if Sarah were so happy, some of it would lift Zipporah over the dry cistern of her own once-dreams. Perhaps, if she could play aunt to Sarah's children, she would not ache for the ones she would not have. Perhaps, if Sarah could live a full and blissful life, Zipporah would not wish for more of her own days when their number was up.

For that split second when they faced the same direction, Urbanus and Sarah, when they took a single step together, it looked so right, felt so right. None other of Sarah's suitors had ever inspired such a thought in Zipporah, but this man could be what she needed. Could love her and lead her, would rule his house with wisdom and grace.

Yet in the next moment, he hung back, let Sarah and Hadriana move ahead. And in the silvery moonlight, he produced by seeming force a smile for Zipporah. "Forgive my curiosity, my friend. But I must wonder what you saw this night. If you would be willing to share."

Rarely did anyone ask anymore, so the interest should have warmed her. Instead, watching the subtle shift in Sarah's shoulders as she realized she would *not* be walking back beside Urbanus, Zipporah went cold.

She knew not what he was about, talking with the servant when he could be getting to know the mistress. But she knew deep within her that it was wrong.

It seemed everything was this night.

fourteen

OTHER THAN AN ECHO OF AN ACHE IN HIS HEAD, BENJAMIN AWOKE
feeling no ill-effects of the nightmare of an evening. No physical ones, at any
rate. But as he splashed water into his face and let Mark help him into his toga,
the gravity of the situation pummeled him along with his friend's heavy gaze.

Yet still it felt no more than a dream. A hazy, half-shadowed memory that
he would not have believed was real if Mark had not worn such thunder on his
brow.

But it was. He knew that. Knew it from the one clear recollection—that
moment he crossed the threshold into her room—and from the bareness of his
brother's finger when they met at the table to break their fast. Samuel really
had given Jonathan the ring...and really would leave it in his hands and secret
Benjamin away.

He did not know whether to be glad his brother loved him so, or furious
that he would consider such an option viable. As if shaming a woman could be
so easily ignored. A woman he loved, at that.

No, he would not abandon Dara to the consequences of their actions last
night. And as he met the gazes of his companions amidst the other inn guests,
he knew they knew as much. Hence the particular shade of their frowns.

It was hardly something to be spoken of in company, so not a word was
breathed until after the meal, when Samuel and Mark both followed Benjamin
back to his room. His brother shut the door and turned to him with a nearly
desperate gaze.

"Please tell me you see reason this morning. That you understand the need
to leave, and quickly."

Benjamin looked from one serious face to the other. How could they honestly expect him to behave so? "I cannot. Surely you understand that. I did
wrong, I misused a woman I care for greatly—I cannot dishonor us both and the
Lord by abandoning her now."

Mark spun to the wall, raking a hand over his hair, and then back again.
"What do you even remember from last night?"

With a sigh, Benjamin considered a chair but dismissed it. He intended to
leave here within minutes, to go to Dara. "I remember a foggy feeling, like a
dream. One clear moment as I went into her room to see her loom. I remember
very vaguely taking her into my arms—but I did not think it real. Not until everyone burst in. Was I drunk?" He thought not—he never drank more than two
cups, never. But what other explanation could there be?

"You only had one cup of wine, that cannot be it." Samuel pinched the bridge of his nose in that habit he had that spoke of too many concerns. "She must have put something in it. The effects looked similar to how Grandmother acted when she had taken one of the potions the doctors gave her to relax her, there before she died."

They thought Dara had done this? Absurd. Was it not? Benjamin shook his head...but he saw no better explanation. She had been the one to put his chalice before him, to pour the wine into it. She had been the one to lead him away. Had she really said the words echoing fuzzily through his mind? Had she told him she was his wife, that she loved him?

He squeezed his eyes shut. "I need to speak with her."

"You need to avoid her, to escape her." Samuel's voice had an edge to it so hard and sharp that Benjamin had no choice but to open his eyes again and meet his gaze. "There was evil at work last night, and you succumbed to it. I realize you now want to make it right, but please, brother, see wisdom. She is temptation for you, and you must flee."

Why, when he had already indulged? Suddenly tired, Benjamin leaned against the wall and dragged in a long breath that did nothing to bolster him. "I love her."

His brother flinched. "You scarcely know her. And how can you say such a thing, knowing she orchestrated this?"

Benjamin splayed his hands. "I know only that it is the obvious answer—but the truth is rarely so obvious. I cannot make assumptions and run away. I will face the consequences of my actions."

"The consequences." Mark's voice fell flat and even. "You realize what those are, do you not? The Law is clear on this. You must marry her."

How could both fear and joy trip through him at that? "I know." And it would have to be now, this very day, before they left for Joppa and Rome. This very night she could be in his arms again, legally and rightly this time...and he would remember it.

"Benjamin." The single word contained a world of emotion, all of which vied for dominance on Samuel's face. It settled on sorrow. "If you do this, you will regret it. I know in my spirit she is not what she seems to you. She is a temptress and a liar."

The flash of anger came fast and hot and brought Benjamin up straight again. "For years, the family has been pushing me to find a wife, to open my heart to love. And now that I have found someone I can feel so strongly for, you disapprove? She is your sister! How can you speak so of her?"

Samuel's larynx bobbed. "She is not my sister. But you are my brother. And I will say or do anything to protect you, just as I have done since a boy of six, when my mistress let me call her mother and welcomed me into her family. Even if you do not thank me for it."

For the space of three pulses, Benjamin clenched his teeth and said nothing, just held the familiar green-gold gaze of the face he had seen nearly every day of his life, the face he knew better than his own, had always, always looked up to. Samuel looked so earnest, so convinced by his own concerns.

But Samuel, no matter how devoted a brother, could not dictate to him. Samuel, no matter how intelligent, could not know everything. And Samuel, no matter how virtuous, had no right to judge *his* decisions.

Benjamin strode for the door. "I am going to see her. She has some explaining to do, but I will not dismiss her and run like a coward. That is not how love behaves."

He decided to ignore the hiss of protests behind him at his use of the word. Though it took effort, which made the anger burn hotter. Who were they to dismiss his feelings, his heart, the yearning of his soul? Mark had never been in love, so maybe he had an excuse for not understanding. But Samuel—Samuel should have. He surely understood the pull of an attraction so strong. He surely understood the way one soul recognized another.

Warm, dry morning air greeted him when his determined stride propelled him out onto the street. Any other day he may have paused to let the sun touch his face, to smile at the way it burnished the city with gold, to draw in a breath of air fragrant with baking bread.

Today, he stretched his legs as long as they would go and set about covering distance. He heard Samuel and Mark behind him but paid them no more attention. Better to ignore their continued whispered pleas for him to stop, to see reason, to join them in prayer before going back to the lion's den.

Lion's den—laughable. He was the only lion about, preying on innocent young women who were foolish enough to trust him. How could he have done such a thing? He had to think that, even with his senses impaired, he would never have acted forcefully. But then, he had not thought himself capable of letting go of reason and conviction long enough to do such a thing at all. So how was he to know?

Oh Lord, please let it not be so bad as that. Please, please let it be that I did not hurt her. If he had, if he had been overbearing either with physical force or even force of will.... He turned the corner and shut his eyes for one second. He had heard only a few years ago the story of how his mother was forced to his father's bed, before Jason Visibullis had a softening of heart and began following the teachings of Jesus. Perhaps...perhaps it was in his blood to take whatever he wanted.

He had always been proud to look like his father, to *be* like his father—the father who had loved Mother so deeply, who had raised her from slavery and wed her despite the protests of his friends, who was one of the first believers, who gave his life trying to save *his* father's. But perhaps being like him in those ways meant being like him in other ways too.

The vendors in the market were just beginning to emerge for the day, to set up their wares and carts and raise their awnings overhead. He wove his way around them, ignoring the scowls when they spotted his toga.

Let them judge. Let them despise. Today he deserved it.

Within a few minutes, he stopped outside Martha's home. Jonathan was not yet setting up his booth—no great surprise. Life for this family, at least, would not go on as usual today. He raised his hand to knock but paused, waited for the others to catch up.

Lord? But he knew not what to pray, and when he turned inside himself to try to feel out the Spirit, all he could hear was the clanging of his own thoughts.

"Benjamin—"

He cut his brother off with a quick, loud rap upon the door. Samuel sighed. Benjamin straightened his spine. He could not summon a smile.

Jonathan wrenched open the slab of wood within half a minute, his eyes just as stormy as those of Benjamin's companions. "So you came back. Here I thought myself the possessor of a very fine ring."

In answer, Benjamin pushed past him, into the dim interior of the house. His eyes were still adjusting when he heard Dara call his name. A second later she was in his arms, which came about her with no conscious command from his mind.

"I knew you would return." She buried her head in his chest, so that all he could see of her was the riot of gold curls.

His abdomen went tight at the hazy, forbidden memories that bombarded him at her touch. He pulled her closer, then, at the weight of many heavy gazes upon them, set her gently away. For her, he found a smile. "Of course I did." He looked over her head to her scowling brother, their mother now at his shoulder. "Could I have a moment to speak with her in private before we talk?"

Jonathan looked about to refuse him, but Martha stepped forward and motioned toward the door. "I expected you would want to—I set out some chamomile and cheese for you on the roof. Take your time."

Dara gave him an uncertain smile as she pulled away, then turned and led him back out the door and around to the stairs. Neither said anything as they climbed up to the roof. Benjamin wanted to apologize. He wanted to ask her if she had, as Samuel insisted, had anything to do with his altered state.

He wanted to take her in his arms again and kiss her until all words vanished.

No sooner had he taken the seat Dara indicated on the rooftop than she fell to her knees before him, covering his feet with her curls. "Dara?" Too surprised to know what else to say, to ask, he merely put a hand on her head.

"Forgive me." Tears clogged her throat. "I know I should not have—I am desperate. Please, my love, please do not hate me. I saw no other way."

"Shh." Looking around, he saw few others out on their rooftops just then, but still he did not want to risk a scene to any who might look. He dropped down to the gritty floor, so that they were mostly below the ledge, and urged her face up. "I know not what you mean, fair one."

Dara turned her gaze on him, her eyes luminous with tears and all the more beautiful for them. "I put herbs in your wine."

All the air seized in his chest. He could not fathom it—Samuel and Mark had been right. "Pardon?"

"We had them from when my father was in such terrible pain, and I..." She averted her face, cheeks flushing. "I knew that otherwise you would never, never put me in a compromising position. But I love you, Benjamin. I could not bear the thought of you leaving without me."

What a muddle were his thoughts. Disappointment, a shade of anger...and pleasure that she would go to such lengths. "You had only to speak to me, Dara. I had already decided to seek a betrothal with you before I left."

He expected instant regret on her part, that she had shamed herself for no purpose. Instead, she shook her head, that desperation she claimed coloring her gaze. "You do not understand. My brother—he hates Romans, hates Christians. He would never, *never* have agreed to a wedding for any reason less than this. He ranted his way through the night, alternating between his insistence that the Roman dog must bear the consequences for what he did to his sister and then shouting I was his sister no longer if I would play the harlot with the likes of you."

He winced, on her behalf rather than his own. "Still. Had you but spoken to me, we could have come up with a plan together, one that did not necessitate sin."

A new surge of tears pooled in her eyes right before she cast them downward, making the brine spill over. "I am so sorry. I spent the night on my bed beseeching forgiveness from the Lord for my actions. And yet I fear he will deny me it, given that I would do the same again. I would do anything to be with you."

Perhaps it should have concerned him more than it thrilled him. Samuel would surely say so. But how was Benjamin to deny her point about her brother's negative bias...or the effectiveness of her chosen method? Now Jonathan would surely not just relent and let them wed, he would insist on it.

Benjamin eased an arm around her and pulled her close to his side. "Dara—"

"You could have left. I almost expected you to. But you came back." She snuggled in and slowly raised her gaze to his again. "Dare I hope that means you want me still? You want me for your wife?"

As if she could not tell. The corner of his mouth pulled upward. "What do you think?"

But she did not smile. She turned her face straight ahead, presenting him with her graceful profile. "I think that somewhere under the pull we feel, you are angry. I think now part of you will always feel manipulated, forced to this, and that resentment will brew. I think that at my first mistake—and I am sure to make many of them in Rome—you will wonder if you made a grave error by giving in to my scheme."

"Dara. No." With a finger under her chin, he turned her face back toward him. "Perhaps I do not approve of your methods. But I...I love you. I want to marry you. And I promise you, I am not the type to let such things fester. I am not the type to blame you."

To prove it, he lowered his head until he could taste her lips, until he could give a promise in kisses rather than words. With the first meeting of their mouths, the fire licked through him again, that primal need to make her his own. How was it possible that he had kept a rein on such urges for so long, but now, with this woman, he was a slave to them?

Dara rested a hand on his chest, right above where his heart thundered for her. "I love you," she whispered against his lips. "I will be the best wife, I promise you. I will serve beside you in all things. I will seek nothing above your happiness, unless the Lord bids it. I will..." Her hand trailed down his stomach, each muscle going taut as she touched it. She held his gaze, though scarlet stained her cheeks as she whispered, "I will bring you pleasure beyond compare."

The fire made a buzz in his head, not so dissimilar from the haze of the night before. He kissed her again, holding her body tight against his. "Tonight. Tonight you will be my wife."

Her smile was a secret, warm and promising. "I already am, my love. In deed, if not in word."

Was it a chuckle that rose to his throat? A groan? He could not tell. "Tonight I will remember."

She pressed closer, somehow—moved, somehow—in a way that made the fire rage. "I already do."

Too much. It was too much, and he was helpless against it. Helpless to fight his instinct when she so readily kissed him, touched him, invited him. And what did it matter? She was right, she was already his. For thousands of years, was it not the action that created a marriage, rather than a few words scrawled on parchment? She was his wife, he was her husband. He had every right to take again what had sealed them together as one last night. He could touch, he could discover, he could—

"Benjamin!" Samuel's voice, not so much loud as sharp, shattered his lovely haze as surely as the Spirit's voice had yesterday. He broke away, having enough mind power only to be thankful that his brother shouted from the ground, not from the top of the stairs. He did not want to imagine the scowl Samuel would send him—disappointed and furious—if he saw where Benjamin's hands had wandered.

He cleared his throat and drew in a breath, put some space between him and Dara. "Coming," he aimed down over the wall. To her he said, more softly, "Come, my bride. We must speak to our brothers and call for a rabbi. I am sorry you cannot enjoy a full betrothal—"

Her quiet laughter cut him off. "I am not."

He smiled as he pulled them both to their feet. *His bride.* "My mother will be pleased beyond words that I have found a wife. Though," he added with a raised brow, "we may want to keep the methodology to ourselves."

She nodded, eyes wide. "Yes. Yes, I think so."

Fingers entwined, they made their way down the stairs and back into the main part of the house, where Samuel waited just inside the door. His scowl was not inspiring. Mark stood just as stone-still, just as rigid, with a frown just as deep.

Sighing, Benjamin looked beyond them to Jonathan and Martha. "Please, allow me to first apologize for what happened last night. I was not myself, though that is hardly an adequate excuse. But I am prepared to take responsibility for my actions this very day and make Dara my wife."

His brother snorted.

Her brother narrowed his eyes and flipped something through his fingers. Samuel's ring—why had he not given it back yet? "You had better. No self-respecting Jew would want her now. What will you give me as a bride price?"

"Jonathan!" Dara stepped forward, outrage in her face. "How dare you? You know as well as I that Father had a dowry put aside for me—"

Jonathan stood, slashing the air with his arm. "You think I will pay the Roman dog for what he did to you?"

"I think your actions bring me more shame than his. And give our brother back his ring!"

Benjamin stilled her with a light touch on her arm, though he had to admit that her vehemence warmed him. "He has every right to feel as he does. Though do give Samuel back his ring, Jonathan. He gave it only as a pledge that we would return, which we have. From here, you are dealing with me, not with him."

"Fine." Jonathan flipped the gold through the air, though it fell far short of where Samuel stood. Bad aim, or did he do it on purpose, so that Samuel would have to move from his spot to fetch it?

He did so slowly, and as he returned the signet to its proper place, he said quietly, in Latin, "You are making a mistake."

Benjamin ignored him and turned his gaze back to the younger of Dara's brothers. How fortunate that he had just met with his steward here the other day, to get a report on what his assets in Israel looked like. He could negotiate with that, without ever touching the bulk of the estate in Rome.

Then, once that was settled, they would call an official to draw up the contract. And within a few hours, Dara would be his wife. Would travel home to Rome with him tomorrow.

It just went to show how the Lord could turn anything to good.

fifteen

DARA'S HEART BEAT A THUNDEROUS TATTOO AS BENJAMIN RAISED her fingers to his lips and kissed them, his gaze latched on hers. Samuel and Mark had stepped out ahead of him, their expressions stout disapproval through the entire affair. But it was done. They were married. The ink had not yet dried on the parchment, but they were married.

Her stomach hurt so much it was all she could do to stand upright. *Married*. Married to this stranger. And no matter whether the master could later challenge it and bring her home, for now it was fact. She was his. This handsome stranger who, yes, lit a fire of desire in her, but who was not the man she wanted.

"I will be back for you in a few hours," he whispered, his voice filled with affection and warmth.

Her throat went tight. She would pack what she could, but that left so much she could not. Still, she smiled and squeezed his fingers. "I will be waiting. Do not tarry long, my love."

With a hopeful smile, Benjamin disappeared out the door with his companions, leaving Dara to turn with a glare for Jonathan. "I hope you are happy. For a second time in my life, I have been sold for the price of a few head of sheep."

Her brother, smug smile still in place, grunted and turned away from her. "You brought this one on yourself, woman. You knew well what you were doing when you lured him to your bed last night."

Yes, but somehow she had not expected her brother to demand recompense in the form of a bride price. And she could not quite explain why it had grated so, other than that feeling of, yet again, being sold off. Never mind that she had put herself in the situation. If she had gone to him with a dowry, at least she would have felt a bit of independence in Rome. She would have felt as though she had something to her name other than a face and body that made men lust for her.

But she *did* have something more. She still had her vision. Who said she could not use it in Rome to earn a few coins, as she did here?

"Dara." Her mother eased forward, expression wary. "You are certain this was his will? That he will not visit his wrath upon us for giving you away when you are not ours to give?"

"She was ours enough to make us a tidy profit." Her insufferable brother fell onto the couch. "The Roman's sheep will make a lovely addition to our flocks. We will have the most impressive in the region."

And getting away from Jonathan was one good thing coming of this. Shaking her head, she strode to her room. The first and most important task was dismantling her loom for transport.

"Dara." Martha again, her voice still hesitant. "What will...become of us without you?"

Dara paused with her hands on the smooth wooden frame. "What kind of question is it you ask? That of a mother who will miss her daughter, one with no answer—or do you wish me to part the veil for you and see?"

The woman's flush was answer enough. Well, then. Letting her hands fall from the loom, Dara turned and took her mother's once-graceful fingers in hers. Closed her eyes. Waited for the flashes. And almost hoped they would show her misery and defeat.

Nothing so dramatic, though, for this woman who had twice sold a child to ensure her own comfort. Nothing so just. She dropped her mother's hand again with a shrug. "You will live as you have lived. If you fail to keep a rein on Jonathan, he will squander everything, but that is hardly a surprise. If you keep him under control, he will only manage to ruin it all after you die."

From the corner of her eye, she saw Martha clutch the fabric around her neck tighter. "What if I...what if I travel with you instead of staying here?"

A suggestion that lit a fire of rage. Dara set aside the shuttlecock, teeth clenched, and then turned back to begin the dismantling. "That is not an option."

"Why not?"

"*Why not?* Are you daft?" She folded the frame, careful not to injure the cloth underway upon it. "Samuel would never allow it."

"But if you—"

"No." Easing the frame up against the wall, she spun on her mother. "*No.* I will not do anything for you. I will not ask the son you abandoned to take you with him. I do not *want* you to come, do you understand? You are a selfish, bitter creature who poisons everything, and I will not have you a part of my life any longer."

"Dara." Outrage colored Martha's voice.

Dara turned to the door. "Do not sound surprised. You cannot expect love from your children when you have never given any to them. Look after yourself—it is all you ever did anyway. If you want to be useful, pack my things. I must hasten to the master before Benjamin returns."

Though she deemed it highly unlikely anything would be packed when she got back, she sped from her room, from the house, without awaiting a response.

The sun was at its zenith, shining bright and warm. Would it look the same in Rome, or would its light color things differently there? Best not to wonder—it made a tremor start in her stomach again. Best to hurry to the master.

Her pulse quickened, and not because her feet did. She had done as he asked. She had given herself to Benjamin, she was now his wife. At that thought, she had to squeeze her eyes tight for a moment. She was married.

And so, surely the master would keep his promise to her. He would gather her in his arms and show her how love could make the pleasures of man and woman even better. He would make her his before he sent her off into the unknown.

Someone hailed her, but she ignored the thin woman and kept up her hurried pace across the city. Today was not a day for anyone else's fortunes. Today was a day to focus on her own. She had long ago sworn off looking at her own futures—it had rendered her unable to make the slightest decision at first—but she did not need to part the veil just now anyway. The master had already told her what to expect.

When she reached his house, she slipped in the back. The slaves nodded to her, and she to them, but she did not pause here either. This time of day the master—assuming he was home—would be inside, away from the heat of the sun. She looked in several chambers before she spotted him, a scribe at his side with parchment in hand.

He looked up the moment she stopped, a smile on his lips. To the scribe he said, "That will be all for today. Take your leave."

Dara retreated to make room for the man and then slipped in behind him, pulling the door shut.

The master lifted his brows. "Well?"

"It is done. I am his wife in word and deed."

His eyes flashed dark yet bright with victory, and a laugh emerged from his throat as he held out his hands to her. "I knew you could do it." When she reached him, he pulled her in, held her close. "I knew that if anyone in the world could fool them, it would be you."

She wrapped her arms around him and let the praise sink deep. Drew in the scent of incense and authority that made everything within her yearn toward him. His touch, his feel made the knots of pain ease...yet set up a new longing. She lifted her face to him, knowing he would see in her eyes how she silently begged him for his lips on hers.

He obliged, kissing her long and deeply, pulling her body flush against his so that her heart cried out *Yes, yes, now!*

But then he eased away, resting his forehead on hers. "When does he come for you?"

"In a few hours."

His hand slid up her side, down again. "We have little time then. We must discuss what you are to do in Rome."

"Discuss?" Her disappointment no doubt rang clear as a trumpet.

A smile peeked out beneath his beard. "Our time has not yet come, my precious one. You are still in a vulnerable situation, and I would put you and our plan in no danger. You must remain above reproach until you have him so firmly in your control that he could not possibly consider putting you away."

Her arms fell to her sides. "When will that be?"

"That is for you to determine. But I suspect giving him a child will suffice."

Tears surged, unbidden, to her eyes. "A child. I cannot know you until I have given him a child? I must go without tasting your love, must toil there alone for years with only a promise of someday? And then what? How will I get word to you? How will I get back to you?"

His chuckle sounded so very wrong, grating as it did against her pain. "Ah, little one." He raised a hand to her cheek, stroked a thumb along it. "You think I am tied to this land? That I cannot find you in Rome when the time is right?"

And just like that, her pain turned to a thrill. "You will follow me? I will see you there?"

"Of course I will. I love you too much to risk you being unduly influenced by them." His kiss this time was soft and gentle, the warmest promise. "You must remain always on your guard, which will get exhausting. You must work at every turn to sow dissent among them, to plant doubts, to turn one against another. Amazing as you are, I would expect no one to do so alone, not for so long a time."

She nestled in. "I will serve you in all things." For a moment, the words—an echo of the ones she had spoken to Benjamin just a couple hours ago—made discord twang within her. But she shook it off and knotted her hands in his mantle. "I will not fail you."

"I know. But you ought not to be alone, and I can hardly follow you now, nor into Tutelos itself. You need a trusted maidservant."

Even while he still spoke, dread coiled. She eased away, wariness no doubt in her eyes. "I have no one I trust enough to bring with me."

"I do." Either not seeing or ignoring her obvious distaste for the idea, he took her hand and pulled her through a side door, shouting as he went, "Tamar!"

No. No, he could not be serious. He did not intend to send his concubine with her. It was unthinkable. He must know how she despised the creature that held the place in his arms she wanted for herself, the one he called when he sent Dara away. He must know how much *more* she hated her right now, when he claimed he trusted her enough to send her to Rome.

Trusted her as much as he did Dara.

She clenched her teeth, gritted them, and refrained from tugging her fingers free of his solely because she knew it would grant her power in the wretch's eyes to be so linked. Dara had at least never seen him holding *her* hand.

Tamar met them in the hallway, her eyes downcast. What did the master see in her? She was pretty, but nothing extraordinary. The same deep brown hair that so many others in the city boasted, the same dark eyes. Her voice never came above a whisper.

"Yes, Master?" she whispered now. The mouse.

"Pack your things." The master came to a halt a few feet away from her, not so much as hesitating on his apparent course. That was something, Dara supposed, that he would dismiss Tamar so easily. "You will accompany Dara to Rome as her maidservant, and you leave immediately."

The woman darted a glance at Dara and went pale. "Master?"

"Was I unclear? Pack your things. Dara has succeeded with the Roman Christian, and I will not risk sending her alone. You must go with her. You must do as she tells you to do and watch out for her. She is our greatest hope."

Dara lifted her chin. "I must be clear on our roles, Master. Is she coming with me as a freewoman who can leave me whenever she pleases? As your bondservant, who will obey me only in the things you have instructed?"

The master waved the question away. "She is not even a full Jew—she is slave, not bondservant. I give her to you. Do as you will with her."

Well now. That was different. Dara's lips curled up. "So be it."

The mouse shrank backward. This time her whispered "Master..." contained a plea that she wisely did not put to words.

He spun away. "You have ten minutes to pack, Tamar. I expect you to serve Dara with dedication and loyalty, as you have me. She will need a friend."

Friend—laughable. But Dara kept her smile in place and leaned into the master's side. "How good you are to me, Master, to look after me so."

He made a shooing motion with his hand, sending the mouse skittering back to her hole. Only once she was gone did he sigh. "I have spent many years molding her into a docile companion. She will obey you and follow your lead in all things, but I pray you, do not use it against her. I know you resent her, but there is no need." He turned to her, gathered her close. "You are the one I have set aside to be my wife someday. She is but a substitute."

A thrill surged through her. Never before had he put her deepest hopes into words so clearly. But then a chill chased after it. *Someday*, perhaps. But for today, she was someone else's wife.

Tamar trudged along after her new mistress, her parcel of belongings small and light. A testament to what her life had become in the past decade. Empty. Inconsequential. Easily tossed away.

Her betrothed husband had done it so easily after the attack, not believing she had tried to cry out. Not believing his own brother would act so unless she had beguiled him. Divorced before she was even wed. A shame to her parents. A shame to her town. A shame, it seemed, to the world, who wanted nothing more to do with her.

And now here she was again. All her obedience, all her willingness to do whatever her master asked, for naught. He gave her away.

To *her*.

Tamar remembered when Dara was a girl, young and innocent and so very beautiful. The child had regarded Tamar with huge, strange green eyes filled with uncertainty. Perhaps one of these days, if Dara ever stopped hating her, Tamar would tell her how she feared for her when the master first brought her home. Having only been there a few years herself, she did not know what lines the man might draw. What hidden predilections he might have. So when he arrived with a child with such obvious beauty...

That fear, at least, had never come to fruition.

She watched the haughty sway of Dara's hips now as she negotiated through the city, obviously knowing each street with perfect memory. Tamar stuck close, lest she get lost. Rarely did she ever leave the house, and she had certainly never had cause to go to Dara's home. And she got the distinct impression that the girl would be happier to lose her than to keep her.

Much as she quailed at the thought of Rome, Tamar quailed far more at the thought of getting left behind and having to face the master again so soon, a failure.

Dara turned down another market street and cast her gaze over her shoulder, scowling at Tamar. "Still there, are you? You could run. I would not tell him."

The suggestion made Tamar's stomach clench. He would know. Did Dara think herself his only seer? His best, by far, but not his only. He would know. He would hunt Tamar down. He would make her wish herself dead.

Nay, better to serve Dara than run from the master. She forced a shaky smile onto her lips. "I will not leave you, Mistress."

Dara made a dubious sound and faced forward again. Only a minute later, she turned to an open doorway. They must be at her brother's house. Tamar followed her inside, the action bringing back decade-old memories. She had prayed she would never again have to walk into a place like this, following a new master—or mistress, in this case.

But why should she be surprised that Jehovah would not hear her? As the master had so succinctly put it, she was only half-Jew anyway, and that made her a dog in the eyes of the chosen.

"Who is this?"

The voice, masculine but young, made her jump. She would have slid into a hiding place behind Dara, but the girl spun away from her. Her glower was aimed at who must be her brother. "A gift from the master."

The young man's brows arched. "For me and Ima, to replace you?"

Dara rolled her eyes. "Do you *try* to be a blockhead, Jonathan? She is my maidservant."

Given the way this Jonathan looked at her, Tamar was glad, just now, that they would leave so soon.

Dara motioned to a curtained doorway. "Through here." She led the way again, through the curtain and into a room with little but a trunk in the center, brimming, and an older woman bent over it.

"That is enough, Mother." No softening of Dara's tone, no thanks for the work the mother must be doing for the daughter. "I will check to make sure nothing was overlooked, and Tamar will finish the packing."

Gaze on the floor, Tamar did not try to look the mother in the eye, nor look for anything but command in Dara's face. If she were going to survive this part of her life, she had a feeling this would be the only way to accomplish it—to be silent, to be a shadow, to be quick to obey and quicker to anticipate, once she learned how.

It would not be so bad. She slid into the place at the trunk when the older woman left it, picked up a tunic and folded it neatly. Perhaps she had never been a handmaiden, but it would without question be better than being a childless concubine. Better than pushing aside the nausea and terror each and every day until her soul went numb. Until her heart went hard. Until what had remained of her spirit snapped and sagged within her.

Better to serve a hateful woman than a lustful man.

She worked in silence, ready to hear and absorb anything Dara said, but not given the chance—the girl remained mute for the first few minutes and then began to hum a psalm of victory. It chafed against the defeat inside Tamar, but she kept herself from wincing and focused on organizing the trunk. When she had finished, she stood beside it, hands clasped before her, and studied the floor.

Not long after, a call of "They are here!" came from the outer room.

Nausea pounced on Tamar again. *They.* She knew not who *they* were, but her purpose in being given to Dara struck her fully for the first time. The girl had married a Roman, a Christian. A man. And here she was, the new wife's new handmaid—at the mercy of a new master.

Jehovah, save me! But he would not. She knew he would not. The God of her mother cared nothing for her, and the gods of her father were naught but lifeless idols. She would get no help in this world from the beings of the other.

"Come." Dara motioned Tamar to follow.

It took her a moment. She made the mistake of looking up, which allowed her to see the way Dara's face changed, the way she put on a sweet smile and made the light in her eyes shine bright and warm. This, no doubt, was the face the new husband expected to see.

A face Tamar recalled. This was how Dara had looked as a little girl, newly arrived at the master's house for a few hours every day. Innocent and pure, frightened but brave.

What had happened to that child in the last seven years? Was she still somewhere inside the heartless woman, behind her, pounding to be let out? Or had she been stripped down to nothing but this mask, to be put on and taken off again?

When the little one had first joined their household, Tamar had wanted to pull her close, to stroke her hair and dry her tears and promise her everything would be well. She had hoped, for one moment soon to be dashed, that the master had brought her a child home to fill her empty arms. But no. He had instead dried Dara's tears himself and taken on the role of father, rabbi, tutor, bridegroom. He had raised up the girl to be exactly what he wanted her to be.

And she had become it all too well.

Tamar stumbled after her now, clasping her hands tighter to try to keep them from shaking. Voices came from the outer room, several of them, and all unfamiliar. Men. Not just Dara's husband, but more besides. Tamar halted when her new mistress did, far too close to three sets of masculine ankles.

She could not help but glance up as Dara, face still sweet and now pleading too, motioned to her. "Benjamin, this is Tamar—a gift from my father's dearest friend when he heard I was heading to Rome. You do not mind me bringing a handmaid, do you?"

Benjamin stood nearest Dara, and his gaze landed on Tamar with some surprise but no darker thoughts coloring it. No suspicion, certainly, of the lie. He was handsome, young, and obviously enamored with Dara. With a bit of luck, his focus would remain on his new wife and stay clear of her. At least until the master came for them.

"Of course I do not mind," he said, voice deep and sure. "It is good to meet you, Tamar. I am certain you will find my house to your liking."

She dipped her head in acknowledgment, but the quaking would not still. Perhaps because of the suspicious glares the other two men sent her. The taller had the look of Dara and Jonathan, strange golden hair and green-gold eyes. Had she not overheard Dara saying she had discovered another brother? This must be he. And he looked none too pleased with the situation. The other wore Hebrew dress rather than Roman, of humbler fabric, but his scowl was no less intense as he regarded her.

Benjamin clapped a hand to his shoulder. "This is Mark, my friend and manservant. I imagine you two will see much of each other. And this is my brother Samuel. Mine by adoption, your mistress's by birth."

Did he expect her to respond? Tamar could manage only a nod.

Dara had clasped her new husband's hand between both of hers and looked up at him with joyful adoration. "I am ready, my husband. My things wait in my chamber."

Little time was spent on good-byes. Minutes later, Tamar was following again. Not just her new mistress, but her new master, her new fellow servant. Men, too many men. She could only hope that if she stayed silent, hunched her shoulders forward, they would forget she was there.

Invisible, she said silently to herself. *Be invisible.*

sixteen

THE DREAM HAUNTED ZIPPORAH LONG AFTER DAYLIGHT BRIGHT-ened the sky, long after the chatter of breakfast had faded to the myriad sounds of the villa, busy at work. She managed to push the images away through most of the morning, but as she walked to the gate, answering a summons, they bombarded her.

Did normal people have such dreams? Dreams where they could feel the force of demons battering them? Where fear consumed them when those dark wings beat at them, when they realized that a smiling stranger's face covered the darkest enemy? Did other people ever have to force their sleeping minds to remember that Jesus was Lord, to claim his name? Did other people ever feel the rush of the Spirit crashing down upon them like a waterfall as they slept, as vividly as he ever did in waking moments?

Zipporah squeezed her eyes shut and drew in a calming breath of the warm spring air. Maybe they were dreams like any other—drawn from her experiences, pieced together from her days, her memories, her fears and hopes. Or maybe a demon had broken through the wall again last night and had pounced upon her while she slept. How was she to know?

"Are you unwell, Zipporah?"

Her eyes came open when she heard Jacob's voice, and she produced a smile. The steward must have been summoned as well, though he had been helping finish Urbanus and Lucius's new home. Progress there had been swift, and according to her father, mirroring progress was being made with Lucius's fight against the Spirit.

"Not at all. Just thinking of an unsettling dream last night."

Jacob frowned, etching lines into his tanned face. "Did you speak of it to anyone? Do you think it from the Lord?"

How could she speak of what amounted to little more than impressions, fears, and relief? She shook her head. "It is nothing I would know how to mention."

He nodded, but from the look on his face—epiphany and pity—he no doubt misunderstood the nature of her imaginings. Probably thought she had been dreaming of Benjamin, whom everyone still knew she cared for, despite her caution in never showing it outright since Anna died.

But her cheeks flushed at what he must be thinking, which would no doubt solidify his thoughts. A terrible cycle.

Zipporah drew in a breath of the sweet, warm spring air and looked to the sky, hoping Columba would come fluttering down to serve as a distraction. The dove was nowhere in sight. Probably off hunting up insects or berries, flying free throughout the countryside.

She would not envy the creature. She would not, despite the thoughts that had surged to the fore again after that exchange with her father and Sarah and Urbanus's family. What could the wide world offer that Tutelos could not, anyway? Nothing. Nothing but danger and loneliness. She was where she belonged. Home. And hardly the only servant never to leave the walls.

Just the only one who would choose to but was refused.

Jacob nodded toward the gate with drawn brows. "A small retinue, but certainly not beggars."

Following his gaze, she nodded her agreement. Four men stood at the gate in the dress of the Greeks, their clothes neither over-worn nor ostentatious. They appeared to span a generation, the oldest of them at the fore, one who looked to be his son at his side—about Samuel's age from the look of him. Behind them, another pair that could easily be father and son, but in the shorter tunics of slaves.

No darkness clung to them, though the light of the Spirit burned brightly only in the leader. Perhaps the others believed with him, she could not be entirely certain. She saw flickers, like a candle in a breeze. Belief warring not so much with doubt, she suspected, as with the tares of the world.

She halted a fair distance from the gate. "They are no threat."

Jacob nodded and patted her shoulder. "Back to your tasks then. If we need more, we will call you."

Sarah no longer needed her help, being happily ensconced with her small wards this time of day, and Zipporah had already finished straightening her friend's chamber. So she sought out her mother and found her humming her way through Mistress Abigail's room.

For a moment, she watched before Ima noticed her. The grace with which her matron moved, the beauty in each line she made with a stretch or bend. It was no mystery where Anna had come by her fairness...only where Zipporah had come by her plainness. How many times had she heard the story of how Mistress Abigail had rescued her ima from the slave docks, where otherwise her beauty would have guaranteed she end up a rich Roman's concubine? How many times had she heard how, at first glance, her abba had known his old friend's new handmaid was the wife the Lord had prepared for him?

Ima rarely left Tutelos, unless it was to accompany the mistress. But *she* never longed for more, not that Zipporah had ever heard. She never once wished to explore the world or make her own mark on things. She served from love, she made this smaller world her own, she knew her place among her family and friends.

Where did one come by that kind of contentment?

Ima turned to put away a brooch and caught sight of Zipporah in the doorway. A smile curved her lips. "Come to help your aging mother?"

Zipporah chuckled and moved into the familiar room, her hands finding by rote the first thing out of place and righting it. "As if you could not run circles about me. But yes, I thought I would lend you a hand."

Ima continued her song, though once at its end she did not launch immediately into another. Instead, she paused beside the window and looked out it with a wistful smile. "How long, do you think, until they get home? My arms yearn to wrap around my son again."

Zipporah smiled too as she stepped to her side. "Soon. A month or so, I should think. If their plans held true, they will be boarding their vessel any day, or could even be now upon it."

Wrapping an arm around her, Ima gave her a squeeze. "We are finished in here. Shall we see if Dinah needs our help?" She reached over to move the curl from behind Zipporah's ear.

"We shall indeed."

When they entered the kitchen a few minutes later, news of the visitors was already buzzing through the room. "Archippus, from the church at Colossae," Dinah said to them by way of greeting. "With his son and their menservants. They have come seeking wives for the younger ones." The cook's still-sharp gaze arrowed into Zipporah. "It is Sarah they will be wanting to meet at the noonday meal. Try to convince her to change into one of her stolas unstained by rolling about on the ground with the children."

A laugh bubbled up and out. "I can try. If such a one exists."

"Perhaps you ought to fetch her now and make her presentable." Ima, obviously repressing a grin, nudged Zipporah back toward the door.

As if it would matter if Sarah's hair were askew and her stola stained—she would still outshine any other young woman this son of Archippus could ever have met. The true question was whether *he* was worthy of *her*. But Zipporah left with another laugh, heading out to where Sarah and her gaggle of enthralled children sat together—by the fountain today.

"...and sometimes an angel would come down and stir the waters. Like this," Sarah said, touching a hand to the stiller waters at the edge of the pool, "only no human hand had touched it. And whoever made it into the water first would be healed of their infirmities."

The younger ones' eyes went wide, but one of the older boys shook his head and looked away.

Sarah was never one to let such a thing slide. "Do you disbelieve the story, Ennius?"

"It makes no sense." And the boy did not mumble his opinion. Arms crossed over his chest, he scowled over the heads of his younger companions. "Did the angel put some kind of power in the water? Why then did it only work on the first to touch it? You have taught us that it is faith that can effect a healing, not some external thing."

Sarah smiled into his frown. "And would you sit for months or years at a time beside a pool, waiting for the waters to stir, with*out* faith?"

"But if it was their faith that healed them, not the waters, why were they not *all* made well?"

"A question I asked my mother when I was about your age, too." A chuckle slipped from Sarah's lips, warm and understanding. "And I did not find her answer very satisfying—that there are mysteries of the Lord we will never understand. But here is the crux of the story, Ennius. Faith *did* make one well, when he put it in our Lord, despite his inability to reach the waters with his lame legs. Jesus commanded him to rise and walk, and up and away from the pool he went."

Sarah looked up, and Zipporah made a subtle motion with her hand.

Her friend patted the little shoulders nearest. "Just as I rise now. Now what of you, little ones? How would you run and leap if you had never been able to walk, but Jesus made you whole?"

The children all jumped up, running and shrieking and laughing their way into the gardens. Sarah ambled Zipporah's way with a smile. "Did you need something?"

"Dinah sent me to fetch you and make you presentable." Smiling, she indicated the smudges of dirt on her friend's stola. "We have guests—a young Colossian Christian in search of a wife from the church. He, his father, and their servants just arrived. Jacob was taking them to your father."

Sarah sighed and looked in the direction of the new building, though it was not within sight from here. "Did you meet this young man already? How does he compare to Nereus or..."

"Or?" Zipporah took her friend's hand and tugged her toward the door. "Urbanus, perhaps?"

A pretty flush stole into Sarah's cheeks, though she shook it away. "He all but avoids me. Have I offended him somehow, do you think?"

How could she possibly have? "No. But the fact that you think of him instead of wondering more about the newcomer tells me much."

Sarah flagged down another servant and asked her to watch over the children, saying nothing else until they were in the dim corridor leading to her chamber. Then she looped her arm through Zipporah's and leaned in close. "I cannot help it. He is older than Nereus, yes, but watching him with his daughters—he adores them. *And* he is handsome, *and* he follows the Way, which I begin to think Nereus never will." She cast a glance over their shoulders as they moved into her room. "I cannot stop thinking of him."

And Zipporah could not stop the smile. "I know. And I have seen him watching you."

"You have?" So quickly did Sarah spin around that she all but rammed into Zipporah.

Laughing, she urged Sarah behind the screen. "Give me the stola."

"It is hardly dirty at all. I do not see why—"

"Do *you* want to face down Dinah?"

The stola fluttered over the screen. "Urbanus—he watches me?"

"He does, like a man who cannot get enough of the sight of you. But then he will always catch himself and turn decidedly away. Something holds him back, and I cannot think what." She pulled a fresh stola out, one edged in blue embroidery that always looked so beautiful against her friend's perfect skin. Tossing it over the screen, she said, "Any other man as interested as he obviously is would have spoken to your father by now."

Sarah's sigh rivaled the north wind in bluster. "Perhaps he likes only my face and finds my personality off-putting."

"Impossible."

"You are biased. I am your dearest friend."

"I am not biased. You are my dearest friend *because* your personality is so endearing." Zipporah moved behind the screen to help tie the matching blue sash and then nudged Sarah back out so she could dress her hair. "I have a feeling he will not be able to fight the pull toward you for long."

Sarah sat with a huff upon her stool. "And yet you make me preen for an introduction to this Colossian."

"Because I do not dare disobey Dinah." Grinning, Zipporah picked up the brush and started at the bottom of the wind-tossed locks. The smile faded. "And because my feelings ought not to be trusted in these matters. Who is to say you will not take one look at this young man and fall in love?"

Sarah herself said it, if not in words than in the shade of pink she flushed as she studied her hands.

"Sarah." Abandoning the brush, Zipporah knelt down and took her hands again. "Is it more than mere liking then? Have you fallen in love with Urbanus?"

"Surely not." Yet she did not meet Zipporah's gaze. "How could I have, when he scarcely ever talks to me? When we have known each other but a few weeks? I would be a fool to give it such a name."

"And yet...?"

Sarah blinked rapidly and looked toward the window, though the action did nothing to hide the sheen of tears. "And yet he is the only one I have ever been able to see myself beside. I can imagine his arms about me, whispering love into my ear. I can imagine adding more children to his precious family, loving them all as my parents love their children, adopted or by blood. I can imagine growing old with him until I know his thoughts before he speaks them."

The familiar ache pulsed and pounded. Zipporah knew those hopes too... and knew the agony of them remaining nothing but imaginings. She would pray it would not be so for Sarah. She would pray it every morning and every night.

Rising, she picked the brush up again. "Then we will show him that he need not turn from his feelings. We will show him you are a woman of beauty, of heart, of wisdom. We will show him you are all he could want in a wife and more."

"But you will still dress my hair for the newcomer."

"I daresay Urbanus will be at the noonday meal too. The efforts will not be wasted."

"Excellent point. Use this one." Sarah pulled a sapphire-blue ribbon that matched the stola from her box of hair ornaments.

Conversation moved to easier things while Zipporah wound the thin band around her friend's head, through her hair, securing and adorning all at once. A few minutes later, the younger stood with lifted brows. "Shall I do yours?"

Zipporah waved her off. "Why would you? I will be serving, that is all."

But Sarah's brows did not lower. "Did you not say the young man's servant is looking for a wife too? What if *you* fall in love—with the chance to see some of the world, if not the man himself?"

Zipporah had no choice but to swat her friend in the arm. To laugh. And to wish it could happen, that she could put Benjamin out of her heart so entirely that she could even consider falling for some stranger.

The weight of warning slammed into her again at the mere thought of him. That sense that she must do more than wish it, want it, that she must accomplish it, or face a greater heartbreak than she had known before.

Sending a prayer heavenward, she kept her smile on her lips by force and shooed Sarah from the room, back down the hallways, and toward the peristylium, from which many voices spilled. They entered together, but when Sarah headed for her parents—and the two Colossians standing with them—Zipporah slipped to the wall alongside her own mother, waiting to be needed. Watching.

The young guest marked Sarah's approach with a light in his eye, as Zipporah had expected him to do. No doubt her beauty won her instant favor, and no doubt when he knew her more, he would like her more. From the way Sarah stood, though, it did not look as though she felt the same attraction. There was no tension in her shoulders, no bashful turning of her head. No flush in her cheeks.

Not until she looked beyond Mistress Abigail and apparently spotted Urbanus. He had been watching her just as intently as the visitor, though he looked away at once upon noting her regard.

Ima chuckled, soft and sweet, beside Zipporah. "Our lovely Sarah will have her pick of the men, I think."

"As well she should." Assuming Urbanus worked through whatever held him in check. Perhaps the Lord would whisper a few words in Zipporah's ear sometime for her to convey to him. Something to help him break free of whatever bonds held him back from the love that awaited him.

Perhaps they would marry. Perhaps they would eventually move back to Corinth. And perhaps Benjamin would give Zipporah to Sarah when that happened, and she could go too. *Please, Abba God. Please do not send her away without me. Please do not leave me friendless.*

If the young man from Colossae sensed Sarah's straying attention, he gave no indication of it. His lips were all smiles, his eyes latched upon her, and *his* stance indicating that if his father arranged a match, he would be well pleased indeed.

Master Titus was, as always, more guarded and harder to read. Did he feel inclined toward arranging a betrothal? From his face, smiling but Stoic, Zipporah could tell nothing except that he played the part of welcoming host to perfection, as he always did when visitors came to their gates.

She cast her gaze around the rest of the room, looking for and finding the other newcomers, the menservants. They stood at the rear wall, exchanging a few words between them, smiling. The younger one seemed to be looking at each maidservant in turn, no doubt wondering if any of them would be a suitable wife for him, and he looked...hopeful. No doubt he would be happy if his master and Titus arranged something with Helen or Mary or Media or Eve.

By the time the gathering moved toward the adjoining triclinium for the meal, the newcomers had fallen in with the Tutelos menservants, and muted jesting reached Zipporah's ears. Soon Mark would be back among that number, which made her smile. Briefly, until she caught the words her brother's friends were saying to the visiting servant.

"If they come to an agreement with the master concerning Mistress Sarah, then it is a safe assumption," young Joseph was saying.

What was? That the master would send a maidservant with them, and that it would be a reasonable expectation that she would be given to this man? Zipporah shifted a bit closer, though she turned her face so she could see them only in her periphery. With all the conversations going on around them, they would not think her listening.

The young visiting lord—she had heard someone call him Balius—must have heard the talk too. He hung back and fell in beside his servant. "My father has had worse ideas, has he not? I think this trip was a wise decision indeed." His gaze lingered on Sarah, a good ways in front of him now, but the sway of her hips apparently no less mesmerizing from a distance.

Zipporah barely refrained from rolling her eyes. Though she supposed she ought not to hold predictability against a man.

Balius looked back toward Joseph. "I assume the young mistress has a maid of her own, yes? And who is that? Deon no doubt wants to know."

Before she could shift behind her father, fully out of their view, Joseph nodded her way.

Deon followed Joseph's indication. No doubt he was expecting the pretty Mary, or the lovely Eve. Media with her generous curves no doubt would have pleased his eye.

But when he caught sight of Zipporah, his reaction came fast and strong. Disgust curled his lip, disappointment darkened his eyes. He turned back around, his low voice barely reaching her. "I will trust the will of you and your father, Lord."

Zipporah felt the weight of Balius's gaze on her still, though she did not look his way. If only she could stop her ears from hearing his murmur. "She is not so bad, Deon. Her figure is fine."

"If one can look that far, perhaps."

It ought not to hurt so. Why should it? She had gotten worse insults before. She had no illusions about her face. She could shrug them off most of the time—had she not done so with nary a twitch when Lucius had called her ugly a few weeks ago?

But Lucius had not been a young man looking at her as a potential wife, he had been a surly guest there half against his will. She had been naught but a handy target for him. For Deon though...

She pivoted, slipped behind her parents, her aim the peristylium's door. Sarah would not begrudge her a few minutes away. Her mother would cover her place, or one of the other maids. They did it often enough, when the gate-keepers called her away. They may even think that was what happened.

Let them.

She needed room to breathe. To pray this pressure in her chest, this churning in her stomach away. No tears burned, but she almost wished they would. Wished she could expel the bad feelings so easily, leak them out through her eyes and move on.

As if he were so handsome, so desirable himself, this Colossian slave. What right had he to judge her lacking? His middle was soft, his brows too heavy, his...his...

"Forgive me, Lord," she whispered as she sped into the hall. She would not, *must* not fall into insulting others to assuage her own injured vanity. If she started down that path, she might never find her way home again.

She made it outside before her breath caught on a dry sob. Ridiculous. Utterly ridiculous to react so to a man she did not know, did not care for, did not *want* to like her.

Except that his reaction was so typical. So expected. So *true*. No man had ever once looked at her and been pleased at the sight. Never. No man would ever be happy to make her his wife. No man would ever want to risk his children having her face.

"Zipporah, wait."

Because it was her father's voice, her feet obeyed. But her hands clenched into fists at her side, buried in the soft white fabric of her tunic, and even the coo and flutter of Columba, finding her shoulder, did nothing to ease her.

Abba's hand landed warm and steady on her arm. "My daughter. Ignore them. They are but arrogant young men, thoughtless and foreign. They do not know you. If they did, they would never even think such things, much less say them."

"Would they not?" She averted her face, let her curls fall from behind her ear. Let them hide her, as her mother always tried to make them do.

How wise her ima was.

He smoothed his hand over her head, over her hair...but made no move to tuck it away again. "They would not. If they knew you, they would see you are the most beautiful of women. One with a heart beyond any young lady's, with a faith as shining as the sun."

"Qualities that may make for an excellent friend—but what man would ever want me for a wife? Freely, of his own will?" She shook her head and stepped away from her father's touch. "Perhaps one could come to love me in time. Perhaps one could even eventually count me a blessing. But how long would he wish, before that, that I had another face, any other face?"

"Zipporah." Censure now saturated his tone.

She spun back to him, met his familiar gaze. "Just keep me here, Abba. Please. Please, get Master Titus and...and Master Benjamin, when he returns, to agree. Keep me here. Do not force me on some man who does not want me. Do not force me to marry. Let me stay here, serve here until the Lord calls me home."

How much longer could she really have, anyway? The battle beyond the walls was strengthening. Sooner or later, a demon would break through. And if it managed it in the form of a man with a knife...

For a long moment, Abba studied her eyes. Wanting, no doubt, to assure her that she would find love as the rest of them did. But reality must have bludgeoned its way past fatherly hope. With a sigh, he gathered her close and pressed a kiss to the top of her head, sending Columba fluttering away. "I promise you, my little sparrow, that I will never give you to any man who does not love you for who you are. You deserve nothing less."

And would get nothing at all, for that was apparently a task beyond the male half of the species. She hugged her father back and then pulled away. "I need a few minutes, if it is all right."

"Of course." He patted her shoulder again, stepped away. But his brows were knit. "Zipporah...you are worth more than rubies. More priceless than gold. You are my greatest treasure, and if a man is not wise enough to think the same, then he is not wise enough to lead your home anyway."

Well, that certainly excluded Deon then. A hint of a smile tugged at her lips. "Thank you, Abba."

Unable to find anything more to say, she turned her feet toward her sanctuary.

seventeen

DARA TOSSED OPEN THE DOOR TO THE SHIPBOARD CABIN SHE shared with Benjamin, growling when her attempt to slam it shut met only with the dull slap of a palm catching it. She spun to find Tamar, as always, slipping in behind her and easing the door closed with a gentle click.

When, *when* would she be alone again? She did not so much mind the hours spent with Benjamin, not just yet. He lit a comfortable fire in her blood, made her forget for moments at a time that the waters carried her farther and farther from the one she truly loved. Time with him was well spent, strengthening the bond between them so she could do the master's work once they reached Rome. And plant the seeds of disagreement between the brothers now.

But the stupid slave was always there when Dara's husband was not, and *that* she tired of.

A friend, he had said. As if they could ever be friends. The wretch may never say an unnecessary word, but Dara knew judgment when she saw it, and it gleamed always in the woman's murky brown eyes.

"What do you want? Go away." She spun for her trunk, though she knew well Tamar would not leave.

The mouse squeaked. "I want only to serve you, Mistress. May I help you find something?"

"The only thing I seek is a few moments of peace and solitude. So leave."

Another squeak, like a whimpering dog. How had the master put up with her all these years? Docile, he called her—more like groveling. Dara tossed her trunk lid up and dug around inside for the fine flax she had put there. She would weave, though she would have to put the loom away again before nightfall.

"Please, Mistress." Tamar's voice was barely even a murmur, so quivering and weak did it ring. "Tell me what I am doing wrong so I can change it. I wish to be a help to you, not a burr."

Hands still empty, Dara stood again, spun to face her. "*Doing*? It is nothing you *do*, slave. It is who you *are*."

Eyes on the ground, Tamar gripped her tunic with shaking hands. "But I am nothing. Why should you despise nothing, Mistress? Ignore me, let me be your shadow. I will care for you and anticipate your needs and—"

"You are a boil." Dara took a step forward, clenching her hands at her sides. "Your very being tries me. He turned to you when it should have been me, poured his love upon you when by rights it is mine."

A shadow flickered in her eyes, and her hands fluttered up in plea. "Do not despise me for that, I beg you. I had no choice. And if I had, I never would have—"

"Silence. All your words prove is that you are the greatest of fools, to admit you would have spurned what I would kill for." Dara snaked out a hand and captured the mouse's wrist, just in time to feel the shiver of fear course through her.

The flashes nearly blinded her. She had been about to ask what use the master really thought Tamar could be—a question answered before she could voice it by the stream of images. Possibilities.

Tamar, weeping in the night as rough hands dragged her toward a circle of outraged men with stones in their hands.

Tamar, hot with fever, thrashing about alone in the darkness, her breath the rasp of the coming end.

Tamar, screaming as figures loomed, advanced, knocked her to the pitching deck. Refusing to scream again as they ravished her, her silence mocking them until their hands bruised, hit, closed around her throat...

Tamar, dead and bloodied on the deck of this very ship, familiar faces slinking away.

Dara let go her wrist slowly. Possibilities. All of them equally bad for the mouse. All spelling misery and death.

Her blood quickened. Would it not be kind of her to hasten the creature's end so she did not suffer? Would it not be better for her to die now than in Rome of a fever, or of a stoning?

The master could not blame her when terrible death was the only future to be had. The master would thank her for pushing her toward the quickest end. The master would know there was nothing else she could have done.

And Dara would be rid of the wretch forever.

"Mistress?" Tamar edged away, terror snapping now in her eyes.

Dara would have smiled, but that would rouse Tamar's suspicions. So she lifted her chin instead, and turned back to the trunk as she called the images to mind again. Daylight, surprisingly, though clouds fisted on the horizon, dimming the light. Sending the sailors rushing about the deck, securing what they could in case a storm blew up. Much like, she realized as footsteps pounded the wood...now.

"You wish to serve me?" she said over her shoulder. "Then go fetch me something to eat. I missed my meal this morning."

A hesitation, no doubt born of panic at the thought of going alone on such a task. But the mouse squeaked her obeisance and slipped from the room.

Dara slid her eyes shut and drew in a deep breath. Perhaps she should have felt some sorrow over the creature. Perhaps she should have felt some regret. But really, what choice did she have? She did not create the visions. She did not write the future.

If the master needed to blame anyone, he would have to take it up with Jehovah.

In her fortnight aboard this vessel, Tamar had never found herself so very alone. Two other families were traveling to Rome as well, and she had ended up sharing a chamber with four other females, happily. They ignored her, they were not a chattering bunch, and it meant she could listen for Dara to emerge from her chamber without being forced into the company of men. She had only gone on deck when Dara and Benjamin did. Only gone to the kitchen with others.

And still she had felt the heavy stares of the sailors.

Was she marked somehow? Did they look at her and know she was easy prey? Why else would they focus such gazes on her and not the other women? Her beauty was certainly not so great.

Thunder rumbled, a sharp crack and a low moan that rolled from the water toward the land. Tamar jumped and then plastered herself to the side when the quick pounding of running feet came her way. Her eyes slid shut.

Invisible. Be invisible.

The laugh sent a million ants crawling over her flesh and proved her failure in her goal. "Well, well, look here." The voice was rough, masculine, unfamiliar. "A pretty little harlot inviting us to take a taste."

"A fortunate day, eh?"

Two of them? She dug her fingers into the wooden planks at her back and forced herself to open her eyes. *Jehovah? Are you there? Do you care?*

She saw only the brutes, which was answer enough. They had the same look in their eyes that Eleazar had that terrible night, the same snarl curling their lips as they looked at her.

Nausea crashed like the sea. Dara would kill her if she found Tamar, even unwillingly, in such a situation. She slid a step to the side, knowing they would see the terrorized pulse in her throat, the way she shook. "Pardon me, please." She strove for normal, but her voice came out so tremulous they probably could not even hear her over the waves slamming the haul. "I am about my mistress's business."

The one said something to the other. Perhaps he spoke in a tongue she knew not. Perhaps the roar in her ears deafened her. Either way, it was only noise, and she knew if she were to escape, it had to be now. Trying—failing, she knew—to put on a cloak of confidence, she turned and took a step. She needed only to get in sight of the others. The whole crew would not stand idly by while two of their cohorts attacked her. Surely. Surely.

She took another step, the panic taking hold of her by the throat when she heard them move behind her. A heave of a breath, and she coiled her muscles, ready to make a run for it. A few feet, that was all she needed to cover. A few feet.

Cruel hands grabbed her, jerked her to a halt even as she struggled forward. Her throat loosed a scream before filthy fingers closed over her mouth.

And she sagged.

"You like to scream?" The rumble that followed was too vile to be called a laugh. "Good. Scream for me."

Tamar closed her eyes. Closed her ears. Closed her spirit. What did it matter? They would take what they wanted, as men always did. Fighting would only get her hurt. And it mattered not. They could do nothing that had not already been done. Take nothing that had not already been taken. She was a rag, used and worthless and cast off as easily as she was taken up.

An echo of a song slipped through her mind, low and mournful. A tune from her father's people, but the words of one of her mother's psalms. Too faint for her to remember them. But they spoke of sorrow, heavy as the hand that forced her to the deck. Heavy as the knees that pinned her down.

Bruising fingers gripped her chin, jerked her head. "Look at me." A clang, those words, tinny and faint in her ears, but they battered their way through, along with some other, undefinable clamor.

Her eyes opened, though they saw only the shadow of destruction and the flash of lightning behind.

Then nothing. Nothing but the surging clouds overhead. Was she dead already? Her soul leaving her body? Part of her hoped so...if only she knew what punishment awaited her hereafter. Where did dogs go after they died? Surely not to Paradise.

When other hands grabbed her, her focus came back as fast as a whip. These hands, somehow gentle despite their insistence, pulled her up, out of the way, spun her around. She could see only the white of a tunic when she halted, but the spin had shown her more.

A flashing sword, a strong, tanned arm wielding it, a jagged knife in the hand of the brute.

She buried her face in the soft white fabric, shuddering when arms closed around her. But these were not bruising. They held her as her father had once done, before she had shamed him. Protected her.

If only she could stop her ears.

A guttural growl, feet lunging, a clang of metal, quick and fierce. Feet shuffling back. Curses, black and scorching.

A clicking tongue. "Now what will you do, when faced with an armed man instead of a defenseless woman?" She knew that voice. Of course she did, but the face to whom it belonged would not surface, nor the name that went with it.

A thud, like knees hitting the deck, but from farther away than the scuffle. "Have mercy on us, Lord. We beg of you."

"Bite your tongue, Janus. You are a fool if you think masters ever show mercy." The brute, that voice.

Truth, those words...except here she stood, unharmed.

A grunt, a shout from the familiar voice, a splash.

The arms holding her tensed, the chest under her forehead jolted forward a few inches. "Samuel, no! He will only take you down with him!"

Tamar turned her face enough to see Samuel leaning over the rail, his expression pained at the splashes. The brute must have tossed himself overboard.

"Master." The one called Janus was still on his knees, his head now touching the deck. "Forgive me for following him. I beg you. Have mercy."

Samuel sheathed his sword and turned. Unable to see his face, she could only try to judge his thoughts by his stance.

It told her nothing, except that he knew how to wear authority.

The arms around her loosened. She glanced up, but now it was only to verify what she knew must be so—Mark, who before had seemed a disapproving, judgmental enemy as he tried time and again to question her on what she could not disclose. He looked down on her now as if she were...a friend? No, not even that. More as if she were a sister.

She had been one once, many years ago. She had not thought she remembered the feeling.

He touched a finger, so softly she scarcely felt it, to the place the brute had gripped her chin. It must be reddened. "He hurt you."

She shook her head and tried to tell herself to step away. Her knees were still too weak to obey. "It is nothing."

Samuel sighed, still regarding the sailor. "You will pass the rest of the journey in chains, while I consider what will be done with you when we reach shore. But I can promise you this—you will never again work aboard an Asinius vessel."

The man's fingers curled inward, but not into a fist. Not in a way that promised violence. In one that pleaded. "I understand, Lord. I submit myself to your will."

A shudder coursed through her. She had said those words once. Had submitted herself to her master. Had given up her will, her hope, her all.

Somehow, she suspected Samuel Asinius would show more mercy to this would-be rapist than she had been shown, who had done nothing of her own volition. She pulled free of Mark's arms and, gaze focused on the wooden planks beneath her feet, turned back to her path.

He stayed her with a light hand upon her arm. Still, it made her shudder now. "You should get below. The storm may be a fierce one."

She halted, swallowed. "Mistress Dara requires food."

"Tamar."

Because his tone insisted, she looked up. Let him search her eyes, as if there were anything inside her soul for him to glimpse through them. The sooner to be released, that was all.

She expected the frown. But not the pain that sparked through *his* eyes. "You have been hurt before, by men not unlike those. I promise you, you will never be so misused again, not while you are of our household."

Perhaps she *was* marked. How else could he know, just by looking at her? She shook her head and looked away. But he would know, she was sure, that she did not deny the observation, merely the promise. No man could promise that.

"Come." He turned with her, touched a hand to her back. "I will accompany you. You need not go alone."

The words wrapped, somehow, around her. Squeezed. And for the life of her, she could not tell whether they felt more like an embrace or a threat.

At the clump of feet outside their door, Dara pulled away from Benjamin's arms. The treads were heavy and several—no doubt the captain and a few of his men come to confess what had happened to Tamar.

The wind had been howling incessantly, the waves crashing, countless feet had pounded continually around them. She had barely made out the scream, and only because she had been listening for it. Benjamin, she was sure, had heard nothing in those first moments after his return.

Smiling, she ran her hands over his chest while she waited for the knock. He and Samuel had been talking privately—about what, he had not yet shared. She would get it out of him. Perhaps later, when she was feigning grief over the mouse's demise, she could ask him to distract her with it.

The knock came, but too light. Timid. The knock of a servant ready to slip in, not of a news-bearer.

The frown knit her brow before the door swung open. Before Tamar stepped in, a tray in her hands. Before Mark and Samuel came in behind her, the thunder in their eyes far louder than that rumbling over the waters.

Wrong. This is wrong.

"What is wrong?" Benjamin stepped forward while Dara's feet felt rooted to the wooden planks. He too wore a frown, though she knew it could not be for the same reason. He saw only his brother's expression, not the flash of future.

"Tamar was attacked." The slave was the one who spoke, his gaze sweeping from the mouse to the master.

That much was right, then. A strange tremor moving through her, Dara sank down onto the bed. It had only been a possibility, it was true...but she had learned how those possibilities work. She knew. She *knew.* If the circumstances lined up, it would happen. And the circumstances had aligned.

What, then? What had gone wrong?

Benjamin had sucked in a breath, immediately concerned. "Are you injured, Tamar?"

The mouse slid the tray onto the table built into the wall and shook her head.

"We came upon them in time," Samuel said. His voice sounded harder than usual, flinty. "There were two of them. The instigator leapt overboard when I disarmed him—the second will remain bound until we reach Rome."

Dara shut her eyes. Wishing, praying the visions would come. Correct themselves. Show her what had happened.

Benjamin's breath came out in a relieved huff. "Praise Jehovah you were there."

Jehovah? *No.* Jehovah gave Dara her sight. Only the enemy could have done this, could have thwarted a true vision. The enemy that deceived these followers of the sacrilegious Nazarene.

"Mistress." The familiar squeak bade her open her eyes. Tamar knelt at her side with a plate of bread and cheese.

Were it not for the audience, she would have flung it away. But they watched her, she knew they did. She pressed her lips together as if fighting off emotion, held Tamar's gaze as if exchanging some silent message. Took her hand as if she cared.

Fingers to palm, palm to fingers. All her mind and spirit focused.

Nothing came. Not so much as a flicker. Dara released the mouse and chose a piece of bread.

Something had gone terribly wrong. If the enemy could thwart her visions, then what good could she do?

No. She would just have to be on her guard. Every moment, every day. She would have to find the small moments, whenever she could. And she would.

Oh yes. She would.

eighteen

ANOTHER WEEK, IF THE WINDS WERE WITH THE MEN. ZIPPORAH SAT back on her heels, eyes focused on the floor she had just wiped clean but seeing flesh and blood faces instead of the mosaic ones under her hands. She could hardly wait to enfold Mark in a giant embrace. To spend a few hours exchanging stories with Samuel. And Benjamin...

She sucked in a breath and pushed herself to her feet. Best not to think of Benjamin.

Her knees popped when she stood, and her back was none too happy with her either. Zipporah shook her head at her own softness. Scrubbing floors did not usually fall to her, but she could hardly stand by idly and watch while Aella, belly round with a child who would make his appearance any day, struggled through it. She had sent the tired servant to rest and promised to finish in her stead.

If only she could have scrubbed her thoughts away as easily as she had the mud from the tiles.

After rolling her head around to loosen taut neck muscles, she dumped the dirty water, returned pot and wet rag to their places to dry, and wiped her hands on her already-soiled tunic. She would check and see if her mother had anything else she could do while she was dirty...otherwise she may slip away to the baths.

Ima, however, was nowhere in the house. On Dinah's direction, she headed outside, feet aimed for the vineyards. Columba greeted her with a coo as he winged by, no doubt on his way to find a tasty worm or berry for his midday repast.

In their usual place in the expanse of gardens beside the villa, Sarah sat with the children. Their eyes were wide with whatever tale she told them today. Far from the narrowed ones of Balius and Nereus, who glared spears at each other from behind the group.

Sarah ignored them both.

Zipporah chuckled and kept her aim true.

As her path took her near the building site of Urbanus's new house, voices reached her. The menfolk all emerged from within a moment later, engaged in some spirited conversation that had Master Titus laughing and Lucius looking thoughtful. When Zipporah's father appeared behind them, she decided on a small detour.

"Abba!"

He paused, greeting her with a warm smile and an outstretched arm. "Zipporah. Do you need something, little one?"

She smiled at the name that had not fit her for many years and stepped to his side, let his arm come around her. "I was looking for Ima. Dinah said she may be in the vineyards with Mistress Abigail."

Titus turned at the mention of his wife, his smile so apologetic that she knew what he would say before he said it. "No, she headed with Abigail and Phillip into Rome, to the markets. On a quest to find a few more pieces of furniture for Urbanus and Lucius's home."

"Is it finished, then?" She turned to survey the structure. Pushed down the pang—as she knew so well how to do—at the thought of a spontaneous trip to Rome. Down into the same place she pushed thoughts of Benjamin.

Urbanus himself stepped from the doorway, his smile not so much bright as content. "It is. Would you like to see it?"

It would likely look like every other small home on the property, but who was she to deny a friend the pleasure of basking in it? "Of course."

Abba patted her shoulder and stepped away. "We were heading in for our meal. Do not take overlong."

"All right." While the rest of the group moved away, Zipporah smiled at her host and stepped to his side. "I daresay it is a far cry from the house you had in Corinth, hmm?"

Urbanus chuckled and led the way inside. "I think its entirety could fit in the atrium of that place. And yet I like this one the more, for having put my own hand to it. My family would think me plebeian for saying so."

He did not often speak of his family, other than those here with him. "Where do they live, the rest of your kin?"

Urbanus nodded toward the window, the hills beyond it, and the city that lay a few miles distant.

"Rome." She paused in his now-small atrium, brows knit. "So close, but you have not left the villa at all. Do you not wish to see them?"

Sighing, he stepped to the window. "It is their decision, not mine. They have refused to acknowledge me since I became a follower of the Way. I pray that someday that will change, but it has not yet. And they will likely all grow even angrier when Lucius makes his decision." He turned back to her, smiling but strained. "He is close, I think. Very close."

She had noted the same thing, and had whispered what she had seen to Master Titus just yesterday, to confirm and encourage him to redouble his prayers. "He is."

Urbanus's pleasure with that lasted a beat, but then it faded into concern. "And Fabia? She so rarely shares what she is thinking in my hearing. Do you know if she is receptive? Can you see that?"

Tilting her head to the side, she studied the man before her rather than the memory of Lucius's wife. He had mentioned before that Septima had not followed him to belief—but she had not realized how deeply that had wounded him. "She listens to Mistress Abigail with patience and an open mind. I rarely see a flicker in her during the ladies' conversations, but I think she and Lucius must discuss it all in depth when they are alone. Her spirit always shines brighter after they are together. They will make their decision as one, I think."

"Good. Good." He nodded, summoned a smile, and motioned her onward. "Let us follow the sounds of the impluvium, shall we?"

Zipporah smiled in reply and let him lead the way toward the trickling water in the fountain. She had forgotten pipes had been run to some of the houses so they need not fetch all their water from the well. That would make their lives easier. And created a lovely chamber besides. She slid onto a bench to watch the water gurgle up. "Very nice, Lord. Your girls will love it. Have you shown them yet?"

"Not since we finished the work. I thought to surprise them with it when it is furnished and ready for them." He trailed his fingers through the little pool, his gaze latched upon the ripples he made. "They will be pleased, I know. There remains only one thing my family needs to be complete—a wife and mother."

Had he finally come to his senses, then? Had he brought her here to seek her advice on approaching Sarah? Zipporah bit back a smile and nodded. "I do agree. You ought to speak with Master Titus at once and then find her—"

"Not *her.*" He faced the fountain for a pulse and then spun toward her. "You."

"What?" She would have jolted to her feet with the shock, if that would not have put her closer to him. Closer to him seemed a bad idea right now, so she merely gripped the stone seat and sat up straighter. "Have you gone mad?"

He came no closer. Indeed, he held up a hand as if willing them both to remain in their places. "Hear me out, Zipporah, please. I realize this is unexpected, and no doubt I led into it poorly with talk of the girls. They are not my only consideration in such things. I need a wife, a helpmeet. Someone to serve the Lord beside me in all things, someone with a heart big and pure enough to accept me and my daughters. I can think of no one who better meets that definition."

"Then you are a fool." Her mother would be appalled if she heard her speaking so to a lord. If she heard her dismissing so quickly the one marriage proposal she was likely ever to get.

But this was wrong. So very wrong.

"Zipporah—"

"No." Shaking her head, she spun to the other side of the bench and stood there, with the stone between them. Not that he seemed at all inclined to reach for her. "You cannot have thought this through. I am a slave, Urbanus."

"You can be freed, as your sister was, you can—"

"I can what? Erase the past that would offend your family, that would push them further from you?" She took another step back. Shook her head again. A curl slipped loose from its binding and tickled her mottled cheek. She shoved it behind her ear and presented the scar to him. "Do you think I can erase this and make myself presentable to your people?"

His determination scarcely covered his resignation. Resignation not at the thought of her refusal, but at this being his answer. Resigned, for some bizarre reason, to the thought of making her his wife. Why, when it brought him no pleasure and was madness besides? Why would he even have gotten the notion in his head?

"You can hide your scars, as you often do anyway. I would not be ashamed of them. I can look beyond them. I promise you, I have no desire for another beautiful wife."

Was this the best she could hope for in life? For someone to look beyond her flaws? To be not ashamed of her? To want her because she was not beautiful?

Tears burned, but she blinked and drew in a deep breath to keep them at bay. "Urbanus, you are my friend. I care for you, for your happiness. And that is why I could never marry you, flattered as I am that you would even consider me as a potential wife."

He lowered the hand held out between them, drew in a deep breath himself. "Do not dismiss it so quickly. Consider it. We could love each other. We get along well, my girls like you. And I can give you your freedom. We can travel together, spread the news of Christ."

Honey, that last promise. But it set up an ache rather than a hope. Because it was not enough to overcome that *could love*, that *like*. She curled her fingers into her coarse, soiled tunic and held on. "No. I thank you, but no."

"Why?" His voice contained none of the pain of a man whose hopes had been rebuffed, just the bafflement of one who met an unexpected obstacle. "Is it...is it because you are in love with Benjamin?"

She took another step back. And took some comfort in the fact that it was anger at her supposed-secret being common knowledge that filled her, and not pain at the mention of the master who would never want her as a wife, even half-heartedly as Urbanus did. "No. It is because *you* are in love with Sarah."

He straightened, raised his chin. The fire of denial snapped in his eyes. "I have no intention of—"

"Your intentions matter little." Only with concentration did she keep her voice from rising to a shout. "Your heart has already decided. You watch her even when you try not to. And you would ask me to spend my life married to a man who cannot help but yearn for my dearest friend? Am I to share your affections with her like some unwanted wife of old?"

A blanket fell upon her, heavy and thick. Perhaps that was all she was meant to be. Like Leah, like Hagar. A stop-gap wife.

But Urbanus winced, and his shoulders sagged. "No. I know what it is like to share a spouse, though Septima did it to torment me. I could never ask you to suffer that. I care too much for you."

So then Septima had not just refused to believe—she had been unfaithful. That, then, was why he did not want a beautiful wife, one who had men always following her. At least he had just realized it. There ought to be solace in that.

Strange how it made her feel raw and bleeding inside instead. "Then let us forget we ever had this conversation."

Half-turning to the fountain, he nodded. Turned his face back toward her without raising his gaze to meet hers. "Forgive me, Zipporah. The last thing I meant to do was hurt you."

Such seemed to be her lot. She forced a smile. "If you want to make it up to me, then go. Speak with Sarah. That is where your happiness lies."

"No. You cannot understand. She is—"

"She is not Septima. She is not just beautiful, you must know that. She is good and strong and selfless."

Urbanus still did not lift his face. "She has a gaggle of men younger than I dogging her steps. She need but crook a finger—"

"But she will not. Ever. Surely you have seen that by now too, as much as you watch her. Surely you see that she guards her affections, that she never so much as speaks to them without her father at hand, and then only politely. She would never betray you, Urbanus. Never."

He made no response other than a ticking in his jaw.

Zipporah slid to the side. "Speak to her. You will not be disappointed, I promise you. Share your fears and let her soothe them."

Urbanus raked his fingers through his hair. "How could she soothe them? How could she promise never to change?"

"The same way she waited these years for the right husband to come to her—faith. Do you think the God who could raise his Son from the grave cannot heal your heart or keep hers steady? Trust him, Urbanus. Trust him to give you both what you need."

His jaw clenched, but he finally looked up. And his eyes gleamed with that certain kind of regret that bespoke clear vision on a matter, for the first time in far too long. "You are right."

She eased away another step. "Speak to her." A trembling had started deep within, and it was only a matter of time before it brought her crashing down. She would not let him see it. She would not let anyone see it. Still, she could build *something* before she came to pieces. "Do it now. This very day."

His nostrils flared. "I must pray first."

"Of course—but you already know the answer. Pray for the strength, for the right words, but do not tarry long enough for the fears to seize you again." She gripped the doorway, ready to flee through it back into the atrium. Just as soon as she had his word.

He stood, a sad smile touching the corners of his mouth. "For a slave, you can be quite the tyrant, Zipporah."

On another day, one further away, she might have jested at the fate he was evading by not bringing her into his house. But she could not manage it just now. All she could do was back into the atrium and say, "Only when it is for the good of my masters. Promise me, Urbanus. You will go now and find her."

His nod came after another moment's hesitation, and it sent her spinning around so she could dart back through the entry chamber and out into the sunshine.

Victory...so why did it feel like such defeat? Her breath shuddered as she drew it in, and the earth seemed to echo it beneath her feet. She would rejoice when Sarah had her heart's desire, when she and Urbanus came to an understanding. That would be the sweetest joy she had known in years.

But why did it require this pain?

"Forgive me, Lord. It is not about me." It was never, it seemed, about her. And she could live with that. She could, if it meant happiness for those she loved, as this would.

But her feet hesitated on their path. She could not return to the villa just yet. Her father would see her distress and try to talk to her, but she could not speak of it to Abba. Not so soon after the Colossian.

Her mother would probably return soon, but she could not speak of it to Ima either. Her beautiful mother would pull the curl over her scar again and say she should have considered it—at least before she knew he was in love with Sarah. She would say, with her mournful eyes if not her words, that it would likely be her only chance at a family.

She glanced in the direction of the ilex, but that was no option either. Not now, when she wanted to avoid those who knew her best. Sarah would look for her there first.

And she could not share this with Sarah. When Sarah sought her out, it would be to tell of her impending joy. So Zipporah must be ready to rejoice with her when they were next in company, and she was not. Not yet.

This pain, it seemed, must be born without a human shoulder for sympathy. Spinning toward the vineyards, where there was always work enough to be done, she squared her shoulders and lifted her chin and promised the tears they could have their release once she was hidden in the wide grape leaves, under the shade of the elms. Once she was free to pray without watchful eyes upon her. Once she was alone with Jehovah.

nineteen

"ONE MORE DAY." BENJAMIN KEPT HIS GAZE ON THE LAND AT THE horizon, land so very close to his own. His hand rested on the small of Dara's back, but the contact never helped him determine her thoughts. All it ever served to do was muddle his. He smiled down at her. "Are you anxious or excited?"

Her smile was small. "Both. Are you certain they will like me?"

A chuckle tickled his throat and slipped out into the salty air. "As long as my mother has been pushing me to find a wife? They will love you."

She looked none too sure, and her uncertainty carried a different flavor than usual. As if it went deeper, was rooted in some place beyond the hints she had shown before. "If Samuel is any indication—"

"He is not. And he is trying." Was he not? They had had a serious discussion just before Tamar was attacked that day, one where Benjamin had laid his hurt bare and begged to know why his brother could not seem to understand what it felt like to be newly married and in love. Samuel had promised to try harder, to in turn lay *his* soul bare before Jehovah and search it for any residual bitterness that belonged to Martha rather than Dara.

Benjamin had noted the change in his behavior, the fewer scowls, but had his brother's mind actually opened? He could not be sure.

Her sigh joined the gusting breeze that sped them home. She darted a gaze behind them.

Benjamin turned and looked too, spotting Tamar and Mark a little distance away. He had instructed Mark to stick close to her, though his friend had not needed the instruction. Not, so far as Benjamin could tell, that they ever spoke. But Tamar had not been alone since that day last week. "You need not worry for her, beloved. Mark will not allow anything to happen to her."

A new note sounded in her sigh. "He can protect her only where she wants to be protected."

That brought a furrow to his brow. "What does that mean?"

Dara shook her head, sending her golden curls swaying. "I would not normally say anything, but as we are now her guardians...she has a history of playing the seductress. Not that I doubt the word of your brother and friend in this particular case, but when one toys with fire..."

Still frowning, Benjamin looked from his wife to her maid and back again. Tamar did not look the part of the temptress, the way she never raised her gaze, avoided everyone she could. "I would not have thought it."

"Mm, I know. I warned her before we left that I would tolerate no such behavior. But who is to say how she acted when out of my sight?"

He shook his head and glanced again at the timid woman. People could hide things, he knew...still. Was fear of his mild Dara enough to warrant behavior so opposite that of which she spoke? He had felt no whisper of warning in his spirit concerning Tamar.

He had felt no whispers at all lately. None except that niggling wonder as to how, in some moments when he felt so very uncertain with his wife, she seemed bold and confident. He had, after their conversation, brought it up to Samuel—which had not been easy. But even the brother who did not like Dara had confirmed that he had seen the proof of her innocence that night.

Reason, then, said he had nothing to worry about. And he would not ever judge her for any past mistakes, if she had made them...but he wanted to know. He wanted honesty between them, but how exactly did one question one's wife on how she knew so well what would please him?

Dara leaned into him, banishing such thoughts. He summoned a smile. "I have no extraordinary insight into a person's hidden motives, I confess. But if Tamar is a danger to the brethren, Zipporah will let us know."

"Zipporah?" Dara drew away, his frown now settled between her eyes. "Mark's sister?"

He had instructed her on everyone's names, but he must not have mentioned everyone's function. Perhaps she had walked her fingers down his chest and distracted him when they were talking. "Yes. She has the most amazing gift of discernment any of us have ever seen. She can look at a person and know his spirit within him."

His wife looked more dubious than impressed. He could not blame her. A hum sounded low in Dara's throat. "Need I be concerned, my husband, with your admiration of her?"

A bark of laughter slipped out—he pressed his lips against it but could not master the smile entirely. "Nay, my wife. You need not be concerned in the least. She is but another sister to me. Although there was a day..." He cut himself off. Zipporah would not appreciate him discussing that childhood infatuation.

Dara narrowed her alluring blue eyes. "A day when what? You thought of her as more than a sister?"

"No. Though you are all the more beautiful when jealous." He leaned over with a grin and feathered a kiss onto the top of her head. "She was the one with such thoughts, but they were short-lived. She was little more than a child."

The line of jealousy smoothed out, and she reached, wove her fingers through his. "Ah. I suppose I cannot blame a serving girl for being enamored with such a handsome, kind master as you. Though I find it hard to believe such feelings would be short-lived. I would pine for you forever, my love, if you left me."

"You need never fear that." Were it not for the audience, he would have pulled her close and tasted of her lips—an ambrosia he knew so well now, yet of which he could never get enough. "You are my forever. I never dreamed of loving anyone so much as I love you."

Her fingers tightened around his, her smile promising kisses aplenty when they returned to their small chamber. "I am the most blessed of women, to have your heart." The smile went teasing, along with the light in her eyes. "Will your Zipporah hate me for it, do you think?"

"No." He laughed it off...and wondered. If he were perfectly honest, he would have to admit that even after he recovered from the ill-fated adoration of the disdainful Leah as a lad, he had been none too fond of the man she wed. And if Samuel were right about Zipporah still harboring any affection for him...

Still. Zipporah was surely beyond such low behavior.

And in one short day, Dara would see so for herself.

"Zipporah? Zipporah!"

Zipporah's eyes snapped open and then winced half-shut again at the on-slaught of light. What time was it? It felt as though she had been asleep for hours already. "Mistress?"

Mistress Abigail, lamp in hand, was kneeling on the hard stone floor beside Zipporah's pallet. It had been so long since anyone but her own parents came to the little room she called her own—she pushed herself up and prayed she had not left it a mess the night before.

But her mistress's troubled eyes did not stray to the belt left on the floor or the heavier blanket tossed haphazardly on her one chair. They remained focused on Zipporah's face. "I have the most terrible feeling. Would you come with me? Would you look for me?"

Her nod came quickly, though she still felt muddled at the unexpected waking. She tossed aside the light sheet that covered her and pushed herself to her feet.

"It is nearly dawn," the mistress said. "I hate to disturb your last hour of sleep, but—"

"It is no matter." But she would not likely return to her bed, so she grabbed up her belt and a strip of leather for her hair, fastening the first as she walked toward the door and scooping her mess of hair away from her face as she stepped into the hall. "My dreams were unsettled anyway." She could not name, now, what had been in them—the images had flown away at the mistress's un-expected voice—but her mind still felt the stirring of unease.

"I awoke an hour ago from the most vivid nightmare." Mistress Abigail shuddered, and the light wavered with her. "I would have been happy to dis-miss it as a mere bad dream, but Titus thrashed in one too. I peeked in on Sarah, and her sleep was also restless—and surely she, so blissful through the last few days since her betrothal, should be having sweet dreams."

Zipporah tried to smile at the mention of her friend's happiness—and did so without trying during the day, when it was so easy to focus on Sarah's joy—but a weight descended. Too fast, too heavy to permit any smile. She tied the leather around her tangle of locks and picked up her pace. Having no reassurances to offer the mistress, she let her sleep-addled tongue remain quiet.

Abigail made no objection, just linked their arms together and sped them both to the nearest door. The night was warm, the sky hinting at morning without embracing it. It was a deep gray, too light for all the stars to shine, too dark to see anything but the barest impression of darker objects that were tree, stone, wall.

Demons. Swarms of them, a column rising from the direction of Rome, others coming from the way of the sea. Streaking across the dark sky, diving at the villa. Flashes of light as the guardians fought them off.

"What do you see?" The mistress's voice came in the softest of whispers, she too facing the walls.

Zipporah's throat was too dry to allow a swallow. "War. We had better wake the others, Mistress, and pray for heavenly reinforcements. I have never seen such an attack on our walls."

"You begin with your parents—I will wake my family first." The mistress released her arm and spun back inside, a prayer spilling from her lips in Hebrew as she hurried away.

Zipporah looked once more to the mottled sky and then ran back to the servants' quarters. It took her ten minutes to rouse everyone and ask them to gather. By the time she herself made it to the peristylium, Master Titus was already leading most of the congregation in prayer.

Sarah had taken a place on the floor near the window, her eyes closed and face lifted up toward heaven. Beside her, bowing until his head kissed the tiles, was Urbanus. Their betrothal was only five days old, but already they acted as a unit. Praying together. Caring for Urbanus's daughters together. And looking at each other with such content expectation.

Something to be thankful for, even as the heaviness bore down more strongly. Zipporah leaned against the wall beside the door, closed her eyes, and focused on the master's prayer.

The sun eventually slipped up, its light pouring into the window and bathing her with warmth. Master Titus fell silent at some point, and a few minutes later Menelaus took up the prayer. Quiet murmurs seeped through the chamber too, the believers whispering their own prayers amidst the main one. So many hearts crying out, standing together. The *amens* and *hallelujahs* mixing with the *please, Lords*. Greek mixed with Hebrew mixed with Latin, with prayer languages sprinkled in that only the speaker and the Lord understood.

Sunlight crept up the wall, finally touching her face. And she heard it, that crystalline singing. Had it come since that first day at the wall, when her eyes were opened? When she passed through their swords and heard the glory for that eternal moment?

No, not like this. From time to time she caught a strain, a refrain, when an angel was nearby. But not so clearly. Not so loudly. Not so that it filled her heart and mind as it did now.

She opened her eyes, slowly.

And was not at all surprised when she stared straight into the face of a messenger, alight with the beauty of heaven, fearsome in his countenance. The angelic face she knew best, the one who had spoken to her before. What was he doing away from the wall?

"Have they retreated?" She barely breathed the words, unwilling to look past his face to the window, where she may see for herself whether the dark ones still bombarded them.

No. How could his voice reverberate so within her, yet obviously make no sound in the room? *They wait, they hover. But they have not retreated.*

She glanced down and saw that his sword was still in his hand, mighty and gleaming. "Why are you in here?"

How to read the face of the warrior? She saw no emotion today, no worry or peace. Nothing to give her a clue what he felt, *if* he felt. Only fierce determination. *Today I guard you.*

Her throat closed off, her stomach clenched. She mouthed the word *why*, though no sound emerged.

Was today the day, then? The day she would die? Could he guard her against the inevitable, or was he here only to usher her into the divine?

At least she had lived long enough to see Sarah happy. She might hope to welcome her brother home again, and Samuel and...and Benjamin, but if that was denied her, then so be it. She had done all she could do. She rose when she was called, she spoke honestly what she saw. If her purpose were finished, then she would cross over into the arms of Anna, into the bosom of Abraham.

The warrior studied her, no doubt reading her emotions more adeptly than she did his. *I know only what I am told—that you are to be protected this day. I obey my Lord and Master.*

He turned, and the song faded, though it did not disappear. His stance was not unlike the one she had seen the men take in their training under Master Titus. Battle ready, on alert. Muscles coiled, ready to strike, even though no threat loomed before them.

A shiver coursed through her.

From the front of the room, Menelaus had opened a familiar scroll and begun to read from Paul's letter. "...we have then different gifts in accordance with the grace given us: if prophecy, then prophesy in proportion to our faith; if ministry, then minister; he who teaches, teach; he who exhorts, exhort; he who gives, liberally; he who leads, diligently; he who shows mercy, show it cheerfully. Let love be without hypocrisy. Despise what is evil. Cling to what is good."

Dinah moved through the room, a tray of bread and fruit and cheese in her arms. Ministering, even as Menelaus read the words, in the way she knew best. Serving the food that the master and mistress provided without reserve. So much, so much they had right here at Tutelos, so much love flowing among them.

So many enemies poised outside their walls, ready to attack.

Some of the congregation moved off soon after, off to serve where they were needed to keep the estate functioning. John Mark took his own scroll of the gospel account and indicated he would read it in another room to any who wanted to listen.

Mistress Abigail stopped at Zipporah's side, her deep brown gaze latching hold of hers and not letting go. Phillip shadowed her, a few steps behind. No doubt he would keep her well in sight all day, even at the villa. The mistress drew in a long breath. "Some of the tension has eased. Are we safe?"

Were they ever? Zipporah swallowed. "The enemy has not withdrawn, but they are holding. Waiting. I cannot know for what."

A crease of worry in her beautiful brow, the mistress nodded. "We must all remain in prayer as we go about our day. And any who feels the need ought to forego their usual duties." She touched a hand to Zipporah's wrist, nodded again. "We will know where to find you if we need you. Go ahead."

She needed no more urging. Pausing only to exchange a tired smile and inclination of her head with Sarah, she slipped from the large chamber and made her way back down the corridors and out into the sunshine. Across the green grass and to the sprawling ilex tree.

Her branch welcomed her. Her dove soon settled on one beside her, cooing along with her prayers. The sun soon dappled its light through the leaves and onto her skin, warming and assuring.

The angel soon stood in his place on the wall. But his stance was different from the others', different from what it usually was. He did not pace his section. And when a dark figure hissed from outside the wall, the way he shifted made it clear he was still standing particularly between it and Zipporah, not just Tutelos in general.

She ought to feel safe. Ought to feel protected. She closed her eyes against the beasts that would devour her if they could and turned her words to prayer. If this were her last day on earth, she would go out with a fight for the Lord.

The sun beat down on them, well beyond warm and firmly into hot, but Dara dared not complain. Not today, when the men's jubilation increased with each step upon the dusty road, each turn of the rented wagon's creaky wheels. She had hoped they would hire a litter for her—she had never been carried around by a horde of men but suspected she would enjoy it—but no. Her husband had merely hoisted her into the wagon along with their trunks and her loom, a grin on his face, and said they would be home within two hours.

Home.

Deep inside, something quavered with yearning. Martha's house had ceased to be home long ago. The master's was where her heart resided, but she had never been able to reside with it. And now here she was, thousands of miles from all she knew, approaching a place that, if all went well, would come crumbling down around her.

But then, *then* she would get to go home.

She prayed as they went, as the menfolk's chatter turned to a babbling echo in her ears, as the mouse curled up in the corner of the wagon and looked as though she would sooner toss herself under the wheels than go where it took her. Dara prayed, and she opened her spirit, hoping images would come.

They did. Flashes of faces she had yet to meet, though some bore resemblance to her companions, so she could guess at who they were.

A woman in her late thirties, still beautiful but for the angry tear streaks down her cheeks as she chased a wagon down a road...a wagon filled with stone-faced strangers that ignored her.

Two older men, one in the dress of a master, screaming at one another. Fists clenched, fists raised. The passion too great to be anything but a brotherhood fractured.

A young man with the look of Benjamin about him, standing in a darkened doorway with lust in his eyes.

A pretty young woman falling to her knees, sobbing, a lifeless girl of perhaps six in her arms, still dripping from the stream that had claimed her.

And then one brighter than the rest, more demanding. Perhaps because Dara saw her own arm within it. Another young woman, this one not so pretty. Her face bore an ugly red welt, her eyes an unholy light. In Dara's vision they glowed a hot white, those eyes, filled with fury and threat. *The witch.* No wonder, then, that Dara saw herself pull out her three-sided dagger. No wonder that she watched herself plunge it into the witch's stomach. And oh, the pleasure of watching that light flicker and fade to nothing.

Dara's hand flexed now, and she let the visions fade, let her eyes focus on the countryside that rolled on before her. Samuel shouted from ahead of them, motioning. A moment later, the wagon crested a knoll and she saw why.

The villa, sprawling behind its stone wall, grand and thriving. The central house, large and impressive, smaller buildings abounding. Vineyards, pastures, fields, an olive grove...too much to take in all at once.

Hers. A smile curved her lips as her husband turned to her, beaming. Perhaps it was the Asinius family who owned the ship they had sailed on, a whole fleet of them, and untold investments besides. But the villa was Benjamin's. The villa was hers.

"There it is, beloved," he said, reaching over the side of the wagon to take her hand. "Your new home, where you will be mistress."

Her new home, which she would tear apart stick by stick, stone by stone. Person by person. Until the master came to claim her. She let her smile grow. "I can hardly wait to meet everyone."

twenty

ZIPPORAH! ARISE!

She jolted at the command from the warrior, leapt down from her branch even before the cloud of prayer had cleared from her mind. Her eyes sought the shining figure. "What is it?"

He extended an arm, pointing his sword toward the gate. *Go. Stop them.*

Stop them? Even as her feet obeyed, her eyes tracked to the heavens. To the swarm of darkness now growing again, to the creatures shooting like stars toward the gate.

To the plume of dust on the road. They would be the ones she should stop, whoever they be. She increased her pace, the heavy leather of her belt digging into her hips as she ran. The angel flew along beside her, his face as unflinching as ever.

Her breath came hard and fast when she reached the top of the hill, less from the exertion than from seeing the wagon already halted at the gate. Praise Jehovah they would hold them there to wait for her, as they always did, otherwise...

She might as well have slammed into a wall, so quickly did she halt when she saw the impossible. The wagon's wheels turning again, taking it not away but within. Toward the villa. "No! What are they doing?"

The angel's answer was to grip his sword tighter and point her toward the villa rather than the gate.

Her heart thudded so fast, so hard she felt the pain of it in her chest. Even before she was close enough to see the darkness, she knew it would be there. Why else would the warrior have roused her? An enemy came. An enemy rode with whoever was in that wagon.

And the cloud of them still outside the walls cackled and cheered so loudly she nearly retched.

She raced toward the villa, lungs burning and belt digging, nearly stumbling once, but the warrior beside her braced her, lifted her over the stone, put her back on her feet. And even glory's song at his touch could not drown out the beating of fear.

No, not fear. He who was in her was greater than this enemy—she had nothing to fear. It was something different that pumped through her, something that had no name. Something that fired her blood with purpose.

She was near enough now, near enough to see sunlight shining off golden curls. "Samuel." But *Samuel?* Samuel came with an enemy? "No. No, Lord, not with them." That would be why whoever was at the gate did not wait to call for her. Why would they? The master had returned, and the master would never bring an enemy with him. But he must have.

She recognized Mark's stride next, noted two unfamiliar, decidedly feminine figures. And there, striding into the villa beside one of them, the unmistakable form of Benjamin.

Benjamin, walking hand-in-hand with a jeering, tooth-gnashing demon.

Her stomach trembled, every prayer she had prayed for him these past months seeming to knot in her gut and press. Every hope, every long-held dream shriveling. Burning under the fire that only increased in her veins. His choice. His choice, wrongly made. His choice had brought tribulation through their gates.

They all disappeared inside as she flew down the hill, her aim the back door rather than the front. It was closer, and the halls would be clear. They all would have heard the shout announcing him. They would all drop what they were doing and rush to meet him. They would all be oblivious to what he ushered in.

"Lord, protect them. Protect your children." She burst through the door, viewed the halls through the shimmering back that now went before her. Barely registered the hand he lifted twice to stop a servant from coming through a doorway and barreling into her. Clearing her path.

Voices reached her ears, but she could not make out what they were saying over the rushing of blood in her ears. Unmistakable joy, though. Shouts of what must be greeting. A happy reunion. *Happy.*

Even as she burst into the entryway, as she saw the crowds rejoicing together, it enveloped her. Regret that she must be the one to speak what no one wanted to hear. That even as she protected them, she set herself apart more and more.

That she would not be one of them today.

"Stop!" The command tore from her lips, from her heart. Did it sound as painful to their ears as it felt to her mouth?

The warrior touched a shoulder here, an arm there, until a path cleared. Her brethren responded, even if they knew not to what. Parted like the Red Sea, but instead of facing freedom on the other side, she faced Pharaoh.

The demon stared at her from hate-filled green eyes, from a mask too beautiful to be ignored, one with golden curls that punched her with their familiarity. The creature's human feet took a step toward her, its gaze latched on her like the wolf's had been all those years ago.

But the warrior lifted his sword, point at its throat, and the woman it controlled came a halt. Smiled. And twined her arms around the man's beside her.

Zipporah swallowed down the betrayal and turned her gaze on Benjamin. He was not hers, had never been hers. But he was *theirs.* He belonged to the brethren, to the Lord. Why, why had he not listened to what the Spirit surely whispered in his ear? She shook her head. "What have you done?"

He narrowed his eyes at her as if unable to process the question. Smiled, actually *smiled* as he gripped the woman's hand. "Zipporah, there you are. Allow me to introduce my wife. Dara."

His wife. Invisible manacles snapped over her wrists. If she was his wife, Zipporah could do little to fight her. She had willingly bound herself to his will. She had trusted him to be her authority. And now *this*.

"She is Samuel's sister. We came by chance upon his family."

Her gaze sought Samuel at that. He was already looking at her, his green-gold eyes intent. He slid a step toward her. "What is it, little sparrow?"

Mark stood at Samuel's side rather than Benjamin's, his eyes focused on her too.

Everyone's, it seemed, were.

She turned hers back to this Dara and the laughing darkness whose name she did not know. "Your *wife* carries a demon. You must get her out of here at once."

The demon's laughter spilled now from the woman's lips. "Darling—I thought you said she would not be jealous."

The fire burned brighter, hotter as she watched the ripple of the words. Watched doubt settle like seeds in the fertile hearts of the congregation.

Her family. Her friends. Her masters. All looking at her with suspicion instead of belief.

Benjamin pulled Dara closer. "You are mistaken." Had his voice always been so hard? No. No, even in that year when he had scarcely spoken to her, it had never sounded like this. "She is a believer as surely as you are. And she is not going anywhere."

"She is possessed by a dark one." Her limbs settled of their own accord into the stance of the warrior standing between them. Spine straight, shoulders back, chin up. One hand fisted as if around a sword. And looking through his brilliance, she saw more truth than ever. "A spirit of divination."

"Zipporah." Her mother slid up to her side, worry in her brow, in the hand she put on her arm. "My daughter, please. She is our new mistress. I beg you, watch what you say."

Zipporah shook off her hand, shook off the worry. Even as it stung like a thousand bees. "I say what is true. I have *always* spoken the truth, and I will not stop when you most need to hear it. This woman is our enemy!"

Mistress Abigail still stood beside her son, the eldest son of her flesh, confliction in her eyes. "You must be mistaken, Zipporah. They have been wed for a month now, he says. He would know, surely he would know if what you say is true."

Benjamin's jaw firmed. "Of course she is mistaken."

The demon laughed again, smug and joyous. Zipporah shivered at the thought of what the others were doing outside the gates. No doubt bombarding them again, determined to get in and help their comrade.

The angel shifted, and Zipporah shifted with him. "How could I possibly be mistaken? When have I *ever* been mistaken about these things?"

Mistress Abigail pressed quivering lips together.

Benjamin glared. "How are we to know? No one else can see what you claim to see. No one else knows if you speak truth or lie."

A blow, one that made her wince. "You think the brethren never tested my spirit? Never weighed it against the word from others?" She raised her sword arm, mirroring the warrior's. "Do the same to her! Test her and see if she is true!"

"Zipporah." Never in the eighteen years she had known him had Benjamin's voice ever sounded so cold, so hard. Like iced-over iron. "That is enough."

"It is not enough." Because the angel edged back a step, she did too. "It will not be enough until you see, until you get that creature away from us. Bind it, cast it out!"

"How dare you!"

For a moment she thought he would lunge at her, this man who had always been her friend, whom she had loved so long. Lunge at her as the Roman had five years ago, with a knife in his hand and a demon behind his eyes.

But his wife restrained him with a light touch and stepped forward herself. Her human eyes, the ones the others would see, all but wept with pity. Pity! But the demon eyes behind them flashed a challenge. "If I need to prove myself, then so be it. Come here, Zipporah. If you think you see evil within me, then bind it and cast it out yourself."

Those invisible manacles weighed heavy on her wrists. The creature knew as surely as Zipporah did that she had no authority over her. Not so long as she was Benjamin's slave and he refused to see.

The warrior half-turned, his sword still pointed at the demon but his free hand now pressed to Zipporah's chest, holding her still. Fire blazed in his eyes. *Not a step closer, or she will kill you.*

"This is absurd." Benjamin tugged Dara back and stood before her, glaring down at Zipporah. "I expect better of you, Zipporah. I expect honor and respect, the kind that comes of knowing each other so well. We have always understood each other, always—so understand me now. You treat my wife with the same honor you show me, or she will not be the one cast out of these walls. You will be."

Zipporah moved not a muscle, though her spirit cried out. He would do it, she saw that clearly. He would turn her away, would use the walls that had held her in all these years to hold her out. Leave her to fend for herself in a world that would be so quick, so happy to abuse and destroy her.

And she could do nothing to fight him. He was her master. His wife her mistress. Either of them could plunge a knife into her chest without consequence in the eyes of the law.

Oh, but there would be consequences here. Here, where God's law ruled above Rome's, there would be consequences indeed. The congregation would split, would shatter, would tear themselves apart.

No. No. Above all, she must serve the brethren. However she could. However they let her.

She took another step back, though her chin would not lower. Her shoulders would not relax. "Yes, Master."

He held up a hand, finger pointed. "I do not want to see you again, do not want to hear another word from your mouth until you are prepared to apologize."

She did not look at anyone else. Did not dare. Could not bear it. So she simply spun. Walked with even, purposeful strides down the same hallway she had run through minutes earlier.

And listened to the heavenly song that filled her ears as the guardian walked with her.

Never in his life had Samuel had to fight the urge to crush a fist to his brother's nose. But then, his brother had never before acted like such a bully. He watched Zipporah stride out, chin still high and righteous certainty in every line of her stance, waited only until the collectively held breath released. Then he took a large, purposeful stride after her. Knowing he would be stopped. Counting on being stopped.

"Samuel!" What he had not counted on was the complete surprise in Benjamin's voice. When Samuel pivoted to face him, incredulity had the gall to fill his eyes. "I realize you always must soothe, but do you really think now is the time?"

Samuel held his ground, held his brother's gaze. Did not look to their mother and father, to their friends or other siblings. Did not look to the smug creature still grasping Benjamin's arm like a leech. "You want to know what I think? I think I *warned* you! I warned you she was not who she said. I knew, *knew* there was something wrong, and you refused to listen! Now you have brought the enemy into the one place we have always striven to keep entirely safe."

Mother eased forward, agony lining her face. "But how could it be true? If she is your sister..."

"Only by Martha's blood, not by Christ's." He folded his arms over his chest and held the gaze that had always been most dear. Never had he put himself at odds with the woman who had saved him, who had loved him. He prayed he would not have to do so now. "Is that now our gauge? Who one's mother is by physical birth?"

"Samuel."

"I am sorry, Mother." That they must face off, but not for the stance he took. He closed the distance between them and leaned down to kiss her cheek. "I am sorry I failed you in that first command you gave me—to protect your son. I failed to protect him from the most dangerous threat we ever faced."

He edged back again, turned his gaze over the entire congregation. A few unfamiliar faces, but mostly the ones he had known for the last twenty-five years, since he joined this family. "How any of you can doubt Zipporah, who has proven herself time and again at the price of her own safety, is beyond me." His gaze settled on her parents. Strong Andrew, who had welcomed him with a smile when Jason Visibullis first brought him home. Beautiful Miriam, who had cared for him with joy and laughter. His question did not need to be asked.

Miriam splayed her hands. "She has always been truthful...but she has also always loved him so..."

Samuel shook his head and turned to face the most of them he could manage at once. "A line has been drawn today. A war has been launched. I stand before you now telling you I believe Zipporah—that her words confirmed what my spirit has told me since we met this woman. I stand with her." He inclined his head toward Dara. How did anyone mistake that gleam in her eye for anything but hatred? "No doubt you will find some accusation to level at me too, likely a lingering bitterness toward your mother. You will find some way to dismiss my certainty, as surely as you just did hers. So be it. My conscience is clear."

Mother reached toward him, but for the first time he did not move into her embrace. And by the tears in her eyes, she recognized that first too. "Samuel, my son. She is his *wife*."

"She is his undoing." He backed up a step and prayed with all that was in him for the strength to do what needed done. "I know you must stay beside the son of your flesh, Mother, at least right now. I know that, I would never ask you to do otherwise. But please, I pray you. Take it before the Lord. Listen to the Spirit. Test her words and actions, her spirit, her fruits. See where they point. Already she has divided us."

Dara lifted a golden brow. "I am not the one walking out, brother."

Samuel breathed a dry laugh and focused on Benjamin rather than his wife. "Will you bar me from your house too, Ben? Will you dictate to me like the slave I once was?"

Benjamin looked stricken, at least. But it was not enough. Not enough to set to rights what he had done. "You are my brother."

"And she had always been your friend and sister, yet you threatened to toss her to the wolves you know well wait to devour her. You struck her as surely as Antonius Merillius, as surely as that boy-loving monster of a master in the markets. Only deeper, because you should be her ally, not her enemy."

He could take no more. Samuel spun again, to the path still cleared from Zipporah. Took a few certain steps before he heard the stirring behind him and Benjamin's outraged, "Mark!"

A lump in his throat, Samuel paused and looked over his shoulder.

Mark was only a step behind him, his back rigid as he faced Benjamin. "You can order me not to follow, not to stand with my sister. And I will obey you. But only because I must. If you give that order, you will be my master...but nothing more."

Some feeling Samuel had hoped never to experience, never to have to define, rose from his gut to his throat. Closed it off, and then pressed against his eyes and nose. A pressure he should not have to feel. A burning he should not have to fend off.

Benjamin swallowed but said no more.

Not until Sarah came through the crowds, a man behind her. Urbanus, from Corinth? Samuel had to blink when he saw their fingers linked. Obviously there was much he did not yet know about the happenings at Tutelos. She stopped before Benjamin, stretched up to kiss his cheek. Her smile was sorrowful. "I am glad you are home, Ben. But she would not lie. No more than she could deny what the Spirit reveals to her."

And then Jacob the steward stepped forward too, his wife with him. He bowed to Benjamin but addressed Father. "I have served with her every day. I know Zipporah's spirit. I do not know this Dara's, but I see something in her eyes that reminds me too acutely of the dozens of other eyes we have turned from our gates. I stand with Zipporah."

No one else followed, not just yet. But as Samuel turned toward the exit again, he knew they would come. Not today perhaps, but they would come. Dara would not be able to deceive the elect forever. Most of them would come to see, as they watched her, what her purpose was. To divide their house. To sow division between them.

Today she would rejoice at the start she had. At the first battle won.

But the war was only beginning.

He did not need to ask where to find Zipporah—some things never changed, even as the years stretched on. He aimed his feet toward the ilex tree, and no one contradicted him. They just strode with him, this small band.

Soon enough the ancient, sprawling tree came into view, its low limbs reaching out, over the wall. For a moment, when he did not immediately spot her on her branch, the fear struck that she had taken Benjamin's threat to heart and had leapt onto the stones and over them. That she had given up on them all.

But no. Rather than sitting, she stood with feet planted firmly on the ground, a breeze that stirred not the leaves whipping her hair around her. Her eyes were closed but her face pointed toward the wall, along with her outstretched arms.

His breath balled. When had his little sparrow grown from an outspoken girl to a warrior of a woman? When had the child chosen for her innocent belief in the Lord become a general in the battle against the darkness? If Anna were alive to see the way her sister had bloomed, she...she...

She would have stayed inside with the others. She would have chosen *it cannot be* over *I wish it were otherwise*.

When they were close enough for their footsteps to be heard, Zipporah lowered her arms, opened her eyes, and turned to them. His heart fractured when no hope sprang up in her eyes, no gladness. Just wariness. She looked at them each in turn. "Did they send you to convince me to apologize?"

Mark leapt through the space between them and gathered her close. "You said nothing that you need to apologize for. We tried to warn him, Zip. We did not know it was a demon, but we knew she was not to be trusted. He would not listen."

She clung for a long moment to her brother. When she pulled away, she looked at the rest of them.

Jacob offered a tight smile. "I wish you were wrong. Yet I cannot doubt you."

"I never thought my brother could be so deceived by a lovely face." Sarah shook her head, her countenance fierce. "I cannot believe the things he said to you."

Zipporah sighed and trained her gaze on the wall. "Nor could he believe the things *I* said to *him*. This day has hurt us all." She moved her gaze, heavy and so very old, to Samuel. "I would have thought you would stay with him. You have always been at his side."

Mark laughed, though it sounded weak. "He was the first of us to call him out and to come after you. We merely followed in his wake."

At that, Samuel opened his arms and, when she walked into them, closed them around her. She smelled of the wind and the dew.

Her arms locked around him as they had done so many times in the past, when she was but a slip of a girl. "You have always been my champion."

Half a smile tugged at his lips. "Someone must be." He kissed the top of her head. "You cannot know how many times I wished you were with us. Especially in Jerusalem, when we stumbled upon Dara's family."

"You think he would have listened to me any more then?" She pulled away, looking tired now as she gazed past him.

He turned, they all turned, though what had caught her attention was well beyond him. And yet...not.

He felt it. Perhaps he did not see what she saw, but he felt it. Felt the shadows pass over him. Felt the press upon his spirit that told him to pray. "Have they broken through?"

"A few. Not the horde of them trying, praise Jehovah, but a few. We must pray. We must pray without ceasing, or they will overrun us completely."

Well then. Later they could catch up. Later he could learn why Urbanus now had a possessive, supportive hand on his baby sister's back. Later they could be family, could be friends.

For now, they must be soldiers. He fell with the others to his knees.

twenty-one

BENJAMIN PUT ONE FOOT IN FRONT OF THE OTHER, FOLLOWED HIS mother wherever she led, but his mind was not on the familiar corridors of his home. It was not with the group of family, friends, and servants who had stared at them with complete uncertainty after Samuel and Mark and the others stormed out. It was not even with his wife, who did not let go his arm as Mother led them on a tour of the villa for Dara's sake.

It was out at the ilex tree, where he knew well Zipporah would have gone. Where the others would have known to find her. Where he had once sat on a branch as she grieved her newly lost sister and spoken to her of the Spirit, of the call to visit the churches, of his wonder if faith had always come easily because he was there for the first baptism of fire.

An echo of pain pulsed through him. When had he last prayed? Fully focused, completely given over to Yahweh, more than a whispered *Please* or vague *Lord*? Not since...not since Jerusalem. Heaven help him, he had drifted, and he knew not how or where.

But that he could repair. Now that they were home, Dara would find her place with the other women, training under his mother in how to run the villa. He would have time alone again to focus on things of the Spirit. He would put that to rights.

But how would he ever mend the break with the people?

"And these are the servants' quarters." His mother looked beyond him and Dara, to where Tamar trailed silently behind, and offered the same warm smile she gave to everyone in her house. "We are glad to have you among us, Tamar, and I know the other young women will welcome you warmly to their number."

Now her gaze focused on him, somehow both firm and questioning. "We have only the one available bed here."

Anna's. Even though she had not slept in it for the year before her death, no one had ever had the heart to fill it. Benjamin sucked in a breath. "Do you think that wise, Mother?"

Now sorrow entered her gaze. Or rather, grew bolder in it. It had been there the whole time. "Do you now think Zipporah violent as well as a liar?" Shaking her head, Mother half-turned away. "She would never take this strife with you out on another. You must know that."

"I never thought she would accuse my wife of demon-possession either." He glanced over his shoulder at Dara's maid, who stood as always with her eyes downcast, her shoulders hunched. Fear flickered over her countenance, he thought—though it looked so very at home there, he could not be certain. Did she walk through all her days in fear, or merely since the attack? He had not paid her much attention. He got the impression she preferred it that way... which made him wonder again how Dara's warning about her could be true.

Dara looked at Tamar too, her lips pursed. And then she smiled. "It will be a good thing, I think. Perhaps the slaves can forge a friendship and Tamar can help Zipporah understand how things are now. Is that not right, Tamar?"

The woman shrank still more into herself. "As you will, Mistress."

His mother pressed her lips together and slid by Benjamin and Dara so she could grasp Tamar's hands. From here, it looked as though they remained limp in Mother's. "You will soon feel at home here, my friend," she promised the younger woman in a whisper. "You will find that in our house, all serve, master and slave alike."

Dara shifted beside him, though she did not let go his arm. "And I look forward to learning at your elbow, Lady, so I might relieve some of the burden from you."

He heard nothing insincere in the words, yet they made him want to groan. In a normal world, one that had not just fractured around him, that would have been his greatest concern right now—ensuring the harmony of wife and mother as Tutelos had, for the first time, two mistresses. Now, he knew not how he could manage it if they ended up at odds over who planned the meals or directed new arrivals to their quarters.

His mother transferred her smile to Dara, though it seemed to him not quite so open, not quite so warm. His imagination, or had Zipporah planted too many doubts?

His free hand curled into a fist, hidden in the folds of his toga. Perhaps it *was* good that Tamar share her room. It would remind her that she was not an island unto herself. She was part of them, one of many, and must make an effort to get along. Too many years now she had been left to her solitude, and look where it led—to her thinking she could level her accusations at anyone.

If a slave had behaved so in the house of some of his Roman friends, she would have been at the least struck. At the worst killed. She ought to be grateful he had only...

No. What was wrong with him? He shook his head, tried to dislodge the thoughts. He would never raise a hand to a servant. How could he, when both mother and brother had been slaves?

Samuel's words returned to him, slicing him through. *You struck her as surely as Antonius Merillius, as surely as that boy-loving monster of a master in the markets. Only deeper...*

But what was he to do? Let her go on accusing his wife of the unthinkable? Perhaps Dara's faith was new, perhaps she had much to learn, but to accuse her of hosting a devil—no. He would know. He would sense it. He would...would...

Would he not?

The doubt fled as quickly as it came, but still he wanted to curse her for making him entertain it. Curse her again for convincing Samuel and Mark of it.

Dara loosed his arm and stepped toward the other two, taking hold of Tamar now. "Come. I will show you there is nothing to fear in your new room. And then once you have settled in, you may return to mine and help me with my unpacking. All right?"

Tamar, with one last glance at Mother, nodded and let herself be pulled toward the closed door. Dara opened it without hesitation, led Tamar through.

Benjamin took a step back. It seemed wrong, somehow, to do this while Zipporah was not within. The room may belong to him, but it had been hers alone for five years now.

But his mother seemed to take no issue with it, and if it were some sort of violation, she would be the first to disallow it. Instead, she sighed and stepped away, drew him with her. Wrapped her arms around him for the third time since they walked through the doors an hour ago.

"My son. I have missed you so."

"And I you." Yet the joy of homecoming was as muted as a lamp held under a basket. Why, why had Zipporah spoiled it all? "Mother..." He pulled away enough to look in her face. "Tell me you do not believe her, not even a little."

A sheen gleamed over Mother's deep brown eyes. She patted his cheek. "Just this morning I woke her up to come see for me, so heavy was the Spirit upon me, telling me to pray. When she told me the demons were bombarding our walls, I believed her without hesitation, because it made perfect sense with what I felt myself. As it always has, every time she has spoken." She shook her head, and a tear slipped out of each eye. "Should I disbelieve now? I want to. I pray she is wrong. But how can I be so big a hypocrite as to dismiss her only when I do not *like* her words?"

"It is not hypocrisy to say she is right sometimes and wrong this time. It is wisdom. No one is perfect. And her own parents did not follow her."

Her own mother had given Dara's rebuttal credence, which made a strange combination of pride and disappointment surge up in him. What man did not like the thought of someone pining for him? But she had told him it was nothing but a short-lived infatuation. He had claimed, all these years, just that. Had believed her.

Mother sighed. "Andrew and Miriam will answer to their own consciences for their decision today—and I daresay will have much repair work to do with their daughter. Perhaps they were following the lead of Titus and me. Perhaps they were afraid of the limb she had stepped out on. I cannot say. But I will tell you this—if you exile Zipporah, they will leave with her. A parent does not confine a girl to these walls for so long only to let her be tossed to the dangerous world on her own."

His eyes slid shut. What a horrendous situation. Why, why had she forced them to it with her brash words? If she honestly had such a concern, why did she declare it before the whole assembly? Why did she not come to him privately and share her worries? He opened his eyes again. "I do not intend to expel her. But I cannot allow her to speak so to my wife. Her mistress."

"Your wife." Why did she sound so resigned as she said it, when it was what she had hoped for all these years? Her smile looked forced. "She is beautiful. I can see why she caught your eye."

Observation or accusation? "She is more than beautiful. She has a seeking spirit, a sweet disposition."

"Good." She stretched up to kiss his cheek and then moved past him. "I will let you two settle in. The meal will be at dusk, as always."

He nodded and leaned on the wall opposite Zipporah's door. Inside Tamar slid open the two drawers, no doubt finding them both filled. She moved to close them again, but Dara stayed her, reached in.

Mother made a surprised squeak from his right. He turned his face, expecting her, somehow, to be objecting to Dara's actions...but she was too far away to see, and the hand she splayed over her chest, the amused reproof on her face was aimed at the end of the hallway.

Phillip leaned in the shadows.

Mother shook her head. "Since when do you follow me around the villa, Phillip? It has been more than two decades since I have turned to find you behind me like this."

The eunuch did not smile. "I have not had to. Now I do."

"Phillip." Her voice sounded weary.

He lifted a brow. "You stay, Mistress, so I stay. But I do not doubt the words of Zipporah. You stay, so I will do all the Lord allows to protect you from the evil now in this house, as I swore before Master Titus, you, and our God I would always do."

His mother did not argue, either because she did not want to or because she knew it was useless when it came to Phillip and his concerns for her safety. She merely shook her head again and continued on her course, the loyal guard falling in behind her.

Benjamin rubbed a hand over his face. So many months he had yearned for home, and now this.

Inside the room, Dara had emptied the contents of one of the drawers, tossing it all carelessly onto Zipporah's pallet. He recognized most of the items—the trinkets Samuel and Mark had found for her these past four years, silly things mostly, the occasional bauble most girls would exclaim over. The tortoise-shell comb, the bronze bracelet. Had she ever worn them, or had she tucked them away and left them there, deeming them impractical for a servant?

Tamar eased her spare tunic into the drawer, though she paused and reached into the corner.

He recognized this too, the wooden figure she pulled out. A small sparrow, carved by one of the brethren training to be a carpenter in Rhegium. It had been the very first thing Samuel had sent home for her, only a few weeks after they first struck out.

Dara took it from Tamar's hand.

Benjamin straightened. "Beloved—why not leave Tamar to become familiar with her new space on her own now? We have much unpacking of our own to see to."

Dara smiled her beautiful smile and tossed the sparrow to the pallet with the rest of Zipporah's things. "Of course, my love. Lead the way."

He took her hand when she drew close enough for him to reach it, tucked it into the crook of his elbow. Tried to bury the new pang when he glanced one last time into the small room.

One of the sparrow's slender legs had snapped off.

Dara said nothing as they traversed the halls again, not until he led her into the chamber they would share and closed the door behind them. He had not expected time to themselves so soon. He had known everyone would gather when they arrived, as indeed they had. He had expected hours of exclamation and information, thought Dinah and her helpers would bring in food, thought the light would fade on them still laughing and talking and learning what they had missed.

But after Samuel and company stormed out, there had been no jubilation left in the others. Most of them had come forward to offer quiet greetings and said they must return to their tasks. A mere half hour and it had just been him as his parents and two remaining brothers, along with Jason's betrothed—who looked mightily uncomfortable. His mother's offer of a tour for Dara had seemed the only option that could break the tension.

As soon as the door shut behind him, Dara pressed against him and pulled his lips down to hers. And for the first time in their month of marriage, no cloud of need punched him, blinded him. He kissed her but then sighed and eased her away.

She frowned. "What is the matter?" At his arched brows, she echoed his sigh. "A foolish question. But my love, I want only to forget it for a few minutes. Please—this is not exactly the welcome you told me I could expect, and I...I need to put it from my mind for just a little while. To remember why I knew coming with you was the right decision."

Poor Dara—a terrible welcome indeed. He brushed her golden curls from her cheek. "I am so sorry, fair one. So sorry you were greeted this way."

Her smile looked taut and frayed. "I knew when you mentioned her we would not get along. Not at first. Not given her feelings for you."

A chill chased down his spine. *The spirit of divination*, Zipporah had said. But no, that was not what his wife meant by the words. She meant only she had a feeling—did they not all have such feelings?

She leaned into him again, though this time she merely rested her head on his shoulder. His arms found their places around her, his hand stroking down her back. So familiar now, yet still so new. She exhaled again, long and slow. "Had she the famed beauty of the sister you all go ever on about, I may be jealous too. But you never loved her, did you, Benjamin?"

A question that made him squirm inside. "Of course not. But not because—I am not so shallow that I think only of beauty." Nor was he so stupid that the irony was lost on him as he said those words to his wife of unsurpassed looks.

"So long as you think only of me." She snuggled in closer, held him tight. "So long as you do not doubt me, do not believe her vicious words."

"I do not doubt you." He could not think of it, not *that*. But as her hand trailed down his side, always so sure of what would bring him pleasure, that other doubt reared its cruel head. He grabbed her hand and eased her a step away. "But while we are talking of unpleasant things...Dara, I must know. Whatever the answer, I will not care, but I must have it so the questions cease. Was there another before me?"

She pulled away another step, fire snapping in her eyes. "You doubt my virginity when I came to you?" Her words were a hard whisper, brittle as glass. "I saved myself all these years, and you *doubt* me?"

Regret pummeled him, but he could hardly unspeak the question. He shrugged, palms up and helpless. "I cannot remember that night. I know only that...that you are certain in times when I would expect shyness. And I would know that *I* need not fear another showing up at my door with a claim to you."

Anger flamed in her eyes, anger and something more, something he could only think to label as resentment. But then it clicked away, and resignation followed. A strange kind of it that made her shoulders square and her chin edge up. "You have nothing to fear. There was a man I thought I loved, a little over a year ago. We...we explored a bit more than we should have, but I never gave myself to him. And he is dead now, dead of a fever before he could speak with my brother."

Jealousy twisted—but she had been honest. She had admitted it. They could move past it. Especially since she came to him again, devotion in her eyes and a private smile on her lips, and settled her hands on his chest. "I repeat, my husband, that I *thought* I was in love. When I met you, when I realized how those old feelings dimmed in comparison..." She tilted her head up, her lips begging to be kissed. "Nothing can come between us so long as we love each other so. Not a ghost from my past, and certainly not an upstart slave from yours."

He bent his head, claimed her lips. Desire came, but no peace.

Her ghost might be dead—but his "upstart slave" would be going nowhere unless he forced her to. And he had a feeling no apology would be forthcoming.

twenty-two

AN HOUR, PERHAPS TWO HAD PASSED BEFORE THE WEIGHT OF THE
Spirit lifted enough for Samuel to sit up. Zipporah's gaze, latched onto the wall,
still looked troubled. But the others looked around them with every bit as much
concern.

Urbanus and Sarah were the first to stand, an apologetic smile on the man's
lips. "Forgive me—I must see to my girls."

Zipporah refocused her gaze, her smile carrying no apology. "Of course you
must."

"Wait." Samuel surged to his feet too, brows raised. He motioned to the hand
yet again on his sister's back. "Do you not have something to tell me first?"

"Oh!" Sarah flushed. And pure joy shone from her eyes like the sun after an
eclipse. "We are betrothed."

Betrothed. His last little sister, soon to be wed. That would leave only Cleopas unattached. And Samuel. He set his gaze on Urbanus, noting the equal joy
in the man's eyes as he looked at Sarah. Samuel had liked him well when he
met him in Corinth. Had admired his dedication to his daughters—but he had
not expected he would someday call him brother by marriage as well as faith.
"Congratulations. When did this happen?" Obviously after their last letter—
such news would not bear being left out.

"About a week ago." Still grinning, Sarah leaned into Urbanus's side.

The man chuckled. "We owe it all to Zipporah, who delivered a much-need-
ed kick to my posterior."

They all owed much, it seemed, to Zipporah.

Sarah left the side of her betrothed husband and went to her friend, wrapped
her arms around her. "Your home is still in that house. Do not be afraid to come
back in."

Zipporah's eyes slid shut. "Soon. Not yet. I am not ready yet."

Sarah nodded, eased away, and then moved to Samuel. Once her arms were
wrapped around him, she put her lips to his ear. "I must help Urbanus with the
children, Jacob has his tasks, Mark will need to see to Ben. Do not leave her
alone yet, brother."

"I will not." He gave her an extra squeeze for always being so very *Sarah* and
smiled as she pulled away.

Jacob moved into the place she vacated, arm outstretched to be clasped. He
slapped a strong arm to Samuel's back as they embraced, its solidity a reminder

of his days as a gladiator. Another life, he called it, but the one that had led him to this family. "It is good you are home. It is good you are out here."

"It is good to be back where I belong." He smiled at Jacob's wife too, as she pulled away from hugging Zipporah, and then turned to Mark. "Ben will need you."

Jacob and his wife headed toward the vineyards. Mark folded his arms over his chest with a grunt and leaned against the trunk of the ilex. "Let him."

"Mark." Zipporah settled a hand on her brother's arm. Censure filled her tone. "He is your master."

"You are my sister."

"And you stood with me. That means more to me than you can possibly know. But please. The wider we let this rift grow, the more the enemy wins. Seek peace, for the sake of the church if not yourself. A body cannot survive long with such a wound."

Mark's sigh was gustier than the wind over the Mediterranean. He pushed away from the tree, though his eyes still looked hard as jet. "If he speaks a word against you, I cannot promise to seek peace."

"Benjamin is a good man." Even as she said the words, disappointment seeped through the conviction in them. She turned so Samuel could see her profile. "He has just made a bad decision."

"A bad decision that affects us all." He planted a smacking kiss on her forehead. "I will come see you later so we can catch up. In your *room*, little sister, not out here."

She rolled her eyes heavenward as only a sister could. "Later, yes. I will return by the time Sarah needs me, you can be assured."

Mark nodded and held Samuel's gaze for a moment before he walked away. A moment that said much—that they had not tried hard enough, they should have carried Benjamin off that night he was too muddled to know what they were doing. They should have trusted their instincts.

Once her brother moved out of the spread of the ilex, Zipporah's gaze fastened on Samuel. "And you will want to go spend some time with your parents."

"I will. But right now I want to spend some with you." He took Mark's place against the trunk of the tree, from which vantage he could see Sarah and Urbanus walking as one. He nodded toward them. "You had a hand in that, did you?"

Zipporah made a sound that crossed a hum with a sigh and rested her shoulder against a branch. "They fell for each other rather quickly."

He lifted his brows. "Not surprising, given what I know of them both. But?"

Her gaze flicked from them to him. "But his late wife had hurt him. He was afraid."

Her voice said something else, something beyond her words. It spoke not of jealousy, either pointed or general. Yet pain echoed. He reached for her hand and ran his thumb over her knuckles, noting a new scar on one of them. "What happened, little sparrow?"

She studied the ground for a moment before looking up into his eyes. Her sigh seemed to release a burden, for her shoulders relaxed. "He proposed to me first."

Not an unthinkable event...were it not for the outcome he had just beheld walking away. Samuel sucked in a breath. "When you knew well he loved Sarah? Why?"

The corners of her lips turned up in a wry little smile he had first seen her wear the last time he was home. "He did not want another beautiful wife."

"He *said* that to you?" Samuel straightened and glared, now, at the back he could scarcely make out at the villa. "Perhaps I do not like him as well as I thought."

Zipporah, however, laughed and put a restraining hand on his arm. "He did not mean to insult me. It is no secret that I am not beautiful."

Words that sounded so strange coming from a warrior queen's lips. "You have always been beautiful. And too strong for your own good. You have told no one of this, have you? You have carried the pain of it tucked away inside."

"It is only a very small pain, in light of the joy I feel for them." But she leaned into him and rested her head on his shoulder as she always had when in need of comfort. He squeezed the fingers still in his, and she sighed again. "I had no one to tell. It is the one thing I could not share with Sarah, and anyone else...we have Colossians among us, and one of them really *did* insult me. It struck me more than it should have, and my parents had to mop up my tears from that. I could not...could not..."

"I know." Even as a child, she had not liked to be the one to receive comfort. Pain had always made her run for solitude rather than loving arms. Still—she needed them no less than anyone. He wrapped his free arm around her and held her tight. "But you have me now, again."

"I know." It sounded like she smiled, though her voice was muffled in his toga. "And I thank the Lord for it. I missed you, Samuel. Even if you are as biased as my ima." She tilted her head up to reveal that smile, mischievous and bright despite the world. "No one else the empire over would ever call me beautiful."

"That is not bias, it is true sight." To prove it, he eased her away and used the fingers still in his to twirl her around. "Look at you. All grown up."

"I was all grown up *last* time you were home."

"And I liked it no more then than I do now." Now, it struck him that she was older than Anna had ever lived to be. He shook it off and narrowed his eyes at the belt she wore, the one he had sent her. "Perhaps that was not such a good idea, it sets your figure off too well. Anna would have been jealous of your form."

Another laugh, and a shake of her head that sent her long curls dancing on the wind. "Anna never had cause to be jealous of me. She never had cause to be jealous of anyone."

And yet she was, of many. Did her sister not know that?

No—Zipporah had always loved her too blindly. But that was a talk for another day. Turning the conversation so fully to Anna would only cement in her mind that she was less, would always be less.

Samuel shook his head too. "She would have been, and of that hair of yours. She always wanted your curls, you know."

Zipporah gathered them together, though the wind snatched them again. "She was only being kind when she said that."

"She was not. No more than I am when I say you and she have the same smile, your mother's smile. Bright as the day and beautiful as the sunshine."

She flashed it again now, though it soon faded to an indulgent half-grin. "I appreciate your effort, Samuel. But waist and hair and smile do not change how the whole is perceived. I am not beautiful." She touched a finger to her scar. "I never will be, and I have no problem with that."

Until some oaf from Corinth or Colossae used such words as a cudgel. Such foolish, untrue words. How could they not all see what stood before them? He tugged her close again and held her to his side. "You are. You always have been, you always will be, and you might as well stop arguing it with me. A scar or broken nose merely adds interest to your face."

He felt her laughter before it emerged, the rumble in her chest that spilled out as music. "Oh, Sam." She slid her arms around his waist and held tight. "It matters not. I will just stick close to you, for you are beautiful enough for the both of us."

"*Beautiful?*" He made a tisking noise and shook his head. "What did I ever do to you, that you use the word reserved for women? I am handsome, fine of face, of ruddy countenance, a head above other men, good look—hey!" He pulled away with a laugh when she dug her fingers into his side, into the place he had always been most ticklish. "Stop that!"

Instead she laughed and reached to repeat the torture. He lunged away, attempted to find her own matching ticklish spot but was foiled by the belt, which just made her laughter redouble.

How good it felt, after this past month—not to mention this day—to laugh. To chase her around the tree as he had been doing since she was a mite. To be *home.*

He had to duck under the branches, had to laugh as she swung herself over one and leapt to another like a red squirrel.

Had to halt when a chill swept over him. *Knock her down. Strike her. You are stronger than she, you could overpower her.* It nearly, nearly sounded like his own thoughts. Except he would never think such things.

Zipporah loosed a resigned exhale instead of a laugh and jumped back to the ground, her gaze latched behind him. "Do not let it bother you, he is chasing it away even now."

It. A demon. Samuel shuddered and watched the movement of her eyes. She traced a path with her gaze, over the wall, and then onto it. "Who is chasing it?"

"One of the warriors who guards us. He has retaken his place on the wall—apparently I will not die today."

His brows pulled down. "Was that a concern?"

"Is it not always?" She turned back to him, but her smile did not look like his little sparrow's. It looked like the warrior queen's again, sad and regal. "Any day could be our last. And I trod a dangerous line on this one."

She had thought she might die but had confronted Dara anyway. Had lived, but at the cost of relationships, yet she could laugh...and keep fighting.

How proud he was to call her a sister, if only by marriage.

A flap of a bird's wings sounded and, knowing well the stories of animals coming at her, he looked up. But the dove that fluttered down did not seem to be in a panic. And it landed, one-legged, on her shoulder as if at home there. She stroked its head.

Samuel's frown gave way to a smile. "A friend of yours?"

"Columba. Did you not meet him last time?" She narrowed her eyes in thought. "I guess he came right after you left. He was injured in a dive from the sky."

A dive from the sky. Aimed at her, no doubt. "And which scar is he responsible for?"

Zipporah chuckled and indicated a crescent-shaped one on her neck, beneath her jaw.

"A bird impales you in the throat, and you make a pet of it."

She grinned. "Just as you would do, O Brother the Healer."

As the dove cooed, a soft laugh won out. "Yes, I suppose I would. Here." He patted her favorite branch. "Sit with me. Tell me all I have missed and let me exaggerate all our adventures for you."

With another smile, she came forward and made no argument as he swung her up, onto her usual seat against the trunk. The bird did not budge from its perch. Samuel's eyes came to a rest directly before him, on the V of fair skin visible under the pure white of her garment.

He had forgotten, in all the excitement.

But now he met her gaze with a grin of his own. "I have something for you. Hold on." He had to extricate his pouch from under his tunic, undo its laces, but then he pulled out the shark's tooth on its leather length. "I brought you a weapon."

Zipporah laughed as he slipped it over her head. "What beast is this from?"

"A shark, or so I am told. I shiver at the thought of one big enough to produce such a fang though."

Her deep brown eyes went wide as she fingered the tooth. "It could have swallowed your ship whole!"

"Let us be glad it did not." He made a fist as if around a dagger and imitated an overhand jab. "I figure in a pinch, you can wield it as a blade."

"A belt for armor and a tooth for a sword. With what will you outfit me next, my brother? A ribbon for a helmet?"

"Well that would be useless. Perhaps a few metal combs, though, could deflect an attack."

Laughter dancing in her eyes, she pressed her lips together and shook her head. Patted the bark beside her. "Sit with me. Tell me your tales."

Samuel hoisted himself up. He certainly had tales enough to tell, enough to entertain them until daylight faded and their stomachs demanded they head in. Until they must face again what this day had wrought.

He wished...but it mattered not what he wished. This was how things were. Benjamin had followed his flesh, had married Dara, had brought her and the demon she carried into their walls. They could not undo it. They could only move on from here. And wherever that might lead them, at least they were back where they belonged. He and Mark now had Zipporah's sight to assist them, and Zipporah now had more allies to lend her strength.

With hope, with prayer, they could trust the day would come that they would be only allies again, no enemy among them. And with more hope, more prayer, perhaps that day would come before the other she spoke of, the one that would cost them lives.

Another chill swept down his spine. And this time, he knew there was no demon on which to blame it.

Never in her life had familiar walls made such dread close over her. Zipporah almost wished, as she slipped down the darkened servants' hall, that she had taken Samuel up on his offer to see her to her chamber door. But she could not keep him any longer from his family. Given the clatter of dishes in the wash pot in the kitchen, they had already missed the meal, but Dinah would have set something aside for him. No matter which side she had decided to take, she would do that for Samuel.

Zipporah's stomach rumbled too, but it also churned at the thought of putting food into it. She needed prayer more than a meal. She would just slip into her room and...

Her feet came to a halt when she saw the light coming from within her chamber. Surely Mark had not come already. He would have been serving Benjamin through the meal and would now be taking his own, catching up with their parents. Unless he, or Abba or Ima or Dinah herself, were lying in wait to try to convince her to join the other servants in the kitchen. If so, she would thank them but decline.

Was it only yesterday she had heard John Mark's voice echo as he read the words of Jesus? *This kind of demon will come out by nothing but prayer and fasting.*

She knew not if the spirit within Benjamin's wife had anything in common with the one of muteness that had seized the boy in John Mark's account, but she knew it was a stubborn one. And a successful one.

A shiver overtook her. She had never been the one to bind a demon, nor to cast it out. The men always did that—Jacob and Master Titus. And she knew she could not do it now, not so long as she was bound by Benjamin's authority. But she could fast. She could pray.

She pushed open her partially closed door, hearing a squeak from within her room as well as from the old hinges.

Half of her things were out of their drawer, lined up carefully, in neat rows, on the top of the small chest that had once held them. Anna's bed, so long empty and stripped, now had blankets and a pillow atop it. And a woman cowered in the far corner as if afraid Zipporah might devour her whole.

Had she seen the woman earlier that day? She could not recall from the gathering. Her focus had been only on a few. But she had glimpsed her just before that, coming in with them. This must be Dara's handmaid.

Zipporah summoned a smile. "Greetings. I am afraid I did not learn your name."

The woman looked to be in her mid-twenties, probably a decade older than her mistress. Perhaps about Mark's age. She kept her face down-turned, her shoulders hunched up, her gaze latched onto the floor. "Tamar."

"It is good to meet you, Tamar." And obvious that the thought of sharing a room struck pure terror into her heart. Well, it was not ideal for either of them, but this was the only spare servant's bed in the villa. "I am Zipporah."

Tamar nodded. "I...saw you. Earlier. I am sorry to intrude—"

"You need not be. You are welcome here." No black figure crouched within this one, no demon tongue hissed from behind hers. They would get along just fine.

Though it seemed to require every ounce of will she had, Tamar slid forward a step and turned her gaze toward the drawers. "I am sorry I..."

A flicker of irritation sprang up, yes, at the thought of a stranger going through her things. But she quenched it and renewed her smile. "I am sorry you had to see to it yourself. Do you need more space?"

Tamar shook her head and smoothed away a wisp of warm brown hair. She was pretty, even with abject fear on her countenance. Zipporah could only imagine how lovely she may be with a smile.

Perhaps if she acted normally, her new roommate would relax. Careful to hum a psalm to assure the woman she was not angry, she headed for the small stand with its two drawers and opened the bottom one. It could hold a bit more without trouble, but all the trinkets would not fit.

No matter. She would find another place for what could not be squeezed in here. She tossed in the combs first, smiling at Samuel's mention of using such things as a helmet. Added the bracelet she had never worn.

Given the faint sound of a foot sliding along the floor, Tamar was leaving her corner. Hesitatingly, but leaving it nonetheless. "Sincere apologies, Mistress."

Zipporah's brows drew together. "I am not your..." When she looked over, her words dried up. Tamar held the little wooden sparrow Samuel had sent her four years ago, with one of its legs snapped off. A chuckle bubbled up and slipped out. "Now it looks like Columba."

Tamar's extended hand shook. "Pardon?"

"I have a pet bird with one leg." She kept her smile in place as she eased forward and took the poor little figure from Tamar's hands. "These things happen, Tamar. It is all right."

Tamar dragged her gaze up. And oh, the depths of agony within her eyes. "Have I one too?"

Now it was Zipporah's turn to say, "Pardon?"

"A demon." Tamar's voice was but a whisper. "Have I one too?"

Too? Dara's maid believed her? Zipporah sucked in a breath and held the woman's gaze. Then looked beyond it. "No. But I see their marks upon your spirit." Like scratches, gashes, oozing the life of her soul. Leaving her bleeding and vulnerable to the next attack. She reached out before she could think not to and touched a finger to the stranger's cheek. "How do you bear the pain?"

For a moment, Zipporah thought Tamar may actually form an answer. She blinked back gathering tears, her lips parted. But then she turned away, her fingers twisting around one another.

Zipporah turned too, to prop the sparrow up in the corner. "Have you served her long?"

She had to glance Tamar's way to see her shake her head, as she made no verbal response.

"Have you *known* her long?"

A pause, and then a single nod. "Seven years."

Since Dara was a child, then. "How do you know her?"

Tamar's fingers were hooks, latched onto one another. Trying desperately, it seemed, to hold on to *something.* "I cannot speak to you of this, Mistress."

"I am not your mistress. And I will not push you." She approached her again, though, and reached out to grasp her hands, to smooth the fingers trying to become a gnarl. "Would you answer me one more question, though—has she been like this long?"

Tamar wanted to retch, wanted to run, wanted to fall to a puddle and weep until it all went away. But the one Dara had called a witch still held her hands—with more gentleness than her own mother had shown after they discovered her shame.

And Tamar's fingers, despite themselves, relaxed within the hold.

She edged her gaze up, a few inches at a time with a rest in between. This Zipporah may say she was no mistress, but she carried herself like one. Shoulders back and chin up, complete surety in her eyes. She may be the younger by many years, but in her presence Tamar felt like a child. A child waiting for a scolding.

Dara would claw her eyes out if she heard them speaking of her. That fire would snap in her gaze, the one the master would call righteous zeal. But there was nothing righteous in it. Tamar had known it all these years, even if she had no words for it.

"How long?" Zipporah asked again. Softly. Gently.

Tamar's swallow nearly choked her. "A long time. All but a few months of the years I have known her."

She remembered the day. Remembered peeking in as she always did when Dara came to the master's house, longing to hold the child in her arms. Remembered his words, raised as if to his God, asking for the power to come upon her. Remembered the way Dara had opened her eyes wide and looked up, perfect trust on her face. The way she had jerked, overcome by the violent spasm, had slipped off her chair to her knees.

She had been different when she rose. A child still, but not. Beautiful still, but twisted. She was, from that day on, too old for her years. Too hard for the soft lines of her face. Too much the master's student.

Zipporah sighed. "It will not be easily cast out then. I did not expect it would be."

A shudder swept over her. They were all terrifying, these people who could see what mortal eyes ought not. Though at least this one did not seem to hate her. Yet. "How...how do you know she...?"

Zipporah's smile was small, soft, sorrowful. "I see them. Spirits, both light and dark. And the ones of people too."

"What do you...?" Did she really want to know? Probably not. But Tamar swallowed again and asked it anyway. "What do you see in me?"

Her smile fading, Zipporah looked at her for a long moment. But not like Dara had on the ship that time when she grabbed her hand. Not like that at all.

Zipporah squeezed her fingers as one would a friend's and then released them. "I see a heart beloved by God."

Perhaps her vision was not so good after all. Tamar shook her head. "Jehovah wants none of me. I am a dog, only half-Jew."

"All Master Titus and Mistress Abigail's children are also only half-Jew. Would you call them dogs?"

Another surge of fear crippled her. But yet the glance she stole showed her only amusement, and patience. Was it possible Zipporah did not mean it as a trick? Tamar shook her head. "Of course not."

"Jehovah loves you no less than he loves them." Zipporah edged back a step, that surety shining in her eyes. "You are his precious daughter. He does not want *none* of you—he wants all of you."

Impossible, as much as the words tugged at her. The great and almighty God would never want her—had she not proof enough of that? Had she not cried out to him until the last bit of hope had drained from her spirit? Never had he answered. Never had he cared.

Zipporah tilted her head, her regard still steady. "It is always hard to see the hand of the Lord through our hardships. I cannot know what you have been through, what you have survived. But you can rest in the knowledge that Jesus suffered as keenly as you. He felt the slice of a whip on his back, the piercing of a crown of thorns in his head. He was crucified—for *you*, to take your sins upon himself as the lamb without blemish. And when he arose, he conquered the consequences of those sins—death. You need only accept his gift."

Was that what these followers of the one called Jesus believed? Tamar could see the allure. She could see why one would want to believe that so perfect a sacrifice had been made. But it had not been made for Tamar. No one would even purchase her a sin offering at the temple. Why would a person offer himself? No. Perhaps Jesus whom they called Christ *had* died for the sins of many. Perhaps he *had* risen from the grave, though it went beyond her comprehension.

But not for her. No one would do that for her.

A rap sounded on the open door, and they both looked up to find Mark filling it, a crooked smile on his lips. "Benjamin sent me to make sure the two of you were getting along."

When Zipporah released her hands, Tamar edged toward the corner. Hopefully he would stay there in the doorway, but if he came in...

Zipporah loosed a sigh that sounded like a dirge. "It is as though he knows me not at all."

Mark moved forward slightly but still halted within the threshold...and sent Tamar a glance that seemed almost—strangely—apologetic before focusing on his sister again. "Are you all right? I know that you..."

She should leave. These siblings could obviously not have a private conversation in her company. But where else on this vast villa could she go? Where would be safe? There were so many people about, all looking at her with suspicion. And she could hardly squeeze by Mark now—he took up the whole space between the posts. Why had she never noticed how broad he was? He stood every bit as large as Eleazar. Was no doubt every bit as strong. She would be every bit as powerless against him if he—

"No." Zipporah's hand touched her cheek again, and though Tamar jerked away, she still felt the peace in her fingers. Just as she saw it in her steady, burning gaze. "You have nothing to fear here. I promise you."

The apology in Mark's gaze intensified. He backed up a step. "We ought to go find Abba and Ima, Zip. I am certain Master Titus and Mistress Abigail would release them from their duties so we could spend some time as a family."

Why did Zipporah look about to refuse? Tamar knew not—but was all too familiar with the pained wariness that swept over the girl's face.

Not sure from where the strength came, Tamar reached out this time and, with shaking fingers, took Zipporah's hand. She should say something too, some words of comfort and assurance. She knew none. Could not make her tongue un-stick from the roof of her mouth. But Zipporah sent her a grateful smile, so perhaps the touch was enough.

As if it had bolstered her, the girl nodded and stepped toward her brother. Mark moved aside so she could precede him out the door. But over her head, he glanced back at Tamar. Smiled.

She was unaccustomed to smiles so warm, yet without expectation. Friendly, absent lust. How long...how long had it been since she had a friend? A true friend, one who cared despite it all? She could not remember. At least a decade, perhaps more. Perhaps not since she was a child skipping through the streets.

Unease chased the thought away, and she turned from the door without returning Mark's smile. She could not find friends here, among these people. She could not. Dara would... And the master—the master would punish her beyond all imagining.

Tamar could not control the shudder. Perhaps she could not bring herself to hate them, to be their enemy. But if she wanted to survive, she also could not be their friend.

twenty-three

"DO YOU STILL LOVE HIM?"

The quiet question may have come from her brother, but Zipporah knew it was one everyone had asked themselves today. Perhaps even a week ago, it would have made her wince, or dismiss it with a laugh, depending upon her mood.

Tonight, it made her lean against the wall just inside their parents' chamber. Exhaustion swept through her. She drank in Mark's beloved features and then looked over his shoulder, to where Abba and Ima both stood, ready to embrace him. But more eager, it seemed, for her answer.

She drew in a long breath. "No." Was it a lie? So long she had struggled, so long she had prayed for that love to be taken from her. So long had the Lord been preparing her for disappointment. But none of that had accomplished what Benjamin himself had in those first minutes home.

"Zipporah." Her mother packed a lifetime of rebuke in her name, matching that in her gaze.

Zipporah pushed off the wall. Apparently rest was not to be had now, here. Which made her heart twist. Where could it be found, if not with her family? "Do not look at me as if I am trying to fool you, Ima. I *did* love him, yes. For too long, no matter how I prayed. But perhaps that was why the Lord had not taken it from me until recently—so that I would pray for him. I know not, except that this last month, I felt something had changed. That any hope that had remained was gone." As if there had ever been any.

"But the heart does not forget so quickly what it held dear for so long. And a jealous heart can see fault where there is none." Ima spoke cautiously now, probing.

What did she want? For Zipporah to renounce what she knew to be true? "Jealousy may have made me dislike her. May have made me hide in my room with tears in my eyes. But it would never, *never* make me lie about the things of the Spirit." Those tears burning now, she shook her head and turned toward the door. Let Mark have his time with them without her to mar it.

"Zipporah, wait." Mark surged forward, blocking her exit. His gaze latched onto their parents. "*I* have no reason to be jealous of her. And at first, when I saw how Benjamin looked at her, I thought it something to smile and laugh over. But the more we got to know her—and when she lured him so quickly into marriage..." He shook his head, his jaw clenched. "Samuel and I knew something was not right, but Benjamin would not listen."

His gaze went hard, harder than she had seen it before. The gaze of a man, not a boy. "He, at least, had the excuse of being rendered blind by his love for her. What excuse have you for disbelieving your daughter?"

"We have none." Their father's voice was low, soft, pained. He shook his head and gripped their ima's hand. "None, except that it is too terrible to be true. It is easier to believe Zipporah is wrong than to contemplate what it means if she is right."

Mark folded his arms. "It will not be easier when Dara tears this church apart."

"No." Her abba moved his gaze to her. "I am sorry we did not follow you out immediately, my daughter. We do not disbelieve you. We will stand with you."

Do not disbelieve... Why could he not say it without the negatives? Why could he not *believe* her? Why did her mother say nothing at all, just come forward and fold Mark into her arms?

Zipporah let her knees go weak, let herself slide down the wall and wrap her arms around her legs. She pasted on a smile and aimed it at her brother, who deserved a more genuine one than she could manage just now.

She would stay for a while. Listen to his stories. Enjoy having him home. Then she would excuse herself to assist Sarah. Retire to her—and Tamar's—chamber.

Maybe the Lord would grant her a night of sound sleep to help her put aside this day. Maybe tomorrow it would not all look so terrible. Maybe she would wake up and find it had been nothing but a nightmare after all.

Or maybe...maybe it was time to take that step away, the one she had refused five years ago. Maybe it was time to ask for freedom from the master she could no longer trust.

Benjamin had scarcely slept all the night long. No, he had lain there in the bed once more familiar than any other and wondered at how soft it was. Too soft. His back had grown accustomed to the hard pallets of ships and inns and spare rooms.

One would have thought, though, that the noises would not have made his ears perk up. Nowhere he had been the last four years had been particularly quiet. So why did he start at each passing footfall, at each muted laugh or whisper?

By the time dawn filtered into the sky, he was weary of remaining still to keep from disturbing Dara. He heard Samuel's door open and click shut again, heard his brother's quiet steps pad down the corridor. Another click, more nearly silent steps followed from either Sarah's or Cleopas's room.

He eased his arm from under Dara.

She stirred, blinked once, and cuddled into the pillow. "Where are you going?"

Smiling, he brushed a curl from her face and pressed a kiss to her forehead. "For a walk. You rest, beloved. I will return to break the fast with you."

A hum was her only answer.

Benjamin slipped from bed and into his clothes. He fastened his sandals and then let himself out of the room.

The halls were empty. Where would the others have gone so early? Samuel may well intend to run the perimeter of the estate as he often did, to stretch out legs too long confined to a ship. Perhaps, if he could catch him, Benjamin would join him.

He headed for the nearest exit and breathed in the fresh scent of home as the morning mist billowed over him. The air had the faintest chill yet to it, though even now the sun burned its way upward, promising heat in the day.

His gaze snagged on Samuel. Walking, not running. With Sarah by his side. Aimed for the wall.

Aimed for the ilex.

Benjamin drew in a sharp breath when he spotted other familiar figures moving the same direction from various points in the villa and outbuildings. Jacob. Andrew. Mark. And was that Menelaus and John Mark? What were they all about?

He took one step toward them but no more. Zipporah must have told them to gather at dawn. Mark had not mentioned it last night, but then, Mark had barely spoken to him at all. And would he even share such a thing, if their intent was to further discuss Benjamin's wife?

His hands clenched. Let them say whatever they would. But he would have his own discussion with Zipporah before he went inside.

Pivoting on his heel, he headed for the opposite side of the grounds.

The birdsong should have sounded like music to his ears. The dappled light of a new sunrise should have inspired poetry in his spirit. The beauty of home, of all that was his, of the Visibullis legacy should have kindled appreciation within him.

But it all reeked of ashes and smoke. He had just wanted to come *home*. To tease Jason about his upcoming wedding, to pretend to groan when Cleopas insisted on sharing his latest song. To tug on a lock of Sarah's hair and ask after Ester's growing family. To hug his mother and receive that proud clap of a hand to his shoulder from Father.

Instead, here he was, alone when he would have preferred company, grumbling when he wanted a reason to laugh.

But he needed time alone, did he not? So then. He would use it. And be grateful for it.

He marched right up to the eastern wall, climbed up the stones, and lowered himself to a seat at the top. Sunrise rainbows streaked the clouds. A better scene for prayer he could not have designed. Why, then, did it take such effort to focus his thoughts upon the Lord? He dragged in a long breath, let it back out. "Father God..."

He closed his eyes and leaned forward, bracing his elbows on his knees. "Father God, I need you. I...I do not understand what has happened. I thank you for delivering us home in safety, I thank you for my family and my wife. But Lord, why did our homecoming have to be like this? Please help Zipporah to see what she has done and repent of it. Please, please mend the rift and help everyone open their hearts to Dara. What am I to do, Father?"

He fell silent, ready and waiting for some stirring within, for some whisper from the Spirit. But the minutes slipped by, and all he heard was the chirping of the birds. All he felt was the coolness of the stones beneath him.

A minute later there came a coo, a beating of wings. He looked up in time to see a dove land on the wall a few feet from him. It had only one leg, but that did not impede it from hopping along, from fluttering to the ground to peck at some insect Benjamin could not see, from returning to the wall with, he would have sworn it, an inquisitive look in its eyes.

Benjamin sighed. "What brings you to my wall, little dove?"

The bird cocked its head, cooed, and hopped backward a few inches.

"I cannot blame you. I would not want to be around me right now, either. In fact, you may want to avoid Tutelos altogether. With the foul moods everyone is in, you may find yourself caught in a hail of missiles."

As if it understood him, the bird took to wing. It flew off into the Italian countryside at first but then swooped upward, around, and back into the air over his land. Perhaps it had a nest somewhere on the property. Or hoped for breakfast from the vineyards.

Oh that his life were so simple. But then, even that creature had suffered.

He faced forward again and stared out, waiting for that whisper that never came, until the sun had climbed upward enough to warm him. The wall grew hard under him, and at last he jumped down, brushed the dirt from his garment, and turned back toward the villa and the ilex beyond it. He had given them an hour, had taken one himself.

But if the Lord were not going to answer him, at the very least *she* could.

He had to make a concerted effort to keep his stride even but not too angry. Stomping would serve no purpose, other than announcing his mood to all. As he moved by the house, he saw figures moving. Servants going about their day, guests and family stirring beyond the windows. Field workers would be trekking toward the rows of crops.

Plodding onward, he spotted a few who had been at the ilex heading off in other directions. Good. He had no desire to confront the group of them. But if Zipporah stayed true to form, she would be the last to leave her sanctuary, and he would still be able to catch her there.

Though apparently, he saw when he drew nearer, Samuel intended to stay behind as well. His brother sat on the branch that Benjamin had once favored, his back against the trunk. Zipporah perched on her own, an arm-span from Samuel.

And Sarah marched toward Benjamin, her face so blank she must be working hard to keep it so. When had his baby sister learned that?

She halted directly in front of him, a pace away, forcing him to stop too. "Why do I doubt you seek her to apologize?"

He knew not whether he wished to sigh, clench his teeth, or roll his eyes. So he kept his own expression as empty as he could. "I wish to speak with her. That is all."

"And ask her what? To deny what she knows, what she sees?" Sarah shook her head, setting her long braid swaying.

How was he to admit he had no questions planned? He just wanted answers. The sigh won out. "You believe her so easily, so quickly. Why? Why do you trust her above me?"

Yet Sarah looked at him with bafflement in her gaze. "My brother, were you to tell me there is a nest in the top of that distant tree, on the topmost branch so far away, I would believe you without question. Because you can see what I cannot. How is this any different? It is her gift, it is how the Spirit has filled her. I cannot doubt it any more than I can doubt the whispers I hear in my own spirit. Any more than I doubt Father's wise counsel and Mother's tender hospitality. This is who she is—one who discerns the spirits, one whose eyes have been opened to what lies beyond."

She took a step to the side, face hard now rather than blank. "Even so, were she the only one to think this terrible thing...but Mark and Samuel agree, and they have spent more time with your wife than the rest of us."

But they were biased against her because of her methods of convincing Benjamin to wed her—not a topic he wanted to open with his little sister, even if she *was* now betrothed to Urbanus. So he merely shook his head and tried to work some words, any words past his tight throat. "They misjudge her, and I trust that in time they will all realize it. In the meantime, I merely want a chance to speak to Zipporah without a crowd of people around us."

"And you will have your way. But Benjamin." She eased near him, touched a hand to his arm. Nothing soft had entered her gaze. "Tread carefully."

"Of course." His stride was purposeful, though, as he continued toward the tree, and a bit angrier than before. He made an effort to keep his face clear. Even put on a smile.

Samuel met it with a questioning glare and made no move to budge from his perch. "Ben. You are out early this morning."

"My bed was too soft." He turned his smile to a grin as he said it, as he would have done a month ago. "I gave up on sleep and opted for prayer instead. It is a beautiful morning."

"Mm hmm." His brother packed a load of dubiousness into that hum.

Zipporah sighed and jumped down from her branch. "Ought I to assume it is I to whom you wish to speak, Master?"

Master. He hated hearing her call him that. It was one thing to get the term from the field hands he did not know so well, but from the people he had grown up with, who had always been his closest friends, it sounded wrong. "If you have a few minutes."

She did not look at him. She just smoothed the length of white tunic below her belt and nodded.

"Zipporah."

At the warning in Samuel's tone, she turned her head. Her smile looked forced. "You know we need to have this conversation, Sam. But I do thank you for your thought for me. And for praying with me this morning. It was an unexpected blessing to have so much company today."

She had not planned the gathering? Possible, he supposed. But Benjamin had his doubts. Doubts he kept from his face as he smiled in what he hoped was reassurance at Samuel.

His brother looked unconvinced, but he slid off his branch. Walked to Zipporah and leaned down to kiss her cheek. "Find me when you return to the villa, little sparrow. I still have not heard the stories for all these new scars." He had taken her hand while he spoke and stroked a thumb over her knuckles.

Benjamin did not see any new scars, but perhaps they were small. And he had no intention of moving closer. No, he just kept that calm smile in place and waited for Samuel to release her hand and walk away. Waited for his footsteps to fade to nothing.

Zipporah did not look up at him. She kept her gaze instead on the ground, an obeisance that ill-suited her. After a long moment, when he said nothing, she swallowed. "I did not expect you would believe me."

The anger surged. "Why should I have? It seems you have lied to me before."

At that she abandoned the humility they both knew she did not feel anyway and raised her gaze, narrowed and obviously baffled. "When have I lied to you?"

He swallowed past the tightness in his throat and jabbed a finger toward the tree. "Right here, four years ago. The night Anna died and I came out to find you."

Her brows knit, but thunder took the place of confusion. "You would hold *that* falsehood against me? The words of a girl trying to protect her heart from further pain, a girl desperate for a friend who would not come near her otherwise?"

"You made a fool of me!" He spread his arms wide. "I defended you. For years, whenever someone would tease, I would defend you. I would say it had passed. And now I return home, and what does everyone say to me? That I must excuse your attack on my wife because you speak from *jealousy*. Have you any idea how embarrassing that was?"

Her face went blank, even emptier than Sarah's had been, and her shoulders edged back. "So sorry, Master, that you must suffer the embarrassment of ugly little Zipporah having feelings for you. Forgive me."

He winced. "It is not—that is not what I meant, and you know it."

"Of course. I know. You are too noble a heart to be swayed by such shallow motives as beauty. Your indifference to me always ran far deeper. And your attraction to your new bride was rather based on...?" She lifted her brows.

He narrowed his eyes. "You do not know her."

"*You* do not know her!" Fury flashed in her eyes, quickly banked, as her hand sliced the air. "I daresay no one does anymore, so long has the real girl been smothered beneath the beast that controls her. Yet you would claim to love her—which is terrifying. What is it, Benjamin, that you love?"

He did not want to understand that terror that replaced the fury in her gaze. But it was too sharp, too brilliant for him to deny it. She believed those words she had shot at them yesterday. And given that, how horrific it must be for her. To think her master had fallen in love with a...a demon.

No. He shrugged off the compassion. "You will not divert me with false questions. We are talking about your motives, not mine."

She dipped her head again. "Very well. Mine, then. Yes, I loved you for too many years. I beg your forgiveness."

How could she make him feel like such an oaf with those words? "Zipporah..."

"I never meant to embarrass you with it. I always knew there was no hope, but it took me too long to learn to school my heart. I have managed it though." She looked up, met his gaze. But he could read nothing in it, nothing beyond determination. "I assure you, Master, that I now love you only as a brother."

He swallowed and lifted his chin. "I have heard such a claim before."

"I was a child."

No longer though. Now that belt Samuel had sent her showcased a woman's curves, as did the chiseled line of her jaw. She was eighteen. But with no betrothed. No husband. No babes.

No wonder she had nothing better to do than shoot accusations at his wife.

Her gaze had gone pointed, and with that too-familiar light in it. "Whatever it is saying to you, I suggest you ignore it."

"What?" He took a step back, unease punching him. And then redoubling. Could he believe her now, when he could not yesterday?

"There are still a few slinking around from when they broke through yesterday."

He clenched his jaw. She would link everything to that, it seemed. To the day before, and to Dara. In Zipporah's mind, every bad thing to strike them would be his wife's fault, and she would sour the others against Dara with her claims.

"You have been too long left to your own devices, Zipporah." The decision gathered within him like a fist, firm and steady. "You need a husband. I will arrange something. Joseph, perhaps, or the servant of the visitors from Colossae—they are looking for wives, are they not?"

"No!" If terror had colored her gaze a moment before, it now overcame her. Overwhelmed. Eyes wild, she fell to her knees and reached for the hem of his tunic. Clasped it in shaking hands until her knuckles went white. "No, please, Master. *Please.* Please do not force me on anyone. They do not want me. No one wants me. *Please.*"

It was as if he watched her from a distance, like a play upon a stage. Interested but detached. He bent down, forcing her hands to let go, and touched a finger to her quavering chin. "And why would no one want you?" The words sounded strange coming from his throat, absent all warmth. How had it come to this, to speaking to her like a stranger? Or like a recalcitrant child? What happened to the friendship born of that shared longing to see the world?

She averted her face. Presented her scar.

He moved his finger to trace the line of it, though when she flinched away, he made no objection. "It is not the scar that would repulse a man, Zipporah. It is the tongue you have still not learned to control. Tell me—has your father let you out of these walls yet?"

Her swallow was her only answer.

It was the only answer he needed. "And why not? It has been almost five years. *Five years* since he issued that command. And what did he say when he gave it? That he would revoke his words when you had learned to control yours. When you had learned when to speak and when to hold your tongue. Obviously you have not."

She held it now though. For a moment at least, and kept her face averted. Then her lips parted. "Five years ago, you offered me my freedom, and I refused. I would have it now."

Benjamin rose with a shake of his head. "No."

"No?" Eyes wide with shock, she jerked her face upward. "You have...you have never denied a slave freedom. *Never.*"

"I have never had a slave in such opposition to me. No, Zipporah." It settled on him with certainty. Cold, hard certainty. "You cannot remain here with an excuse to defy me and my wife. You bound your will to mine, by your own choice. By your own choice, you submitted yourself to me—and not just in times when we agree. This is the true test."

Her nostrils flared, her hands clenched into fists. But this time, she held her tongue.

He eased a step away. "Know this, Zipporah—you will learn. You will learn how to be a part of this family without giving offense. Or you will leave us little choice. If you want your freedom, you will have to take it outside the walls of Tutelos. If you stay, it will be with an obligation to obey."

With one last look at her bent back, her bowed head, he pivoted on his heel and headed back for his house. And told himself he was acting like a responsible master—not like a monster.

twenty-four

WHEN DARA AWOKE, THE BED WAS EMPTY BESIDE HER AND THE SOFT sounds of Tamar's footfalls met her ears. She had a vague recollection of Benjamin saying he was taking a walk. Blinking her eyes open into the soft morning light, she saw the mouse pouring water into a basin.

So then. The slave survived her night with the witch. How very disappointing.

Dara made no effort to rise just yet. Instead she relaxed, closed her eyes again, and focused. It took a bit of effort. That clanging in the back of her mind had worn an ache in her head, and she had to force it aside. Silence the part of her that just wanted to go home and forget all about causes and sacrilegious zealots and husbands and masters. She had work to do.

And she was off to a good start at it, so far as she could tell. Her mere presence had caused a fracture—who would have thought? The witch might have it backward, but proclaiming it was exactly what Dara had needed.

A demon. She tossed back the covers now, stormily, and swung her feet to the floor. If either of them had a demon, it was *her*. Dara had seen the fire of it in the girl's eyes, just like in her vision.

Good to see she still got *something* right, anyway. And so, perhaps, the rest of those images were true as well.

Yes, she had work to do.

Tamar squeaked, jumped, looking torn between running away and rushing to assist her. When Dara lifted a brow at her, she leapt forward, a clean tunic in hand. "Good morning, Mistress."

"Yes it is." Her first morning as mistress of Tutelos. She smiled and held it in place even though Tamar refused to meet her gaze. "Did Benjamin's mother send over the stola, as she said she would? I want to wear that today. And you will dress my hair in the Roman fashion as well."

Tamar's eyes went wide. "I...know not how, Mistress."

"Then learn." Spotting the unfamiliar cloth folded on the table, she pointed. "The stola. Unless you are incapable of helping me with *that* too."

Though her hands shook, Tamar rushed to the table and exchanged tunic for stola. Dara strode to the screen. "What happened with the witch last night? Did she accuse you as well?"

Eyes focused on the cloth, Tamar shook her head. "She was...she welcomed me warmly."

"No doubt she thinks to turn you against me." Dara pulled yesterday's tunic over her head. And acknowledged the talons of resentment in her stomach for what they were. She would attack the mistress and welcome the slave, would she? Dara snatched the stola from Tamar's hands and shook it loose, pulled it over her head. "But you are not so foolish as to betray me. Are you, Tamar?"

"Never." Faint as her voice was, it at least sounded sincere as she helped smooth the cloth into place. "I will serve you faithfully, as the master instructed." She spun out of the screen. "Mistress Abigail sent a variety of sashes as well. What color do you prefer, Mistress?"

Dara followed the mouse out, though her gaze scarcely touched on the array of ribbons. She fingered the material of the stola—inferior by far to what she could produce herself. She would have to use some of her own cloth to make something in the Roman fashion. "The green."

As the master instructed. She played the words over in her head as Tamar tied the green sash around her. What exactly had he intended when he gave Tamar to her? Surely he knew they could never be friends. Dara would sooner be alone in this camp of the enemy than forced into company with *her*.

But the master always knew best. He had known that, for whatever reason, Tamar must come with her. Or perhaps it really was a sign of his love for Dara—that he did not want her to be alone, no matter that she would prefer it.

Well, she knew one thing beyond all doubt. When he came for them, when he took them home and made Dara his wife, Tamar would not—would *not* come with them. Dara would not suffer his concubine remain in their household. Perhaps wives aplenty the world over shared their husbands, but not Dara.

There was surely a way to usher in one of those other terrible fates she had seen for Tamar. They could not *all* be wrong. She would see the woman died as she ought.

Or...or, if for some reason that failed, she would find some other way to leave her behind. A smile curved her lips as she sat upon a stool. He had given her to Dara, after all. She could do as she willed with her. Sell her. Give her to the state.

The master would be displeased with her if she did that—but she would find a way. A way that, if she could not claim it was beyond her power, she could say was for the best.

When the door opened, when Benjamin strode in, when Tamar shrank away, Dara's smile grew. Perhaps that was her answer. The mouse obviously had a fear of anything male. It would be torture for her to be given to a man again.

But would a responsible mistress not see that her maid was cared for? That she had a husband to protect her?

Benjamin grinned at Dara and came over to drop a kiss onto her lips. "It suits you, fair one. You will put every Roman woman to shame with your beauty."

"You flatter me, beloved." She rewarded him for it with a smile, but the look in his eye did not escape her. And was no doubt not *for* her. He looked half angry, and the other half determined. Were she to speculate, she would say he had just come from an argument. Though she dare not guess with whom. "Did you enjoy your walk?"

He forced a smile. "It is a beautiful morning. Perhaps after the meal you would like to explore the grounds a bit."

She made sure her returning smile was bright and easy. "Perhaps so."

It took Tamar forever to get Dara's hair into something that resembled a Roman style, and had Benjamin not still been in the room, she would have told the mouse in no uncertain terms what she thought of her abilities. But instead she simply smiled anew at its completion and turned to her husband. "Shall we break our fast?"

"Certainly." He stood from whatever scroll he had been reading and offered his arm.

He seemed disinclined to talk as they walked, which suited her fine. She took in the halls through which they passed again, acknowledged her inner battle. They were beautiful halls. Well-constructed and well cared for. Benjamin was no doubt proud to call it all his, to know that his father, and his before him, and his before him, had tread the same tiles and stone.

And she could almost be proud to be its mistress now. She could almost imagine a world where she would look with concern on every nick and scratch, where she would bustle about from dawn to dusk seeing to the guests and servants and family under its roof. She could almost see herself living out the rest of her days in a place like this, without that burning voice in her head—the master's voice—forever chanting that she must destroy it all.

Almost.

But her fate lay in other halls. Not quite so grand, it was true, but *home*. Something this place could never be.

As they neared the same room in which they had eaten the night before, the chatter of many voices seeped into her consciousness. Quiet compared to yesterday, muted as if by morning, but she recognized a few of the tones.

And the faces even more so, when Benjamin led her to the entrance. Cleopas, who stared at her—the young man from her vision. How easy it would be to smile his way, speak a few words, and pit him against his brother. Jason and Deborah, who would not look at her. Division there already, too. Abigail and Titus, who both wore smiles—guarded ones—when they spotted her and Benjamin. Sarah, whose countenance went blank when she realized who had arrived, which spoke as loudly as a glare.

And behind her, the witch. With a pitcher in hand, but that hardly excused her presence. Dara looked over at her husband, but Benjamin did not seem to notice her. Or, perhaps, care that she was there.

She drew a breath through her teeth. That would not do at all. *He* may not remember his command of yesterday, but everyone else would. And if he went back on it so quickly...no, that would undo the work she had so carefully wrought.

And so she squeezed his arm to get his attention, then halted him a step inside the door. Said, just loudly enough for those nearest to hear and repeat, "It is all right, beloved."

Benjamin paused, his expression more perfect than he could have known. Question, but that thunder of disquiet still in his eyes.

Dara nodded toward Zipporah. "I know you said she could not be in your presence again until she apologized, but please. Let her do her duties and serve. I do not mind."

On the contrary—let the wench pour for her, bring her food, learn her place.

Chagrin flashed through his eyes. At forgetting, she suspected, but no one else would realize he had been about to take his seat without hesitation over the forbidden presence. Then he smiled, warm if small, and covered her fingers with his. "What a gracious heart you have. Come, sit."

She let him lead her to her place by his side. Let the whispers work their way around the room. Let the seeds sow deeper. She glanced the witch's way only once, ten minutes later, when Dara felt the scalding weight of her unholy gaze.

The witch knew. She knew Benjamin would have said nothing. She knew exactly why Dara had spoken.

Dara lifted her chin a notch and raised a plump date to her lips. Let her know. She could do nothing. Nothing but help slam the chisel and widen the crack in her precious Tutelos.

Then they would see who was left smiling when this so-called church lay around them in ruins.

Mist clung to the hills, shimmering white in the strengthening sun and cooling Zipporah's skin as she prayed. Under her knees, the earth was damp and smelled of last night's rain and the promise of life.

She had closed her eyes as soon as she knelt under the ilex. The sounds of the others joining her had hovered on the edges of her perception, but she had focused on the prayer. On the Spirit whispering over her with the breeze. It had been necessary to shut them all out—otherwise she would have fretted over who was there this morning. And who was not.

When she opened her eyes again though, when she beheld the soft light rising through the mist, everything in her—heart, throat, stomach—went tight. Her mother was here, kneeling beside Abba. It was the first time in these five long days that she had come.

With Ima's addition, that made a dozen of them under the sprawling branches of the ilex. And they must have all sensed, as she just had, the lifting of the hand of the Spirit. Everyone was stirring, shifting, rising.

Samuel cupped a hand under Zipporah's elbow and helped her to her feet. She smiled up at him, though he would no doubt see the strain in it. Because even now, her mother wore regret on her beautiful features.

How tempting it was to flee before Ima could say whatever she must intend to, given how her lips pressed together. Zipporah knew not if she could bear more doubt from her mother. Her mother, who should have been the first to defend her. Who she had thought knew her better than anyone else.

Samuel's hand moved from her elbow to her back, a silent encouragement as her parents came her way. Abba, at least, smiled as brightly as usual. And touched a hand to Ima's back in much the way Samuel did hers.

What a strange parallel.

Her mother summoned up a smile and came forward to wrap her arms around Zipporah. Though she barely had time to hug her back before Ima pulled away a bit, searching her eyes. For what? Her breath slid out. "I am sorry I did not come before now."

The apology only made Zipporah's insides squeeze tighter. She could not wrap her tongue around any response.

Her mother did not wait for one. "I want you to know—it is not doubt that kept me away. I know I said...I feared..." She sighed and shook her head. "The Lord has dealt strongly with me for my reaction that first day. And yet, still, I feel that my place is inside with the mistress for morning prayers. I feel...I feel quite certain there is something I will have to do within the walls. But I need you to know that is the only reason I will stay within."

She should believe her. Zipporah could see the sincerity in her eyes, the faith in her heart. Yet somehow it did little to heal up the hurt place in hers. Showing it, though, was not an option. Not now. She produced a smile of her own and nodded. "I understand, Ima."

Clearly, Ima saw through her words. Her eyes snapped, her lips pressed together. She reached for Zipporah's hands, gave her fingers a squeeze. "How could you? Yet I pray you will. And I am encouraged in seeing you out here, so very strong. I never...I never thought you would lead us. Perhaps I should have. Perhaps I should have seen it long ago."

Lead them? Zipporah took a step back, forcing Samuel's hand to move. He could have dropped it, given her room, but instead he slid his arm more firmly around her. She shook her head. "I am not—"

"Hush, Zipporah." Samuel's voice held a smile, and he gave her a squeeze to punctuate it. "There are some things you, even with your deepest vision, cannot see. But the rest of us can."

Abba nodded his agreement. "They are right. And to show you how...to make it clear..." Her father cleared his throat and straightened. "Abigail has promised Dara she would take her to Rome today. Sarah is going, as is your mother and several other ladies. You may go. If you want."

Her breath caught in her lungs. He was...he had...she could *go*? To Rome? Outside the walls of Tutelos? No doubt she looked like a fool with her mouth gaping open—though no more a one than Sarah looked from her place five paces away, with eyes wide as she made a giddy bounce.

Zipporah was free. She could go. She could—

A flash of light brought her gaze up from her parents, to the wall. The warrior, the same one that had shadowed her five days ago, had drawn his sword. Not, however, to chase away any dark creature near the walls. Nay, he faced *her*, his look forbidding.

The wind stirred, rushed. And she heard the voice so clearly inside, that command from the Father that overrode the permission of Abba. *No.*

A shudder coursed through her. She wished, oh how she wished she could ignore it. Could pretend she had not heard and march gaily along with Sarah and their mothers and...Dara?

She sucked in a long breath and tried to absorb some of the comfort from Samuel's arm. "Thank you, Abba. Ima." She could not force a smile, yet peace flowed through her. "But I think that would not be wise. Not today, not if Dara is going."

Sarah deflated, but Abba smiled and stepped forward to plant a kiss on Zipporah's forehead. "You are wise indeed, my daughter. But we will find another time. Soon. I promise."

"We certainly will," Sarah said, rushing forward and linking her arm through Zipporah's. "I will think up the perfect thing for us to do. It must be something special, to mark your return properly."

Now the smile came, and a chuckle with it. "You can gather ideas while you are there today. But focus first on the cloth for your wedding garment. I know you have months yet to prepare, but it will take many hours to embroider it properly."

Sarah flushed and glanced over to where Urbanus spoke with Jacob. "I think I will bring the veil Benjamin sent, so I can be sure to find something to complement it."

The group began to disburse, some heading for their homes and the fields, the rest toward the villa. Zipporah sent Sarah back to Urbanus's side with a laugh and then sobered as she refocused on her mother. "Ima...watch her closely today."

Ima lifted her brows. "Sarah?"

"No."

She needed make no more clarification. Ima's gaze went serious too, and she nodded. "I intend to. And have been already. I have seen her several times now flirting with the other young men when Benjamin is not nearby. Insulting the other young women, though cleverly enough that they always laugh. They will feel the sting though, I am sure."

Samuel's arm steered Zipporah back toward the villa, too, then fell away. "Have you spoken more to Tamar, little sparrow?"

"Nothing of consequence." Zipporah fastened her gaze on the backs of those in front of her. "She fears her."

Mark fell in on Zipporah's other side. "Dara apparently told Benjamin that Tamar has a history as a seductress. He thought he had better 'warn' me." He shook his head. "I cannot fathom that he believed her for a moment. I have never seen a woman so timid around men as Tamar. She has obviously been hurt."

Ima, though a step ahead now, turned toward her son. "Many of us here have been hurt. But we will show her love. We will show her that healing can come through the Lord."

They could all agree with that, and from there conversation turned to plans for the day. Ima asked if Zipporah needed anything from the city, Samuel announced his intentions of working in the vineyards this week. Easy things, normal things.

How quickly life went on, despite the cracks they all knew laced their foundation. But then, what choice did they have?

Once they reached the villa, the group went its separate ways until the meal. Samuel turned to Zipporah with a grin. "You will be at loose ends with Sarah gone. You could charm some food from Dinah at midday and come share it with me in the vineyards. I have yet to tell you of our adventures in Greece."

Sweet Samuel, always so careful to make her feel included. She grinned back. "Perhaps I shall, if I find myself in the mood for a good fable."

With a laugh, he gave her a playful shove in the arm and turned toward the entrance. "I will see you at noon."

Mark alone remained at her side now, and he had a strange look on his face, as if he heard something afar off. Perhaps he did.

"Mark?"

"Hmm?" He blinked, focused on her, but his countenance did not ease. "I think..." Without finishing his thought, he spun and headed back around the corner. Curious, Zipporah followed him.

Their aim seemed to be the fountain. She heard the flowing water before she could see it—and saw the shadowy figure hunched beside it before she noticed the human forms. Was that Deon, the Colossian's slave, into whose ear the dark one whispered?

She could only pray that the anger that flamed up was directed at the demon and not the man. Though she was none too sure.

Mark went stiff as the statue from which the water spouted—his gaze was not on Deon, but rather on the elbow that was all that was visible of a second person. He hissed out a breath. "Tamar."

The name was all the impetus either of them needed, it seemed. They both strode forward.

Deon's voice filtered through the water sounds. "Come now, do not play bashful." He had her hand in his, though now that her face was in sight, the terror in her eyes was clear as the sun burning off the mist.

Mark muttered a choice word but then put on a mask of calm. "Tamar, there you are."

Deon turned to them, thunder in his brows. "Excuse me—we were having a conversation."

Zipporah felt the smirk settle on her lips. She looked not at him, but at the demon that had its claws in his shoulder. "I bet you were. You have no authority here, beast. This villa has been claimed in the holy name of Jesus. Be gone with you."

She was vaguely aware of Tamar jerking her fingers free and retreating to Mark's protective side. She noted the confusion that possessed the slave's face. But mostly she focused on the growl that emerged from the creature's yellow-fanged mouth, the hatred that flashed in its eyes.

The door has been opened. Its voice sounded like the crackle of flames on damp wood, hissing as it consumed.

"Not for you. Not for this man. I said be gone, in the name of Christ Jesus."

Deon regarded her as though she were mad. "What?"

"She is not talking to you," Mark answered, low and exasperated.

The creature howled, released Deon's shoulder...and coiled. She knew in a heartbeat he would not sling himself into the sky. No, he would come at her, and she had no idea what he might be able to do to her on his own, without human hands and human weapons to aid him.

"Lord Jesus, save me!" Her cry came out no more than a whisper.

Yet before she even finished it, she heard the song. She saw the flash, the glimmer, the comfort of a sword slicing down before her. The demon had already launched himself toward her, but the gleaming angelic weapon sent it tumbling.

For a moment, she watched the light chase the dark away, back toward the wall.

Then she looked back toward the man, and that flame of anger burst into an inferno. "And you! How long have you claimed to be a Christian? Yet can you not tell the voice of an evil one from your own thoughts? Can you not hear the whisper of warning the Spirit surely sent you when it came near?"

"Evil one?" Deon frowned, swallowed, and backed up a step. "I know not—I...I was only talking to her."

Zipporah motioned to Tamar, who still shook visibly. "Does that look like a woman who was merely being talked to? Does she look inclined to be charmed? What thoughts were going through your head, Deon? Were they pure and holy?"

He edged away still more, red creeping up his neck. "I did not intend..."

She took a step toward him, hands balled in the white fabric of her tunic. "This is not a world where you can go around without intention. This is not a world where faith can be easy and lukewarm, do you not see that? We have too many enemies always waiting to devour us and lead us astray. You must decide now which voices you will heed. Who you will serve. Your master's faith will not save you, do you understand that? You must fight for Jesus too, or else you fight against him."

His legs collided with the fountain wall, and though his arms flew out and wheeled, it was not enough. A second later he fell with a splash into the pool. Had she not still been so mad, she may have laughed. As it was, the water that sprayed her only cooled her down a degree.

Deon, hair dripping and tunic soaked, stared at her with wide eyes.

She huffed out a breath and stepped forward with her hand outstretched to help him out. "My apologies for losing my temper."

He did not accept her aid. Nor, it seemed, her apology. He made no move at all, just sat there with the statue spitting a continual stream down his back.

So be it, then. Later, she would no doubt wish she had bitten her tongue to begin with or come up with more compelling words of apology. At the moment, she could manage no more. With a roll of her eyes, she turned away.

Tamar still stood half-behind Mark, as close as she could get, it seemed, without touching him. Her shaking had eased, though her eyes were still wide and she clutched a length of red fabric as if it would anchor her.

Mark grinned.

Zipporah let one corner of her mouth tip up for her brother. Confident he would see Tamar back inside, she strode away.

She heard the splashes begin after she had taken a few steps and had managed only ten when she heard Deon's "Wait! Zephyra!"

She would *not* get angry again. "My name is Zipporah."

"Right. Sorry." His sandals squishing with every running step, he came up beside her. "You...you really see them? Demons and angels?"

Apparently the water had not cooled her enough after all. "Why does everyone always ask that as if it had never happened before? Have you not heard all the stories of Jesus and his followers casting out demons? Could they have done it without knowing they were there, without seeing them? Or do you think a person must be thrashing around and foaming at the mouth if he hosts a demon?"

"I...have never thought of it."

She came to a halt and spun to face him. "And why have you not? Because it is easier that way? Well it makes it easier for *them* too, when you are unaware. Perhaps you ought to think of *that.*"

His larynx bobbed with his swallow. "What was it doing?"

The frustration left her in a gush when she saw the fear in his eyes. The breath she drew in was to calm herself, and to force herself to form her answer with more care. "Speaking into your ear. And digging its talons into your shoulder."

He flinched, and his left hand rose, settled on his right shoulder. Over the very spot the creature had clawed. She could see the marks in his spirit, much like she had seen scars throbbing within Tamar. They could heal, with faith and prayer. But without it? Never. A person could bear those marks forever, and it made them a target for continued torment from other dark ones.

He pushed aside his tunic, craned his neck, and winced.

Zipporah sucked in a sharp breath. Red welts lined his shoulder, bright and bold. On his physical man, not his spiritual one, yet aligned. Blood oozed from a few places.

He met her gaze with glazed-over eyes. Because she feared he would topple over in the next moment, Zipporah stepped to his side and grasped his arm. "Samuel!" Where was he now? Had he gone inside? Was he in his chamber? "Samuel!"

"It hurts." Shock saturated his voice. "It is bleeding."

"I know. Come. Samuel can help." She steered him back toward the fountain and again called out, "Samuel!"

He must have heard her through the windows, for she no sooner got the stumbling Deon back to the fountain than he came running out, concern knitting his brows. Mark and Tamar had disappeared.

"What is it?" Samuel halted on Deon's other side and helped her lower him to the edge of the fountain's pool, where he could sit.

Deon moved his fingers away from the wound.

Samuel measured the injury with a steady gaze and gentle fingers. "It is not so bad. What happened?"

Zipporah's mouth had gone dry. "A demon clawed him."

His fingers stilled, and Samuel's gaze swung over to her. "And his body bears the marks? That is possible?"

She could only shrug and motion to the evidence. "Apparently."

"It is the strangest thing." Deon's voice still sounded tinny, faint. "I did not feel it. Not until she told me what it had done. There is no blood on my tunic. Why did I not feel it until then?"

Samuel shook his head. "I cannot say. Perhaps because you did not believe it until then."

Zipporah straightened and wrapped her arms around her middle. If awareness, belief brought the spiritual so firmly into the physical, then she dared not wonder what may have happened had the angel not arrived so promptly.

Samuel must have been thinking along similar lines. He caught her gaze again, and his green-gold eyes had gone worried. Then he helped Deon to his feet. "Come inside. I have a salve that will help with the sting."

If only he had one for the deeper hurts.

twenty-five

ROME WAS TERRIFYING. TAMAR KEPT AS CLOSE TO THE GUARDS AS she could, but even the two giant, muscular eunuchs could not make her feel safe amid the throngs of strangers. They had been here only two hours, and already she had five times heard the cry of "Thief!" echo down one street or another. She had seen a motley collection of common folk barreling down an alley, crying out about a collapsing building. She had heard curses in more tongues than she knew the names of.

Try as she might to focus on the pleasant things—the public fountains, the grand architecture with its gray-white columns, the food smells that may have been tempting had her stomach not been a churning ball—it was no use. Every time she fixed her eyes on such a thing, a sneering, leering face would obscure her view.

Or Dara would say something sly and cruel.

Her mistress was having a grand time, it seemed. The bustle that made Tamar want to sprout wings and fly back to the villa must have fed Dara's energy. She all but glided down the streets, head held high as she collected the stares of passersby like a child might collect stones or shells. When they paused for lunch at a stall that sold skewers of meat, Dara's gaze tracked to another stall just beside them.

Tamar's stomach knotted still more. A fortune teller. The woman was middling in years, dressed in layers of wispy fabric and a collection of necklaces draping her neck. She called out to those who walked past, "See your future!"

Despite the warm air, a shudder coursed down Tamar's spine. The woman must be a fraud, to have nothing but a booth along the street. The true seers, the ones who had proven themselves over the years, would have private places of business. They would not have to call out to pedestrians—customers would come to them.

Of all that was different between Rome and Jerusalem, she was certain that was the same.

Dara must have been thinking something similar. She had that calculating look in her eye, the one she usually kept hidden around Benjamin's family.

Tamar was not the only one to note it. Mark and Zipporah's mother looked from Dara to the fortune teller and back again. Was it suspicion in Miriam's eyes or simply curiosity? "You probably did not see these things on such blatant display in Jerusalem, Mistress Dara."

Dara focused her gaze on Miriam without bothering with more than a partial smile. "Only occasionally. Such imposters were usually removed quickly."

To make room for the true diviners—Dara, and the others the master employed. The ones that, according to Zipporah, heard the words of demons, not of God. How, then, did they know the future so well, so often?

"They were supposed to have been removed from Israel centuries ago." Lady Sarah nibbled at her meat, her gaze cool and direct upon Dara. "Yet how strange that whenever a king of old decided to call on one, there they were. It seems evil is always lurking just around the corner."

Tamar felt her brows knit, though she should have taken care to keep her countenance clear. Mistress Abigail noted the expression at once and gave her a warm smile. "What is it, Tamar?"

Dara would not be pleased with her if she spoke. She ought to hold her tongue now and ask her question of Zipporah later. Zipporah would answer her with no judgment. Yet her mouth opened, and out came the words swimming around her mind. "Forgive me, Mistress, but I was not raised in Israel—I do not understand these things. In Greece where I grew up, oracles were held in high esteem. Yet the Jews claim they are evil. If that is so, then how are they so often right?"

Mistress Abigail's face was a work of beauty, even as sorrow veiled it. "Because ours is a world where evil is always at work. Where it can speak what it wants to happen and then influence men to make it so. And if we trust our history, it is often successful until a true man or woman of God intervenes."

"Like the prophet Elijah facing down the prophets of Baal." Dara's lips curled into a terrifying grin as she provided the example. No doubt imagining herself the good prophet.

Tamar tried to press her lips together to hold back the next question—but her mistress would already be angry with her. Why not make it count? She cleared her throat. "Forgive me another question, then. But how is one to know a true prophet from a false?"

Lady Sarah breathed a laugh and motioned at the fortune teller. "Well for starters, true prophets of God do not prophesy for coin."

Tamar could feel the hatred in Dara's gaze. Perhaps her mistress felt the burning in her palm of the payment she had always demanded.

Though likely not. Her mask of a smile in place, she said, "The prophets had to receive support from someone."

Though the older women looked about to speak, the younger lady beat them to it again, challenge gleaming in her deep brown eyes. "God provides for those to whom he speaks."

Dara lifted a golden brow. "And does he or does he not often choose to do so through his people?"

"For their needs, yes. But he is quick to strike them down when they try to profit from his word."

Was he? Because the master's house had only increased in opulence with each seer he sponsored. And the Lord had done no striking that she could tell.

Perhaps Jehovah defined "quick" differently than Tamar did.

Dara pasted on a smile that looked so sweet the other women surely knew it was honey-covered poison. "I will defer to you, my sister. I do not know nearly as much, it seems, about false prophets."

Tamar wished for a shadow to hide in. Why, why did her mistress have to say such a thing in that tone that implied the young lady was the one with the ungodly connections? Why must she antagonize these people every minute of every day? Tamar could only hope Dara would grow tired soon from the effort and give her a few days' reprieve.

Lady Sarah did not appear offended. She just turned up one side of her mouth and said, "I suppose that depends on what you mean. I daresay you know far more about them, *sister*. But it would seem you do not call it by the right name."

"Sarah." Mistress Abigail's hissed warning did nothing to slice the tension pulled taut between the two young women.

But Dara looked now to her husband's mother with a sad smile. "You need not chide her, Mother. We all know where she stands already—she proclaims it every day when she goes outside with her handmaid and breaks her brother's heart anew."

Sarah rolled her eyes, and somehow she made the gesture look dismissive instead of petulant. "I am not the one in danger of breaking Benjamin's heart. But I do tire of a conversation that amounts to little more than bashing my head against a wall, so if I might take Phillip with me, I shall just venture to that shop right there."

The fairer skinned of the eunuchs exchanged a glance with Mistress Abigail that must have contained silent words. Without more than that moment's hesitation, Phillip ushered Sarah across the street.

They left Mistress Abigail with a sigh upon her lips.

Dara wasted no time in turning her false smile on Miriam. "Forgive me if I offend you by referencing your daughter's activities so, Miriam. I confess I forgot you were of the same family—she bears little resemblance to you."

"She has her smile," Mistress Abigail replied before her maidservant could open her mouth. She put on her own, though it was strained.

"I am afraid I have not seen that particular expression upon Zipporah's face." Dara exhaled, as if it injured her to think of it. Then she brightened. "Benjamin told me about everyone during the journey though. He mentioned how beautiful your elder daughter was—she must have taken after you a great deal."

Another topic that could easily move to sorrow—which Dara no doubt knew. But again the mistress stepped in, chuckling. "I will never forget the song Cleopas wrote for her wedding day. He was, what, thirteen at the time?" She shook her head, her grin genuine now. "That boy has a way with words, but he seems to think their sole purpose is to evoke laughter."

"It is a gift," Miriam agreed. She finished her skewer and tossed the stick away. "I will go find Lady Sarah, Mistress."

"Thank you, Miriam."

Tamar edged a little closer to the remaining guard and ate as quickly as she could force it down.

Dara kept to the edges of the room. For now. The villa was bursting with people—the faces she had gotten to know over the last fortnight from the church, but many more too. Romans, visiting Jews, strangers who spoke in languages she had never heard.

It seemed that when the Asiniuses threw a wedding, all the world turned out. Even if the rain forced them indoors.

Jason and Deborah, the bride and groom, were far out of Dara's line of vision at this point. As was Benjamin. For a few panicked moments she had stood here alone, on the outskirts, wishing he were at her side. Wishing for a hand to hold in this sea of people.

But that was foolishness. She knew how to navigate such seas, and with the reminder she straightened her shoulders, lifted her chin, and set about catching gazes.

One, in particular. When young Cleopas—two years her elder but referred to so often as the baby brother that she tended to think of him as such too—sauntered into this room from some other crowded chamber, Dara let the confidence slip from her shoulders again and rounded them in seeming-discomfort. She sidled forward just a bit, so he could see her past the guests chattering away in Latin in front of her. And she waited.

A minute later she felt him draw near. "Did Benjamin abandon you in this throng?" As always, his tone carried half a laugh in it.

Dara drew out a smile, one that met his half-laugh with half-uncertainty. "He was stolen away by...a Roman friend. Nereus, perhaps?"

"Ah." Cleopas's grin won over his mouth as he surveyed the packed room. "No doubt Nereus wanted to complain of the injustice of pursuing Sarah for a year only to have Urbanus swoop in and steal her heart."

Sarah had a collection of admirers, did she? Dara dug her fingers into her arm. She was beautiful, she supposed. Though she seemed to take no care with her appearance, and she did not bear herself with any awareness of her beauty. How had she managed to make the men fight over her?

No matter. Sarah was not her concern just now. Dara held her arms against her middle. "I suppose your sister's wedding shall be next. Your poor mother will be bone-weary after it all."

Cleopas chuckled. "She thrives on it, and do not let her tell you otherwise. I daresay this reminds you of your own wedding." He motioned to the crowds.

Dara made her smile go tight. "No. Our wedding was small and quick, so I could travel with him. Only my mother and brother and the priest were there, and Samuel and Mark, of course."

His brows lifted. "You had no week-long celebration?"

"No." Her tone went wistful on command. "Part of me wishes we had waited until we arrived to wed, so that I might have gotten to share those traditions with your family. Perhaps then I would feel more a part of it. Although..." She sent him a sidelong glance and a shy smile. "Who knows how things would have turned out had I come merely as Samuel's sister?"

His neck went red, but she had to give him credit—he did not stumble for words. He merely cleared his throat and kept his grin in place. "Let us hope you would not have fallen for Jason, or you would have had a fight on your hands with Deborah."

She used her chuckle as an excuse to lean a bit closer. "Did you write a song for them, Cleopas? Your mother was telling me of how you composed an ode to Anna when she and Samuel wed."

He only glanced down at her for a second before focusing on the crowd again, but it was enough. Enough to see the desire in his eyes. "I did. They laughed for at least twenty minutes after I sang it."

He sounded pleased—should she try to turn it into insult instead? No, not just now. She would keep her focus on flattering. She touched a hand to his arm. "It is a gift, to bring such joy to people. Perhaps...perhaps someday you will write a song for me."

His larynx bobbed as he swallowed. "Perhaps I shall."

Zipporah stepped around the tall Roman, jar of wine in hand. Clenching her teeth so tightly she feared she would grind them to nothing, she speared Cleopas with a glare. "Wine, Lord?"

He had always been a friend. Not so close a one as Samuel, they had not the shared interests she had once claimed with Benjamin. Certainly he did not care for her as Sarah did. But they were of an age, she and Cleopas. They had toddled about the villa together. She had napped beside him when they were children.

He should know better. And he should not look at Zipporah now with irritation, not when *he* was the one standing there promising to write a love song to his brother's wife.

His smile was tight. Not the usual Cleopas smile. "No. Thank you."

Dismissed. Never in their eighteen years together had Cleopas dismissed her with that tone that other masters reserved for the lowest of servants.

But then, most servants did not ask questions of their masters in the tone she had used either, she supposed. She moved her gaze to Dara, knowing well what she would see in her eyes. Dark satisfaction, gleaming from both woman and demon. Zipporah held up the wine. "Mistress?"

Dara inclined her head, no doubt to showcase those golden curls for Cleopas. "No. But you may fetch me a cluster of grapes."

It pleased her to make Zipporah serve—she had already proven as much over the last few days by sending Tamar on some errand and then asking Zipporah to do the meanest of chores.

She would not be accused of neglecting her duties to the household. Certainly not today, when every pair of hands was needed. "As you wish, Mistress."

Without waiting for any further command, she spun and headed for the exit, pausing only four times to refill a lifted glass. The guests, it seemed, looked straight through her...but they noted her wine jug. By the time she made it out of the chamber, the jug was empty anyway. She headed for the kitchen, though Dinah could be heard a corridor away, barking out commands in a voice to rival a general.

A smile won her mouth. It froze when she turned a corner and ran headlong into Benjamin.

He steadied her with all the care he would give a wooden beam and looked through her just as his friends did. "Have you seen Dara?"

She wanted to bristle. Wanted to snap. Wanted to do something, anything to remind him that life had not gone on as normal. That she was not just another servant caring for just another wife. To remind her own heart that it had once felt...something. Anything other than this cold dread that more trouble was on the horizon.

She settled for stepping away and studying the ground. "She is where you left her, Master. Cleopas is with her."

Innocent words that he obviously found no fault in. With nothing more than a nod, he strode away. No reference to him holding her as a slave by force. No reminder that he was determined to force *her* upon some unsuspecting groom soon. No question as to whether she and Dara were getting along.

Just as well. None were topics she wanted to discuss. Still, it left her with a sigh as she continued on her way. And with a strange twinge in her chest. Silly as it felt, she missed loving him. Missed thinking about him with affection instead of this pervasive disappointment. Missed...missed believing in him. Thinking that, no matter what, they could always depend on Benjamin.

They could not. They could depend only on the Lord.

The kitchen was a hive of servants dashing this way and that, in and out. All of Tutelos's, and some that had arrived with the guests as well. She spotted a tray of fruit ready to go out but knew better than to pluck a cluster of grapes from the careful arrangement. Just as she knew better than to heft the whole tray—others could well pick it dry before she got to Dara. So she headed instead to the work counter.

Dinah met her with lifted gray brows. "Are you here to offer your hands, or have you need of something?"

An hour of quiet would be nice, with no noise beyond the cooing of her dove. She smiled. "Mistress Dara wishes grapes."

Tamar stepped near, a furrow in her brows. "She told me she would not eat for another couple hours."

Zipporah met Tamar's gaze but said nothing. She needed to say nothing.

Tamar nodded and wiped her hands on a towel, reaching then for a fresh bunch of grapes. "I will take it to her. It is not your duty, m—my friend."

Zipporah nearly smiled. She liked to think they were becoming friends, odd as it seemed, but Tamar still persisted in calling her "mistress" when they were in their room. No matter how many times Zipporah corrected her. "I will take over for you in here, then."

Dinah stared at her for a long moment, though her hands did not still from their stirring. "We need more cheeses brought in from the storehouse. Though if you go out, you will get wet and muddy, and you would have to change before you rejoined the feast. And dry out your hair, lest it brush against the guests."

Grinning, Zipporah abandoned the fruit and leaned over to smack a kiss onto Dinah's cheek. "You spoil me."

"Nonsense. I give you the tasks no one else wants." With a wink, Dinah motioned toward the exit. "Check with Jacob before you go, see if they need anything else while you are out there."

"Certainly. And thank you." Not giving anyone else the chance to assign her any other job, she raced for Jacob. He directed her to the mistress, who added a few other items to her list. And then she stepped out into the steady rain.

The noise of the villa faded away, muted as the fog. Out here was only the rain drumming on the tiles of the roof, strumming on the marble, pattering into the fountain. The ground, so greedy this morning, now refused the moisture and forced it into puddles.

The road would be a mess. The vineyards would need tending as soon as the sun came back out. The weeds would try to choke the life from the crops. After the wedding, after the rain, the work would redouble.

But just now, she stood there and let it soothe. Let it wash away the fear. Then she headed for the storehouse.

Though she looked around for Columba, he was no doubt hidden away in a branch somewhere, out of the torrent. No one else stirred.

A psalm found her heart and her lips as she strolled through the rain. "They will fear you as long as the sun and moon last, through all generations. He shall pour down like rain upon the grass, like showers that water the earth. In his days shall flourish the righteous, peace shall be abundant, until the moon ceases to be."

A shadow moved in the doorway of the storehouse, making her stop short, her song going silent. When the Colossian slave stepped into the dim afternoon light, she frowned. "Deon? Have you need of something?"

Given his expression, he was sheepish but not ashamed at getting caught out here. Which meant...what? Not that he did anything wrong, but something he nevertheless did not want to be observed doing.

She peeked over his shoulder, half expecting to see Eve within. They had announced just the day before that his master would wed one of the Roman daughters who had visited frequently during their stay, and that Deon would take Eve home with him when they went.

Deon stood aside to let her in and motioned toward the rear corner, where

Archippus had been laying up stores for their return voyage. "I was seeing to our stock, that is all."

"In this weather?"

A glance his way showed he had pursed his lips in thought. At length, he heaved out a breath. "It was necessary. We leave at first light for Ostia so we might sail with the evening tide."

She pivoted to face him fully. "Does the mistress know?" A foolish question—the mistress knew all that went on at Tutelos. And yet, the secrecy...

Deon hesitated a moment and then shook his head. "Master Archippus did not want to make a fuss before the wedding. He plans to speak with Lord Titus and Lady Abigail tonight, after all else have retired."

She sank to a seat on one of the barrels. "Why so sudden? I thought Lord Balius and Livia would wed before they left."

"Her family has agreed to travel with us so the wedding might take place at Colossae." Deon studied the packed earthen floor for a moment and then met her gaze. "The master does not wish to stay any longer. Not with Lord Benjamin's new wife here. She...she tried to tempt Master Balius away from Lady Livia."

Her eyes slid shut. "I know not what to say."

"What *can* you say? You warned everyone of what she was. Nothing she does ought to come as a great surprise."

At that, she looked up. It never occurred to her that the Colossians might believe her. They had never joined her for prayers under the ilex. They had never spoken to her at all, aside from Deon at the fountain, and a few casual exchanges since.

But she had watched the fluttering of their spirits. How Balius's had dimmed even below its usual flicker for a few days last week, and how Deon's had brightened, strengthened since the demon's claws had bit him.

He picked up the basket they kept out here and handed it to her, obviously knowing her purpose. "Master Archippus thought from the start that you were right. He told us that first night to be on our guards, especially around her. Master Balius and I..." He shrugged and motioned to the oiled fish.

She shook her head and moved to the cheeses. "I know. It was beyond your reckoning." Since he followed, she handed the basket back to him and set about filling it while he held it.

"No more. Eve has said you have seen them since you were scarcely more than a child. That, I confess, I cannot reckon. How does it not overwhelm you?"

"It is just the way it is." She reached next for an amphora of seasoned olive oil. Darted a glance at him. "And it is the way it is the world over, Deon. You can leave Tutelos and the particular demon that Dara hosts, but you will not be escaping it. They are everywhere."

"Yes. But at home, Master Archippus will have the authority to refuse entry to his house to anyone he does not believe to be truly of the brethren. Here, he can do nothing." He shifted the basket, used his free hand to wipe his damp hair off his forehead. He was not a handsome man. His middle was soft, his brows too heavy.

But he had listened. He believed. He had been changed. Zipporah nodded and added dried dates and figs to the basket. "I will pray for you all. On the journey, and beyond it."

"Thank you." He turned when she did and followed her back to the door. But he paused at the threshold and stopped her with a light touch upon her elbow. She looked up to find him frowning. "Zipporah...it is not safe for you here. I have watched her since..." He touched his shoulder. "I have watched how she watches *you*. She may bide her time now, but she will attack you sooner or later."

He said it so simply. As fact.

Fact that settled perfectly in line with what she had known for so long. Sooner or later, Dara would lunge. Sooner or later, Zipporah would die. What could she do but nod? "I know."

Deon gripped her elbow now. "You need to leave this place. Master Archippus agrees. Livia—she has no handmaiden, and Eve knows not how to perform those tasks. You could come with us. He could speak with your mistress and masters tonight."

Yes, he had changed a great deal in such a short time. Of that she could be glad. She smiled but put some space between them. "I thank you for your consideration, Deon. It means much. But my place is here. My family is here." And Benjamin, she suspected, would not release her to them.

He shook his head, his eyes rejecting her words now as they had her face the first time he saw her. "Do you not understand how serious this is? She is your mistress. She could kill you. *Kill* you, and your parents would have no recourse, not unless Lord Benjamin decided to punish her for it. Which he would not. You know this. You see how she has manipulated him."

And there, again, that pang of disappointment where affection had once lived. She nodded again. "I know."

"You know." His fingers slid off her elbow. "You know, but you stay here anyway."

She looked out into the driving rain—streams of silver flashing, splashing, splaying. "I have felt for years now that the time will soon come when I must lay down my life for the Way. I am prepared. I will serve the Church faithfully for as long as I can, and then I will go gladly into the arms of Christ."

She only prayed that, somehow, when she went, she would leave the church here better off. That she would help them find freedom again from the evil that sought to destroy them. Or if it was not hers to help, then that her death would serve some purpose toward that end.

"Here." Deon handed the basket to her, his face tight and mournful. "I am not quite finished here, or I would help you in."

She gave him a smile and looped both arms through the heavy basket's handle. "I will manage nicely."

He stepped back into the shadows. "There are hours yet before my master will speak with the Asiniuses. You could think on it."

She could. But she did not need to. The resonance of the Spirit told her what she had always known.

Her place was here. Here she lived. Here she would die. The only question was when.

She stepped back out into the rain and let it anoint her.

twenty-six

TAMAR GATHERED HER MISTRESS'S CURLS AND TRIED TO SMOOTH them into place. She snuck a look at the reflection in the bronze mirror but did not dare catch that metallic green gaze.

Dara looked smug. And when Dara looked smug, it was always a bad, bad day.

She reached for a ribbon. And prayed, silently but with all that was within her, that she would be able to produce the style the mistress wanted today, quickly and without faltering.

"It has been two months since we left Israel, has it not? Am I counting right?"

Her voice, slow and contented, made fear tie a knot in Tamar's throat. The thick curls sprang loose from her fingers. "It...it has, Mistress. Perhaps a week more." Three days since the wedding feast. Two since the Colossians had left.

"Two months." Dara all but hummed the words, the corners of her mouth tipping up. "That is long enough to know, is it not? To be certain?"

Tamar's hands shook around the coil of curls she tried again to wind into order. "Of...of what, Mistress?"

The metallic eyes in the mirror rolled. "You are as observant as a rock, Tamar. Have I once sent you for rags?"

The knot in her throat dropped to her stomach. "You are with child." The words, even out of her own mouth, sliced her through.

How unfair it was. Dara, who did not want to be with her husband. Dara, who did not want to belong to anyone but the master. *She* carried a child, Master Benjamin's child, which she no doubt wanted only for another means to control him. *She* was with child, must have gotten with child almost immediately, while Tamar had obeyed the master's every whim for a decade and had never once been blessed with the stir of life in her womb. Never once had felt the quickening of hope that came with counting the days since that last time of impurity.

Never once had been given something for which to live.

"Ow! Be careful, you wretch!"

Tamar dropped the hair she had pulled too tight and took a step back. "Apologies, Mistress. I am sorry. So very sorry."

"Fool." Dara scooted away, gathered her offended tresses, and tossed the ribbon to the floor. "Never mind, I shall wear it down today. Go. I will think up how to tell my husband this blessed news."

"Yes, Mistress." Tangling her trembling hands in her tunic, Tamar fled the chamber, not so much as slowing until she had closed the door of her own and could squeeze her eyes shut against the hot tears.

The small chamber was empty. Zipporah had been up and out for half an hour already and would be gone at least as long yet. Tamar had a few minutes of quiet, of solitude. Time to pull herself together.

Though as she slid down the door, she felt like she was falling apart.

The first drop rolled down her cheek, dripped off her chin, and fell like rain on her arm. How many times had she beseeched Jehovah for a child? A son, a daughter—she cared not which, she only wanted someone to hold. Someone to love. Someone who would look at her with trust and warmth instead of cruel, cold lust.

Perhaps she would get to hold this one. Perhaps Dara would let her be nursemaid. Surely the mistress would not want to soil her hands with spit-up and excrement. Surely she would not pace the floors at night with a wailing infant. Surely, surely she would push it upon Tamar.

Please, God. Please.

A shudder overtook her, violent and nauseating. Afraid she would retch, she doubled over until her cheek pressed to the cool floor.

The poor babe. Why had God allowed an innocent life to come to that...that witch? Dara would not know how to love her child. She *could* not, not with the demon controlling her. She would use the poor thing as another tool, one to toss aside when she was not in the mood to play the role of doting mother.

Tamar dug her fingers into the grooves between tiles. "Jehovah, protect that precious life. Guard it, insulate it from the evil it shares a body with. Please, Jehovah. Please. I know you cannot be bothered with me, but the babe is innocent. The babe is begotten by one of your children. Protect it for Master Benjamin's sake. For his mother's and father's."

She held still for a long moment, as everyone did during morning prayers, but she heard no answer. Did they? She had watched them closely every morning, had watched the moving lips, the outstretched arms, the faces sometimes upturned and sometimes pressed to the floor. How did they know when the Lord answered them? How could they be sure Jehovah heard their cries?

She heard them now in the hallway behind her, feet shuffling along. She must join them, as she had every other morning. But this morning she would not just sit there and watch. This morning she would pray, silently but with her whole being.

A quick dash of water from the basin was all she could do to freshen her countenance, but hopefully no one would pay her any mind. Head bent low, she slipped out of her chamber and through the hallways until she ducked into the large room where others were already gathered.

She took her usual place in the corner, far enough away from where Master Titus would stand that she could usually only hear half of what he said. This morning she did not try to make out any of his words. She took to her knees, bent her head, and let her hair fall forward into a protective veil.

Please, Jehovah. Please.

The ache would not lessen. The hurt would not ebb. Occasionally a new emotion would slice through her—jealousy, bitterness, despair—but they were only flashes. Lightning against the roiling clouds of desperation within her. The driving need to do anything she could to protect that child.

A touch upon her head made her jump and brought an abrupt halt to her begging. She sat up, wiping at the tears she only now realized fell again.

Miriam knelt at her side, but facing the opposite way so that she looked right at her. Concern warmed her eyes as she stroked Tamar's hair away from her face like...like her mother had once done. "Tamar." Her voice was quiet enough to be inaudible amidst the prayers of the others, to be just for her. "What is it, child?"

She clenched her teeth, flared her nostrils, and did not dare open her mouth. If she did, a sob would surely heave its way out. With no other recourse, she shook her head.

Miriam's lips turned partway up in a soft, gentle smile. "I understand. But may I tell you a story? I have felt for days that you should hear how Mistress Abigail and I came to be here, but with the wedding, there has been no chance to speak with you."

A story of two beautiful, happy, blessed women beloved by their God as well as their men? She could only latch her gaze onto the floor.

Miriam scooted a bit closer. "Mistress Abigail was born free. But her father died when she was seven, and her mother a year later. Her mother's second husband sold her—to a Roman officer. Cleopas Visibullis was a good man, one who loved the true God, and his wife Ester loved Abigail like a daughter. Their son, however, was not inclined to view her as a sister when he returned from Rome."

A finger touched Tamar's chin. She obeyed the silent beckon to look up, into intent brown eyes.

Miriam shook her head. "Andrew was a slave in the same house. He had asked for Abigail to be given him as wife, and the master was about to consent. They were looking for her, in fact, to tell her the good news when they discovered the young master, Jason, had forced her to his bed against her will."

Tamar sucked in a quick breath. "The mistress was...was...?" But she looked so at peace. So happy. So...so unafraid of the men that were always around her. Tamar had seen her countless times go willingly into the arms of Master Titus.

Miriam tilted her head. "She did not cry out. She knew Andrew would come, and she knew Jason would kill him if he did. So some would say that the guilt was hers."

The tears surged again, and she had to drop her gaze to try to blink them away. Miriam did not insist she raise it again.

"But Jason changed, perhaps for love of her. As she grew with his child, as he listened to the stories his father told of a rabbi named Jesus, he wanted to make things right. She was freed, and they married, so that his son might be his heir."

Her breath quavered. "Master Benjamin."

"Indeed. Jason never met his son—he and his father were both killed in an uprising. It was at the trial of their murderer, Barabbas, that Mistress Abigail first met Jesus for herself. At his crucifixion she felt a drop of his blood land on her and was forever changed. And there her birth pangs came upon her. Master Titus was a friend of Jason's, another centurion, and he took her home and cared for her. Then brought her here, to Rome, to claim the Visibullis estates for her son. Together they learned of the Way to salvation. They learned that Jesus came to save not just the righteous Jew, but the gentile as well. The slave. The woman, not just the man. He cares for each of us."

Tamar's chest went tight. A tug, a twist. She glanced up, only for a second, but it was enough to see Dara glaring at her from across the room.

She did not dare. She could not believe.

Miriam picked up Tamar's hand and held it between both of hers. "My story is different, but much the same. I was born a slave. When my master returned from a trip and noticed I had grown up, his wife did not take kindly to it. She sold me, well before he had a chance to do more than sneer at me once or twice. But the slave-trader." A shudder racked her, and now it was Miriam who studied the floor.

Tamar curled her fingers around the hand under hers. She had her own nightmares about a slave-trader.

"He did not defile me," Miriam whispered, "but only, as he pointed out many times, because I was worth more as a virgin. He kept my hair long, kept me well fed, so that some rich noble would pay a higher price to buy me for his bed."

They must all be the same, those traders. The one who had bought Tamar had decided to teach her how to please a man, since she was *not* a virgin but had nothing but terror from her memory of the encounter with Eleazar. All, he said, for a higher profit. Her stomach churned at the memories. "Were you? Bought by a noble?"

"No. Mistress Abigail saw me first and paid a ridiculous sum to have me for her handmaid, to save me the fate she had suffered herself." Her smile should be bright at that, but instead it was small and tight. "And yet my first night with her, Titus's father came into my room in a drunken stupor and forced himself upon me."

"*No.*" It came out a fierce whisper, from somewhere deep within. Somewhere that cringed away from the thought of this sweet, motherly woman suffering what Tamar had.

Miriam met her gaze and held it. "I will not pretend it was as bad as it could have been. I had been asleep, so he did not resort to violence. In the world of such horrific violations, it was an easy one."

Tamar shook her head. "There is no such thing. He may not have bruised your body, but you cannot tell me it did not bruise your soul."

Without hesitation, Miriam nodded. "It did. Yes. I felt I had failed my new mistress before I could even prove myself to her. I felt I had been stripped of any worth I still had. I felt...I felt like a maggot. Vile and unlovable."

More brine spilled from Tamar's eyes, and it was all she could do not to say, *Yes. Yes, that is how I feel.*

"I assured Mistress Abigail I was not troubled by it, and she let it go. Largely because she was having her own problems with Master Titus by then, whom she loved, but whose family had made it quite clear that he would be disowned if he wed her."

Miriam shook her head. "Some time later, after they had worked things out between them, the mistress's family from Israel arrived, Andrew with them. He...he will tell you he knew at first glance that I was the reason Abigail had been snatched from him. Because his heart was meant to love me." Her smile remained muted. "Mistress assured me that Andrew would not hold the sins of another against me. She assured me she wanted me only to be happy. But I knew it was her will that I marry him, and so when he pursued me, I made no objections. But Tamar."

Their gazes twined again. Again she shook her head. "Inside, I was screaming. Every time he took my hand, I had to fight back panic. When he kissed me, I could feel only Caius's disgusting mouth."

She understood. Tamar was not the only one to suffer so...yet Miriam, too, must have moved beyond it. She, too, went willingly into her husband's arms now. She smiled up at him with perfect love.

How? Did time accomplish this? Was a decade not enough to lose the fear? Did it take two? Or perhaps it took love—something the master had certainly never offered her. He had craved her body and her obedience, not her comfort. "What changed?"

"Andrew did, first. He was no fool, he knew I did not enjoy his embrace. He took me aside one day and said he would not ask for my hand, not when I obviously had no feelings for him." Even now, Miriam's sigh sounded frustrated. "But I *did* have feelings for him, buried under the fear and hurt. I just could not figure out how to break free. I confessed as much, told him what had happened with Caius."

She waited, but the older woman did not go on for a long moment. Tamar squeezed her hand. "And he...?"

"He prayed with me." Now her smile was soft and content. "They are not magic, these prayers. Especially when one feels so surely that one is unworthy to approach the throne of God. I would never dare go before an earthly king. I would never, at that point, dare speak against my mistress, who was kinder than I thought any mistress the world over could be. How could I approach God, except when I beseeched him on *her* behalf?"

Tamar swallowed. How indeed?

"But as Andrew prayed with me—not just that day, but every day for weeks afterward—I began to see God loves us. Even us, broken and leaking vessels though we are. We are not his subjects, chores he must attend. We are not mere supplicants bowing before the king. We are his children. And he loves us with perfect love, not with the faulty love we parents often fail at on this earth. He loves us so much that he sent *his* Son to give his life for mine. Can you imagine? Can you imagine loving anyone so much that you would give up your own child for them?"

Her empty womb ached, echoed in her heart. "No. I cannot."

"Exactly. Yet it is true. The mistress and master saw that Son die with their own eyes. They heard the first reports of how he rose from the grave, conquering sin forever. They felt the first flame of the Spirit. Andrew and his late mistress saw him rise into the heavens and then heard the miraculous sermon by Simon Peter—the one that each man heard in his native tongue. But if I were to believe he did all that, that he did it for *them*...I must also believe he did it for me. And if he would, if he would sacrifice himself for me—if he could love me so much, then there must be something inside me worth loving." She lifted one hand from their knotted fingers and touched Tamar's cheek. "Just as there is something inside you."

She wanted to argue. Wanted to insist that they were wrong, all of them. Fooled, deluded. But how could she? How could she deny that these people had found what always evaded her? But then, how could she grant its truth for them and yet cling to her own sense of worthlessness?

They were not so different. She had thought herself the only one here to ever suffer so at a man's hands, but she was not. Miriam had been raped by a beast. Abigail had been forced to a master's bed over and again.

Not so different, except that they had, eventually, risen above it. One to the role of mistress, another still a slave, but both with a contentment Tamar assumed was beyond someone like her. Someone like *them*.

Yet one crucial difference remained, scored into her consciousness by that terrible green gaze. Miriam's mistress no doubt wanted her to believe. Wanted her to find happiness and peace.

Tamar could see it beckoning, could recognize that quaver within as a promise of truth and mercy. But if she took the step toward it...if she put her hand in the outstretched palm of this Jesus they spoke of...*her* mistress would kill her.

Or worse, send her back to the master.

The sun had fully recovered from the wedding day's rains. Now it beat down, scorching, determined to dry up the mud it had let sneak into its domain. Zipporah positioned the water pot on her head, let its weight settle over her frame, and headed for the vineyards. Samuel would be working them, as he had been doing nearly every day lately. Training the vines up the elms and along their stakes, making sure no leaves lay in puddles to molder and rot.

When there were no people to tend, it seemed the plants suited him well.

Dinah had given Zipporah the task of water-bearing at first, she suspected, to free her from the wedding preparation and cleanup that Zipporah was none too fond of. But even though the guests had all returned to their homes and the villa had been put to rights, she did not mind continuing with the task. It had been one of the first chores she had been given as a girl, and she had always liked it. There was something satisfying about bearing a burden to a destination and quenching the thirst of hard workers. When they smiled at her, it was with gratitude uncolored by any other concerns. No worries of whether their mistress were possessed by a demon or not. No questions of whether Zipporah ought to be trusted. Just water.

She spotted Urbanus and Lucius and Fabia outside their house, the little ones running ahead of them, toward the villa. Another something over which to smile. Just yesterday Lucius and Fabia had professed to the faith.

New brethren. Yet she suspected their addition did not make the mistress forget that other brethren had fled in recent days. Archippus's household, yes, but not only them. Their leaving seemed to trigger something. Other families had departed in their wake, claiming it was time to see to the homes they had scarcely visited in the past few years.

But she knew. Zipporah did, and surely Mistress Abigail and Master Titus knew too. They left because what had once been a safe haven was now just like the rest of the world. Why, then, should they stay?

She glanced up at the shadows passing overhead. Sometimes dipping low, sometimes circling. The guardians fought them back as much as they could, but the dark ones broke through more often these days. No doubt because there were more of them, and they had renewed strength after the one within Dara had come.

They seemed especially interested in a portion of the wall near the vineyards. Zipporah squinted against the blinding midday sun but could not see what had garnered their attention. There were half a dozen of them swooping and hissing, and two angels fending them off.

Her feet had changed course before she realized she had given them the command. Still, the sound told her who they targeted before her eyes did.

Cleopas. She recognized the way his fingers moved over the strings of the lyre and the low hum that seemed wordless until she drew near and could make out words interspersed through the melody.

She caught "hair of spun sunshine" and "emerald eyes." And somehow she suspected he did not write a song for his eldest brother.

Anger wanted to spark again, but she did her best to stamp it down. To focus instead upon the sorrow. Lowering her jar to the ground, she cleared her throat to get Cleopas's attention.

He glanced down at her from his perch atop the wall with the same irritation he had sent her at Jason's wedding. His humming ceased, but his strumming did not. "Do you need something, Zipporah?"

No shame, no embarrassment. Could it be his heart was pure as he composed this song to Dara's beauty? She moistened her lips, praying it was so. Knowing that, if it were and she accused him falsely, the sin would be on her head and not his. Drawing in a deep breath, she fit fingers and toes into the cracks between the stones and hefted herself onto the shoulder-high wall beside him.

The warning burned in her spirit. She had avoided getting too close to the wall for years, always stopping a few feet away. Certainly never climbing atop it as the others of her generation always loved to do. But battling the warning was the insistence that she must meet him where he was, must speak to him.

She did her best to smile. "Composing a new song?"

He sent his eyes heavenward before focusing them on his instrument. "Do not pretend you came here just to make conversation. You have scarcely said a word these weeks that was not condemnation of my brother's wife. You are here to poison me against her."

The demons hissed and jeered.

Zipporah swallowed, refusing to let the untruths hurt. Even if they did. Even if she had *not* said a word of Dara to anyone unless they asked her opinion. Not since that first day.

Arguing would not win his heart back to the straight path, though. Much as it would satisfy her. "I want to poison no one. I want only to help heal this rift that has sprung up amidst the brethren."

His fingers went still, and the silence of his song reverberated through the hills. "The rift you caused, you mean."

She sucked in a slow breath and held on to her calm with tooth and nail. "I cannot make you believe me, Cleopas, I know that. But surely you can at least admit that *I* believe what I said. That I would not have said it otherwise. And if I believe it, what was I to do but speak?"

"You could have held your tongue—though we all know that is a skill you have not mastered." He shoved to his feet, his balance never wavering as he towered above her on the stones of the wall.

She hoped that was unfair too...but knew it had been true in the beginning. She had grown though, had she not? She had learned when to fight and when to hold her peace.

She hoped. Without the same steadiness, she stood too. "I did not come over here to fight with you. Or to talk of her at all. I only wanted to see why the demons were clustered along this portion of the wall—"

"Now *I* am hosting demons?" His outrage looked genuine.

She could hardly blame him. "No! No, not hosting them. They are merely here, no doubt trying to influence you—it happens all the time, Cleopas, I am not accusing you of anything. I just...I just want to make certain you are aware of them so you can combat them."

The assurance did not seem to placate him. "What exactly do you think they are trying to influence me toward?"

This was not going well. She should have kept walking toward the vineyard and merely prayed for him. She slid a foot backward over the uneven stone, wanting more distance between them but not entirely sure she could get off the wall with even a semblance of grace. "I...I know not. It just seemed that at the wedding, she was implying an interest and I—"

"And you do not trust me to know better than to seek an involvement? You do not think I remember that she is my brother's wife?"

What she thought was that she knew lust when she saw it in a man's eyes—not from personal experience, but from protecting her sister and Sarah. She knew that though Cleopas would not—*please, God*—ever act on such thoughts, entertaining them at all would be counted sin. And would come between him and his brother.

She swallowed and lifted her arms a bit to help her balance. "I think the fact that she would say such things to you ought to tell you something."

"What it tells me is that she is lonely and feels rejected by the people who should have embraced her—the people swayed by *you* to keep her at arm's length." He swung out an arm. No doubt just in demonstration, but his hand struck her biceps.

It did not hurt. But it pushed on her, forced her shoulder back, her back to bend, her hips to sway, her legs to react. A step back, that was all she needed to keep her balance.

Except there was nothing behind the foot she moved. Then nothing beneath the other as the rest of her body followed her foot down, off the wall.

She heard someone scream her name, though Cleopas's lips did not move.

Then a crack. And darkness.

twenty-seven

SAMUEL STRETCHED HIS LEGS OUT TO THEIR FULL STRIDE, PUMPED them faster than he could remember pumping them before. Barely feeling the ground he pounded, he flew toward them even before he saw her tip. Before he saw her fall. Before he saw her head strike her water jar, snap forward, and then lull.

Before she slumped, motionless, to the ground.

His throat burned from screaming her name, but he did not remember doing it. Just heard it echo into nothingness as his heels kicked up mud behind him.

Cleopas had already jumped down from the wall, already knelt beside her by the time Samuel reached them. Horror already contorted his brother's face.

Samuel barely glanced at him. He fell to his knees in the soft earth. Had she fallen anywhere else—*anywhere* else—the ground would have cushioned. She would have been no more than bruised. Why, why must she have come down right upon her pot?

"Zipporah." Her name came out tortured, so that he scarcely recognized his own voice. His hands shook as he slid one under her neck, feeling for each segment of her spine.

She could not be dead. She could not, Jehovah would not take her from him too. Samuel put his other fingers to her throat, felt for the pulse.

Steady. Relief sagged him.

"I did not mean to hit her arm." Cleopas's voice shook as much as Samuel's hand. "I meant only to gesture, not to touch her at all. I did not—"

"Hush, Cleo." At least Samuel sounded only haggard, not angry. He had no room to be angry. First he had to be sure she would be all right. "I saw, I know it was an accident. But it does not change the fact that she is injured, so please. Hush."

Her spine felt normal. Aligned, no obvious injuries. But already his hand was sticky with the same blood that dripped from the cracked jar. He moved his fingers slowly, probing until he found the knot, and the gash.

The moment he touched it, she gasped and moaned and tried to roll away from him. He stilled her with the hand that had been at her pulse, pressing it to her waist to keep her where she was. "No. Stay still, little sparrow. Let me make sure you are well."

She did not open her eyes. She did not say his name. She went limp again, sagging against his knees.

His fingers flexed against the leather of her belt, against the metallic studs.

Please, Father God. Please spare her. Please. Do not take her too. He could not bear it.

"She was right." Cleopas's hands fisted in the loose soil. "She was right, and I argued with her."

The warmth of her life still oozed out onto his hand. He looked over to his brother. "Focus, Cleopas. I need you to run to the villa and prepare a table for me. I will need water, bandages, my stitching supplies. A basin, and my salve. Can you do that? Can you get that ready for me?"

Cleopas nodded, lips pressed together.

"I do not think her spine is injured—I will carry her in. You run ahead. Hurry."

Cleopas did not argue now. He pushed himself to his feet and sped off.

Samuel took a moment just to breathe. Just to pray. Then he slid his arms carefully under her and lifted her, inch by inch, until she was in his lap, her head on his shoulder.

When he looked down into her face, his heart twisted. He tightened his hold, held her against him, and rested his forehead on hers. "Wake up, little sparrow. Come back to me."

The spreading warmth against his arm was her only answer.

He needed to get her inside. As smoothly as he could, he stood, repositioned her slightly, and pivoted toward the villa. Each step felt like it moved them farther away instead of closer. The weight of her in his arms scarcely registered, but the one upon his spirit seemed to push him into the ground.

It was hardly the first time he helped carry her in, unconscious or bleeding. Hardly the first time his needle would flash through her flesh. Hardly the first time he had investigated gashes and knots on her person.

But never had it hit him like this. Never had he wanted to just sink down to the earth and hold her to his chest. To whisper into her ear until she roused. To kiss her until she kissed him back.

His feet came to a halt. He looked down into her still, unresponsive face. "Heaven help me." When had this happened? He had always loved her. How had it shifted?

"Samuel? Zipporah!"

Miriam's cry shook him, and he strode forward again. He had gotten her halfway to the villa, apparently. Her mother flew toward them, agony in every feature. "What happened? Cleopas said she fell from the wall and struck her head. Is she well? What was she doing on the wall?"

Samuel shook his head. "She has stirred but not awakened. Perhaps she will not until I get the wound stitched—that would be a blessing for her. I believe she and Cleopas were talking. He had his lyre."

Miriam swiped at her cheeks. "I had thought these days behind us. She has not suffered more than a few scratches and bruises in so long."

"It was an accident. Nothing more." Except there was obviously *something* more. Cleopas said he had been arguing with her—and Samuel could not recall the last time Cleopas argued with anyone.

But she had not seemed to be the aggressor. He had watched them when their rising caught his eye. Cleopas was the one moving in anger, Zipporah had tried to retreat.

And then that whisper in his spirit to run, as fast as he could.

"I will get the doors for you." Miriam leapt ahead to do as promised, holding the main door wide for him and then, once in the cool interior, darting around him.

Trusting she knew where Cleopas had set up a table for him, he followed in her wake. She did not head down the servants' hall though, as they had done that first time he had stitched Zipporah's face. Nor to the room that had once been a makeshift medical chamber, before he left—and which was no doubt in other use now.

She turned down the hallway with the family quarters and craned her head around. "Cleopas said he would set it all up in your room, if that is acceptable. Your supplies are already there."

Having her in his room ought not to make his stomach go tight. Not when she had been there countless times before, when it was Anna's room too, and certainly not given that she was coming there now unconscious.

And yet he could not deny the reaction. Heaven help him, indeed.

For Miriam, he produced what he hoped was a reassuring smile. "Of course it is acceptable." To prove it, he increased his stride and soon sidled through the doorway, Zipporah's sandal-clad feet leading the way.

Within, Cleopas was still spreading a sheet down on the table that usually sat under the window with scrolls and his small surgical tools upon it. It would not have been large enough to hold a full-grown man, but Zipporah, he saw as he set her gently upon it, would just fit.

"Dinah will bring the water any moment." As he spoke, Cleopas set the salve, the silk thread, and the needle upon a smaller table. Then he met Samuel's gaze. "What else can I do?" His voice had gone soft and pleading.

Samuel had hoped for, expected a moan as he set her down and by necessity jostled her head. She made no sound, no move. His fingers settled on her cheek, the tips brushing the old scar running from eye to chin. "Pray."

With a single nod, his brother backed away. "I will let everyone else know to pray too."

"And I will assist you, Samuel." Her face set, Miriam stepped to his side and took her daughter's hand. "Just tell me what to do."

Within a few minutes, the water had been delivered and they did the best they could to clean the wound, catching the red-tinted water in a basin. Then Miriam moved to the other side of the table and helped hold Zipporah on her side, back to Samuel, while he prepared the silk and needle.

Her smile trembled. "Do you remember how Anna hated the sight of blood?

That first time Zipporah was attacked, I thought Anna would faint too at the sight of you stitching her."

He chuckled. A small sound, far from mirthful. But it must have loosed something in Miriam. Her shoulders relaxed, and the lines around her eyes softened.

He settled on a stool directly behind Zipporah's head. "I remember well. I was not certain if she was more angry at the interruption to her wedding or distraught that her sister had been hurt."

Miriam's chuckle was just as soft and half mournful. "She could be so self-ish sometimes—but she loved Zipporah. That always won out. Largely, I think, because Zipporah adored her so totally. She never saw anything but Anna's virtues."

"I know." He pressed the torn flesh together with one hand and slid the needle through with the other. "Anna never believed her though. About her vision."

"I know." Miriam sighed and smoothed Zipporah's hair down again, away from his ministrations. "It is good to be able to speak of her with you, Samuel. To see life in your eyes again. We feared...we feared you would never recover from her loss."

Samuel focused on the needle, on the silk, on the wound from which blood still wept. "It was hard to forgive myself. So many times I was called away from her to tend someone else, yet when she was the one who needed me, I could do nothing. I could not save her. I could not save our son."

"Some things are not within our power. Sometimes death cannot be cheated."

Too true. He had always known it, but knowledge had made it no easier. He made his last stitch and held out his hand. Miriam placed his bronze spring scissors into it. A snip, and the excess silk dangled free from the bloodied needle. "There. Though I daresay it will scar."

Miriam breathed a laugh. "Her hair will certainly cover that one, whether she wants it to or not." Laugh fading to a smile, she kissed Zipporah's forehead. "Stubborn girl. I love you so."

Samuel's stomach went tight again. "I can clean up. You should go fetch Andrew."

She rose even as she nodded. "I will not be long."

"Let us pray she is awake by the time you return." He sat for a moment after she left, letting his gaze take in the curve of Zipporah's shoulder, the dip of waist, the rise of hip.

A test. Though he was not sure whether the band around his chest meant passing or failure. He knew only it was new when he looked at her, and that he had not felt it in years, not really. Desire, quick and intense.

In part it thrilled him, proving him still alive inside after all.

In part it terrified him, when he considered the pain and possible rejection that desire brought with it.

He rinsed her blood from his hands and tools and then cut of a square of clean cloth, folded it, and pressed it to the wound that was still seeping. With his other hand, he wrapped a long strip around her head to hold it in place.

Then he sat in Miriam's chair, rested his arms on the table and his chin on his hands, so that his head was on a level with Zipporah's. "Sparrow." He wanted to run his fingers over her cheek, down through the dark curls tumbling over her shoulder, trapped at the top by the bandage. He wanted to lean over and see if her lips tasted as sweet as they looked when she smiled.

He wanted, mostly, for her to awaken and smile. "Come back to me, my little sparrow. Wake up. Tell me to stop worrying for you." Maybe, when her eyes were open, these urges would fade. She would just be his little sister again, as she had always been.

But no. When she opened her eyes, she would be the warrior queen. And he would love her all the more, and not in the same old way.

"Oh, Father." He knew not what to pray, but he closed his eyes anyway.

A long minute later, her breathing hitched and her hand settled on his head. His eyes flew open to find hers fluttering. "Zipporah!"

Her eyes were unfocused as her fingers stroked through his hair. "Was she jealous of your curls too?"

"What?" He caught her hand when it slipped away, pressed his lips to her fingertips.

"Anna." She said it on a breath, as if she were still half-asleep. Then she blinked again, and the glassy look faded from her eyes. She frowned, her fingers curling around his. "My head hurts."

A laugh slipped out. "You should see the water jar you fell into. Dinah will go on for days about how you broke it." After she fussed for days over Zipporah.

"Water jar." Her frown deepened. "I...I remember walking toward the vineyard with it. Did I trip?"

"No." He laced their fingers together. A move he would have made before this shift inside, but now it felt different. Deliberate. "You paused to talk to Cleopas. He was on the wall, and you climbed up too."

"I did?" Her eyes narrowed. "Why would I do that? I always avoid the walls."

He shrugged. "All I know is when I looked up, you were both standing upon it. He bumped you, and you fell. Your head struck the water pot."

The minuscule movement of her head was no doubt meant as a shake. Her gaze found his again. "I cannot remember."

"That is normal. We will have to watch you closely—head injuries can be tricky." Loss of hearing, loss of vision, loss of speech—all results he had seen from this sort of commotion of the brain, as Hippocrates had called it.

None of which he could suffer seeing in her. *Please, God. Please.*

Her brows were still knit. "Is Cleopas all right?"

His laugh felt like relief. "He is worried for you, that is all. And feeling very bad for being the cause, however accidental, of your fall."

"He had his lyre." She blinked again, and pursed her lips.

He had to work at swallowing. "Do you remember anything else?"

"No. But that is enough to tell me what I must have been thinking." She pushed up onto her elbow—obviously a bad idea. She gasped in pain, her eyes went wide, and she all but fell onto their joined hands. "Aaah. That water jug had better be in pieces already, or I will go after it with a hammer."

Even as his heart thundered with alarm—and that something else that came of her being pressed to his arm—he smiled. "That is my Zipporah." And it was no wonder at all he had fallen in love with her. The only mystery was that it had taken him a full month of being home to realize it.

Samuel had prescribed quiet and dim light for her headache—a medicine Zipporah accepted with a relieved sigh as she sank down onto the pallet in her room. Her mother helped her to a comfortable seat, set a glass of water nearby, and then left with a promise to check on her in a bit.

Zipporah embraced the silence with closed eyes. Her head pounded, more fiercely with every noise or flash of light. Her body wanted her to lie down, but the thought of putting her head, even the side of it, upon the floor held no appeal. The flat pillow she called her own would not provide nearly enough cushion. So instead she pulled the chair close and rested her arms on it, then the pillow, and finally her throbbing head.

The pain had just dulled to an ache when her door slammed inward, crashing into the wall.

It might as well have crashed into her skull. A whimper escaped her lips, and she clutched at her temples. Her vision blurred when she looked up.

Even so, there was no mistaking the figure that fumed her way into the small chamber.

"Mistress!" Tamar scurried in behind Dara, her eyes wide and apology in every line of her posture.

Dara picked up the nearest thing at hand—a wooden cup long since emptied of water—and hurled it to the floor. "How *dare* you! The best day, the happiest day since I arrived in this godforsaken den of heretics, and you *ruin* it!"

Zipporah could only stare. Had she done something else in that bit of memory that was missing? Something to offend her? Because she had otherwise not even been in the same room with Dara until now.

"Mistress." Tamar put herself between them. Her hands trembled, and for good reason. Dara looked fit to throttle her. "Your day is still a good one, your husband is overjoyed."

"No." Dara's voice went icy to match the cold radiating from her eyes. The blackness within her seethed and snapped its teeth. "My husband is now with his family praying for *her* instead of shouting our joy for all to hear."

Zipporah's head still felt so foggy. She could scarcely grasp the words. Benjamin was praying for her—that at least made sense, however surprising it was. But as for their joy...

For a moment Dara's golden curls blurred in her mind with Anna's long, thick braid. She heard, instead of the hiss of this mistress, her sister's exasperated sigh. *As always, your timing is impeccable.*

The time she had returned from Rome with a bloody nose. When Phillip had carried her in, when they had interrupted Anna in Samuel's arms, when she told him...Zipporah's eyes slid shut.

Dara carried Benjamin's child.

Hearing Tamar shift, Zipporah opened her eyes again. Her chamber mate had moved closer, so that all she could see was the back of her tunic.

"You know it was accidental, Mistress. She did not plan it, did not even know of your news. She certainly would not have chosen to be injured so."

A slap sounded, reverberating through Zipporah's pulsing head, filling the room and knocking Tamar over a step.

Dara's glare rained down. "Do not ever get in my way again, you little mouse. And you." She thundered nearer, crouched down, and grabbed Zipporah by the chin.

The sudden motion made her vision blur again.

"I know exactly what you are, you witch." Her fingers pinched, tried to crush. "*You* are the one who is the enemy of Jehovah, and make no mistake. I will wipe you out. I will eradicate you. And everyone here will cheer when they are free of your poison."

Another blur, and then the door slammed shut again. The dizziness it caused had not quite stilled when it opened again more quietly. Tamar must have gone out.

But no. A soft hand soothed back her hair, Tamar's scent drifted past her nose. And masculine legs entered her vision. They bent, and Cleopas's face filled it instead. He studied her for a long moment.

She wanted to assure him she was all right. That, whatever words they had spoken on the wall, she did not blame him for the fall. But speaking around the pain would take such effort.

He sighed. "You were right."

She tilted her head. She knew only what she thought when she heard the lyre. Had she accused him? Or did he speak of something else entirely?

He gave her a smile that was but an imitation of his usual bright grin. "I will be at the ilex in the morning."

She forced her tongue to work. "You need not come just because you feel bad, Cleopas." She motioned toward her head.

"I know." His smile went lopsided. "But I need to come." He rested a hand on her shoulder for a beat and then stood. A moment later there was empty space before her again, and the soft squeak of her closing door.

Zipporah closed her eyes. Was it one more warrior fighting on their side... or one more push to drive the separation wider?

twenty-eight

BENJAMIN ROLLED HIS NECK TO RELEASE THE KINK AND SAUNTERED over to the window. Sunset streaked the sky into a rainbow and cast a red glow onto Samuel's hair. His brother stood staring out at the sun-bathed world. No doubt worrying about Zipporah—he was always anxious when anyone struck their heads, what with the cases of the injured going to sleep afterward and never waking up.

A fate Benjamin certainly did not wish on her, especially not with all these bad feelings between them. He wanted only for her to let go of her foolish notions about Dara and focus her energies on something constructive.

He leaned into the opposite side of the window. "Are you all right?"

Samuel darted him an inscrutable glance. "Well enough. She only scared a decade or so off my life, by my best estimate."

Benjamin chuckled. "If it makes you feel any better, her injuries have now interrupted a second man who was getting the most excellent news from his wife."

At that, Samuel turned and regarded him fully. If only his smile did not look half-sorrowful. "Congratulations, Ben. You will be a good father."

"Thank you." He sent his gaze out to the sunset-tinged hills again, hating that he had to seek so hard for something to say to his brother. When would things return to normal? When would they all forget Zipporah's accusations and accept Dara? Maybe the child would help. Surely.

And that did remind him of something Samuel would no doubt have an opinion on. He had been meaning to broach the subject with their father for weeks but had not found the right moment. "Speaking of Zipporah...I have been thinking."

Samuel stiffened beside him. "Why do I have a bad feeling about this?"

"It is nothing bad." Yet under the determination, he could not deny an unease. She had never been one to blindly obey. He could not be entirely certain she would in this, either. "But all these weddings do serve to remind me that she is well past the age when she ought to have been married. Sarah will wed Urbanus in a matter of months, and then what? A marriage ought to be arranged for Zipporah too."

Samuel's face hardened until it looked like it was chiseled from stone. "Do not, Ben. Do not do it."

He felt his own face go stiff in return. "It is my duty to see she is provided for."

"Not like that." Samuel stepped close and pitched his voice low. "When have we *ever* dictated who will marry whom at Tutelos? And why would you use Sarah's marriage as an excuse, when you know well she will beg you to send Zipporah with her, when and if Urbanus leaves?"

"I only—"

"Want to get rid of her. And in a way you know well would hurt her. If you are going to bind her to some man she scarcely knows or does not like, you might as well sell her. Is that next? Will you take her to the slavers?"

Benjamin took a step back, anger snapping. "Do you think me such a monster?" But was he any better than that? She had asked for her freedom, and he had refused her.

The muscle in Samuel's jaw pulsed, but then he relaxed. "No. Forgive me—it has been a long and trying day."

And Benjamin's motives had not been so bad. "Sam...she needs a life of her own. Perhaps if she had one—"

"No." Only Samuel's eyes went hard this time. "Please. If not for her sake, then for Sarah's. For mine. For her parents'. Please, Ben. Just...focus on your own coming child. Leave her alone."

Benjamin drew in a deep breath. "Would that I could. But what will be left of the church in a few months if I do? We have had so many leave lately—you surely see how it has upset Mother."

"Yes." Samuel folded his arms over his chest. "What I fail to see is why you lay it at Zipporah's feet."

Much as he wanted to mirror his brother's pose, Benjamin refused. Instead, he leaned against the wall again. "I asked the younger of the Colossian slaves why they were departing so quickly. The only answer he gave was 'Zipporah knows.' He said I should ask her, if I really wanted answers. How would you interpret that?"

Samuel blinked. "That he had already had a conversation with her about their reasoning. Did you ask her?"

"Not yet. Would you suggest I do so now?"

Now his brother sighed, stepped away, and held up a hand. "Please just let this drop. I beg you."

Benjamin said nothing to detain him. It seemed they had little left to say at all.

The sun hurt her eyes, and the pain in her eyes triggered that slicing one in her head, proving a lie those words Zipporah had just spoken in the kitchen with a smile. No, she did not feel back to normal. She had thought she had earlier, when she rose at sunrise and made her way to the ilex tree—the first time in three days she had managed that. But the sun had been softened by haze then, not glaring at her from the heavens.

The headache was a better alternative, though, than staying inside another minute. She repositioned the basket on her hip and set a course for the vineyards. If she did not hurry, Samuel would be on his way inside to check on her, and he would no doubt forbid her—again—from doing more than lifting her own bowl to her mouth.

Yet let it be noted that *he* fled the room within five minutes this morning when the conversation turned to the news Dara and Benjamin had finally shared the evening before. Obviously the endless chatter from all the women grated on him too—or perhaps reminded him too much of the very-similar words that had been exchanged when it was Anna sharing their good news.

She shifted the basket again. Dinah had put no more in it than usual, but it felt heavy. At this rate, Zipporah would end up on her pallet for a nap this afternoon. She had hoped to avoid that today. But then, that too would be better than the pitying looks people kept sneaking at her. The ones only Sarah had put voice to.

"Are you upset? To know she will have his child?"

Her best friend was allowed to ask, because she did not wonder solely because of those spent feelings; she also wondered because of what it meant for the church, for them all. A valid question, that last. And it rendered the first irrelevant. She had no room for jealousy, not with that sick feeling in her stomach that wondered if to Dara the child was but another rope to tie around Benjamin. Sarah understood that.

The others could keep their pitying glances to themselves.

Her pace had slowed. With a huff aimed at herself, she increased her stride and pushed all other thoughts from her mind. Samuel. A meal. Nothing more. She would smile and convince him she was well, lure him into telling her some exaggerated tale, and then let him talk her into resting. It would speed the afternoon by.

The outbuildings were soon behind her, the wall to her right, and the vineyards spread out ahead. She traced the rows of elms and vines with her gaze, searching the fanning leaves for the gleam of golden hair.

She saw instead a dozen bare backs gleaming with sweat in the blazing sun. Bronzed, the lot of them, proving this was not the first they had stripped to the waist in their labors.

Her gaze snagged on a particularly well-defined back. Largely because the man turned as she looked on, showing a well-defined front that could have been used by the sculpting masters as a model. How hard must a man work to achieve such muscles? Perhaps he threw the discus. Or trained with weighted bags. Or...ran, she realized as she finally glanced past the chest.

Samuel. She squeezed her eyes shut, but his image was still seared on her eyelids, and it still made her throat feel dry. She would shake it off. It was not as though she had never realized before how beautiful he was, how perfectly sculpted. She had just never seen him wearing so little.

Maybe this was a bad idea after all. She would just turn around and...

He spotted her. He went still, lifted a hand to shade his eyes, and no doubt bit back a few choice words. So much for slipping away unnoticed. With a deep breath to brace herself for the lecture sure to come—and against that sleek form of his—she strode onward.

He greeted her with a quirked brow and unsmiling lips. "What are you doing out here in this sun, and carrying a heavy basket? I said I would check on you at noonday."

"Have mercy on me." She injected an overdone plea into her voice and set the basket down. On a normal day, she would have tossed herself at his chest and fisted her hands in his tunic just to complete the image of a distraught supplicant. At the moment she was keenly aware that that would put her hands directly upon his too-appealing muscles. No, she would just settle for an exaggerated expression upon her face and hands clasped before her. "If I have to listen to one more conversation about the coming babe, I will not survive it."

His smile was every bit as compelling as the rest of him on display. "I thought you would plead a headache and spend the day in your chamber, or with Sarah."

"I may not be the busiest servant on the villa, but I can only withstand so much idleness. I have had my fill of it the last few days." She picked the basket up again and held it between them. "Will you eat with me, so I do not have to carry this heavy thing back?"

His eyes went narrow, though the smile did not fully fade from his lips. He took the basket and stepped to her side, touched a hand to her back. "Into the shade with you, at least."

She let him guide her to the nearest elm and would have sat quite happily at its base, but he stilled her with a hand to her elbow and turned her to face him. He put the basket down and then framed her face in his hands, tipped it upward to his.

The dryness returned to her throat. Until she realized he was just peering into her eyes as he had done each day since the strike to her head.

Of course that was all he was doing. Why would she even for a moment think otherwise? This was Samuel. Anna's husband. Her brother. Not...not... She drew in a breath through her nose and shoved whatever this was down. Mentally stomped on it and hefted a few blocks of thought overtop it. Her brain must have been truly scrambled by the fall, that was all.

"Do I pass inspection, O Wise Physician?"

He stroked a thumb over her cheek, his smile crooked. "Sorry. My hands are dirty—though if you had waited for me to come in and wash up..."

"I am not concerned with a few streaks of dirt."

He let out a slow breath. "You still have shadows under your eyes, and I can see the pain within them. But they are reacting normally to the light." His hands dropped to her shoulders. "Promise me you will rest when you go back in."

"You have my word." She had seen him greet Anna a few times after working the vineyards, before he had washed up. Always, if he touched her, it was on the bare part of her arms, where she could easily brush the soil off. Never on her pristine white stola. His fingers now, though, splayed over the gathered seams of Zipporah's garment, no doubt dirtying the shoulders.

Streaks of dirt really did not bother her. So why did the comparison seep into her mind, past that block she had just put on such thoughts? She obviously needed a larger one. She would have to send her mind to a marble quarry and chisel out a better slab.

"Sparrow." He bent down to put his face on a level with hers. "Are you all right?"

Why could she not summon up a smile? The headache, that must be it. Just the headache. "Not as well as I thought, that is all. But not so bad compared to yesterday."

He made the same "poor creature" sound in his throat that he had when they found a lost kitten, when Zipporah was no more than five. His lips found her forehead, and his arms came about her. As he had done, as they had done countless times before. Embracing him was as familiar as embracing her own father.

Except that this time, her cheek was pressed to a bare chest, slicked with sweat and sun-warm, and her pulse was not behaving itself.

"Sorry," he said into her hair, even as he gave her a squeeze. "I am sweaty."

She shut her eyes. He was Anna's husband, her brother. And she would not be a fool about a man again. She wrapped her arms around his waist and held on. "I will survive it."

She hoped.

She strolled along, her hand in Benjamin's, a smile upon her lips. But Dara scarcely heard whatever her husband prattled on about. What did she care about crops and vintages, new wineskins or old? She had taken on some of the household planning, but only because it suited her ends. Though it had proven more difficult than she expected to irritate Abigail and Dinah and Miriam. They were surely frustrated with her when she insisted on change with a sweet smile, but it had yet to cause any division among them.

Benjamin laughed over something, so she did too, and leaned into his arm.

She must act quickly. As quickly as she could. Being already with child, perhaps she had a hope of escaping this place within the year. Perhaps the master somehow knew and was already on his way. Perhaps now she could be his, before the babe growing inside her made her stomach swell up and her beauty fade.

Benjamin squeezed her hand. His sigh sounded happy. "It is so good to be home. Whatever the problems we face, we are at least here. I am blessed indeed to have all this, my family, a beautiful wife." He grinned down at her. "And now our first child on the way. I never imagined it. I think I always thought such love was beyond me, that I would never feel this way."

Foolish, predictable man, to mistake physical desire for love. But she would not pity him. It suited her well, and she could understand that longing for touch, that craving. She enjoyed having his hands on her, feeling his lips trail over her.

But love—that was reserved for the master. She had to find a way to get word to him, or receive it from him. That, however, would require escaping the villa. Just for a while.

Renewing her smile, she swayed to a halt so she could stretch up to kiss him. "I know exactly what you mean. I had always hoped to find a husband who would love me, but to find one of the faith...and then all this." She motioned to the despicable villa. "I can still scarcely fathom it, and I certainly do not deserve it." She settled her hand upon her abdomen, though the only indication she felt of life within was the occasional bout of sickness. "But it is reassuring to think that my child will not want. That he will have the holdings in Israel, this villa, and...have you anything in Rome itself? You never mentioned it."

But if she could get back to the city, it would be a simple matter of earning a few coins. And with money, she could get a message to the master. Everyone here was too careful, knew too well the prices of everything, not to notice if she secreted away enough of his money to do what she needed to do. And the last thing she needed was them discovering she was in correspondence with a man in Israel.

"No, not in the city." He led her onward again, toward the setting sun. "My abba's family sold off all its holdings there when my great-grandfather fell out of favor with the emperor. Which is just as well. With a half-Jewish father and full-Jewish mother, the state would likely have stripped me of it when they expelled all the Jews from Rome, even though I was born a citizen. But Father— Titus—has holdings still in Rome. He inherited the Asinius house there when Caius died. If ever we need to stay in the city, we use it. Otherwise we lend it to visiting friends."

The Asinius house. She had heard nothing about it particularly, but Benjamin had told her of Titus's father. A drunken lecher, from the sounds of it, but a wealthy one. A consul. His house would no doubt meet her needs quite well.

She wove her arm around his and gave him her sweetest smile. "Could we stay there sometime, do you think? I so enjoyed visiting the city for a few hours. And I confess, I would appreciate some time on our own."

He smiled, but she read no indulgence in his eyes. "Perhaps sometime, beloved. There will be business in Rome to keep me busy soon. But I hate to leave Tutelos for more than a day so soon after we got here." He kissed her, lightly and absently, and turned them back toward the villa. "Perhaps in another month or two."

To push now would achieve nothing. But two months? That would not do at all. She would simply have to find a way to get him to leave sooner.

twenty-nine

THE ARGUMENT, IF IT COULD BE DEEMED SUCH, SPANNED AN ENTIRE corridor. Samuel kept his seat on the edge of the impluvium, quite happy to be lost in the sound of the indoor fountain's trickle but still paying half-attention to the ongoing debate.

"They will not come. They have made it clear." Urbanus sounded as weary as Samuel felt.

But he had a full day's work in the vineyard as excuse. Urbanus had only this quarter-hour conversation to blame. Though granted, Sarah could exhaust anyone in such time.

His sister glared at her betrothed. "They may have made it clear in the past that they do not approve of your conversion, but have we not been praying? Is it not a lack of faith if we do not at least invite them, give them the chance to take part in our day?"

Urbanus took her hand, his face drawn. "No. It is a desire to spare you heartache. I know you wish to help me reconcile with them, my sweet one, but it will hurt you too much when they refuse. Which they will do, as they have always done."

Zipporah, a pitcher in hand and a smile on her lips, paused at Samuel's side to refill his cup of watered wine. "Will she wear him down, do you think?"

Samuel tried only to glance up at her. His eyes would not submit to so short a perusal though. They insisted on taking in every detail. It had been a week since the accident—the pain, she said, had stopped. His yearning to gather her close and test her lips had not. "I dare not guess. She is stubborn. But he loves her well, and knows well their refusal would hurt her."

"We shall see, I suppose." With a chuckle, she moved off to refill other cups.

Samuel shot to his feet, not so tired after all. If he sat here until the meal was ready, he would only follow her with his gaze and memorize each movement. Which was an utter waste of time, given that he had already memorized them yesterday. And the day before. No doubt any onlookers were, at first, willing to think he was making sure she had fully recovered. But if he kept it up, they would start to wonder.

All well and good—but he would speak to Zipporah before any whispers could work their way to her. She deserved to be the first to know of his love for her, not the last. Pushing to his feet, he abandoned his eavesdropping and headed for the portico. The sun was waning, not so hot now. A chaise out of doors would suit him well.

He had been praying about how to broach the subject, what her reaction might be. Thus far, the Lord had given him no instruction. But he would keep praying, waiting for an answer. Until then, he would say nothing—and guard his glances.

No one else was out here now, but he would be able to hear when the meal was announced. He settled onto a chaise that gave him a view through the window if he sat on its side instead of reclining. The series of rooms beyond it were all open, and he could still see the gathering in the impluvium. Zipporah crossed his line of sight, her head tilted back in laughter as the eldest of Urbanus's daughters bounced around her.

Oh, Lord. Instruct me soon.

A deep, familiar chuckle interrupted his prayer, and Andrew appeared beside the window. On the outside, though Samuel had not heard him come up. The man crossed his arms, his eyes smiling along with his lips. "It has been many years since I have seen that look on your face, my son." He peered inside, but he would not be able to see Zipporah now. He turned back with lifted brows. "Who has earned it?"

Samuel swallowed. Had it been Father, perhaps he would have admitted it freely. Perhaps, in fact, he should seek him out for advice. But Andrew?

The man's face softened, his arms dropped. He took a step closer and then sat beside Samuel on the chaise. "It has been four long years. It is time for you to move on, to find another wife. We know this, and we will rejoice with you when you do."

Tell him.

Samuel dragged in a long breath, testing the voice. Pouring a prayer onto it. Peace filled him as he met Andrew's patient gaze. He nodded. Still, he had to swallow and suck in a fortifying breath before he could speak aloud what his thoughts had been screaming for seven eternal days. "I am in love with your daughter."

Andrew sighed—not the reaction he had hoped for. "We all know how you loved Anna. But she is gone. She would want you to find someone else to spend your life with."

A laugh slipped out, too cynical. "No, she would not. She was always the first to say I would mourn her forever if anything ever happened to her." He winced and dug his fingers into the wooden seat beneath him. No doubt that had sounded far too bitter. "I do miss her. I did love her. But I was not speaking of Anna."

"You..." Andrew trailed off, his eyes went wide. He scooted a bit to face him more fully. "You mean Zipporah?"

Samuel looked through the window again, though she was still not back in sight. "When I saw her fall off the wall..." He shook his head. "She has always been special to me. But not like this."

"Samuel." Andrew's hand landed on his shoulder, pulling his attention back to his earnest face. "You know I would welcome you as my son again with joy. But you do realize, do you not, how carefully you must tread with her?"

Samuel's brows knit. "What do you mean? I would never hurt her."

"No—I know that. But..." He moved his hand away to motion with it. "She adored her sister. She not only assumes you still love her, I do not think it has once occurred to her that you would ever find anyone else." He shook his head, the set of his mouth worried. "Especially not herself. She does not think any man would ever want her."

"If they do not, then they are fools. She is..." His words dried up when he caught sight of her again.

"You really love her." It was a statement, yet filled with awe. "You are sure of it, it is not a passing fancy."

"I am sure." So sure that it made his every other decision in life seem wavering in comparison.

"Despite her scars."

Samuel's head jerked back to face Andrew. He knew he must look fierce, but his companion did not flinch. "No. Not *despite* her scars. I love her *for* them—they are testament to the spirit, the heart, the faith that sets her above all others."

Perhaps Andrew had meant it as a test. Because now he smiled, certain and calm. "Then take my advice, my son. Convince her first you can love. Then that you love her." He stood, again clapping a hand to his shoulder. "I can think of no one more worthy of my precious Zipporah. I will be praying for you."

"That I appreciate." He stood too—it must be nearly time for dinner. Though when he looked through the window again, a sight met his eyes that was so rare he could only gape.

Andrew turned too, his eyes going wide when he also spotted Mother flying through the rooms with pure fury on her face, Benjamin and Father both dogging her heels. "Do we run, or do we see what has happened?"

"Oh, we stay. I have not seen Mother in a rage in...years." Too many to count. All his memories of her face contorted in that particular way, in fact, dated back to when they first arrived in Rome, when Benjamin was but a babe.

Benjamin did not look quite so intrigued by it. Rather, desperate. "Ima, please. She did not mean it as it sounded."

Andrew hissed out a breath between his teeth. "He called her ima. This is bad."

"Mm." Samuel backed another step away from the door, pulling Andrew with him. "We need not ask who the 'she' is, I suppose."

Mother charged through the exit, not seeming to notice them, though Father sent Samuel a look that seemed to say, *It has finally happened.*

"Ima—"

"No." A step away from leaving the portico already, she spun, a finger pointed at Benjamin's chest. "I stood with you, with her. Despite my suspicions, despite that warning inside, I trusted you. I was willing to accept her, to be patient with her. I have said nothing—*nothing*—through the many times she insulted me over this past month. The times she insinuated I could not run this villa, the times she implied I was less for having been a slave."

Benjamin's expression turned from pleading to confusion. "She did *what?*"

Their mother's hand sliced the air. "But I will not stand by while she insults my children!"

That explained the ferocity.

"And your husband," Father added, the corners of his lips twitching. "Do not forget that part."

Mother glared at him. "I am not in the mood to be amused, Titus. Do not jest with me."

"I cannot help it. You are so beautiful in a rage." He moved behind her and put his hands on her shoulders. Perhaps to steady her, or perhaps to keep her from charging all the way to Ostia and booking Dara passage home here and now. He kept his gaze on Benjamin. "You really think your wife did not mean what she said?"

Benjamin sighed, but he looked conflicted. Which was enough to make Samuel shift a bit closer. His brother usually defended Dara without any hesitation at all. Now he splayed his hands. "She...she must have been parroting her brother Jonathan's thoughts, that is all. No doubt they slipped out before she could think to stop them. He hates Romans and makes no secret of it."

Mother still looked stiff as granite. "She called my children—your brothers and sisters—dogs. *Dogs!* Because their blood is only half Hebrew. Tell me, what does she think of Jacob, the man who has served you so faithfully? Does she hate him, too, because he is Samaritan? And if she thinks so lowly of those who are only *half* Roman, how does she feel about the full Romans among us?"

Benjamin passed a hand over his hair. "She cannot have meant it. How could she, when she loves me, and I am part Roman too?"

Their mother's silence stretched and snapped. She inched back, closer to Father, the glint in her eyes shifting so subtly, but so profoundly, from anger to pain. "I wonder if she does. Please, my son, I know you do not want to hear this—but you should wonder too."

Benjamin's face went hard. "No. I will not question her devotion because of an opinion on Romans."

"Then question it because of the way she has tried to entice half the men here." Mother swallowed, and a Stoic mask came over her face. "It is why Archippus left. He did not think his son strong enough to refuse her if she made more than a passing offer."

Benjamin's fingers curled into his palm, and the war raging within flashed through his eyes.

Their mother's chin edged up. "Have I ever lied to you? Ever?"

Samuel saw Benjamin's pain. The clutching at denial. The need to refuse it, to cling to what he thought he knew.

An arrow seemed to pierce his own heart. Dara would destroy him, if she could. This man who somehow loved her, this brother Samuel had spent twenty-six years protecting. She would try to be his undoing, and if they all left him to her devices, she might just succeed.

Abba Father, give him your strength. Give him your wisdom. Lend him mine, if I have enough to help him.

Because it was the only way he could think to aid, Samuel stepped to Benjamin's side.

His brother's shoulders sagged. "I know not what to say."

"You need not say anything to us," Father replied, his voice low and quiet. "But to your wife, you had better pray for the right words."

Benjamin's head shook. "She makes mistakes. She says things she ought not—I know this. But can we not be more patient with her? Think how hard it is on her, to come to a new place like this, to be accused within her first few minutes here of hosting a demon. No one has tried to make friends—"

"Many have tried." Mother's voice went cool again. "None have succeeded. Benjamin, whether the accusation is correct or not, Dara needs to be gotten in hand. She is not the only one here who arrived in Rome knowing only a few. She is not the only one to receive a mixed reception. But tell me, is it the Way of Christ to respond as she has? To insult and allure? To condemn a person's blood?"

"She is still a babe in the faith. She admits as much. And you know as well as I that she is far from being the only Hebrew Christian to have a hard time accepting the gentile members of the church." Yet for the first time, Benjamin sounded as though he were trying to convince himself.

"But *she* is mistress of this villa. It is her responsibility to welcome, not to offend."

Father squeezed Mother's shoulders. That muscle ticked along his square jaw. "Everyone needs time to think through how we will all live in peace. If I might suggest it, Benjamin, you could take her into Rome for a week or so. Stay in my house. Perhaps a bit of distance will help everyone see the situation more clearly."

More like give the women time to calm enough that they did not go at it tooth and nail.

Benjamin let out a puff of breath, his gaze going unfocused. His fist clenched tighter. "A fine idea, Father. I will let her know. And I am sorry, Ima, for what she said to you. I will speak with her about that too."

Mother turned partially toward Father, exchanging one of those looks that seemed to say something in a language only the two of them spoke. She nodded.

Father sighed and nodded too. Then looked up at them, from Samuel to Benjamin. "Do as the Lord leads you, Ben. But we will do the same. We will be joining Samuel and Sarah for morning prayers at the ilex from now on."

No victory surged within Samuel at that. How could it, when their parents looked so resigned? He had never wanted to be pitted against his brother. Never.

They said no more. Mother pivoted away from the house again, and Father tucked her hand into the crook of his elbow and led her away, though at a far more sedate pace than she used a minute before. Andrew slipped back into the house with a silent glance of encouragement.

Samuel turned to his brother. "Ben—"

"Could she have known, do you think, that they would react that way? That they would ask us to leave for a while?" A strange, pained glint lit his eyes. "Could she have guessed at the one thing that would upset Mother enough to give up on her?"

Ben spun back to the house, though he made no move to enter. Merely looked at it, as if seeing through the walls. "She asked me a few days ago if we could go to Rome for a while. I said now was not a good time."

Samuel let his breath ease out. He must step carefully, he knew that...but he also recognized that look on Benjamin's face. It had no doubt been on his own the first time he had pressed a kiss to Anna's throat in that way he thought she liked, and she had pushed him away. Had said, "I am already with child. Must you touch me?" It was the look of unwanted realization about the one you loved.

His brother met his gaze. "Would she do that?"

Samuel swallowed, knowing well he asked it brother-to-brother, friend-to-friend, not as one would to the person who had become one's adversary on an issue. And so he must put aside his thoughts on this particular woman and find a more abstract answer.

Not so hard to do. "I think some people know no way to communicate other than through manipulation. I would be tempted to attribute it solely to too-beautiful women, except that Mother and Ester and Sarah prove that generalization false."

The sorrow did not so much as flicker within Benjamin's eyes. If anything, it deepened. "What of Anna?"

It was Samuel's turn to stare without seeing at the house. "I do not think she would have purposefully offended my parents to get her way, but she certainly employed similar tactics in other situations, yes. But I knew of that tendency before we wed."

Benjamin snorted a laugh. "I never saw it in her. Perhaps I am incapable of noticing such things until they club me." He rubbed a hand over his face and shook his head. "You loved her though. She loved you. That did not have to come into question."

Samuel turned back to the chaise and sank down onto it. "I loved her. She loved me. But it was still difficult sometimes, Ben. Marriage...our parents make it look effortless, but it is not."

His brother looked at him strangely. "I thought—I thought you two were blissfully happy. I never saw you argue."

How had the conversation turned to him and Anna? But it had, and he would not lie. He pinched the bridge of his nose. "We did not argue. When she did not like something I said or did, she had more subtle means of showing her displeasure."

"Like forcing those around you to push you into doing what she wanted?" Ben shook his head and plopped down in the same place Andrew had been a few minutes before. "She is my wife. She carries my child. But I suddenly realize that I scarcely know her."

Now was not the time for an *I tried to warn you* lecture, but Samuel could think of nothing else to say. So he just sat there, beside his brother, and hoped his presence would speak for him.

thirty

NEVER IN HIS LIFE HAD BENJAMIN FELT AS HE DID WHEN HE DRAGGED his feet into his chamber. Dara had not joined everyone for dinner. Which he learned only through the report of Dinah, since he had not come back inside either. He had just sat there beside Samuel for an hour or more, trying to pray, trying to understand. Trying to believe that Dara had a good reason for acting as she had.

She waited for him in their room. The moment he stepped in and eased the door shut behind him, she sprang from her seat before the loom and flew across the floor. Threw herself onto his chest. Cried tears that wet his toga.

And he felt nothing. Nothing. He could not even convince his arms to come around her.

"I am so sorry," she sobbed against him. "I did not mean it. I do not know why I said it. I have felt so odd lately, I do not know if it is because of the baby... your mother said it could affect my moods. Oh!" The sobbing increased. "I have made an enemy of her! What have I done?"

His hands finally lifted, by rote more than design, and settled on her back.

Dara did not seem to notice his lack of response. "She will not want to teach me anymore. She will not want me with her children. She will not want me here at all!"

And there it was. His cue, he supposed, to let her know she had won. "Father recommended a bit of distance. He suggested we go to Rome."

Her tears slowed, her hands curled into his toga. "This is not how I wanted to go."

"Is it not?"

She drew back, a flash in her glistening green eyes. "How could you ask that?" Her voice sounded plaintive.

He moved his hands to her arms, meaning to set her back and put some space between them. Instead, his fingers gripped her as a coal fanned to life within him. "What were you thinking? You have been here a month, you must have known. You *must* have known that the one thing that would anger my mother so acutely is an insult to her children."

He released her abruptly, relieved to see no red marks upon her arms. Even so, he spun away, hating the thought that he might have hurt her. Hating that everything within churned and roiled and refused to find a resting place. Hating that all he could think of was hating.

Her fingers, small and warm, touched his arm. "You are angry with me. I deserve it."

The right words. Yet if he looked in her eyes, would he see true remorse or calculation? Was he even wise enough to know the difference? He did not turn to find out. The emotion drained from him again. "What did you say to Balius?"

"What?" She sounded genuinely surprised. "Who...the Colossian? When?"

His gaze fell to the tile floor. The same mosaic stared back at him that always had—an angry Neptune setting the sea aswirl. He had ceased to see it years ago, but just now it seemed an echo of his own soul. "According to his father, you are why they left. He said you tried to tempt him." And Benjamin had blamed it on Zipporah. What had he thought she had done, really?

A derisive breath brought his gaze up to his wife. So very beautiful, even as she stood there with a dark gleam in her smoky green eyes. "You think I would have said anything improper to *him*?" She shook her head, contempt curling her lip. "Some men, Benjamin, think every word from a woman's lips is an invitation. Perhaps you would prefer I never speak to your male guests?"

She had a point. He had witnessed firsthand with his sisters, with Anna, how that could happen.

Yet his mother knew it too, had been parrying unwanted advances most of her life. She too would know what it looked like, and she would be the first to champion someone who found herself in that situation.

But liars and temptresses she had no patience with.

He splayed his hands. "I want to believe you, Dara. But you just proved tonight that you are capable of saying things I thought you never would. You just manipulated my entire family into anger with you so I would take you to Rome. How am I to trust you?"

Her shoulders came back, and it was as though a mask dropped from her face. Gone was the repentant, sweet woman he had married. In her place stood one cold, angry, and poised. "It is the only way I know."

So then. His arms fell to his sides. "A lesson learned well from your mother, I suppose."

"I am not like her!" Fury blazed across her face and seemed to lift her, make her fly at him in a very different way than she had a minute ago.

This time he caught her, caught the arms she had raised, ready to strike him. She was stronger than he would have thought, but he had spent his youth wrestling with brothers. He held her arms easily enough and, when she made to kick him, backed her into the wall as gently as he could manage, given her flailing.

"Stop it. Stop! You will injure yourself and the babe."

She looked ready to bare her teeth and gnash at him. "I am not like her! I would never sell my own child!"

All this, for the sake of what Martha had done to Samuel? It did not feel right. Nothing about this evening felt right. He eased off, slowly, testing. "Good to know, since your child is mine too."

As suddenly as the rage had ignited, it fled. She slumped against the wall, eyes downcast...and yet he wondered, now, which was the show. Whether to trust the rage or the repentance. "I am sorry," she murmured.

He stepped away, his limbs feeling heavy and useless. "You are my wife, Dara. We are bound together for life, and that is not a pledge I take lightly. We will get through this. We will find our way. But I need to make something clear right now—you will not manipulate me like this again. I will take you to Rome because my parents need me to, but this is your last victory through such means. Do you understand that?"

The quirk of her brow was pure haughtiness. "I understand. You are the tyrant, I am the subject."

It should not grate. Yet it did. "I am the husband. You are the wife. I will honor you and love you and care for you—but you must respect me in return, or our life will be nothing but contention."

"As you will, Lord."

Benjamin turned away. He would find Mark. Share the news that they would be staying in Rome a while. And pray with all his might this was just the shifting emotions of pregnancy and not something far deeper turning his wife into a stranger.

———

Pain pierced Tamar's stomach, inspiring her to pull her knees to her chest and pray. Not for herself—the pain was not real, she knew that, just a reflection of the anxiety of her mind—but for everyone else. For Master Benjamin, who obviously knew not what his wife was capable of. For Mistress Abigail, who had looked so hurt and furious when Dara had insulted her children. For the whole group here, who strove so hard for peace.

Peace was an illusion. Nothing more.

Tamar leaned her head back against the wall of her chamber and tried to keep the worry from her face. Zipporah and Miriam would notice it. They always did. And she suspected they had decided to pass an hour in here with her solely because they worried for her.

As if she deserved worry. She deserved nothing. She was here only as a slave to their enemy, meant to be a helper to a creature out to destroy them.

But oh, how she wanted to be something different. How she wanted to tell them that Dara was no better than they—that she, too, had been sold into bondage. But the master had kept her to be his wife someday, not just a slave. Perhaps that made it different. Perhaps that *did* make her better. How was Tamar to know? All she could be certain of was that if she whispered the words burning her tongue, her mistress would know, and they may well be the last words she ever spoke.

Zipporah's laugh pulled Tamar's attention back to their small chamber. Miriam was braiding her daughter's hair, showing extra care as she neared the injured place. What would it be like to have a mother who still loved her? One who came to visit and fuss over her hurts?

A knock on the door interrupted that musing, which was just as well, as it would end only in more aches. Zipporah shot Tamar a look, as she always did when a knock came. Awaiting permission before she bade the visitor enter. Tamar would never dare forbid it, but she appreciated the question. She nodded.

"Come in," Zipporah called.

The door opened, and Mark filled the doorway. He did not enter—he never did, not when Tamar was here, though she had come in a few times to find him lounging about with his sister, laughing and teasing. He always left when Tamar joined them.

She wished it did not relieve her so.

This evening, though, his gaze fell on Tamar, not his mother or sister. "Benjamin asked me to find you and let you know so you can pack for yourself and Dara—we are going to Rome tomorrow, to stay for a week or so."

Mistress Dara—in Rome so long, with stretches when she would no doubt be under no watchful eye? A massive hand seemed to take her by the heart, squeeze and press and completely eclipse the discomfort in her stomach. She could not breathe. She could not speak. She could only shake her head.

"Tamar!" He entered now, apparently, given that he appeared before her downcast eyes, knee-to-knee with either mother or sister. She did not glance up to see which. "What is it? What is the matter?"

Could he not see? He did not like Dara, did not trust her, yet did he not see?

"Tamar?" Miriam's voice came from her side. Miriam's fingers found hers and wove through them. "Tell us what frightens you so."

The hand on her chest lightened, words tumbled into her mouth. She clamped her lips shut. She could not speak of the mistress's business here. Much as she wanted to, much as she *needed* to, she could not. She swallowed back the truth and squeezed her eyes shut when the hand pressed again.

"You need not tell us everything." Zipporah's voice now, soft and low. "We all respect the bonds of master and servant. But tell us what you can, please."

"She will..." That much slipped out without her permission, but then she had to cast around for words that were safe. For truth that was not too true but not too false. She risked a glance at Mark and found his brow creased in concern for her. "Did the master say why?"

Mark looked more serious than she had yet seen him. "Mistress Abigail and Master Titus requested he remove her for a while, so they might calm down. They were very upset."

Of course they were. She had known the moment Dara got that look in her eyes before she spoke that her words would be poison. But they surely did not realize they requested the very thing she had been after. How could they? They had not heard her that morning, pacing her chamber and mumbling about her need to get to the city.

The pain in Tamar's stomach redoubled. Dara would go there so she might tell fortunes, of that Tamar was certain. She would likely bring her customers into whatever house they were staying at, when Master Benjamin was out about other business. She would order Tamar around just to prove that she was a mistress and not in need of the coin she would insist upon, and then that horrible, suffocating cloud would descend. The one that Tamar was just beginning to realize was missing from this place.

"I cannot." She pulled her knees closer to her chest and pressed her forehead against them. "I cannot go back under that cloud of oppression, it will undo me." She had finally tasted a sampling of freedom. Not of her person, not from her bonds, but her spirit—since Miriam shared her own and Mistress Abigail's history, she had begun to feel as though she might find a place here. Somehow. Some way.

But if she left it, even for a week, that inching in of peace would be destroyed. She would be alone with Dara again, at her mercy. No advocate, no other women who understood her even when she had told them nothing.

"You need not be alone." Zipporah took her other hand, laced their fingers together just as her mother had done. "Abba God will go with you."

"Abba." She whispered the word, but even she heard the scorn, the disbelief in her voice. She had not called her father by the Hebrew term, of course, but it meant the same. And her pater had not wanted her. Why should Jehovah? She shook her head, and her fingers tightened around theirs. "My father sold me."

There was nothing, surely, they could say to that. And indeed, for a long moment the silence crackled.

Then Mark said, "Tamar," in a voice smooth and quiet. "Mistress Abigail made sure all of us children studied the Greek philosophers. Aristotle spoke of the form—the *eidos*. I imagine you are familiar with the idea."

Every Greek child knew of Aristotle. But she failed to see what he had to do with God.

Mark shifted, settled to a seat on the floor. "The eidos is the ideal, correct? That heavenly thing that embodies what an object ought to be. The perfect table, that never breaks and is completely level. Whose surface never splinters. That which all earthly tables aspire to be. Yes?"

He spoke of *tables*? She tilted her head up just enough to see him beyond her knees.

He looked so intent, so...invested. "God is the eidos of a father. The perfect father, whose love never fails. Who never does wrong by his children. Our earthly fathers are but men. Some good, some bad, all sinners. They will all fail us at one point or another—yours, it seems, in a way that can never be forgotten. But Jehovah does not."

"I am nothing to God." She had not intended to speak, to give voice to the words that had burned so long within her. But there was no holding them back now. "How could I be? He does not hear me. He does not see me."

"He sees you. He loves you." Zipporah settled her other hand on Tamar's shoulder. "He loves you so much that he has used the evils of men, the trials you have suffered, to bring you here. Here, where you could finally find a family to love you too. Here, where you could learn how much he longs to welcome you into his embrace. Where you could learn that he offered up his own Son—for *you.*"

Why did everything go tight within her? Why did the pressure of that hand pull now, rather than weigh her down, why did it seem to urge her on, up, to a place she did not know? Why did she *want* to believe?

"I cannot." It was the truth, but it pierced to say it. "If I do, she..."

Miriam brushed a hand over Tamar's hair. "And if you do not? Is it any better?"

She let her eyes go unfocused. Dara may just be angry enough to kill her if she discovered Tamar believed in what she deemed a heretical religion. And if the master returned and found out—it did not bear thinking about. Death would be a relief, then.

But was it any worse than living each day like this, for the rest of her life? Having nothing but pain and fear to hold her, when peace waited just beyond her reach?

Her breath eased out in a soft gust. The hand on her chest now felt like a spreading warmth.

Miriam's arm slid around her shoulders. "Do you believe that God is above all gods? The living God, the sole creator of heaven and earth and all that is within them?"

To that she had to nod. She had long known the gods of her father were nothing but lifeless statues.

"Do you believe he sent his Son, Jesus, to this earth to serve as a perfect, eternal sacrifice for the sin of mankind?"

That required more thought. Before she came to this place, Jesus had been nothing but a story. One told with hatred and revulsion. But did not that very hatred always kindle the fear of evil inside her? But these believers of the one they called Christ, they were different. Pure, peaceful, and good, even in their imperfections.

She nodded again.

Miriam leaned close. "Do you believe he did this for *you*? That he not only died to pay for your sins, but he then rose from the grave so that you, Tamar, might triumph over the death that comes of sin as well?"

Such joyful longing filled her that she scarcely knew what to name it. "I do. I do believe."

Miriam's head rested against hers, and Zipporah's fingers squeezed blessedly hard. "Then welcome to the family of God," the younger whispered, her voice tight with restrained happiness.

Happiness—for *her.* At welcoming *her* to the family. Tears stung Tamar's eyes, but they were happy tears this time. Tears of blessed surprise.

"You will not go alone to Rome, my daughter," Miriam said. "You will go with the Lord, and he will make a way before you. He will protect you, and he will ease your fears. God is for you—none can stand against you."

A prayer. A blessing. And for the first time in her memory, Tamar could smile as she whispered, "Amen."

COLUMBA COOED IN HER EAR, SINGING HER A PSALM, IT SEEMED, ON this hot and hazy day. Zipporah hummed along with him and tossed another weed into the pile. Sweat trickled down her back, but after being unable to work while her head recovered, it felt lovely to dig her hands into the earth and know she accomplished something.

And it did not hurt that the villa had felt so peaceful yesterday and today, with Dara in Rome. A bit of guilt niggled at the thought—she turned it into a prayer for Tamar, for Mark, for Benjamin. And, when the niggle turned to a stab, for Dara too.

She rocked back on her heels and used her wrist to push aside a strand of hair that had come loose. That guilt was well deserved. She had prayed a lot *about* Dara in the past month. How often had she prayed *for* her?

"Do the weeds bring you such epiphany?"

She looked up, over, and smiled as Samuel swung his long legs over the garden wall and sat on its edge. "There is much truth to be found in green stems and dark earth."

"There is indeed." He grinned and rested his forearms on his knees. His hands, she noticed, were spotless, and he wore his tunic and toga instead of his work clothes. "I intended to head back out to the fields myself, but I was sidetracked by a rather nasty burn on young Mina's hand."

She sent him a knowing glance and bent back to her weeding. "Not to mention that the villa is rather peaceful today, and you are in no rush to leave it."

His chuckle for some reason made her aware of the dirt staining her garment, of the sweat no doubt making it stick. "I confess it, but only to you." Then he sighed, and his mirth seemed to leave him with his breath. "Benjamin seems finally to be aware that she is not forthright. It is a good step, I should think—yet when I saw the heartbreak in his eyes, it did not seem good. I know not what outcome could bring happiness to him."

A question she had asked herself too. What could he do? Divorce her, send her home? Jesus had not looked kindly upon such things, not unless vows had been broken. And now with the babe...

Zipporah shook her head and tossed another weed onto the stack. "I know not either. Part of me says if he could just be free of her, he would be the better for it. Yet that feels wrong of me."

"I know what you mean. Some part of me hopes she just goes away, that Ben can find his happiness elsewhere. Yet I feel base for those thoughts. And I wonder if he would, or if the pain of it all would be too great. If his only hope is in somehow winning her."

Possible, she supposed. But only through Christ. "I suppose some only find one love in life."

"I imagine so."

Yet the way he said it, as if he could think of no examples, made her hands still and her gaze seek him out again. "Your grandmother Ester certainly never sought another after her husband died."

"True." His eyes were at once thoughtful and expectant.

"And you have not pursued any other but Anna."

Hesitation filled his countenance—rare, in her company. "Zipporah..." He looked out to the hills, drew in a breath, and then met her gaze again. "Just because I have not up to now does not mean I have no intention of doing so."

Her chest constricted, though she could not pinpoint why. "I...I suppose you will. You are young yet. You will want companionship, and an heir."

"I want more than that. I want a wife I love with my whole heart, one who can love me so with hers."

For a moment, she could hardly tell what was weed and what was vegetable. "Of course. Forgive my surprise, it is just—you loved her all your life."

He breathed a laugh, though she kept her gaze on the plants rather than looking at him. "Not like that."

And now she felt silly. "Well of course not—you are older than she, and when she was a child...but you know what I mean."

"Yes, I know what you mean. But it is not how you must think. I never considered her for a wife, sparrow. Not until our fathers approached me and asked if I would marry her, to protect her."

She had wrapped her hands around a stalk but could not pull. Her gaze lifted, tangled with his. "It was not your idea? She said...or perhaps I assumed. But she loved you always."

Samuel nodded and ran his clean fingers through his shining hair. "So they said when they spoke with me, that she wanted to marry no one else." His eyes slid shut. "And yet too often I wondered why. Sometimes it seemed she barely tolerated those things I always thought defined me. That she loved me despite who I was, rather than for it."

"Samuel." She abandoned the weeds and went to sit beside him. "Why would you think that?"

He took her hand, not seeming to notice the rich soil caking it. "She resented it every time I was called away to attend someone. Or not resented it exactly, just would sigh and act so longsuffering. As if it required all her patience to allow me to do what I had always considered my calling."

His fingers flexed over hers. "I loved her. She loved me. Had she lived, we would have had a full, rich life together. We would have learned how to balance each other. But she died. I could not help her, I could not save our son. She died, and I was left wondering if she would have been happier with someone else. If she would have *lived* if another had been her husband."

"No." The reassurance came easily, without thought. "She was happy with you, Samuel. She never wanted anything in life but to be your wife, to carry your child." And yet how well Zipporah understood his question. How well she understood the pain of thinking you were not loved for who you were inside.

"She wanted to be my wife, to have my child, but that felt different than wanting *me*." He met her gaze again, his eyes soft now. "I spent years wondering. Wracked by guilt. It was a long journey out of that valley, but I have finally emerged on the other side. I am ready to move on, little sparrow. To build a life with someone."

She ought to be happy for him. She ought to smile and squeeze his hand and assure him she was glad for him. She ought to be thinking of him, not of how this would affect her. Not wondering if she would lose him as a friend, a brother when he set his sights on some beautiful young woman.

"What is it?" His other hand had come up, and only when he touched it to her cheek did she realize a tear had slipped from her eye.

And she could not wipe it away herself without smearing mud all over her face. She tried using her wrist, but he batted her hand away and did the job for her. Which was at once sweet and humiliating. She kept her eyes focused on the wall opposite them. "Forgive me. I am being selfish. I want you to be happy, Samuel, I do." And why would she have ever thought that her friendship would be enough to make him so? "I just...you are one of my very best friends. I suppose I fear how things will change when you begin spending your time seeking a woman's hand."

"You need not fear that." He released her fingers, but then his arm came around her and pulled her close. "You are one of my dearest friends too. I promise you, she will not take me away from you."

"She." Now Zipporah turned her head, the tears burning dry. "You already have someone in mind? And this is the first you mention it?"

He had the gall to smile. "I only just realized it myself a week ago."

"Oh, so while I was suffering from that fall from the wall, you were falling in love with someone?" Hearing her own words, she slapped a hand to her mouth. If she were trying to prove herself a petulant child, she was succeeding.

Samuel laughed and pulled her close again, kissed the side of her head.

Zipporah slumped against him. It should not hurt. She should focus on his joy. "Who is it?" Try as she might, she could not think of anyone he had spent much time with since he returned.

He sighed into her hair and then eased away. "I think that is a conversation for another day, little sparrow."

Given her behavior thus far, he was probably afraid she would run off and attack whoever it was. Not that she would, but she could certainly use some time to adjust to the idea of him finding another wife before she had to face said woman. She nodded. "Soon."

"When you are ready." He stood, giving her braid a playful tug that she ought not to have felt all the way in her heart. "I promise I will not declare myself without your knowledge."

Her eyes slid closed. He was too good, too considerate, too perfect a friend. He should not have to coddle *her* on matters of his own romance. And yet she could not make herself turn around and assure him he need not wait on her. She could not, it seemed, be that selfless just now.

She waited until his footsteps faded away and then fell back to her knees in the garden, determined to take her frustrations out on the weeds. Columba's cooing failed to soothe her now. The sun felt even more scorching. But the tightness in her chest kept her yanking at stalks, praying work would ease it.

It could not. She knew that. Work could never take the place of a friend who could make her laugh, a friend who had always known when to follow and when to give her time, when to hold her close and when to let her go. But that friend would soon focus all his attentions on another, and she would be left with her weeds. She would be alone. So alone. Sarah would be consumed with Urbanus and his girls, and then Samuel with this *she*. And though he had always had time for her when Anna was his wife, that was different. Then she had been his sister. What would she be now?

Nothing.

Columba's song changed, signaling her to an approaching figure well before she heard the familiar steps or looked up to see Sarah stepping over the wall. Zipporah offered her a nod but could not manage a smile.

Sarah sank down onto the very spot Samuel had occupied. "The children begged for an hour inside out of the sun. I thought I would see if I could convince you to come in as well. You could surely use a respite."

"I am fine."

"Are you?" Amusement soaked Sarah's voice as surely as perspiration soaked Zipporah's tunic. "You look hot and angry. And I thought you would be happy to have a bit of peace this week."

"I am." At her friend's snort, she tossed the last weed from that row into the pile and sighed. "I was. Until Samuel came to see me."

Sarah's brows went up. "*Samuel* put you in a foul mood? How on earth did he manage that? He is usually the one to pull you out of one."

"And that is the problem." Zipporah pushed herself to her feet and bent to heft the pile of uprooted weeds. "While he was gone, I got along well enough. But as soon as he returned I fell right back into depending on him, and now what am I to do?"

Sarah blinked with exaggerated deliberation. "Did I miss something?"

Tossing the stalks across the wall into the pile she had begun earlier, Zipporah sighed. "He is getting married."

"*What?*" At that, Sarah shot to her feet. "What do you mean? To whom? When?"

Seeing her friend's anger managed to cool her own. Zipporah motioned

Sarah back down and plunked down beside her. "I know not who, but he said he has fallen in love with someone. He will eventually approach her, and that will be that. No woman would possibly deny him, nor any father."

She could feel Sarah's gaze, steady and probing, on her profile. "And you are upset because...you will miss his company? Because you will feel alone?"

Zipporah blew out a breath and tried to rub some of the dirt off her hands.

Sarah bumped her shoulder into Zipporah's. "Or is it something more? Have your feelings for him—"

"No." She shot back to her feet and stomped to the next row. And wanted to tell herself that he was Anna's husband, that she should not even think such things...but he was not, anymore. He was Anna's widower. He had stripped Zipporah of that wall to hide behind. Yet it did nothing to change reality. "I have learned my lesson. No more yearning for men who think of me as a little sister."

Sarah's next snort sounded suspiciously of laughter. "And do you believe yourself when you say that?"

"Please, Sarah." She crouched down again and let her knees find rest on the warm earth. "If there is something for me to deny, let me deny it—he already loves another."

For a long moment, the only sound was of Columba chirping a warning to a crow that flew overhead. Then came the low whoosh of Sarah's sigh. "I feel so strongly that happiness awaits you. I just wish I could see in what direction it lay, but the Lord has not revealed that."

Of course he had not—because Zipporah's happiness waited impatiently in Paradise, and that was a glimpse of the future he would not burden her best friend with.

Zipporah dug her fingers into the earth and let it anchor her.

For the first time in months, Dara felt free. No husband looking over her shoulder, none of his friends waiting to catch her slipping, no mouse of a slave hovering behind. It was just Dara, the sunshine, and the throngs of Rome. How alive she felt as she maneuvered through the crowds!

With coin in her purse that she earned herself. And oh, how delightful it felt to let the visions flow again. To embrace who she was instead of hiding it behind sweet smiles and lowered lashes. She had not fully realized until she strode these streets with only a hired eunuch to attend her how stifling, how chafing life was by Benjamin's side.

She needed more. Stealing the clients of the street fortune tellers was easy, but it did not pay well. She may have earned enough to send a message to the master, but she could easily earn more. Enough to take herself into the markets without the watchful eyes of Abigail upon her, cautioning her against excess.

She wanted excess. After these months of pretending, she craved it. Required it. Turning to the guide and guard she had hired for the day, she lifted her brows. "You have lived here all your life?"

The slave, his eyes without a spark to tell he was alive, nodded.

"Then you surely know where the true seers live. To whom do the nobles go? The senators?"

A muscle in his jaw pulsed, and irritation snapped at Dara. She had only a few hours more while Benjamin was out. A few hours to accomplish what she must and then bask in it. By sunset, he would return from his visit to his friend, and if she were not safely ensconced in the Asinius house as she had sworn she would remain all the day...

The slave must have seen her building anger. He jerked his head to the left. "There is a woman named Caelia, a former slave. They say when her master died, she followed his spirit and unlocked the world beyond, and now she can see all."

The cloud descended, pictures flashed. Yes, that was where she must go. Caelia had the clients she needed—and gave them more than visions, it seemed. Dara felt the sneer form in the corners of her mouth but held it in check. She had no compunction against taking business from a harlot. "Lead me that direction."

The eunuch obeyed with a grunt and led her, surprisingly, back toward the Asinius house. They bypassed it, turned on the next street, and he motioned to a large building with a jewel-trader as the storefront. "She rents the rooms behind there."

"Very well." Dara would wait here then and watch for the harlot's customers to come out. Then it would be a simple matter of stopping them, amazing them by recounting whatever this Caelia said to them, and correcting it.

She waited twenty minutes, her impatience mounting with each passing second. At last, a tingle swept up her spine, and she saw someone emerge from the back of the building. "Finally." She took a step forward.

The eunuch's arm shot out, halting her. She opened her mouth to rebuke him, but his nod made her aware of the sudden bustle in the street, and of the horses clopping their way. Horses—a sure sign that whoever came was powerful.

Whispers reached her ears just as a vision filled her inner eyes. Emperor Nero. And much as she wanted to catch a glimpse of him with her physical eyes, the vision gave warning. She turned, lifted the cloth she had let fall to her shoulders, and covered her hair.

"Wise of you," the eunuch said, his voice quiet. "The young emperor is well known for his...appreciation of beautiful women, and I daresay he would be enamored with finding a young woman with hair as fair as his own. Stay hidden a moment longer. He seems to be paying a visit to Caelia."

Dread sank into her stomach, coupled with hope. "The emperor visits the seer?" Then it could have gone badly for her had she tried to undermine Caelia.

The eunuch snorted. "It is not her second sight that enthralls him, I suspect. The emperor is also well known for his frequenting of harlots."

Dara studied the wall of this other building until the slave said, "He has gone in. I suggest you return to your home now, Lady, before he comes out again."

Much as she wanted to argue, the risk was too great. With a sigh, she turned and cast one last look at the alley leading to Caelia's.

Her gaze snagged on a man who stood in the center of the alley, staring at her as if he had been waiting for her to turn. Her throat closed off, and she pulled her head covering tighter. Usually she did not fear men, but this one must have arrived with the emperor. That meant this one was dangerous.

She took a step away, but her feet seemed stuck in mire. His gaze held her trapped, and a corner of his mouth tilted up. He moved toward her.

Swallowing proved difficult. He was a young man, perhaps in his thirties, with hair of the darkest brown and eyes to match. It still felt odd to see so many clean-shaven jaws around her after spending her life surrounded by Jewish men who wore their beards proudly, to mark them clearly as not Roman.

She wanted to look away, but something within her cried out. Made her step forward instead of away. Her eyes narrowed as he drew nearer, near enough for her to see into his eyes.

His smile evened out. "I have been looking for you."

Her heart leapt within her, and it was all she could do to keep from falling to the ground at his feet—or launching herself into his arms. "Master!"

He chuckled and closed the last of the space between them, his hand finding hers. "Surprised to see me?"

With the emperor? Assuredly. But then, she had always known he was capable of anything, of finding power where by rights there should be none for him. She held his fingers tight and searched his eyes again. "I scarcely recognize you, Master." Different hair, lack of a beard...how could they make him look so much younger?

But then, she had long observed that he seemed to age in reverse.

He cast a glance over his shoulder. "I have an hour, if you have."

"Yes." Waving off the eunuch, she pulled her master down the street. "We are staying just a street over, and Benjamin will be gone several hours yet. There is no one there but Tamar." She regretted saying the name as soon as it left her lips.

But the master did not even seem to have heard that part. "How goes your task? Are you managing with the heretics?"

"They are people like any others." She shot him a grin. "Easily manipulated. Easily torn apart."

"Good." Pride swelled his voice as she hurried him along. "And your husband?"

"I have done all you instructed." She leaned closer, looked up at his smooth jaw. Desire knotted her belly. Much as she had always loved his beard, this new look was all the more attractive. Perhaps because he had made the change solely for her, so he could find her. In a whisper, she said, "I carry his child. It is safe for us, Master."

The eyes he turned on her were hot with that primordial fire. "I prayed it would be so. Then we need wait no longer, beloved. Today you become mine."

TAMAR TRIED TO CALL TO MIND ONE OF THE PSALMS SHE HAD HEARD the women at Tutelos singing. She hummed out the melody, though only a few of the words surfaced to her mind. Words like *praise the Lord* and *his glory.* Words that brought a smile to her lips.

The halls echoed with her footsteps, so very empty for a house so very large. She imagined that in years past slaves would have been bustling every which way, going about the business of their master. Today there was only her—even the cook was out in the markets to restock the store room. The fear wanted to sneak in. Tamar could feel it, hovering there just outside her spirit, trying to find a claw-hold.

She clung all the more tightly to the peace within. Trusting in Jesus would require a lifetime of practice, but she would not falter so soon. She would not slide so quickly back into the unworthy, incapable wretch. By the grace of God, she would not.

Flowers out in the back garden caught her eye as she walked by a window. Dara was unlikely to thank her for it, but she would pick some and put them in water in her and Master Benjamin's room. A few minutes of her time, but a gesture that meant something to her, even if it would mean nothing to the mistress. To Tamar, it was a sign that she obeyed the dictates of the Lord, to serve with a faithful heart.

And from what she could gather, the master and mistress could use something to sweeten their chamber. They had hardly spoken to each other since that night at the villa. She had been praying for them. It still felt strange to beseech Jehovah with the thought that he heard her, but she would learn. It would help to rejoin the congregation when they returned to the villa. At the thought of morning prayers, a smile worked its way from heart to lips. That would be a new experience, now that she believed. One she could hardly wait to partake in.

Flowers in hand, she hummed her way down the corridor that housed the family rooms. Master Benjamin and Mistress Dara had taken the one that, the master said, had once belonged to Master Titus. She had already straightened it that morning but would go through it again now, to see if there was anything else she could do to make it welcoming.

Laughter from within stopped her, but too late. She had already opened the door, had already stepped halfway inside before the sound penetrated her hum. When had the mistress returned? She had not seen or heard her, but then, the house was vast. Had Tamar known she was back, she would have knocked, would have—

The flowers fell from her hand. The bed was rumpled, and even now a man's naked back retreated from her view.

A back not so broad as Master Benjamin's, nor so tall.

Her gaze landed on the mistress, still in the bed with bare shoulders peeking from the sheet. "What have you done?"

She did not mean to say the words, and regret of them surged through her when Mistress Dara narrowed her eyes. Tamar ought to have fled immediately and prayed her entrance had not even been noted. She ought to have feigned ignorance that it was not Master Benjamin enjoying the pleasures his wife offered so freely.

She ought to have done anything other than stand there and let the outrage of it seep through her. A few days ago, escape would have been the only thought on her mind. Why then, today, did she stand rooted long enough to shake her head? Why, when the mistress glared at her with that silent but unmistakable promise of punishment, did she lift her chin?

Tamar spun, yanking the door shut behind her and actually relishing the noise of its slam—she, who had striven for silence for so many years, only hoping to go unnoticed. Wincing for the sake of the flowers she crushed under her foot, she strode down the hallway again, not sure where she intended to go until she had stormed into the back garden again.

"Tamar?"

She did not even jump at the voice. Perhaps because Mark's calm, even tones had grown so familiar. Or perhaps because the outrage still flowed too strongly through her. She turned to find him just emerging from the kitchen, his brows drawn.

"Are you well, Tamar? You look...angry." Which no doubt baffled him.

It baffled *her*. She had not dared to be angry in so very long. Why should she choose today to let it strike her, when punishment for it was so sure? Dara would not forgive her interruption, her discovery of what had surely been meant to be a secret. She would at the least devise a punishment worthy of the master. Perhaps even kill her.

A strange peace seeped through the anger. For once, death held no terror.

She drew in a long breath and shook her head. "It is Mistress Dara. She...I..." She pressed her lips together, though her nostrils flared in compensation. Giving up on words, she sank onto a warm stone bench.

Mark approached her with the same caution he always employed, other than those times when he must rush to her rescue. She slid to the end of the bench and indicated he should join her. Judging by the arch of his brows, he had not expected the invitation.

Another odd surge of peace. Did his presence not cow her because they were outdoors, or had something already begun to heal inside?

Mark sank slowly onto the bench beside her, as if expecting her to shoot to her feet and run away. "Has she done something?"

"Of course she has." A breath huffed its way out, and she shook her head. "She has sinned, and I will be punished for it. But for the first time in a decade, the thought does not strike fear into my heart." She angled a look up at him. The familiar, strong jaw, dark hair, gentle eyes. "Is it normal, when one comes to belief? To feel so much...braver? So soon?"

A soft smile touched his lips. "It is different for all. But we are supposed to change when the Spirit dwells inside us, yes. We are supposed to trust where before we feared. It is not always easy."

"I have feared for so long. Being free of it, or at least partially free of it...the whole world looks different."

Mark's smile brightened but then faded away. "If ever you need to talk about whatever caused the fear to begin with, I am here. Or my mother or Zipporah, of course, when we go home again. Or any of the others, really—but you need not hold it all inside any longer. We are your family."

Her family. Tears of gratitude stung her eyes. "Thank you—I have not had one in many years." She could tell from the look in his eyes that he wanted to ask what had happened to strip her of her blood family. And the fact that he did not, that he merely smiled again, was what made her open her mouth. "I was betrothed. Over a decade ago, when I first came of age. To a Jewish man, at my mother's insistence." Her eyes slid shut. "Then a month before the wedding was to take place, his brother attacked me."

"Tamar." His voice wept for her.

She opened her eyes again and stared at the wall at the edge of the garden. "They did not believe me when I said I cried out, they did not believe he would have done such a thing unless I enticed him. They said I was a shame to both families. And so my father sold me."

He shook his head as his eyes filled with sympathy. "I cannot fathom how a father could do such a thing."

She knotted her fingers together. "I have given up asking that question—it has no answer."

Mark leaned forward and braced his elbows on his knees. "I am so sorry you had to suffer that."

"That pain may have faded by now. But the slave-trader...he thought I would fetch a better price if I were skilled in certain areas, given that he could not sell me as a virgin." Heat crept up her neck, but she would not carry the shame of it any longer. She would *not*. It was not her sin then, and it certainly was not her sin now, with the Messiah's blood having covered it. "He sold me in Jerusalem to a religious leader. I was his concubine for ten years."

She looked up again, met Mark's eyes. And found, as she expected, only compassion. No condemnation. His gaze looked hopeful as he asked, "Was he kind to you?"

Her breath came out as a laugh with no amusement. "No. He did not want my affection, he wanted my mindless obedience. I was an animal to be trained. Please him, and I was granted enough food and water to survive. Displease him, and I was stripped of that, of my clothing, of my bed..." She shook her head. "He never raised a hand to me. I often thought bruises would be easier to suffer."

Mark looked to feel the pain she had once felt—and the anger she had just experienced minutes ago. "This is the man who gave you to Dara? He was...a friend of her father's?"

She had no idea if the story of friendship was true—perhaps it was, perhaps that was how he knew her. "He never spoke to me of his friends. But yes, he gave me to Dara."

Mark's brows were still knit. "Had you children you left behind?"

"No. I am barren." A curse—life surely would have been different had she a child to love. And yet a blessing now—she knew well the master would have sent her with Dara, even if she *did* have children. And how much worse would it be to leave them than to never have had them?

"I am sorry." He straightened again, and his hand moved toward her. An inch, no more, then he curled his fingers and rested them on his leg.

He wanted to comfort with a touch. She knew it, and she felt no fear. But she could not quite bring herself to reach out to *him*. That, it seemed, would take more than two days of faith to accomplish.

She turned her head so that she could see the house again. Was the man still inside, or had he slipped out? "Is Master Benjamin home too?"

"No, not yet. We ran into the cook in the markets, and I helped her home. Ben will be another half hour or so." He leaned back and caught her gaze again. "What has she done? Do you want to talk about it?"

For a moment, she held his gaze. And, trying to recall how Zipporah and Miriam handled such things, sent a silent inquiry toward heaven. But no strange peace came this time. Just a sorrowful pang and a tightening in her chest. She shook her head. "I cannot. I am sorry." She could not tell this kind man that her mistress had betrayed his master.

"You need not apologize—it is not yours to tell." He faced forward again and drew in a long breath. "Would you like some company, or do you need some time alone?"

"I...I would like you to stay." Her wonder at herself no doubt came through in her tone, but her companion merely smiled.

And for the first time in too long, she just sat in the presence of a man without fear. Without calculating a path of escape if he should try to hurt her. Without a desperate cry to the Lord that she was sure would go unheard.

For the first time in too long, she could listen to a man talk and find the strength to laugh at his jests, to add her own stories to his. They spoke of nothing important, just of childhood memories. And it felt like healing.

Perhaps that was why when, sometime later, Master Benjamin stepped into the garden with a frown, she still felt no fear.

He looked torn as he exited the house. Not so the mistress, who followed him out. The look on her face was pure smugness. They advanced upon the bench, stopping a few feet away.

Master Benjamin glanced back at Dara, then faced Tamar with that conflicted look again. "Tamar...Dara has told me something quite disturbing. I would hear your answer to it."

Behind him, Dara folded her arms over her chest. "She will deny it, but I caught her in the very act."

Dread sank into Tamar's stomach—yet it felt distant, as though it happened to someone else. "Of what am I accused?"

Dara lifted her chin. Benjamin sighed. "She says she caught you in a compromising position with a man."

Mark shot to his feet. "It is a lie, Ben! You must know that." His voice carried outrage, though Tamar did not look up to see if his face matched. She kept her gaze on her mistress and rose slowly.

Master Benjamin, in turn, kept his eyes fastened upon her. "Tamar?" He did not look inclined to believe it...yet he still asked. Because it was still Dara's word against hers, and Dara was his wife.

Tamar held her arms out by her side and let them fall again. "Does it matter what I say? She will punish me regardless."

"*Punish* you?" Feigned innocence on her face, Dara splayed a hand over her chest. "I merely want to protect you from the dangers of immorality. You are my responsibility, Tamar. I must see to your soul, not just your physical well-being. This behavior must stop."

She had a plan. She must, though Tamar could not think exactly what it was. But she was certain it was a plan Dara had thought up long ago. She had just been waiting for an excuse to execute it. Tamar straightened her shoulders but tilted her head forward in deference. Waited.

Dara gripped her husband's arm. "What was it you said Paul instructed? That if one cannot control oneself, one ought to marry?"

She felt the blow in her stomach, and it forced the breath out of her.

Dara's lips curled up into a smirk. "That is the only answer for her, since she needs the arms of a man so desperately."

Tamar's fingers knotted in her tunic. Of course that was her plan. Cast her own sins upon Tamar, punish her in the way she knew would hurt most, and guarantee she could never return to the master.

A blessing, that last part. But a husband—her stomach churned at the thought of yet another man who could do whatever he wanted to her, whenever he wanted it. Another man to call her a disappointment for her barrenness and to treat her as nothing more than a means to his own pleasure.

Mark shifted, eased forward, put himself in the same protective stance he had when that Colossian slave had been snarling at her. "Ben, you know this is a lie. You know she has never shown anything but fear toward men."

Dara laughed, incredulous and mocking. "How little you know her, Mark.

You no doubt do not realize she was her master's lover for years. That her father sold her because of her immoral behavior." Her eyes narrowed. "But if you are so keen to defend her, perhaps *you* should be the one to marry her."

Master Benjamin must have clenched his jaw, given the pulse of the muscle there. He half-turned toward his wife. "Dara. This is not your decision. I will not force a marriage on Mark just because—"

"Force it?" Another mirthless laugh. "Have you not seen the way he looks at her? I would not be surprised if he has already tasted of her favors."

"Dara—"

"Master." Mark had edged a bit more in front of her and even held out an arm, low but steady, as if to keep Dara from lunging at her. "Ben, we both know that accusation is false. Just as we all know this is your decision, not your wife's."

"Beloved." Dara pressed against him, trailed a finger up his arm. "You promised me when we first wed that Tamar would remain under my authority. This is best for her. I *will* see her married before the week is out."

Silence beat its wings for a moment. Then Mark lowered his arm and rolled back his shoulders. "So be it. Let it be to me. I would be honored to have Tamar as my wife."

No doubt Dara wanted Tamar to cry out, to break, to shatter. To back away from him in horror.

She would not give her that victory. Instead, she slid closer to him. Made herself reach, albeit with shaking hand, to touch her fingertips to his arm.

Master Benjamin's hand had formed a fist in the folds of his tunic. "We will discuss this."

"What is there to discuss? She is mine to give, and I give her to him. He can take her to his bed this very night." Evil delight flashed in Dara's green eyes as she said it.

Master Benjamin did not so much as flinch. "No. That is not how things are done in my family. Servants' marriages are celebrated with the brethren, not done in secret." He shrugged away from Dara's touch and took a step toward the door. "Mark, please come with me."

Mark nodded yet did not follow. "May I have a few minutes with Tamar first?"

He looked from Mark to her and nodded. "Of course. Dara." He held out his arm, but it looked to Tamar to be more order than invitation.

Looking pleased as the master had when he reduced her to begging for a sip of water, Dara spun on her heel.

Mark waited until they disappeared back into the house and then turned, slowly, to face her.

She pressed her lips against a quiver. A man ought to be joyous when he turned to his newly betrothed. Not look as if he had volunteered to take the punishment of another. And yet she knew why he had done it—because he wanted to protect her from some other husband who would not understand her fears.

He held out a hand. It took her a long moment to convince herself to rest her fingers against his palm. But when she looked up into his eyes, she found them as gentle and kind as ever. "Mark, I...I appreciate what you are trying to do. But please, do not sacrifice your future for me. I cannot be the wife you deserve."

His thumb swept over her knuckles, warm and soft. "You deserve to be loved and cherished. To be shown that not everyone is cruel and hateful."

He had already shown her that, he and his family and friends. She shook her head. "Not like this. Please. You are handsome and kind, thoughtful and strong. You ought to have a wife whose heart is whole, who can give you children and go happily into your arms. I am too broken."

He raised her hand, slowly and deliberately, and feathered a kiss over her fingers. "Perhaps someday the Lord will have healed you enough that you can come to me as a wife does her husband. But if not, I will be your brother and protector, Tamar. I will never hurt you as your betrothed's brother did. As your master did. I swear it to you."

Try as she might to blink them away, tears burned her eyes. Why would he resign himself to life with a wife he would not touch? Yet say he hoped someday he could? Did he desire her or not? "That is not marriage. It cannot be what you want."

"It is not about what I want." He sounded as though his throat were tight— the only indicator he gave of an internal struggle. "It is about what the Lord wills, and I am certain of this. He wants me to show you his love. I must trust that he will give me the strength to honor my promise and the heart I need to love you as you need to be loved."

The tears slipped out, and she did nothing to stop them. "Why would God ask you to sacrifice so for me?"

When he smiled, it loosed another spring of peace inside her. "Because I am willing. And because you are his precious daughter."

She did not deserve such love, either from God or his servant. Yet the fact that both would offer it broke through some walled up place inside. With the same deliberation Mark had shown in raising her hand to his lips, she eased closer to him and wrapped her arms around his waist.

No love filled her, no desire, no warmth. But she did not want to run away.

For today, it was enough.

thirty-three

SAMUEL TURNED AROUND AND SLAMMED DIRECTLY INTO HIS LITTLE sister's glare. He halted, given that she blocked the path down the corridor, but smiled. He had a feeling he knew what inspired that particular scowl, and he would enjoy having a bit of fun with it. "Good afternoon, Sarah. Did you need something?"

Her brows lifted much like their mother's often did. "I believe you have something to tell me."

"Have I?" He made a show of looking toward the ceiling in consideration. "No, I do not think so."

"Samuel." Now her eyes went wide. "Would you keep secrets from your favorite sister?"

A chuckle slipped out, and he leveled a finger at her nose. "You are allowed to call yourself such only because Ester is not here. And yes." He tapped his fingertip upon the tip of her nose, since it seemed always eager to butt in where it did not belong. "I have been keeping secrets from you all your life. You ought to be used to it by now." He sidestepped her, though he knew well she would not leave it at that.

Indeed, she spun and fell in behind him. "Zipporah said you have fallen in love with someone—that you intend to marry this someone. You cannot mean to keep *that* a secret!"

Yes, exactly what he suspected. He did not bother to restrain his smile. "I do, actually. At least until I have had a chance to ascertain whether she returns my affections."

"I can help you!" She leapt into his path again, her eyes far too bright. He could only pray it was because she took an interest for Zipporah's sake, and not just at the thought of helping make a match in general. "Tell me who it is, and I will talk with her. I can subtly sound her out."

Another laugh escaped, and he stepped around her again. "Am I an adolescent in need of a mutual friend to speak with a girl? Nay, sweet sister. I will handle it myself."

"Samuel." Her voice faded to serious. She reached out to still him this time, and her gaze was as sober as her voice. "We all thought you still in love with Anna."

"Hence why I thought it necessary to speak first with Zipporah." He leaned over and kissed the top of Sarah's head. "If you want to help, then pray for me, Sarah. Pray my lady loves me as I love her, or can learn to. If she turns me down, I know not what I will do."

There, the light in her eyes shifted to pure sisterly fierceness. Which proved it had been something different to begin with. "Well of course she will, whoever she is. No woman of sound mind would turn you down. You are perfect."

Perfect? No. A perfect man would not struggle so to forgive the mother who had abandoned him. A perfect man would not be so relieved that his sister by blood was gone for a few days, not when she took his brother with her.

A perfect man would not have to bite back a curse when he realized Zipporah had passed by the end of the corridor and he had watched her too closely. Sarah's gaze had followed, and now she wore a pleased, knowing half-smirk on her lips.

He growled and leveled that finger at her nose again. "Not a word, little one. I will be the one to tell her, and it will be when the Lord whispers that she is ready to hear it."

"I promise." And she giggled and launched herself into his arms, trying to squeeze the very life out of him. "I knew happiness awaited her. I knew there was someone who could love her for all she is."

He gave Sarah a long squeeze. "She has always thought of me as being Anna's. It will take time for me to convince her of my heart. I need you to—"

"Stay out of it. I will, I promise you. But I will pray." She stretched up onto her tiptoes to kiss his cheek, then stepped away, still grinning. "I will plan my wedding with a lighter heart, knowing she will not be lonely for long."

The Lord had poured blessing upon him when he put Samuel in this family. He grinned back at his sister. "Keeping your heart light has always been one of my goals. Now off with you. The children are no doubt wondering where you are."

He watched her scurry away with a shake of his head. He still expected to see a child when he looked at her, this youngest sibling planning her wedding. Now in a few short months she would become a mother to Urbanus's girls, and no doubt mother a few children of her own soon thereafter.

The thought brought an influx of unwelcome images. Anna, large with child, discomfort on her face. Anna, that last night of her life, when the pains were too great upon her. Anna, her eyes lifeless as the midwife cut her open, only to pull out a babe already blue.

He had taken his son from the woman's hands. He had tried every trick he knew to get the tiny boy to breathe, to stir. He had prayed every prayer of a desperate heart.

But the Lord had said no that night.

Samuel's feet headed toward the nearest exit, but the suffusion of sunshine on the portico did not cast away that inner chill. Much as he knew how useless it was to seek reasons in these things that were an inescapable part of life, he had tried. And though he thought himself well beyond that, the questions came again now. Covered with a new guilt as he anticipated joy on the horizon.

He wanted Zipporah as his wife. When he caught sight of her striding toward the gate beside Jacob, desire surged unlike anything he had felt for Anna. He loved her depths, he loved her spirit, he wanted nothing more than to hold her close and be the other half of her. But if his prayers had been answered that night, if Anna had lived, then this love would have been impossible. Would either have been sinful or never have bloomed.

Did that mean he was glad his wife had died? The question was a razor-sharp talon. For a long moment it festered as he watched Zipporah shrink into the distance. The sun scorched him down to his soul.

"Samuel?" Mother's voice broke through the heat, soothing as it always had. Her hand came to a rest on his arm. "Are you all right? You look troubled."

Samuel sighed and looked down into the face he had always looked up to. Who better to speak to of such things? "Did you ever feel guilty, Mother? For falling in love with Father after Jason was killed?"

A hint of a smile settled in the corners of her mouth. "You were too young to remember my torment, I suppose. I hope. But I hope you ask now because your heart is ready for spring again."

His gaze returned to Zipporah, though she and Jacob were far enough away now that had he not known it was her, there would be no telling. "It is. And yet I find myself thinking that had my prayers been answered and Anna lived..."

"My precious boy." She urged him forward, angling her steps toward the smattering of small houses between the villa and the vineyard. As usual, she carried a basket that proved she was about some task, not just out for a leisurely stroll. "Death is a part of life—one of the hardest parts, but we all face loss. We all feel as though part of ourselves dies with our loved ones. And we all must decide if we will keep our place among the living—which means moving on to other joys, other pains, other triumphs and losses—or if we give up. I will never forget the fear that my mother Ester would give up when she lost her husband and son."

She looked over and up at him, her eyes agleam. "I felt that fear again after Anna died, when I saw that hollow look in your eye. I feared for you for so long."

Such a familiar refrain. He shook his head. "It was as much guilt as grief. Had she her choice, I would not have been a physician. I always thought my gift was of healing—but the one time it could have blessed her instead of causing her frustration, I could do nothing. And now..." He reached up to wipe away the sweat inspired by the summer sun. "We have discussed this before. How you never loved Jason as much as he loved you, because of how your relationship began. Yet you had come to care for him, to respect him, certainly to honor him. When you fell in love with Titus in the wake of his death..."

"A love that could never have been had Jason lived." She nodded, sending her thick braid swaying. "When one looks at it a certain way, one would think I was glad, then, that my husband had been killed."

His sandals crossed from paved path to grass. He met her gaze again and knew, hearing the words from her mouth, that looking at it that way was not right. "Did you ever think of it that way? Feel guilty for it?"

"At times, yes. But the important thing to remember, Samuel, is that your life did not end that night. You are still here in the land of the living, and if you are living the full life the Lord wills for you, you will find joy again. It is not a betrayal of what came before. It is a praise to the Father for sending rain after the drought. For giving food after famine. It is a new gift. One I have been praying for four years Jehovah would prepare you for and send to you."

As they crested the knoll, a breeze swept up to meet them, cooling his skin and his spirit both. "I am ready for it."

She smiled, brighter than the noonday sun, and looped her free arm through his. "I am glad. We must soak up all the joy we can in life, whenever we can, to hold us through the dark places." Her smile dimmed, and she leaned into his arm. "We have enough of those always waiting."

"You think of Ben and Dara?"

"In part." She gave his arm a squeeze. "And of you, having to face your mother again. I wish I had been there, to stand between you. It is a foolish wish, I know—you are a grown man, you do not need me to protect you any longer. But..."

"But you are my mother, and it is your instinct." He reached to cover her arm with his other hand. "It is what makes you my mother, rather than her."

Mother drew in a long breath, looking at him rather than their path. "I have wanted to speak with you of this since you returned, but the time had not felt right. It must have been so difficult."

"More so than I expected." His gaze caught on a bird soaring overhead. Was it Columba, or some other nameless dove? "I thought I had forgiven. Forgotten. And I should, I know I should. I look at Dara and the darkness inside her, at the bitterness of her brother Jonathan, and I am so glad I was not raised by Martha. And yet..."

"And yet it still hurts to think that she would do what she did. I still cannot fathom how she made that choice. How she looked into your beautiful, innocent face and devised such a terrible plan."

He shook his head and slowed their steps—they drew near to the houses far too quickly. "I was her son. I remember little of that time, cannot call up an image of my father, but he must have left us with nothing. Otherwise she would have kept me near as the heir to it, as her security. We must have been in dire straits for a son to be burden rather than hope. In a few short years I could have started earning for her, working honestly, providing for her." The air he drew in tasted of the unknown. "Or perhaps she knew he had a brother in a better position. Perhaps she thought her only hope was to marry him, but thought he would not if I were around. He would have no obligation to give an heir to his brother if I were there."

"Whatever her reasoning, I am so grateful the Lord brought you to us." She came to a halt, and her face reflected the tight control of emotions churning within. "You were my hope in those early days. You were what kept me going when Jason and Cleopas were killed, when Ester lay unresponsive in her bed. You were a blessing beyond compare when Benjamin was born. You were the first to thaw Titus's heart when he struggled so against his Stoic roots. Much as I cannot fathom her motives, I also cannot fathom life without you."

The words soaked in, honey to his spirit. A truth he had known but must have forgotten to hold dear, especially in this past month when his mother was so torn between her children. When she had stood beside Benjamin.

But she would have stood beside Samuel too, had he been the one to bring home a wife like Dara. He knew that. She would always give the benefit of the doubt until she could not any longer.

"I cannot fathom life with another family." But his brows knit. "I am not certain I have forgiven her though. The wound must have festered all these years, and now...how can I be sure? I never want to see her again, I feel it as a pain whenever I look at Dara and see Martha in her eyes. How will I know when I have let the Lord's mercy cover it as I should? I am trying, but..."

Her countenance thoughtful, Mother led them onward again. "Perhaps it is different for everyone. But for me, when I have finally let go the hurts, my outlook changes. I stop taking pleasure in the thought of their meeting justice and paying the price for their wrongs and start praying they will find the saving knowledge of Jesus."

Conviction pierced. Since his words with Zipporah yesterday, he had been trying to pray for Dara's salvation. But Martha's? "I will try. Though I confess I cannot imagine those people ever embracing Christ."

His mother's smile was small but triumphant. "Everyone said the same of Saul of Tarsus. Now Paul is one of the greatest voices of the church."

To that, he had no rebuttal. Just the weight of knowledge that he still had far to go to want to welcome Martha or Dara into his family.

Benjamin's steps were slow as they traveled the familiar city road. He had walked this part of his current path many times through the years, but seldom with so heavy a heart. He could only pray it came solely from the state of his own house and not a premonition of how this meeting would go.

Urbanus's family was unlikely to listen to him anyway—why bother trying to talk to them for his sister's sake?

Because it gave him a reason to leave the house. Painful as that was to admit to himself.

Mark edged to his side from where he had followed a step behind. "Ben, you do not seem eager to go. Perhaps we ought to stay home."

A glance at his friend did not give a hint as to why he would suggest it. "You think they will not hear me out?"

Mark's face was tight. "I think...I think you ought not to leave your wife at home alone."

A sigh built in his chest. "Not so long ago you did not like me spending so much time with her—now you do not want me to leave her?"

Mark presented his profile and the ticking muscle in his jaw. "I do not know what happened yesterday before we returned, but it had Tamar upset and angry. She indicated it was because of Dara but said no more."

They were at odds—Benjamin had suspected it for some time. More than once he had entered their room to find the maidservant standing with her head down and shame in every line of her posture while Dara halted mid-scold. His wife would never tell him what the problem was, merely said she had taken care of it.

An ache bloomed to life behind his eyes. "About Tamar." They had not had a chance to discuss it last night. Dara would not leave his side, and it was not a conversation he wanted to have with his friend in any company, even hers. "You need not do this. If Dara is determined to find her a husband, she can find her another."

"No." Mark's voice was firm, and at peace. "I want to marry her."

The ache doubled. Whenever he had bothered giving any thought to what kind of girl Mark might wish to marry, it had not been one who could not meet anyone's gaze, who seemed as though she would be happiest by disappearing. "Do you love her?"

"I care for her. Deeply. I think...I think I could love her easily, if I let myself. But I do not intend to do that unless she wants me to. Ben, she—" He cut himself off with a huff, obviously debating what to say next. He seemed to choose his next words with great care. "She was mistreated by a few men in her life. It is why she is always so afraid of us all."

That did not ease the ache. It just added confusion. Abuse and fear...that did not fit well with Dara's insistence that Tamar was of loose morals. "But you would marry her."

"To protect her. But I promised her I would never hurt her as they did. That I will not..."

Benjamin widened his eyes. "You will not what? Touch her? Mark, have you any idea how difficult that will be?"

His sigh said he did. "God will have to grant me the strength, since he is the one who asked it of me."

Another ache, this one in his chest. God had not asked anything of Benjamin lately. Or if he had, it had gone unheard. "Why would God ask you to marry outside the brethren? It is not a wise idea—"

"He did not. She believes." Yet the moment he said it, he came to a halt and stopped Ben with a hand on his arm. The throng continued around them, heedless, though they moved to the side. "She does not want Dara to know yet. Please, say nothing to her."

"Why not? Dara would rejoice—"

"No, Ben. She would not." Exasperation combined with defeat, now, on his face. His shoulders slumped. "I should not have said anything. Please, I beg you. Do not tell your wife."

Was this, then, what life would be? Mark married to Tamar, Benjamin married to Dara, and because the women were at odds, the men would be too? Even if everyone else accepted Dara eventually, if she defeated whatever it was that made her mother come out in her and manipulate, Mark would still not like her, not if Tamar did not. Not if they married.

But what was he to say? He rubbed at the base of his neck, as if that could alleviate the strain. "All right. I will not tell her. But Mark, I..." He paused when his friend lifted his brows, when he realized that Mark expected some warning, some argument, some negativity. He bit back those words and found new ones. "I pray you will be happy together. That you will love each other as your parents do, and mine."

More, he wished him a marriage that did not involve looking at his wife one day and wondering if he had made a mistake.

Mark nodded, his expression softening. "Thank you. I pray the same. I know our path will not be easy, but I trust it is the one the Lord wants us on."

Surety Benjamin did not have anymore. He had been so certain at first, when she had consumed his thoughts as none other ever had. So sure she was the one he had waited for. How could he be so sure then, and so uncertain now? When he had not questioned at all until so recently?

He turned again toward the corner, trying to force his mind back to the task awaiting him. Urbanus's family, not his own. That was his focus for the day. Maybe, if he could accomplish something for his sister, he would feel better about his own problems.

At the corner, a commotion brought them to a halt. Benjamin strained upward to see over the heads of other pedestrians. When he caught sight of the unmistakable golden head sitting atop a horse, he lowered back down and exchanged a glance with Mark. "The emperor."

Mark's brows knit. "I heard he was in this part of the city yesterday too."

"I do not like it." But he mumbled that sentiment in Hebrew, lest anyone around them hear it and report it. Thus far their family had managed to stay out of the sights of Nero, unlike his predecessor. When Mother had refused the advances of Caesar, he had expelled all the Jews from the city. The conviction at Tutelos had long been that safety for the church lay in not attracting the attention of the emperor, whoever may claim that title.

He looked around and, when he spotted a familiar face from his school days, sidled through the crowd. "Vitus! Good day."

He and Vitus had never been close as boys, but friendly enough to greet each other as men. The Roman turned to him, seemed to take a moment to place him, and then smiled the warm but uninvolved smile of a near-stranger. "Benjamin. It has been years."

"Indeed." And they knew so little of each other's lives that he saw no point in wasting time pretending to ask about each other's families. He instead nodded toward the horses clopping proudly down the street. "Do you know what brings the emperor's retinue here so often?"

Vitus stepped close enough that his snort of a laugh would not find any other than Benjamin and Mark on the crowded street. "The charms of a prostitute who claims she is also a seer, from what I am told."

Unease punched him in the chest, though he could not think why. "In this section of Rome?"

"The rabble invades every part of our lives, do they not?" Vitus sneered and waved a hand in the direction the horses were headed. "This woman was apparently a slave to the Asinius house before the consul fell over in a drunken stupor and never rose again. She found lodging nearby after his death."

Benjamin sucked in a breath. That would explain the unease—it had been the Spirit warning him. And realizing it sent grateful warmth through him in the wake of the terrifying news. It must be Caelia. She was the only one who had not run away in Caius's last months.

Vitus looked at him strangely for a moment, then understanding lit his eyes. "I had forgotten—you have ties to the Asinius house. Not to Caius though, was it?"

"His son, Titus, married my mother when I was but a babe. He raised me."

"Ah, yes, I remember now. But they never spoke after the son converted to one of those strange religions and the father's drunkenness grew worse than ever." To Vitus, it was obviously nothing more than gossip.

Not so to Benjamin, who had heard often enough the stories of how acutely Caelia hated his mother—enough to plot with Caius to have her sent to the arenas when she heard Father planned to marry her. And the thought of that woman sharing a bed with and filling the ears of the emperor...who knew what poison she might speak against them?

But it had been a long time ago. Perhaps he ought not to assume she still wanted to destroy them.

The retinue had passed, and Benjamin had no desire to let this acquaintance see his unease. He pasted on a bright smile and nodded his thanks. "Ancient history, though I am surprised the emperor would dally with a woman so much his elder. She is my mother's age."

Vitus laughed. "She must be particularly skilled. And is now quite popular, I understand, since Caesar began visiting her. Perhaps I will try to see her myself someday, her age notwithstanding."

It was a chore to manage the derisive laugh when his stomach had gone so sour. He half-turned away. "I will leave that one up to you. It was good to see you again, Vitus. I hope all is well for you and your family."

"Quite. And I hope the same of yours. Good day, Benjamin."

He turned the direction opposite that which the royal group had gone and motioned Mark to fall in beside him again. "I do not like it."

"Neither do I. When the group passed, I had the strongest sensation of warning—we must pray, Benjamin."

"Indeed. After I speak to Urbanus's family I will write a note to send to the villa too. I know not if that woman still has hatred in her heart for us all, but better to pray if she does not than not to if she does."

"Agreed." Yet rather than worry, contentment blanketed Mark's face. He even smiled. "It is good to see that light in your eyes again, my friend. The one that goes beyond the day's troubles."

And it was good to hear that whisper in his spirit again, even if it spoke warning rather than peace. "I may have been distracted, Mark, but I did not lose faith."

"I know. But in the heat of battle, a moment's distraction can be one's undoing. Your family has taught us that well."

He wanted to argue that they were not in battle, that *his* distraction would have no such dire consequences...but the words stilled on his tongue.

They were always at war. He knew that. He could only pray now that the Lord would show him how to heal the wounds most recently inflicted and help his wife to fit into the fold.

Thirty-four

DARA WATCHED THE MASTER PULL HIS TUNIC BACK ON AND REACH for the toga she never imagined him deigning to wear. The muscles across his back rippled. Another flood of desire swept over her.

Then nausea followed on its heels, and she had to roll off the straw mattress in search of a chamber pot to retch in.

What are you doing? The voice battered at her thoughts like fists on a door. *He is not your husband. Adulteress!*

The same voice that had tried to steer her away from seducing Benjamin. The same stupid, childish voice that always tried to keep her from doing the master's will. But she would silence it, as she always did.

She retched again, gagged.

The master's hand smoothed down her hair and trailed over her back. "Does the babe make you sick often?" Compassion saturated his voice.

"No." Other than some mild upset, she had not yet experienced this kind of sickness. "Or it had not, yet. I must be reaching that point." The women at the villa had already filled her to overflowing with stories of what to expect. When to expect it. The joy that would greet her at the end of the pain.

Joy—joy was here, now, in the master's arms. Joy would be *his* child, someday. This one was just a means to their goal. When she went back to Israel with the master, she would leave this quarter-Roman, half-Christian whelp with whomever remained of the Visibullis-Asinius family. *They* would want it. They could have it.

He lifted her and helped her with her stola, his every move slow and loving. And against this backdrop of an abandoned servant's room in a corridor no one was likely to come to in the Asinius house, he looked like a king. Better than the emperor himself.

She wrapped her arms around him and pressed her cheek to his chest. "I know not if he will leave again tomorrow. How am I to get word to you?"

"Do not attempt it—it is too great a risk. I will watch the house." His fingers trailed through her hair as he had always loved to do. "How long are you in Rome?"

"He said a week or so." But surely he would spend another day away before they returned to the villa. She could find a way to force him to it if she must.

"You must not dread your return." He trailed his lips down the side of her face. "You still have much work to do there."

"But Master, why did you come if you did not mean to take me home?"

He drew back, his eyes sharp as her dagger. "Do you tire so quickly of our cause, Dara?"

"No! No. I am dedicated, Master." She gripped his toga. So much like Benjamin's...yet with a different border. Did it mean something, or was it merely decoration? Either way, the wool was not nearly so fine as what she could weave. Why had he not used some of the cloth she had made for him? In Israel, he had never worn anything her hands had not created. And she knew well she had left him with enough to make a toga.

His shoulders relaxed. "I know you are. And that is why I came, to encourage you and help you. That is why I took on this new name—for you, and so that we can defeat the Christians together. I will find you at Tutelos, my love. I will get inside if I can, and if I cannot, then I will meet you outside the walls. You will know where." His lips found hers. "You will know when. Be attentive."

She could only nod, kiss him again, and then stand aside when he made for the door. Much as she wanted to detain him, he had said when he slipped over the back garden wall that he had only an hour. She dared not try to interfere with whatever other tasks awaited him.

He slipped out silently, unseen. Dara trailed him down the closed-up corridor and watched him slink his way through the garden and back over the wall. She stood a moment, watching where he had been, but the sun was too hot. She soon turned back toward the cool of her chamber.

And came to a halt when she found Tamar standing outside the room, regarding her steadily.

Had she seen the master leaving? She must not have, or she would have been shaking in fear, her eyes on the floor. A smile touched Dara's lips. He had not once asked about her, about how the mouse fared at Dara's side. Still, she wished Benjamin had let her send the woman to Mark's bed last night. The sooner she was his wife, or someone's wife, the better Dara would feel.

And the more miserable Tamar. What a happy turn.

Her smile felt like a smirk as she glided past the slave. "Daydreaming of being in Mark's arms?"

Tamar followed her through the door. "You mean it for a curse—Jehovah will turn it to a blessing."

With a scornful laugh, Dara spun to face the mouse...who did not look like a mouse today. What had gotten in to her? "Jehovah cares nothing for you. You are naught but a dog come to beg crumbs from his table, and he will kick you away as the pest you are if you dare to beseech him. He has no use for a castoff whore."

Her chin did not quaver, her shoulders did not hunch. Tamar merely walked over to the pitcher, poured its water into a basin, and added a few drops of Dara's favorite perfume. "An odd choice of name to throw at me, Mistress, when you are the one who smells of another man." She added a wash rag to the water. "I suggest you wash before your husband returns."

She would have ordered Tamar to ready the water—but the fact that she did it on her own, and had the gall to command her to use it, made Dara want to dump it onto the floor instead and make her clean it up.

Had she the time for such indulgence, she might. As it was, she had no idea how much longer Benjamin would be gone and did indeed need to wash away all the evidence of her time with the master. Chin high, she strode forward and grabbed the rag from the water, rang it out. Sat. And snapped, "Do not judge me. You cannot possibly understand my actions."

"That is the truest thing you have ever said to me." Tamar moved behind her and gathered the mass of her curls. Her reflection in the bronze mirror looked sorrowful. "I cannot understand why you would do this to your husband. He loves you."

The water was warm. How had Tamar known she would need it? Had she seen her meet the master? Or just guessed, when she disappeared, where she had gone? Dara wiped it over her face, down her neck, and over her chest. Places where the master's mouth had caressed her so recently. "He loves only the image I showed him. And if he is fool enough to believe it real, that is his own fault."

Tamar's reflection shook its head. "He is a good man. You will break his heart."

"He is the enemy." She spun on her stool so she could glare up into the familiar face that looked so very changed. "We have been here a month, you have surely heard enough to know why the master sent us here. These people are heretics. They take the Holy Scriptures and twist them, defile them, try to rewrite them to say that some nobody from Nazareth fulfilled prophecy. That he rose from the dead, as if such a thing were even possible. They are the enemy of Judaism. It is my duty to try to stop them."

Tamar reached slowly for the brush. "I am only half-Jew, as you and your master are always so quick to point out. But perhaps you ought to take a lesson from my Greek heritage. When you try to silence a teacher, as the Athenians did Socrates, all you do is make the teaching spread like wildfire."

"*My* master? He is your master too." She turned back to the mirror so Tamar could get to work on her hair.

"No." The word rang soft and sure. Too soft, too sure. "He gave me to you. You married Benjamin. *He* is my master. And by wedding me to Mark, you are effectively binding me to his house forever, even if you leave it. You know that very well. We both know it is part of your plan to be rid of me, one way or another, so you can have your master to yourself." She stroked her fingers through Dara's curls, gently despite the defiance in her stance. "I pray he will treat you better than he treated me."

As if she needed such a prayer. "I am his chosen bride. He loves me. You were but a convenient harlot, a tool with one purpose."

For a long moment, there was no sound. Then came a quiet, "I know what I was. I know what I am. I know who I serve." Saying no more, Tamar reached for a ribbon. In but a few minutes, she secured the style she had been unable to achieve a month ago. And without another word, she slipped from the room.

And left Dara to fume. Never would she have thought that weak, fearful Tamar would speak to her in such a way. She would find some way to punish her for her insolence. She would...she would...she smiled. She already had the best punishment imaginable in the works. A few more days, and the mouse would marry the slave. She had seen Mark watching her—perhaps he had not made any move before yesterday, but when she was his wife, he would do as any man would. He would take her to his bed with pent-up passion and little thought to her feelings on it. He would take, he would demand.

It would wipe the defiance from Tamar's face in minutes. She would be a mouse huddled in a corner again, as she was meant to be.

It would be enough. Dara freshened her washcloth and pulled up her stola, running the warm cloth over her legs.

If only you could wash away the sin as easily.

She jerked up at the voice, spun on the stool, but no one was there. Yet she had the distinct feeling, the gooseflesh-raising certainty that were she not bound by human eyes, she *would* see someone. Someone that would no doubt have the look of the glowing-eyed Zipporah from her vision.

A shudder overtook her. Demons. Servants of this Jesus that would undo all their careful work, if they could. "Get away from me," she whispered into the empty space. "You have no authority over me."

For a moment, her vision seemed to clear, to open, to expand. For a moment, she caught a glimpse of a man that would tower over men, one clad in armor that put the Romans' to shame, with a sword pointed directly at her chest.

Despite herself, she pushed away, until the dressing table bit her back. Had she seen him before? No. Of course not. And yet, breath heaving, she had the impression that he had stood before her just so on other occasions.

The man vanished, fading back into nothingness. But his voice echoed in her ears again. *She will yet be ours.*

"Never!" Her voice sounded strange to herself, garbled and low.

No response came, but it was a long moment before she could make herself relax. Her hands shook as she stood. Her stomach felt ready to roll again. Needing solace, she crossed to the loom she had insisted on bringing to the city with her. Her fingers took up the shuttlecock, freeing her mind.

But the visions did not come. None that mattered, anyway. She could see strangers on the streets of Rome, but those she *needed* to see were dark to her. She had no glimpse of Tamar or Mark or Benjamin or Zipporah. Of the rest of Tutelos. She could not see the master in his new role, nor herself interacting with any of them.

"Please." Her fingers stilling, she shut her eyes and cried out to Jehovah. "Please, do not cut off my sight. It is all I have. I cannot do your work without it."

There, finally, a flicker that showed promise. It was the villa, stretching out into the rolling hills. Vineyards and farm fields, servants' houses and outbuild-ings. A tree growing close to the wall, its branches stretching low and thick over it, into the freedom on the other side. And there the master waited, a blanket in his arms ready to be spread out.

She would find him there. She knew not when, yet, but she would find him.

When the door opened and Benjamin walked in, she jumped. And covered it with a smile. "My love. You are back earlier than I expected."

He scarcely glanced her way. Which made her realize that he had not touched her since she insulted his family at the villa. No matter how she hung on him in the evenings, he would keep his focus on whatever scroll he had in his hands and would read until the exhaustion of carrying his whelp caught up with her and she fell asleep.

One part of her was glad. Another fearful. How would she control him, if not through the distraction of pleasure?

"We are cutting our visit to the city short," he said even as he moved to his trunk in the corner. An old, battered thing that had obviously seen much of the world. "Tomorrow we head back to Tutelos."

"So soon?" They had been here only four days. She had hoped for at least one more chance to see the master before they left.

Benjamin turned, slowly and with deliberation. His gaze, when it tangled with hers, was fierce. "Will you argue with me? Or just devise some means of manipulating me into staying longer?"

The master would find her at the villa. Perhaps not in the next couple days, but surely soon. He would crave her touch as much as she craved his. For her husband, she put on a meek smile. "Of course not. Whenever you are ready, I am ready. I merely wondered if there was a reason for your change of plans."

"Several of them." He turned back to his trunk and dug around inside it. "The best one being that Urbanus's parents are willing to see him, though I do not know how long their good favor will last. I must speak with him and encourage him to act quickly."

"Oh, how pleased Sarah will be!" She brightened her smile. Pretended to care. And called to mind again the image of the tree stretching over the wall to the master.

Zipporah could hardly believe the words rattling around in her head, even with the evidence before her. There, beside Dinah in the kitchen, they stood. Mark and Tamar, their hands clasped together. Proclaiming to their parents and friends that they intended to wed within a week's time.

It was the right thing. She could feel it in her bones, in her spirit. Their hearts had aligned, somehow, and they would complement each other. They would find happiness out of sheer determination to be what the other needed.

And the joining of their hands was all the proof Zipporah needed of that. A week ago, before she turned her heart over to the Lord, Tamar would have shied from that touch in terror. Today she clung to Mark as if he were her lifeline on an uncertain sea.

"It must be so soon," Mark was saying to their ima. "Dara is determined. Had she her way, it would be done already. Ben insisted we wait until we could be with our families."

Ima frowned at the mention of the new mistress, but a smile eclipsed it in the next moment. "Well, whatever her reasons, we are so happy to welcome you to the family, Tamar."

Zipporah smiled too, nodding along with her father and Dinah and Mistress Abigail. Though the smile nearly faltered when Samuel's hand came to a rest on her back. She had been trying to ignore his presence at her side—or rather, the unwelcome way her pulse accelerated at it—but it was impossible when he touched her.

Though she knew not why she had to react so. He had put his hand on her back innumerable times over the years. Innumerable times since his return home even. It had never affected her so before.

But then, before she had never known he intended to marry another soon. When he was betrothed to Anna it was different—it meant he was to be her brother, so of course he would treat her as warmly as Mark did. But now? Whomever he had set his heart on, she would no doubt not care for him being so friendly with another girl, even one whom no one would ever consider a threat to his heart.

She should enjoy the familiarity while it lasted. In a few months' time, she would probably rarely speak to him. He would be busy with whatever pretty bride he had selected.

It should not hurt so much.

Dinah drew Tamar into an embrace. "Forgive an old woman her happy tears," she said as she held her close. "Andrew is like a son to me, Mark like a grandson. I am so happy to see him wed. To welcome the next generation."

Tamar's smile wobbled, and the blood drained from her face. "I should—you should all know now, so you are not too disappointed." She looked at Mark, as if for added strength. "Mark already knows. I am barren. I was...I was my master's concubine for ten years, and I never..."

Oh. Zipporah leaned into Samuel's side, her own heart pierced as that knowledge settled in between the cracks in her sight. That was part of the pain she had seen in Tamar's spirit. Not just the childlessness, but the relationship with her master. He must have been cruel. Those were the marks on her spirit.

Wounds already healing. She focused on where they had been, but in place of the mottled, angry welts, they looked more like long-faded scars from childhood. The Lord was working quickly in her. No doubt because she had so little pride to get in his way. Hers was a spirit ready to soak him in, so desperate had she been for his healing touch.

Dinah touched Tamar's face with a capable, weathered hand. "I know that pain well, my child. But the Lord fills our empty arms with family, even if not of our own flesh. He gives us husbands to love us." She transferred her smile from Mark to Mistress Abigail. "Daughters and sons to help nurture into adulthood. And sometimes an unexpected miracle of birth. Not for me, but you are young yet. Never discount what the Lord may do."

How brightly the hope and faith burned in Tamar's spirit, where only fear had been before. She nodded, her eyes wide as she soaked in the words. "I know he will care for me. He has already proven it so many times since bringing me here."

Ima stepped forward and wrapped her arms around both Mark and Tamar, Abba following to clap a hand to their shoulders.

For a moment, she could have mistaken Tamar for Anna. So very pretty, with her glossy dark hair swaying against her perfect face. Her ima would finally have a beautiful daughter again, one that looked more like her than Zipporah did.

She edged back but could not move more than an inch. Samuel's arm encircled her more securely, and the way he squeezed her forced her gaze up and into his green-gold eyes. Eyes that, as always, looked at her with far too much insight.

"Are you all right?" He asked the question quietly, so the others in the kitchen would not hear.

She summoned her smile back up. "Yes. I am proud of them. I think they will have a strong, happy marriage. And Tamar will fit well in our family."

"Yes, she will." He inclined his head toward hers. "But do not think I cannot guess where that led your thoughts, little sparrow."

She sighed and elbowed him in the side. "Must you know me so well?"

His chuckle warmed her from toes to ears. "Yes, I must."

Her abba looked up and over at them and grinned at Samuel. No doubt thinking their laughter was in joy for Mark. And she *was* so very happy that he had found the Lord's will for him in a wife. It may not be like they had expected, or even as they hoped, but it was good and right. Love, she knew in her soul, would come quickly for them.

Samuel grinned right back at her father and moved his hand up her back to grip her shoulder. "Another wedding. Tutelos seems to be overflowing with them these days."

"Indeed it is." Mistress Abigail pressed a hand to her head, but her eyes were alight with contentment. "I can scarcely keep up with it all."

"Ha! That will be the day."

Abigail hummed a laugh at her son's observation and then turned at the sound of footsteps. Benjamin stepped into the kitchen, his gaze going straight to Mark and Tamar. Apparently seeing their smiles put him at ease. His shoulders relaxed, and he slid into the row of them at the back of the room, on the other side of his mother.

Mistress Abigail's smile was not so bright as she turned to her firstborn. "Where is Dara?"

"Resting. I went to speak to Urbanus. He seemed wary but sounds as though he is willing to go talk to his family in a few days' time."

"That is good. It was thoughtful of you to visit them, Benjamin."

He sighed instead of smiling. "That is not all that brought me home early. Caelia is still in the city. She has apparently become a harlot and claims to be a seer—Nero has been visiting her."

Samuel's fingers went tight on her shoulder.

Abigail sucked in a breath. "We must find Titus. Come."

They slipped out amid the continued laughter from those surrounding Mark and Tamar. Zipporah looked up at Samuel and saw his jaw had gone tight. "Caelia?"

He shook his head. "An evil woman. She was a slave in the Asinius house. Father bought her, but when he left for Jerusalem, his father took her. She hated Mother, blamed her as being the one who changed Father. It is she who gave Caius the idea to have Mother sent to the arenas." He shook his head again, more slowly. "I do not remember everything from those days, but I remember the dark light in her eyes. Much like..."

Phillip must have slipped into the kitchen when his mistress left. His face grim, the eunuch stepped into the empty space at Samuel's side. "Like an aunt I had in Germanica. And like Dara. I can guess at what you would see inside her, Zipporah."

And such a woman had captured the emperor's attention? Zipporah pressed a little closer to Samuel's side. "Yet another something for which we must pray."

"Indeed."

"On the first of the week then." Ima's pronouncement stole Zipporah's attention, given that she had spoken it loudly and had turned to include their group huddled at the back of the room. "That gives us three days to sew you a new garment and prepare a small feast."

Color suffused Tamar's cheeks again. "Oh, you need not go to any bother for me."

"Of course we must." Zipporah stepped forward, wishing she did not feel the lack as a gust of icy wind when Samuel's hand slid off her shoulder. She advanced until she had joined her family and could reach out to grip Tamar's other hand. "It is our pleasure."

Dinah spun away. "I had better get to planning."

"As must we." Ima led Tamar a few steps away from Mark and Abba, motioning Zipporah to come with them. "Come, girls. We have wedding garments to sew."

Tamar smiled as they left the menfolk behind and exited into the hallway. "I cannot tell you how much it means that you welcome me so warmly. I know this is not how you imagined your son entering into marriage."

"The Lord always outdoes my imaginings." Her mother led them down the servants' hall and into the room she had always shared with Abba. "I believe I still have some linen stored away. It will be perfect."

Zipporah sank down onto a cushion. "I will help as much as I can, but you know my stitches never meet your approval, Ima."

Her mother sent her a teasing smile. "You need more practice, that is all."

Tamar found a seat on an unadorned wooden chair and clasped her hands in her lap. "I need your prayer. I...I have come far in the short time since you prayed with me about giving my life over to Jesus, but I have far yet to go. I still bear the effects of an attack when I was younger and the pain my master added to it. Mark understands my fears and swore he would not touch me until I was ready." She squeezed her eyes shut. "He is too good. I want to be a wife to him, the kind God intended. I want to give the Lord a chance to provide the miracle of a child to us. But I still feel nothing but repulsion when I think of it. He deserves better than that. He will not accept an offer I do not want to make."

"Oh, Tamar." Ima abandoned her search and sat on the second chair, wrapped an arm around Tamar's shoulders, and pulled her close. "Of course we will pray. You must be patient with yourself. Give yourself time to heal."

Zipporah scooted over to them and covered Tamar's clasped hands. "We will pray without ceasing. And though I cannot know when full healing will come, I can see such progress within you already, my sister. Your faith is bright and innocent. God will deliver you from these chains."

Her ima blinked against a sheen of moisture in her eyes. "Just trust in his timing. Sometimes he works more slowly than we would like, sometimes more quickly than we would dare to hope. But always in a way that will perfectly achieve his purposes."

Tamar's eyes slid shut. She rested her head on Ima's shoulder like any daughter would and gripped Zipporah's hand as her sister seldom had. "I can scarcely reckon why Jehovah has blessed me so, to give me the family I always craved. But I am so grateful."

They sat like that for a few minutes more. When they stirred, it was to return to the task of sorting through cloth, drawing it out, measuring it against Tamar, who stood up and posed like a statue.

Zipporah smiled and, at the knock on the door, turned to open it. Mistress Abigail entered. Her eyes still looked strained, and Zipporah wanted to ask her what the master had said about that Caelia woman. But now was not the time.

The mistress touched a hand to Zipporah's cheek, tucked that always-falling curl behind Zipporah's ear. And then smiled and turned to Tamar. "I was going to rearrange the rooms so that you and Mark might have your own. He said you may wish to stay with Zipporah for a while yet, until you have had the chance to adjust. It is a sudden arrangement, after all. We all understand this."

Tamar's spirit fluttered like a candle in the wind—then grew all the brighter with renewed resolve.

Yes, the Lord would heal her more quickly than one might expect.

"He is so very considerate. But I wish to stay with my husband."

Mistress Abigail nodded. "Joseph has greeted the news of his roommate's marriage with a request for Media's hand as well. If you heard any squealing a moment ago, that was her agreeing. Given that Eve has left us, they can move into Media's room, and you into Mark's."

Zipporah would have her space to herself. Funny how it made her feel lonely all over again, when she had treasured the solitude for so long.

WEDDINGS FOR SLAVES. DARA KEPT HER EXPRESSION SWEET BUT also kept to the edge of the room. She could hardly believe that the entire villa came to a halt for this just as they had for Jason's wedding a few weeks ago. It was not nearly so grand, and no one from outside Tutelos had come, but still. Tamar and the other slave girl had been fussed over and beautified, and now they both stood by their grooms with brilliant smiles.

She had not thought the mouse such a good liar. But she looked happy—an impossibility. Dara knew well how she hated the attention of men, and her smile would turn to whimper that night.

Tamping down the pleasure at that lest it show on her face, Dara eased her way around the perimeter of the room. She needed to get away from all these merry-makers. She would go outside. Try to find the tree she had seen in her vision.

That would require getting around Benjamin, who stood near the exit. But he was beside Urbanus and looked to be in deep conversation, so perhaps that would suffice to distract him. As she neared, she heard him chuckle.

"Of course I am glad, but I would have been gladder had you gone two days ago."

Urbanus's smile was muted. "I thought it wise to fast and pray first. Then we did not want to miss the wedding. But hopefully they will not turn us away, given that your sister and parents will go with me."

"Well we will be in prayer for you here, rest assured."

Pray—that was all any of these people ever wanted to do. She slipped through the door with a shake of her head. What did they think to accomplish by constantly crying out to a God that was surely too infuriated with them to hear them? Nothing. They wasted their time and no doubt angered Jehovah more with each passing day.

Which suited her fine. The sooner he smote them from the earth, the sooner she could go home with the master.

But not with Tamar. She smiled again. She could stay here with Mark and rot when her world fell in on her. Perhaps even be killed when Tutelos was torn apart. What a shame that would be.

The sun was hot again today, and the outdoors was still. All the field workers had been given the afternoon off to celebrate the two marriages, so there were none to question her as she meandered, for only the second time, beyond the villa's immediate circle. Other than when Benjamin had shown her all that was his, she had stayed near the main house. There was nothing for her in the fields or vineyards or grove.

Or there had not been, before. Now she headed for the wall in the direction that seemed to promise its nearest point. She had heard them all mention that Zipporah and her group met to pray at an ilex tree on the edge of the property, and this was the direction from which they always seemed to come. A few minutes of walking, and her pulse hammered. There, that was the tree. The tree from her vision. And as she drew near it, her heart quickened still more, and the vision filled her eyes again.

He was here.

With a glance over her shoulder to be sure no one had followed, she took off at a run for the tree. A hop onto the low-hanging branch that stretched toward the wall, a quick scurry onto it and another jump down.

Into the master's arms. He caught her with a laugh, spun her around, and then his mouth found hers. "Things look quiet within the villa today."

"They are all at...a wedding." She would not ruin the day with mention of whose. She slid her hands up his chest, onto his shoulders, and pushed at the heavy toga. "They will not miss me for a good while."

"Good." With a tug, he untied the sash around her waist. "I can come again tomorrow, but then it will be several weeks. I am needed in Rome."

Had he not kissed her again, she may have asked what tasks could possibly keep him in the city so long. But what did it matter? Today he was here, tomorrow he would be back, and if then she must suffer his absence again, she had better soak in his presence while she could.

Darkness had fallen. Another maid had offered to see to Dara's needs that evening, and so there was nothing to keep Tamar away. She was half thrilled. Half terrified. And entirely determined to make her wedding night a good one, if not a typical one. *Jehovah, help me*, she prayed as she tucked her hand in Mark's and let him lead her from the celebration, toward the familiar corridor and the unfamiliar door that would now be hers. *Help me be a wife to him. Help me love him. Help me want him.*

Her husband—she made a point of thinking of him as such all day, and each time it sent a strange quiver through her—looked over at her with that soft smile of his. "Are you certain you wish to stay here so soon? It is a small room, there is not much privacy to be had."

Countless times over the last three days she had nearly gone back on her decision and announced she would stay with Zipporah for a while after all. But something within her always stilled her, checked her. Assured her that this was the best path.

She returned his smile. "The more time I spend with you, my husband, the more I admire and respect you. The more at ease I become." These last few days she had even taken comfort, if not pleasure, in the feel of his fingers wrapped around hers. "I want to be your wife in every sense. I know not how long it will take me to be able to offer you that with joy, but I feel strongly that the time will be shorter if I am with you more. That we will the sooner love each other." And she prayed that once she loved him, she would long for his arms.

His thumb stroked over her knuckle as he opened the door to his chamber. Someone had lit a lamp. The oil must have been perfumed, for a sweet smell filled the space, light and pleasant. Her things had already been transferred, apparently. There were her tunics, folded on a shelf. Her few belongings given places of honor.

How strange to walk into a room she had never stepped foot in and feel it was home. That it had always been home, all these long years when she yearned for something other than the life she led. After Mark eased shut the door behind them, she leaned into his side and even rested her head against his shoulder. "Thank you. For all you have done. For all you are doing. I am honored to be your wife."

"And I to be your husband." With the slow movements he always used with her, he lifted a hand and stroked it down her hair.

A pleasant shiver raced down her spine. No man had ever caressed her hair like that. She had seen the master do it to Dara, but never to her. Never for her. It would have been too loving a gesture, too giving.

She tilted her face up to study his. So handsome. So strong. He could have asked for any maiden here to be his wife, and any would have been thrilled. Why had the Lord given him to Tamar? She did not know. But she was glad. So very glad.

She lifted her hand to touch his face. And her fingers did not shake. Perhaps that was what made wonder light his eyes. After only one swallow, she found her voice. "Will you kiss me?"

Now wonder shifted to surprise. "You want me to?"

Would he think it permission to take more, more than she was ready to give? No. Not Mark. She meant it as she nodded, as she came up on her toes.

She was glad she had found the courage to ask when he lowered his head and brushed his lips so very lightly over hers. This was what a first kiss was meant to be. Soft and loving, not hard and bruising. Sweet and promising, not domineering and demanding. She kissed him back, looped her arms around his neck, invited him deeper.

Praise filled her soul. Not fear, not repulsion. Just praise. Praise and worship and awe, and the first budding of what she could only call love for this man God had given her.

He kissed her long and slowly, and when he eased away, he looked content. His smile was satisfied. He did not paw at her clothes or shove her to their pallet. He just held her there, against the door, and smiled.

She smiled back. "We can sit." She motioned to the carefully made bed on the floor.

His breath hitched. "Are you certain?"

"Unless you do not want to, if it would be too difficult. I know sitting and kissing is not a normal wedding night."

His smile bloomed again, and that hitched breath emerged as a low rumble of a laugh. "My wife. It is so much more than I dared to hope for so soon."

They found a comfortable place against the cushions, and she settled at his side, in his arms. She rested an arm over his abdomen and leaned in to kiss him again.

She could spend a lifetime here, with him. It would be good. It would have joy. Pain would come too, because it was part of life, inevitable, but it would be bearable. Because she would have, finally, love. It made the hand he settled on her side feel warm and secure. The taste of his lips like honey. When she pulled away, it was with a smile, and he wore one too. "This is nice."

But would it be enough for him, tonight?

His eyes said yes. "This is perfect."

It was.

Her brother and new sister were smiling and happy. Sarah was on her way to Rome with Urbanus, his daughters, and her parents, to meet his. The sun shone, the ground smelled sweet, and Columba fluttered to a rest upon Zipporah's shoulder.

It should have been a peaceful day. Yet her spirit thrummed like a harp string pulled too tight. And somehow she was not surprised when the familiar glowing warrior flew from his spot on the wall and came to a rest before her.

He said nothing. But his sword was in his hand.

Zipporah's throat went tight. "What am I to do?"

His lips made no move. But his eyes lifted, and his gaze landed beyond her. She turned to where, by the fountain, Samuel and Benjamin stood with Mark and Tamar. Talking and laughing and looking like evidence that all was right with the world.

But it was not. A stone settled in her stomach. Where was Dara?

Get them. All of them. Go to the ilex.

For prayer? The stone sank deeper into her gut. Benjamin had not come with them to pray since he got home. He would not want to come now. Tamar had joined them the last few days, since her betrothal to Mark, but they had been quiet, relaxed sessions. Insight without urgency.

Not so today, not given the angel's behavior. But in the heat of battle, soldiers must learn quickly. Perhaps it was time to show her what kind of prayer the church needed for survival.

Lord, if I need words, give them to me. She squared her shoulders and strode toward the group. But her tongue would not untwist. Words would not come. When she reached them, they must have seen something on her face, for all fell silent and stared at her.

She did the only thing she could think to do. She reached out and took

Samuel's hand. Met his gaze, then Mark's, then Tamar's, and finally Benjamin's. Then she turned and walked toward the ilex.

Samuel came without needing so much as a tug upon the hand she held. She had known he would. He always came when she needed him. He always lent his strength when hers felt insufficient.

And now he lent his voice too. A simple word aimed at the others. "Come."

They came. She heard them, heard their feet stepping in time to hers. An unexpected unity, that, one that sent a shiver through her. Soldiers on the march.

She saw the battle raging the moment the ilex came in sight. Just beyond it, over the wall. Demons swooped and dove and climbed upward again in a frenzy of black glee. Angels shouted, held their ground on the stone hedge and yet tried to get in a swipe when the dark ones got near enough.

All the battles she had beheld, but none like this. Never had the demons looked so...excited. Their screams were filled with the flip of joy, dark instead of light. The same excitement she imagined filled the cries of the spectators in the arenas when lions ripped a hapless victim to pieces.

Samuel's fingers tightened around hers. "What do you see?"

"Evil." She clung tight to his hand. "Evil in the throes of ecstasy."

Benjamin's steps increased, and he came up on the other side of her. His profile looked taut and worried. "Why do I have the feeling it is Dara? I have not seen her for an hour—she is supposed to be resting in our room." For the first time since he returned home, he looked at her as he used to. As a friend. One who trusted her. "Is she all right?"

If only she had an answer to give him. "I do not know. I do not know that she is involved at all. I see only the demons cavorting beyond the wall by the ilex tree."

She saw the twist of his features, but Samuel must have interpreted it faster. He stepped in front of Zipporah, reaching to halt his brother. "Ben, do not act rashly. We will go together, and we will pray as we do."

Benjamin seemed not to have heard. Before Samuel even finished speaking, he took off at a run for the tree.

"Ben!" Samuel took off after him, his fingers still tangled with Zipporah's. She had no choice but to keep pace, though never would she have thought her legs could pump so fast. Still, he pulled away from them.

No doubt without her struggling to keep up, Samuel could catch him. "Go." She dragged in a breath around the burning in her lungs and squeezed his fingers, then released them. "Keep him on this side of the wall."

When Sarah and her parents and Urbanus had crossed through the gate earlier, she had felt no alarm at all. Yet the thought of Benjamin leaping over those stones that marked the end of their property, the edge of their protection, made it all come back. That first day, Samuel and Anna's wedding. When she first saw the demons and the warriors, when she had known so clearly that if Master Titus crossed beyond the gate, he would be at the mercy of the evil ones.

They must stop him. They must. If the master of Tutelos jumped headlong into that frenzy of evil, it would not end well. "Jehovah, protect him!"

He was already at the ilex, leaping onto the branch that he had always favored. Running along the limb, straight for the wall.

"Ben, no!" Samuel reached the tree too, ducked under the branch to run along it. Too late.

Benjamin's cry rent the air, a scream without words. One that needed none to fill the skies with pure, raw agony.

"God. Jesus." It was all the prayer she had breath for, though her spirit cried out with every pounding of foot on earth.

Samuel was over the wall too. Lord protect him, the demons were swooping at them like vultures, and the angels were, praise be to God, leaving their posts to fight them off. She could hear shouts, masculine and feminine, over the screeching of the beasts.

The tree was beside her, and Columba left her shoulder with a startled chirp, finding a roost on a faraway twig. Her breath shook as she drew it in. Her hands shook as she levered herself up onto her branch. But her feet found their footing and carried her toward the wall.

She stepped onto it, the scar at the back of her head throbbing when she did. Her last time atop the wall had not gone well. And the last time she had crossed it...

"Stop! Get off him!" Dara's cry sounded more demon than human, and she clawed at Benjamin. Her stola was falling from one shoulder, the sash that should have anchored it in place nowhere in sight.

Benjamin leveled a fist at a man who wore only a tunic. A toga still lay on the blanket under their feet.

Dara shrieked again. "Master!"

The man lashed at Benjamin, the blow sending him back a step. Giving her her first full look at the man. Or rather, at the yellow-eyed creature within him.

Benjamin charged at him again, though Samuel caught him. "Ben, stop! Do you not know who he is?"

"That is right." Dara's fists pounded at her husband's back. "He is my master—you have no right to hurt him!"

None of it made sense. Not the words she spoke, not the hissing of the demons, not the way the man stepped backward instead of coming at them again. He looked to Dara, but if they exchanged any message, it was none Zipporah could hear. Then he turned and ran.

Dara stumbled back a few steps and fell onto the blanket. For a moment, her face reflected rejection, pain. Then the gnashing teeth within her formed a snarl upon her lips, and she fumbled around the spread-out cloth. Pulled up a dagger that glinted in the sun. And staggered to her feet.

"No!" Zipporah jumped from the wall, landing between Dara and the brothers. Benjamin still fought to break free of Samuel's hold, growing more violent by the second. No doubt she meant the blade for Benjamin, but she could as easily find Samuel with it. Terror clanged.

"Get out of my way, slave!" Green eyes and yellow both glinted with hatred. She held the dagger with all the ease of one who had used it before, and with pleasure.

"No." Though a skitter of fear coursed through her, she kept her place and held up her hands. She had to try. She must, though she still felt those manacles around her wrists. "I will not allow you to destroy this church. In the name of Jesus, I command you to come out!"

The demon laughed, and the woman with it. "You? You have no power over me, witch."

The skitter turned to a full wash. She had seen so many demons cast out. They always, always responded to the name of Jesus. Even if Zipporah had no authority, Jesus did. Why did she not respond at all? "Whatever is bound on earth is bound in heaven."

"Yes." Dara raised the dagger, and it glowed in the sunlight. "And on earth you are bound to Benjamin, bound to *his* will. Slave." She lunged for her, her face contorted to match the ugly beast within.

An angel dropped between them, sword raised, but the flock of cavorting demons swooped at him, forced him a step to the side.

Just a step. But it gave Dara a way in, and all Zipporah could do was lift her arms.

Dara slashed downward, her aim obviously Zipporah's stomach. But the thick leather of her belt deflected the blade. Dara shoved into her, and Zipporah took a step back, pushed the woman away. On the wall she saw Mark and Tamar, but they could not rebuke this thing inside Dara any more than she could.

"Samuel. Samuel!" Her hand sought the shark's tooth around her neck, pulled it over her head.

Dara was on her again, her screech filling her ears. The dagger arced downward, aimed this time at her eye.

She turned her head at the last second, but not enough. It bit her cheek, slashed it again from another direction. It was all she could do to pull her arm back enough to put some force into it when she jabbed the tooth into Dara's shoulder. "Samuel!"

The blood blinded her.

Thirty-six

SAMUEL HAD NEVER TUSSLED WITH HIS BROTHERS, NOT BEYOND their training at Father's hand. It felt so wrong to push at Benjamin, to deflect a punch and try to land one of his own. "Let him go!" But the shout seemed not to reach his brother's ears. "Will you die for this? For her?"

"I will kill him!" Benjamin's cry tore at his heart. "He was with my wife! He was lying with my wife!" He shoved Samuel back, tried to dart around him.

Samuel jumped into his path again, grabbed his shoulders again. "I know that." He had seen the evidence as clearly as Benjamin had. But he had apparently seen more than his brother could process. "But did you not see him? Did you not recognize him? He is the emperor's oldest friend. If you kill him, Nero's fury will come down upon us all!"

Another heart-ripping cry, another lunge, but no swinging fists.

Samuel pushed against him, half-holding, half-fighting. And looked up. "Lord, no."

Zipporah had leapt down, and Dara stood before her with a raised dagger. Their words sounded like clanging cymbals in his ears, all but a few.

Bound on earth.

"No. No! Benjamin, let me go." He pushed again, wildly this time, but his brother's arms seemed to tangle more tightly around him.

He saw her lunge. Saw Zipporah stagger back, Dara still on her, though she made no cry of pain.

No, she just cried out his name.

Samuel shoved at Benjamin, but his brother must have mistook it. He shouted again, shoved him back. Samuel ducked a blow and watched that dagger arch again. "Ben—Ben, free her. Set Zipporah free!"

"What?" The request apparently kindled new rage. He kicked out a leg as he swept out his arm. Samuel did not see it coming until he had landed with a thud on the ground.

He should...he should get up and rebuke her himself. He had never done it, but...but he must save Zipporah.

"Samuel!"

He pushed up, and his fingers closed around something metallic. A disk. A coin. "I bind you!" He shouted it as loudly as he could, though his voice sounded breathless and light. "In the name of Jesus, I bind you!"

Dara jerked, though he could not tell if it was at his words. She clutched at her shoulder, where blood dripped from between her fingers.

Benjamin pulled him up, fist raised.

Samuel held the coin in front of his brother's face. "Sell her to me. Give me Zipporah."

Confusion overcame the anger, though his hands did not release him. "What? Why?"

"Because she has no authority over your wife so long as you are her master! Give her to me, please. *Please.*"

"I…"

They had no time for this. Dara let out a scream and staggered forward again. Samuel shoved the coin into Benjamin's chest. "Will you take this for your slave? Just say yes."

Looking dazed, Benjamin took the coin. "All right. Yes."

He would have tried to shout to Zipporah, but it was not necessary. She must have felt it. She shuddered the moment Benjamin said yes and seemed to grow before his eyes. She stood there straight and true as an arrow and raised her hand toward Dara. "Be gone from her. In the name of Jesus, I command you to come out."

"No!" Dara convulsed, jerked back as if she had run into a wall. "No, she is mine! *Mine!*"

"She is not! Leave her now!"

Such a screech left Dara's lips as he had never heard before, and she slashed at the air with her dagger.

Benjamin finally turned, his eyes going dead as he watched his wife fight what they could not see.

Samuel surged forward, to Zipporah's side. Blood flowed freely down her face, covering her right eye. He could not tell, through the angry red river, where the wound was. "My sparrow." He snatched up a length of blue cloth from the blanket and pressed it to her face.

She held it there but kept her gaze on Dara.

That woman screamed again, dropped the dagger, and staggered back. Her feet caught up in the blanket, and she fell down onto it, her limbs jerking and twitching.

Benjamin stalked by and came to a halt at her feet. Samuel drew in a quick breath, not sure if he should try to restrain his brother again or let him do whatever he willed. And felt that *Stay* resonate in his spirit. He pulled Zipporah close to his side.

Benjamin's fingers curled into a fist. "How could you do this to me?"

The flailing Dara hissed at him. "You? You are nothing. He is my master. I belong to him, not to you!"

Movement at the wall caught his gaze. Mark had jumped down and was helping Tamar lower to the ground.

Benjamin spun away, then back again. "That man? *That* man was your master? How can that be, when he has never left Rome and you have never come to it until you did with *me*?"

Another jerk, and her head snapped to the right, then the left. "He...he is a Jew. A religious leader. Ask Tamar, she was his whore!"

Tamar, clinging to Mark's side, shook her head. "The man I saw running away was not my master."

"Of course not." Benjamin bent down and snatched up the toga, shook it before Dara's nose. "This is the toga of a senator, Dara! A *senator*. A Roman. The oldest friend of the emperor, not a Jewish priest. Not—not the man we saw you with in the market in Jerusalem. *He* was your master, was he not? The man who found you after that time we met in the upper room?"

Dara made no answer. A garbled sound came from her throat, and she fell backward to the ground.

"It does not want to leave her. Its claws are so deeply entrenched...pray. We must pray it out of her." Zipporah loosed the blue sash and left Samuel's side, went to kneel beside the thrashing woman. The woman who had just sliced her with a blade not two minutes before. Now Zipporah took her hand, bent until her forehead was only inches over Dara's face, and prayed words in a language his ear did not know, though his soul did.

Love for her nearly felled him. Not daring to close his eyes, he turned his spirit toward prayer too. Mark and Tamar made their way to him, and Mark's hand landed on his shoulder. Linking them. Praying with him. He led the knot of family over to Benjamin and added him to the chain.

His brother shivered, his shoulders sagged. But he did not step away. "It was true. God forgive me."

Samuel gripped his shoulder all the tighter. "He does. You know he does. Pray for your wife, my brother. She needs you."

Benjamin sank to the ground, then stretched prostrate upon it, his back heaving. Samuel knew the Lord would accept those cries even more readily than eloquent words.

A minute later Zipporah straightened a mere second before Dara jerked up, shrieked, and then sagged to the ground as if lifeless.

Zipporah wiped at her eye. Blood, not tears, stained her fingers. "It has left her. And has left such wounds within her I know not how she will recover without asking for the power of Jesus's blood to flow through her."

Samuel moved to her again and helped her up. His stomach twisted at the sight of that red river still flowing strong. "I must tend to that, my little sparrow. Now."

Tamar appeared, the stained blue length in her hands. "Here." She had folded it carefully and now handed it to Zipporah. Tamar's face held unfathomable pain as she regarded her mistress. "Why would she have thought that man was our master?"

"Your master was hers too?" Mark shook his head and sank to his knees beside Benjamin, whose shoulders still shook. "I do not understand."

Tamar sighed. "He bought her seven years ago. He had many seers in his employ, but she was his best one. He meant her to be his wife—but not until she had helped him destroy the Christians. He had been telling her all these years that she must serve him first by marrying another, then she would be his." Her gaze went to the distance, where the senator had disappeared. "That man looked nothing like him. My master was at least a decade older, shorter, broader."

They all looked to Zipporah. She shrugged. "He had a demon. That is all I know."

Tamar drew in a long breath and moved to Dara's side. "Perhaps now she will be the girl I first met again."

Zipporah looked about to answer, but then she swayed. Samuel caught her, swept her up into his arms. He had longed to hold her again, but not like this. He had prayed never to have to carry her in like this again. "Mark, Tamar—can you two see to them? I need to get Zipporah's bleeding stopped."

He barely paused for their assurances before lifting her to the top of the wall, climbing up and over, and pulling her into his arms again.

"Do not fret." Yet her head lolled against his shoulder. "I feel strange."

"You have lost much blood." *Lord, strengthen her.* He held her close and prayed wings onto his feet.

"You saved me. How did you..." Her good eye slid shut, then opened again. "How did you...I felt as though shackles had released. Her authority over me broken."

His solution now made his neck heat. "I...bought you from Benjamin. I tried to get him to say you were free, but he did not understand."

"You did." Her fingers curled into his toga, and she tilted her red-streaked face toward his. "You always understand." Her smile looked, somehow, faded. "I am honored to belong to you."

Fear stabbed him in the stomach. "Stay with me, sparrow. Hold on."

It should not be such a danger. Head wounds always bled so, this one looked no worse than others he had seen. Not so bad as the gash to her head from the jar, nor as the first time a blade had marred her face. Yet that glazing of her eyes...

She convulsed, her whole body curling inward, and Samuel broke into a run. Hard as his feet pounded, her muscle spasms worsened. Terrifying. He burst into the villa minutes later without seeing it, without knowing if he passed anyone, without registering anything but the path to his chamber and its surgical tools—and the continual shaking, jerking, and spasms of Zipporah.

She went still. Even more terrifying.

He slid her unresponsive body onto the same table he had stitched her at a few weeks ago, but he could not reach for his tools, for his balms, for his potions.

He could only shut his eyes, fall to his knees, and press his hand to the wound. "Heal her, Lord Jesus. By the power of your precious blood, heal her. I know not what is wrong, but I know she needs you. She needs your touch. She needs your power. Touch her!"

His hand felt hot, and not from the sticky warmth of her blood. The heat came from within, pulsed, spread. He felt it move from his wrist to his fingertips, felt it surge from him to her.

She sat up with a gasp, heaved. He grabbed a pot and managed to get it to her just before she retched. Once the heaves had passed, she wiped at her mouth and handed the pot back. "Sorry."

Sorry? He breathed a laugh and put the pot aside so he could pull her close. "No. Do not be sorry. You frightened me so. Are you well?"

"Better now. I felt so strange. Dizzy, then this pain seemed to eat up my insides." She pulled away, her fingers over her lips. "I think I need some water."

Water. Yes. He could get her water. He moved to his pitcher and poured some into a cup, added a few herbs that would help take the bitter taste from her mouth. As he watched her first rinse her mouth and then drink, it was all he could do to keep from crushing her to him again. Run his hands through her hair. They flexed now in anticipation of its silken curls wrapping them.

He needed a drink of water too. "I had better stitch you up. The bleeding has slowed, but I still cannot tell what damage might have been done to your eye."

"I think it is fine." But she sat there, still as stone, while he dabbed at the blood and examined her eye, while he got out the silk thread, the shining needle, the bronze scissors. She no more than flinched when he took the needle back and forth through her torn flesh.

By the time he snipped the excess thread away, though, his hands shook. He put the tools down and braced himself on the table, an arm on either side of her, and rested his forehead against hers. "You seem determined to add still more interest to your face. It is in the shape of a cross."

Perhaps she smiled. From this perspective, all he could be sure of was the light in her eyes. "I suppose I must take what I can get."

"Zipporah." He pulled back, but not by much. He could not stand to put more than a few inches between them. He could not stand the thought that, yet again, she could have been killed. Could have been snatched from him. He lifted his hands, still bloodied from her face, and buried them in her hair. Tilted her head back.

And kissed her with all the passion he never thought he would feel, until she set it kindling.

When his lips touched hers, Zipporah could not quite fathom what was happening. And when they parted, parted hers, when he drank of her mouth as if she were water and he a man crossing a desert, she thought perhaps she was still unconscious and dreaming it all. Because surely Samuel—beautiful, strong, perfect Samuel—could not possibly want to kiss *her* like that.

Her hands clutched at his toga, pulling him closer. If it were a dream, she would enjoy every moment of it before she awoke. She would relish this fire that swept through her before it gave way to the pain sure to come. She would kiss him as she had not let herself admit she wanted to do before reality intruded and reminded her that he loved another.

"Wait." She pushed him away, trying to catch her breath, trying to figure out why he looked at her like that, when it was *not* a dream. She should loose his garment, scoot away. But she could not. "What of the girl you love?"

The slow curve of his lips made her breath abandon her again. "That would be you, my sparrow."

Dizziness swamped her, making her clutch him all the tighter. "Me? That... that is impossible. How could you be in love with me?"

"How could I not?" His hands were still cradling her head. Now they tilted it, and he kissed her temple, where the old scar began. "You are the strongest woman I have ever seen." His lips followed the scar downward. "The most selfless, the most faithful."

He bent his head, urged hers back, and kissed the scar Columba had given her, on her throat. "The most amazing." He rose again, his gaze capturing hers, his mouth a breath away. "And the most beautiful woman in the world."

She could not breathe. Could not move. Could do nothing but sit there and try to find the lie in his eyes. But there was only sincerity. He believed it. He somehow looked at her and saw beauty where there was none.

Her heart welled, crested, overflowed. She loosed his toga so she could splay her fingers along his clean-shaven jaw. "You *must* love me, to think that." To give to her the title she had thought belonged unequivocally to her sister.

"With all of my heart." He touched her lips again with his, more softly this time. "And it is the truth. When I look at you..." With a little groan, his hands moved to her back and pulled her flush against him, and he kissed her deeply once more, making the blood sing in her veins.

Her thoughts had gone muddled by the time he pulled away, resting his forehead against hers again. "I know you have not been thinking of me as I have been of you. But give me a chance to claim your heart, my sparrow. I beg you. I know I am not my brother, but I will love you for the rest of your days. I will do all in my power to make you happy. I will never need anything but to claim you as mine."

She let her fingers trail up into his golden hair. "I do not want you to be your brother. And I believe you already *can* claim me as your own. How much did you buy me for, anyway? You could not have had any money on your person."

His neck went warm under her hands, which made her smile turn to a grin. Samuel did not look quite so amused. "I have no idea. I found a coin on the ground but did not even look at it. But I will free you. This very moment—"

"I think not." Laughter in her throat, she wrapped her arms around his neck and her legs around his waist. Given the flash in his eyes, perhaps that was a move she ought not to have made. But his arms closed around her, and he kissed her again, so what did it matter? So long as he did not pull away just yet and get out a scroll and ink. She was not ready to let go of him.

A moment later, though, the door swung open and he pulled away from her, leaving her arms empty.

Tamar did not seem to even notice what she interrupted. Her eyes were wide, and she held Dara's dagger between two fingers as if it were a cobra about to strike. "Zipporah. Is this what she cut you with?"

Her blood still stained it, it ought not to be a question. She nodded. "It is an odd looking blade. Has it three sides?"

"And poison always upon it. I have watched her dip it more than once." Letting the weapon fall to the tile floor with a clatter, she hurried forward and took Zipporah's hand. "Are you feeling all right? Any cramping, any pain? Dizziness?"

Her stomach dropped to her feet. "I am well."

"You are not well!" Samuel shoved a hand through his hair, torment on his face. "That is what made you convulse, what left you unconscious when I carried you in here!"

Was it peace she felt, or had she gone numb from the mere thought of it? Zipporah shook her head, digging her free fingers into the table's edge. She would have preferred tightening them around Samuel's. "Perhaps. Probably. But I am well *now*. Your prayer, Samuel. You prayed healing over me, and I swear to you. I feel better than I have since my fall from the wall. Even this does not hurt." She touched the new wound, with its raised skin and silk thread crossing through it.

Samuel sank down onto a chair and buried his face in his hands.

Tamar drew in a deep breath. "You ought to be thrashing on the floor by now, near to death. It works quickly, from what I have heard her say. It is how she protected herself in Jerusalem, walking so often between her home and our master's."

Samuel pushed to his feet again and paced to the door. He was just turning back when Zipporah's parents appeared at it and came in. A moment later, her ima's arms were around her and her abba's around them both.

Everyone seemed to speak at once, a babble of exclamations and disbelief and concern and relief. She did not try to make sense of it. She just let them hold her, assure themselves she was well, let Samuel and Tamar offer their explanations.

She had not realized Samuel had been struggling with Benjamin the whole time. Or that when Tamar and Mark first tried to come over the wall, something had held them immobile. But when the retelling was done, one question still remained. "How is Dara?"

Her parents exchanged a glance, then looked to Tamar.

Her sister shook her head. "She has not awakened yet. Master Benjamin carried her in and is sitting with her. He is...barely responsive himself. Hollow."

She looked past her family, to Samuel. "You should go to him."

"No. Not yet." He slid past her parents, back to her side, and anchored his hand at the back of her neck again. It felt so right there, so warm and steady and comforting. His eyes shone with all the love he spoke of as he gazed deep into hers. "I am not leaving your side until I am confident this poison has left your system."

A smile started, despite the seriousness of his gaze. She was hardly going to argue with him wanting to stay with her. "Well then. We will both go."

He breathed a laugh. "That is my sparrow." Leaning in, he pressed a soft kiss to her lips, there in front of everyone.

A collective gasp sounded. Or not quite collective. When she peeked at her family, she saw that Abba looked not a bit surprised. Rather, he was grinning as he slung an arm around her mother. "I take it you have had the conversations we discussed."

He had known? Her own father had known Samuel had fallen in love with her, and he had breathed not a word?

Though when Samuel ran his gaze over her face with such love, she had to admit this was the best way to discover it. From him, in a way that could leave no doubt. He lifted her off the table and, once assured that she stood steadily, tucked her to his side.

She could get used to it there.

He nodded to Abba. "There are words yet to say. But I think I convinced her of my heart."

"Then if I might offer one more bit of advice." Her father's smile faded. "Your brother is in no state to see your happiness right now."

Samuel sighed and slid his hand back around to its traditional place on the small of her back, putting a little space between them. She would have preferred to remain closer, but his obvious displeasure provided consolation.

As did the fact that he nodded the others out ahead of them and, a few steps from the door, paused to lean down and kiss her again, quickly but with heat enough to send tingles down her spine.

"To hold me over," he whispered against her lips.

She indulged in a smile before forcing her mind to those among them with nothing to smile about.

thirty-seven

BENJAMIN SAT WITHOUT MOVING, HIS LIMBS ALL HEAVY AS MARBLE. His eyes remained fixed upon Dara, who, were she not breathing, would look dead. She was laid out upon their bed, her hair askew and her stola still loose around her. Her stomach was still flat under it, though soon enough it would round with his babe.

Or was it his at all? How long had she been sneaking off to meet this...this *master* of hers?

He blinked, swallowed. And wondered who this woman was he had married. Had taken to his bed so readily, had sworn his love and devotion to. The woman he had defended against his family and friends.

About whom he had been so very wrong. Who was she? And who would she be when she opened her eyes? Would he know her at all? Would she know him? Or would she look at him with the eyes of a stranger, this woman whose body he knew so well?

"Here." Mark handed him a cloth, damp and cool.

His hands took it. But he knew not what to do with it.

Mark sighed and motioned to his jaw. "You have a bruise forming from your tussle with Samuel."

Another blink. He had been fighting with his own brother. Not an argument, not a wrestling match meant only for fun or training. He had struck him, been struck in return. All because of that murderous rage that had blinded him when he saw another man's hands on his wife. Another man's mouth caressing hers.

Lord, forgive me. Forgive me, forgive me, forgive me. For so much. For everything. For what I did. For what I failed to do.

Noises came from outside his door, but he did not stand to investigate. It opened, but he did not look up to see who entered. He just kept watching Dara. The way her chest rose and then fell again. Up and down. Breath in, breath out. Life. But he felt so far from alive.

A scrape of metal coming to rest upon wood startled him enough that he glanced over. Tamar slid a dagger onto the table. Was it the one his wife had wielded? The maid's nod seemed to say so. And when she glanced behind her, he did too.

Menelaus had come, and Jacob. Miriam and Andrew and Dinah. Jason and Deborah, Cleopas. And Samuel, with a hand on the back of Zipporah.

He was on his feet without any thought of standing, his gaze on the two bloody gashes forming a cross on Zipporah's cheek. The long one skipped over her eye and cut into her eyebrow. It was a miracle Dara had not taken her eye. "You are hurt." His wife had attacked her, while he was fighting off his brother so he could try to murder a senator. And he had not even noticed it at the time.

"It will heal. How is she?"

The only possible answer was a glance toward the bed. Her still form spoke for itself.

Jacob's hand landed on his shoulder. "Do you want to send to Rome for your parents? If all goes well there, they will not be home until tomorrow, at the earliest. If you need them—"

"No." He did, of course he did. But he had brought this on himself. He would not ruin his sister's chance to meet her betrothed's family because of his own selfishness. "The Spirit will send them if they need to come." Heaven knew they all listened for his voice when Benjamin did not. They, when they felt a messenger from the Lord barring a door, would not barge directly through it as he had done.

His chair welcomed him again. "I am sorry. I did not heed the Lord's warnings, and I brought evil into our midst. I did not listen to the brethren." He looked back up to Zipporah, scarred more than ever. Because of him.

Sold today, because of him. Because he could not fathom why his brother would demand her freedom. Peddled for an assarius that he had let fall again to the ground—the same price as two sparrows outside the temple.

His head bowed. "I am so sorry, Zip. I have hurt you most of all."

"Another scar for my collection is nothing. And I am told this one's shape is quite meaningful." He looked up in time to see her touch it, see her smile. "It can serve as a reminder of the sacrifice our Lord made for us all."

"But I called you a liar. Did not trust in the gift I knew well you had."

"You loved her too much to see it. That is understandable."

He shook his head. She should not be making excuses for him, not now. "I sold you."

At her parents' gasp, she was quick to add, "To Samuel! That is all. I could not cast out the demon, not so long as I was bound by Benjamin's will. Samuel realized the problem and bought me. To save me. To help me."

To Benjamin's shame. He should have realized it too. Should have freed her long ago, when she asked. Should have bound the beast within Dara himself.

Should never have married her. His head sank lower, until his hands had to support it, his elbows digging into his knees. He should have listened to Samuel and Mark. Never looked her way, honored his brother's wishes.

"Benjamin." Menelaus crouched down now to be at his level. "You made a poor choice. But there is no sin so great that the blood of Christ does not cover it. No mistake so big that the Lord cannot use it for good. We will pray. Without ceasing, all night. And then we will wait to see what the Lord does with this situation that looks so impossible."

Even the support of these, his brethren, shamed him. "I thank you. All of you. And appreciate those prayers. But if you would leave me for now, I..." He drew in a shaking breath and let it ease back out. "I have much praying I must do alone. Please."

He listened as they all filed out again. Then he slid to the floor, pressed his face to the cool tiles, and wept.

Darkness had fallen. No dinner had been served, none had been wanted. Everyone in the villa, everyone on the grounds had been found and notified. Everyone had spent the evening on their knees. Zipporah had knelt beside Samuel, her fingers most often clasped in his. Sometimes her thoughts strayed his way, her lips thought of his kiss.

But mostly she kept her mind focused. On Dara, and on Benjamin. On his family even now in Rome, seeking unity where a rift had long stretched. On their church body, that staggered now rather than running the race.

But they were not beaten. They were not destroyed. They would rebound and be stronger than ever.

She stood to stretch her back and relieve her knees, and the world swayed around her. Samuel's hands cupped her elbows so quickly, he must have mirrored her every movement as she rose. She smiled into his worried frown. Both of his worried frowns. And then blinked until only one handsome face stared down at her. "Stop worrying," she whispered. "It is not the poison."

"Then it is the loss of blood. You need to eat something, and to rest."

Her mother appeared at her side and turned her toward the door. "He is right. You can pray more in your chamber. Do not neglect yourself, my daughter. We need you strong and healthy. This will be no easy path we are upon."

"I will see she does as she is told." Samuel offered her mother a tight smile and tucked Zipporah's hand into the crook of his elbow.

Ima nodded and stepped away, peace in her eyes. She approved.

Of course she approved. She had approved him for Anna, so obviously she would think him good enough for Zipporah. Though, she admitted to herself with a frown as he led her out, most would argue with good reason that she was far from good enough for him.

But he loved her. If he loved her, that was all that mattered. His parents would welcome her. The world would not, but he would not care about that. And if he could wave it away, so could she.

He led her down the darkened halls without a word, into the kitchen. A lamp burned here, as it always did. Enough that she could see the vegetables still out from the interrupted preparations, the bread waiting to be sliced.

Samuel nudged her to a chair. "Sit, sparrow. I will get you something."

She sat and leaned onto the table, her hand going to her neck. Her fingers searched, looking for the leather band to toy with. Nothing. She jerked to her feet. "My necklace. I must have dropped it after I stabbed her in the shoulder. It is still outside the wall—"

"And will be there still tomorrow." He cupped her face between his palms and brushed his thumbs over her cheeks, careful to avoid the wound. "I will find it for you at first light. I promise."

And if it were gone...well, he had given her a far greater gift today. She sighed and covered his hands with hers. "The belt deflected her knife. The tooth held her at bay. You set me free."

"I could have lost you." He let go her face and wrapped his arms around her, held her against his chest. "When I saw you had jumped down—"

"I had to. She had that dagger, and..."

The low lamplight caught the lift of his brows, washed them even more golden. "And you had to save Benjamin."

"No. Well, yes." She let out a gusty breath. "I suppose I would have tried had it only been him—he was my master, and master of Tutelos. My friend. But no. My thought was for you. The way you two were fighting, she could have hit you by mistake."

"Me." Why did wonder color his voice? Why did his eyes look so disbelieving? "Do you...do you think someday you could come to love me, little sparrow? As I love you?"

Why did he sound so uncertain? "Let me think." She screwed her face up into an exaggerated show of consideration. Then grinned. "Yes."

His fingers trailed up her spine. "Yes? You think you will?"

Laughter rumbled in her throat. "No. Yes, I already do."

He held her close, buried his face in her hair. "You are certain?"

"Very certain. Why would you doubt me?"

His hands reached her shoulders and then slid back down, leaving a trail of sparks in their wake. "You loved him all your life."

Had she? With the way she longed for Samuel in this moment, she could scarcely remember those years of longing for Benjamin. And would she have ever set her sights on her master had Samuel not been Anna's? She had always thought him the more beautiful, inside and out.

She smiled and pulled his head down. "You were out of reach."

He kissed her again, until her pulse matched his, until she could hardly breathe, until her knees went weak and she sagged against him.

At which point he pulled away and urged her back into the chair with a frown. "Food. You need food. You are too weak."

She chuckled but leaned back against the wood. "That time was your fault."

The lamp illumined his satisfied smile and caught his arms as he turned to put together a plate of simple food. He knew all her favorites. He chose them for her with care. He served her with a smile, this new master of hers.

She could not tamp down a grin as she bit into an apple slice. He would free her by this time tomorrow, she knew that. Would likely go back to his room and draw up the paper now. But for this moment, she rather liked knowing she was his. Under his protection, his authority.

Another wave of dizziness washed over her, but she did her best to hide it and reached for the watered wine he had provided. Her mouth was parched.

Her stomach empty. That was all. God had healed her with Samuel's prayer. Of that she was certain.

While she ate, he put the kitchen to rights, stowing away the vegetables and bread Dinah had left in her hurry. "I will never forget the first time I stepped foot in Dinah's kitchen, in Jerusalem. Benjamin's father had just bought me, had just introduced me to Mother. Who, even that first day, had welcomed me to her side as a son. Had promised me that I would be a brother to the child she carried. Then she took me to the kitchen, telling me she had a job for me." He glanced over her way, a hint of a smile on his shadowed lips. "I was determined to work. My—Martha had warned me I would have to. So Mother delivered me into Dinah's hands and said, 'He is to help with the tastings.' As if this were the most menial task in the house, tasting Dinah's cooking before it reached the table."

Well able to imagine Mistress Abigail tending a small Samuel's pride, Zipporah laughed. "And Dinah put you upon the table, gave you that very serious face of hers, and fed you until you were bursting."

"Have I told this story before?"

Another laugh. "Probably. More, I know her."

He wiped off the work surface and returned to her side, giving her half-empty plate a look stern enough for Dinah. Then he sighed. "I would have been happy as a slave in this house. But they made me a son. An heir. Equal to the children born of their flesh."

She reached for his hand. Familiar fingers, around which hers fit so comfortably. "Had they not, I daresay I would be dead right now by the hand of your sister."

A shudder coursed through him. "She is not my sister."

"The demon was not." Abandoning the food, she stood and lifted a hand to rest on his face. "Dara is. She will need you."

He moved his head, kissed her palm. Closed his eyes. "Must you force me to be a stronger man than I want to be right now? I just want to focus on you. On us."

She traced the contours of his face. The strong jaw, the hollows under his cheekbones, the slender nose. Masculine perfection. "That would be lovely."

He opened his eyes again, and they were resigned. "But it is not our lot. Not yet."

She wished it were. But she shook her head.

And because he was Samuel, the man she had always loved but never dreamed of calling her own, his eyes went peaceful in the dim light. "I want you for my wife, little sparrow. But it would be too cruel to my brother to announce a betrothal when he is mourning his own marriage."

"I know." Perhaps it made her sigh. But it was right. She turned with him toward the door. With food now in her belly, exhaustion settled on her shoulders. "We are in a night of weeping, and it may last a long while. But when the morning comes, we will have that joy."

"And in the meantime," he said, grinning now, "a few stolen kisses to sustain us."

"A few *daily*, I hope you mean." Though they were hardly stolen when her parents knew and approved, were they? "I will have to tell Sarah. She will be pleased."

Samuel laughed and led her down the hall the brief distance to her door. "Sarah will not be surprised."

She came to a halt with an exaggerated huff. "You told her too?"

"No. She saw me looking at you." He pulled her flush against him, pressed her back to her door. "Apparently I wear my love for you on my face."

"Oh." A thought that set a warm glow alight in her chest. "I like that."

He laughed again, soft and intimate, and traced his lips over hers so lightly, so gently that she felt like a feather. Then he pulled her weight off the door and opened it. "You need to rest. Promise me you will."

"I will rest. I will pray too, but I will rest." She backed into the doorway but leaned against the threshold rather than entering fully. "Will you return to the gathering?"

His face went solemn. "Not just yet. I need a bit of private prayer time as well."

She nodded. Her pallet called to her, but she was loathe to leave him. "Samuel. I love you."

"It cannot be half so much as I love you, my little sparrow." He kissed her forehead, her nose, her mouth.

"Do you really want to argue with me right now?"

He laughed again and backed away. "Good night. Rest well, my love. Tomorrow you will need your strength to face what comes of today."

Nodding, she eased into her dark room. "Good night."

Her door closed silently, and she moved without needing any sight to her pallet. The chamber still felt empty without Tamar's things, without the knowledge that she would soon come in. Zipporah had not even had a chance to speak with her new sister today to see how she and Mark had fared on their wedding night. But they had looked happy this morning, before the world fractured. That surely meant that whatever path they had decided on, it was the right one.

She settled onto the straw tick, the smooth blankets, and closed her eyes. The stitches pulled against her flesh when she did so. In a few days they would start to itch—always her least favorite part of an injury.

So trivial, compared to the pain Dara would be feeling. And Benjamin. *Father God, pour out your succor upon them. Protect Tutelos from any other demons that may try to come in and enter her again, protect her so that she might finally hear the truth. Draw her unto you. Strengthen Benjamin. Knit them together.*

She wanted to pray more, her spirit cried out within her, but she felt her mind going fuzzy. Her limbs growing heavy.

A blinding light jerked her up, though whether it was seconds or hours later she could not be sure.

The familiar warrior filled her room, sending his light into every corner. He held his sword toward the door. *Get up. Go. Now.*

She stumbled to her feet, her legs still awkward from sleep. "What is it? Can I know? Where must I go?"

Go. The dagger.

The dagger? She fumbled for the ring on the door, tugged, but her arms were weak and as awkward as her legs. "I am healed of the poison. I know I am." Another yank, and the door whooshed open.

The song filled her, then the angel stood before her in the hall. *Yours is not to die alone in your room. Yours is to give your life for the Father's glory. Go.*

So she was to die tonight after all? When she thought for sure Samuel's prayer had defeated the poison? It made no sense. Her feet propelled her down the dark hallway, though she had to put a hand to the wall to stay steady. How would dying with others glorify God?

The wall vanished. She had reached the intersection. Were she to turn to the right, she would find the gathering, where her parents were no doubt still praying with the others.

Her feet took her to the left. She needed Samuel. If she were going to die, it would be with him. He would never forgive himself if he were not there in her last moments to pray for her. To try whatever he could. Maybe...maybe it would glorify God if she could somehow give *him* healing in her last moments. Though how she could do that she could not fathom.

She found his door, and urgency dug its claws into her throat, made her push it open even as she knocked. Made her breath heave as she stumbled in and shut it behind her. Her knees shook. She had to lean against the solid wooden slab once she was inside.

Lamps were lit. Samuel stood at his table, parchment before him but un-marked. He wore his tunic, his toga cast off. After the second it took him to register her presence, he flew toward her. "Zipporah! What is wrong? You look as you though have seen an apparition."

"Only an angel." She found enough strength to push away from the door, into his arms. "I cannot be in my room. I cannot die alone."

"Die?" She expected panic to nip at his words. Instead, they were strong and sure as he held her close. "You are not going to die. You were right, the poison would have felled you hours ago if it were going to. You are healed."

"He said 'the dagger.' He told me to leave, that very second." She wrapped her arms around his waist and held on. "Let me stay with you."

"Sparrow." Now his throat sounded tight. "You cannot stay in my room."

"Have you freed me yet?"

She looked up to see his frown. "Not yet. I was just getting ready to."

"Then I can. I am your maidservant. By every law in the known world, you have every right to me. There is nothing immoral in your maidservant staying in your room."

His fingers pressed against her back. "You are right. Though I will not—you will be my wife someday, not my concubine. I will free you in the morning and pretend, tonight, that you do not set fire to my blood."

So long as she could be with him. "So I can stay?"

He nodded. When a shiver of relief swept down her, he pulled away a few inches and tipped up her chin. His brows were drawn. "You are frightened. I do not recall the last time I saw you frightened."

She should not be. The thought of death had never affected her so before.

But then, before she had known she would not leave anyone behind to mourn her to the depths of their soul. Before, she had not heard words of love fall from Samuel's lips.

Today had changed everything. "I am not ready to die."

His frown dug deeper. "You are not *going* to die."

She lifted a brow.

He rolled his eyes. "You know what I mean. We all die, but I speak of *now*. You are not going to die tonight. You are not going to die anytime soon."

She pressed her quavering lips together.

His hand fell away from her chin. His nostrils flared. "What do you know?"

"Nothing. Nothing for certain, just..." She focused her gaze on his tunic. She could not bear to watch anticipated sorrow race through his eyes. "I have long felt I would give my life for the Way. The angel confirmed that tonight. He said my part was to die for the glory of the Father."

"That does not mean soon. You can give your life for him when we are both so old we cannot remember our own names."

The optimism brought a mirthless laugh to her lips. "To God's ear, my love. But I have always thought it would be sooner rather than later."

"No." His hand was in her hair again, against the back of her head. He forced her gaze up. "No. The Lord would not give us this love just to take it away so soon. I have to believe that. I have to trust in that."

How she prayed he was right. She made no objection when he pressed her close and held her there. "If it comes tonight, then I praise him for letting me experience this first. And if it is not tonight, then I will praise him for every day I get to spend with you."

"Sparrow." He must have felt her shaking. He lifted her, carried her to his plush bed, and set her gently upon it. Then, obviously knowing the objection about to trip off her tongue at the thought of him leaving her, he settled at her side and held her close again. And whispered fiercely in her ear, "You will not die tonight."

thirty-eight

DARA OPENED HER EYES TO DARKNESS AND A YAWNING EMPTINESS inside her. Like the fiercest hunger, yet dull. A throb rather than a slice. An echo rather than a scream.

Nothingness. She stretched out her fingers and felt soft blankets beneath her. Turned her head and acknowledged a pillow. Listened, and heard steady breathing.

Familiar. Yet wrong. She bolted up in the bed and looked at the chamber gilded here and there with moonlight. Not her room. Not her home.

A shudder made her stomach want to heave. What was dream, what was real?

She touched her hair—long, no evidence of the time she took shears to it after her abba died. She wiggled her toes—so far away. She was grown, then. It had not been a dream. Thomas had really come, had really put money in her mother's hand, had really led her to his home. Until then, he had only visited them a few times. First to laugh with her father, then to make sure, after his death, they had enough to get by. Then to buy her.

Then...then...what?

She pressed a hand to her temple, willing her mind backward, or forward, or whatever direction it needed to go. Then she bit back a scream when the images came too fast, too strong, too fierce. She doubled over, unable to breathe.

Too many pictures. Too many faces contorted in misery, yelling at her, begging her, laughing with her. Too many possibilities. Too much violence. Too many hands on her. Too many questions, with that certain knowledge that the answers had once been there. That when daylight had kissed her face, she could have closed her eyes and seen the future. She could have known the mysteries.

But she had not seen this. She had not been able to guess such emptiness awaited her. What had happened? How had her soul been so stripped?

She pressed her forehead into the bed. Thomas. Her master. She had loved him. He had loved her. He promised they would marry, but first...first Benjamin.

Jehovah God! Her stomach hurt. Her lungs hurt from the weight of air on them. And her head, her head felt as though it might split in two. Benjamin. The hands that had been on her. The breath that sounded now from the floor beside her. The man who had taken her from all she knew. All she was. Who had looked at her with murder in his eyes.

When? How long ago was that? She pressed her hands to her temples, squeezed, but the pressure in her head did not ease. It could not have been long ago. It was the last thing she recalled. He had tried to kill her master.

No. Not her master. She straightened again, willing the darkness to yield answers as it used to. Willing the vision to come. But her eyes saw only shadows and moonlight and the glint of metal. It had not been Thomas. Yet...yet it had. Not his hands, but his words. Not his face, but his eyes.

The glint of metal.

Yes. Yes, that she knew. Dragging a breath in, she scurried to the side of the bed, to the table. To the dagger she remembered as if from a dream. Blood still stained it, dark as the night. Not Benjamin's.

The witch's. The witch who had jumped from the sky and stripped her soul bare. Left her with nothing. Left her empty and alone again, comfortless and blind. Without a master. Without a purpose.

Her hand closed around the cool metal handle. She would take it back. The witch should already be dead from the poison, but she was not. Her voice echoed through the hollow places inside, rattled around in the darkness. She was still alive, while Dara felt so very dead.

Her bare feet came down on cool tile. Another sensation both familiar and strange. Those feet knew the way to the door, her hands where to find the ring, her arms how hard to tug. Yet the memories felt foggy. Shrouded.

A sob heaved its way up. She caught it, mostly, let nothing out but a gasp as she staggered from the room, her dagger in hand.

This was not how life should be. This was not how hers was meant to unfold. It had all been so clear. That afternoon, the one that shone in her mind so bright, she had known. She had seen it, had seen it all, it seemed. When she kneeled at her master's knees, feeling so lonely, so worthless, so abandoned. He had promised her life. He had promised her the power that came of knowing a truth no one else could. He had promised that she would never awake again and doubt who she was and what she was meant for.

He had lied.

Another gasp broke free. She smothered it with her other hand and turned a stumble into a run. The power had entered her that day. Had opened her eyes. Had filled all the battered and broken places inside, shored them up. What right had the ugly slave to steal it from her? It was all she had. All that set her apart. All that made her grow in Thomas's eyes from one more slave, one more seer, to a woman worthy of becoming his wife.

Now what was she?

"Nothing." Her voice sounded strange to her ears. Too low. No, too high. No...just *wrong*. Running now, she sped down the corridor of family chambers, skidding to a halt at its end. Light glowed from straight ahead.

What was it the voices had said while the darkness cradled her? That they would be praying. That they would pray all through the night.

Dara backed up a step, gripping her dagger tighter. Would Zipporah be with the group? Maybe. But maybe not. She was hurt. Benjamin had said she was hurt. The dagger had struck her—in the face. Those images came now, fuzzy and red-tinged. Even had she somehow not been felled by the poison, she would need to rest.

Dara's feet turned to the right, down the corridor that housed the servants' quarters and led to the kitchen. Her feet knew the way. Her hands knew the door. Her eyes knew where in the room to look. Her arm raised, ready to strike.

"No." Empty. Just like Dara. "No." She kicked at the pallet just to make sure. Nothing. Just like Dara. "No!"

She could not find enough air to fill her lungs. Her head felt ready to split in two. Her knees gave out and then struck the hard floor. The sobs caught her, strangled her, and forced their way out.

What was she to do? She could not go on as nothing but an empty vessel. She could *not*. There was no point.

They had taken everything from her. Everything. She had failed Thomas. She had—she had somehow given herself to the arms of a Roman with the master's eyes. She had lost all she was. No one would want her now. Not Thomas, not the Roman, not even Benjamin.

She was undone. Destroyed. Erased.

Her fingers tightened around the dagger until her knuckles hurt. If she could not have revenge...then she would have an end.

Squeezing her eyes shut, she choked on another breath and lifted her arm. It shook, but that would not matter. If she did not die right away, the poison would eat her alive. It would mean incredible pain, but not for long. Another hour of torment, no more. Then it would be done. She would be released from this terrible reality.

She clasped her other hand atop the first to steady herself. Tensed her muscles. Plunged the blade toward her stomach.

"No!" The shout seemed to come from all around her, in the very same moment something knocked her over and sent the dagger clattering over the floor. "Dara!"

Benjamin. She knew his voice, his scent, the feel of his body on hers. What she did not know was why he stopped her. "Get off! Let me finish it!" She slapped at his shoulders, clawed at them, but still he pressed her to the prickly straw tick she had landed on. "Let me die!"

"Stop. Please." His voice sounded every bit as agonized as she felt.

But why would he care? "Leave me alone." Struggle as she might, thrash and flail, she could not dislodge him. Neither hand nor foot could find the dagger. Another sob tore through her throat. "I want to die. Let me die."

"No." He caught the hands she tried to gouge him with, levered them back and pinned them above her head.

Why must he be so strong? Why must she feel so useless against him? This morning, she would have known how to twist and arch to make him aware of this body. Now she was scarcely aware of its changes herself.

His breath shuddered on its way out. "I cannot let you die."

If she could not escape him, she could at least refuse to look at his shadowed face. She turned her face to the side and went lax. "Why not?"

He did not relax, not even after that question had hovered in the air for an eternity. He gave her no chance to surge up and knock him away. "Because you are my wife. I loved you."

She surged again anyway. Perhaps it was like attempting to knock over a stone wall with one's shoulder, but she had to try. "You did not love *me*. You did not know me."

Just the faintest hint of light reached them from the corridor, but it was enough to find the agony on his face and highlight it. "Will you tell me it was that—that *demon* I loved?"

Demon? She tried to arch her back, to lift him away from her, but to no effect. Demon was such an ugly word. It could not be the right one. It could not be how best to describe that power that had given her purpose these seven years.

She should tell him it was. Lie. So simple. Her tongue had done it so many times now. She remembered each one—foggily. She was a master at it. She was...she was...she was nothing. And the lie would not settle on her tongue anymore. The idea of it tasted bitter, turned her stomach.

But when would the truth be sweet again? Never.

She shook her head. "The woman you loved was a fabrication. A lie created to allure you. Nothing more. She never existed."

She could feel the defeat roll through him, muscle by muscle. He rose, still pinning her down but no longer pressed against her but for his hands and knees. Still he was impossibly strong. Or perhaps she was impossibly weak.

"If I let you up," he said in what was more breath than voice, "you must promise not to try to injure yourself."

Her silence must have lasted too long as she tried to find one of those lies and speak it.

"Dara." He squeezed the wrists he still held. "Promise me. For the sake of the..." He was off her so quick, she could not even respond to it. Off her and kneeling at her side. "Is it even mine? The babe?"

Babe? Panic bore down on her fast and hard, and now she twisted not to escape him but *it*. The parasite growing inside her. "Get it out! Make it go away—I do not want it, I cannot!"

"Dara—"

"*Please*—your witch can get rid of the power, surely she can rid me of a leech."

"Child!" His shout would surely bring the entire villa down on her. Good, maybe someone else would kill her. Kill *it*. "It is a child, not a leech."

"I do not *want* it!" As if she could be a mother—the very word made her want to retch. "I do not want *you*. I hate you! I did not want to seduce you, I did not want to marry you, I did not want to come to this godforsaken land with you. *Let me go!*" She lunged in the direction the dagger had clattered, though she could not see it in the darkness. She would find it. She would plunge it into her stomach, into her womb, before he could stop her. She would—

She was jerked backward, landing on his legs, his chest pressed to her back, his arms iron clamps around her. She tried to use her head to bludgeon his, but even in the dark he must have been able to see that move coming. Only air met her head, and a shoulder that gave not so much as an inch.

She slumped again as the tears strangled her.

"If you do not want me, do not want our child, then why did you do it? Why did you seduce me, why did you marry me?"

Because her arms had not obeyed her. Her legs had not been under her control. If they had been, she would have run back to Thomas and begged for him to find another way. "He made me."

"The demon?"

"Stop saying that!" She turned her head so her hair would insulate her from him. "Thomas. My master."

"Why?"

"Are you a fool, to have to ask? I was to destroy you. Because you are a Christian. The protector of all the Christians in Rome. The enemy."

And he had touched her. Had planted his seed in her. She swallowed back rising bile.

"A brilliant plan." If his voice were any indication, he was nearly as dead inside as she. "Except you failed. And now you are my wife."

"I am not your wife!" She shook her head, grasping at that thought with the single ounce of hope left inside her. "Jonathan had no right to give me to you, only Thomas could. He is my master. He bought me. Only he can give me."

An incredulous breath puffed from his lips, at her ear. "You just said he made you do it. Told you to seduce me. To marry me. If that is not permission to wed me, I know not what is."

It was too true to deny. He had given her away. Forced her into the arms of a Roman dog. He loved her no more than her mother ever had.

And even the Roman with his eyes, with his words, had abandoned her that morning. Run off, left her to the dogs and witches when she needed him most.

There really was no point then. No reason to live another day. She let her limbs go boneless.

Benjamin's head rested against hers. So heavy. "Is the baby mine?"

"Yes." She closed her eyes, though it made it only a shade darker. But that other face greeted her, that other set of Roman hands. She wanted to vomit. Who was he, the master who was not Thomas? "I am an adulteress. You should have me stoned. Please."

His arms slid down hers, coming to a burdened rest upon her lap, still trapping her hands. "I would never do that. Especially not when you carry my child."

No point. No purpose. "You cannot force me to live. I will starve myself." It was the only threat she had the energy to make. The only one she had a hope of carrying through.

She wanted oblivion. Non-existence. She closed her eyes, let her head rest against his shoulder. Oblivion. Even if only for a few hours.

It took an eternity for daylight to come to his bed chamber. Benjamin's muscles ached from sitting so long without moving, but he dared not rise. Dared not shift, lest he wake her and send her on another flight toward something she could use as a weapon. Scarcely dared to breathe.

He could only pray. Sit there on the hard chair pulled up beside the soft bed on which she lay, restrained, and pray. As he should have done when he met her. As he should have done when Zipporah saw the evil inside her. As he should have done every day since.

Dawn had finally come. It lit her loom in the corner, the angry Neptune on the floor. But it brought no illumination to his spirit. No solutions. No answers as to how he was to convince his wife to live and deliver their child when she obviously wanted so desperately to die.

No clue as to how he could undo all the damage he had wrought.

An hour after daylight, a light tap sounded on his door. He could not bring himself to move, but he did manage a hoarse, "Enter."

Familiar footsteps. Samuel. "How is she? And how are you? Did you sleep at all?"

"Some. When I should not have." He forced himself to shift, straighten his spine, and turn to acknowledge his brother.

Samuel had not come alone. Zipporah stood with him, half-behind him, with a tray of food in hand. And behind her, Mark and Tamar hovered in the doorway.

The new cuts on Zipporah's face screamed an angry red this morning. Benjamin had to look away as she slid the tray onto a table. "She awoke at some point in the night. I had fallen asleep on the floor, praying. I heard her stumbling down the hall so got up and followed." He darted another glance to the girl he had once called a friend. "She went to your room, Zipporah, with the dagger. She meant to kill you."

The others gasped. He pressed the heels of his hands to his eyes. "Then she tried to take her own life. Begged me to let her die. Told me I could not force her to live, she would starve herself if she must."

"Ben." Samuel's hand came to a rest on his shoulder, solid and warm. "Why did you not send for someone to sit with you after that? You need not carry this burden alone."

"It must have been before you left the gathering, Zipporah." Tamar's voice, soft yet more confident than he could remember hearing it before. Although he seldom *had* heard it before.

"No, I do not think so." At Zipporah's cryptic tone, Benjamin looked up again. Her gaze was fixed on Samuel. "That makes more sense. The angel was not warning me of the time the dagger had already cut me, but of the time she yet intended it to. It did not occur to me."

Mark, his fingers linked with his wife's, stepped nearer his sister. "Angel?"

"You were awakened by the warning. You cannot be expected to reason through it all perfectly." Samuel smiled, though it looked more sorrowful than anything. "I told you that you would not die last night."

Praise the Lord the angel had warned her. Had she been there, Dara would have been upon her before Benjamin could have stopped her. He had barely arrived in time to keep her from turning the blade on herself. He slumped again. "I know not how to deal with this. What to do. She carries my child, but she does not want it. She is my wife, but she hates me. She would rather die than face life without the demon inside her. I do not understand it."

But Zipporah might. He looked her way, ready to beg her to see into his wife's spirit and share whatever she saw.

He did not need to ask. Her eyes were already fixed on Dara, and she already eased her way to the bed and sat upon it. Her gaze fell to the strips of linen he had used to restrain her.

"I knew not what else to do. To keep her from hurting herself if she awoke again, if I had fallen asleep again." Not that he had.

"No doubt a wise decision, Lord." But she loosened one of his knots from Dara's wrist and then cradled her hand. "Such pain. Some of the wounds are so very old. I could not see them before, beyond the demon. But they are clear now. Only Christ can heal such wounds." She squeezed Dara's hand and then moved one of hers to his wife's shoulder. "Did no one tend this?"

"What?" He stood. Zipporah pointed to a mark on Dara's shoulder with blood dried around it. "I did not see it. She was injured?"

"My shark's tooth. It was all I had to defend myself." Without getting up, she reached for the basin of water and a washcloth. "It is not deep, but it could still fester."

He opened his mouth to say he would tend her, or Samuel could. To caution her against being the one to touch that washcloth to the wound.

Before he could get out a word, Zipporah had already done just that, and Dara awoke with a hiss of pain. She arched against the linen strips holding her down, and her gaze flew straight to Zipporah. Hatred filled it. In the next instant the back of her newly freed hand connected with the maid's right cheek, with its inflamed flesh.

Zipporah did not so much as whimper. She merely caught the offending hand and held it again. "Easy, Lady. I am trying to tend you, not hurt you."

"I do not want to be tended." Dara's voice emerged hoarse and bitter. "Especially by *you*."

"I know that. And so I will go to Samuel's chamber and get his ground ilex acorns for him—he will want to apply some to your wound to ward off infection." She stood up, graceful and patient. "And I will pray for you."

Dara turned her face toward the window and closed her eyes again. "I do not want your prayers."

"I know. But you will get them." Zipporah turned to Benjamin. "You will need help. Do not be afraid to ask for it, nor refuse to out of pride. Let the church weep with you, so that we might rejoice with you when this night has ended."

He could do nothing but nod.

She caught Samuel's hand on her way by, though for only a moment. "I will leave the acorn paste outside the door, along with bandages."

"I will join you at the ilex in a bit," Samuel said. "Do not venture over the wall without me—I will help you find the necklace."

Zipporah sent Samuel a challenging, half-amused glance.

His brother narrowed his eyes. "Humor me. Yesterday is still fresh in my mind."

She actually smiled as she turned. "Yes, Master. As you will."

Benjamin hesitated a moment, then took the place Zipporah had vacated on the bed. Dara did not even look at him. Her hand was lax now, but he did not try to touch her. "Dara? How are you feeling this morning? Can I get you some water? Breakfast?"

"Nothing."

At least she answered. He had expected her to ignore him. He nodded. "Perhaps a bath or—"

"Just leave me alone." She turned her head again, apparently to glare at him. "If you want to do something for me, give me a chamber where I can have privacy and stay away from me."

His mouth was so dry. Or perhaps that was his spirit. "I cannot do that, Dara. You tried to kill yourself and our baby. You will not be alone again."

Her answer was to turn glassy eyes away once more.

Tamar eased up to his side. "We will help you, Master. I will sit with her during the day."

"We will all help, however we can." Mark motioned toward the tray of food. "For starters, you must eat. And then rest. We can watch over your wife for you."

No. How could it be right that these people he had refused to heed would be the ones to see him through this? He dug his fingers into his leg. But he could not tend her alone. And Zipporah's latest insight still echoed through the room. It seemed the first step to healing the rift he had caused was to lay it bare and let them tend it.

He nodded and looked up at Samuel. His brother offered a hand to pull him up. Unable to think of any alternative, he took it.

thirty-nine

SAMUEL TRIED TO THINK OF IT AS JUST ANOTHER WOUND ON JUST another shoulder, but it was challenging. Perhaps Zipporah could greet her with calm and respect after learning that, even without a demon, Dara had tried to kill her. He found it a great deal more difficult.

But he would do his part and give his brother a chance to step out of the room for a few minutes. And he would pray that this knot of resentment inside would loosen. He focused on her shoulder, dabbing the damp cloth around the puncture. Zipporah was right that it was not so deep. No stitches would be required. But already it was hot and swollen. The acorn paste was definitely required.

Dara's fingers dug into the mattress as he cleaned the blood away. She did not look at him. "How is she still alive? The dagger was poisoned."

"So we heard." He strove to keep his tone even, prayed the Father's love would fill him, since he could manage none of his own. "No doubt it was a strong potion, too. But God is stronger. She was convulsing and had lost consciousness when I brought her in. I prayed for her."

Her head rolled his way now, eyes narrowed to green slits. "You prayed for her, and poison had no effect? Ridiculous."

"Yet there she stands, living proof of it." He did not have to force the smile. "Jehovah healed her."

She snorted and sent her gaze to the ceiling. "He obviously did nothing for the wound itself."

"Because she can fulfill her purpose on this earth quite well with a scar. But not if she is dead. The Lord gives what we need."

Tamar slid the jar of boiled, ground-up ilex acorns onto the table. He reached for them, even as his pulse accelerated at the thought of Zipporah outside the door, slipping away to go back to the tree.

Focus. He must focus. He opened the jar and used his finger to spoon out some of the paste. When he smeared it over the wound, Dara looked at him again.

"You look like my abba." Her voice sounded different, young. The voice of a child, saturated with the pain of losing that father.

He looked into her eyes and saw himself as a boy, still raw from the loss of *his* abba. He remembered trying to cling to his mother and being pushed away. Always pushed away. *You cannot help me,* she would say. *You do me no good at all.*

Always about her, what her children could do for her. It made his head hurt, and his heart. He drew in a long breath through his nose and held her smoke-green gaze. "I am sorry your father died. I am sorry he left you with her. I am sorry she sold you."

"She told me I was worthless. That a daughter would be only a burden." She blinked back tears but kept tracing his face with her gaze, over and again. "I did not understand. My abba left us well enough off. We had the flocks, the house in the countryside, the one in the city. He had put money aside for my dowry. He had Jonathan to carry on the family name. Abba had always loved me. He called me his little darling, his precious one. Why did my ima hate me so? Why was I such a burden?"

Samuel shook his head and gripped her hand.

Her lips puckered with restrained tears. "Thomas came a few times to check on us, and she—she always made it sound as if we barely got by. As if we were desperate. We were *not.*"

"Perhaps she hoped he would marry her."

She jerked, her eyes went wide. Then her gaze went unfocused. "Perhaps she did. Perhaps that was why she hated me all the more when he offered, instead, to buy me."

Her master—Thomas. The man she seemed to love. The man at whose name Tamar shrank behind Mark, gripping his hand with what looked like desperate force. Obviously a Jewish man. How had she mistaken the senator for him?

Dara's gaze went to the window, the foot of the bed, and then back to his face. "Jonathan shares Abba's features," she whispered. "But he never reminds me of him. He is *her* son, through and through. You, though. You look so like my abba. Even your eyes."

It was hard to swallow. "He was a good man." He had to have been. Just like the father Samuel barely remembered.

She blinked rapidly. "You hate me."

The words, spoken so softly, with such mourning, broke something inside him. Because he *had*, he had hated her as he hated Martha. He had resented her for digging her claws into his brother, for trying to tear apart their home and their church. For trying, even when free of the demon, to kill the woman he loved.

He had hated her. But that made him like Martha. He had despised her. But that made him like the beast that had been inside her. And he wanted no part of the darkness. He wanted to show her love, love for the girl who had been abandoned and disdained and sold into the hands of evil. Love, like her abba had shown her.

And like his Abba God did.

He gripped her hand and leaned down. "No. No, I do not hate you. Not anymore. You are my sister."

She gripped his hand back, and for a moment life sparked through the tears in her eyes. Then it faded away, and her fingers went lax again. "It is not enough. I do not want this life, Samuel. I cannot be a wife and mother. You should wipe off whatever this paste is and let the infection come. Let it kill me."

Benjamin slid back into the room, almost wishing he had stayed in the hall. Almost wishing he had not heard that last exchange—one that first lit hope and then dashed it. She would rather die than stay here. With him. With his child. "Dara."

His brother straightened and turned on his chair, but Benjamin could not look at him. He could not look at any of them. Perhaps he could not say, right now, that he loved this woman begging for death. But she was still his wife. Still the mother of his child. With some effort, he schooled his face into the Stoic mask he had learned at Father's knee—though it was only a mask. The whole point of the philosophy was recognizing what you could not influence. This though...this he *must* influence, or she would die with his babe.

"What if..." He must wrap his tongue around the words, but they killed him a little as he formed them. "What if I offered to release you? If you will just stay here long enough to birth the baby, then...then I will equip you with money and slaves for protection and...and let you go wherever you will. You can start again. Wherever you please."

It was a wise deal to strike. It would guarantee she would not try to harm herself. It would give them time to minister to her. But it shattered Benjamin's heart into a thousand shards when he saw her eyes spark with life.

Dara was silent for a long, throbbing minute. Then she swallowed and lifted her head. "You would grant me a divorce?"

He winced at the word. How must she hate him, that she would prefer that disgrace over life with him? He focused his gaze on the floor. "If you wish it."

"I do."

He nodded without looking up at her again. "Then I would."

He edged backward a step, away from the bed. That whisper, too long silent, said he was doing right. But why, then, did it hurt so much? Every moment she considered it, her fingers toying with the edge of the sheet, sent those shards of his heart digging in, piercing. He dragged in a shaking breath. "Will you agree? You will not harm yourself or the babe, and in return I will provide your freedom."

Dara closed her eyes, worked her jaw back and forth, dug her fingers again into the bed. Benjamin could almost see the possibilities that she would be weighing. Months yet here, where she was so miserable, but then an open future. Money enough to take her somewhere where no one knew of her, no one would know she had been married before.

Where she could forget him. Forget their child. Leave him here to deal with the consequences of their actions on his own.

At length, she jerked her head in a nod. "I agree to your terms."

Benjamin managed only one nod of his head. The Stoicism was slipping. The mask would come off, and if she looked at him, she would see the tears gathering in his eyes. She would see how, even as he was glad she had chosen life over death, he would have to grieve her as if she had succeeded in plunging that knife into her stomach last night.

It felt as if she had plunged it into his. Pivoting on his heel, he left the chamber again. The others would tend, would minister. And he would take his turn at that too.

Just not yet.

Samuel turned back to the supplies Zipporah had brought him and picked up the bandage. With quick, gentle motions, he bound his sister's wound. Then he pressed his fingers to hers and waited for her to look at him. Tried to see only her, and the hope of winning her to the Lord, rather than the agony that had flashed through Benjamin's eyes before he slipped out again. "I will be back to visit more later. And every day. For now I must attend some other business."

"Thank you."

It was the first sincere appreciation he had heard from her since they met. He stood with a nod, catching Tamar's gaze to give her an encouraging half-smile.

Mark followed him into the hall. "Samuel. A moment."

Samuel paused, his brows lifting at the tone of his friend's voice. "Is something wrong? Beyond the obvious."

Mark pulled the door shut and studied him for a long moment. "Tamar said that yesterday—that you and Zipporah…"

Clearing his throat, Samuel drew him farther from the door and pitched his voice low. "Have you a problem with me falling in love with your sister, my friend?"

"No." Yet still he scowled. "What I take issue with is her spending the night in your chamber, given those feelings. Or will you tell me she did not? She was not in her own, she did not return to the gathering—"

"She was with me." And even knowing he had done nothing wrong, embarrassment clawed at him. "She came to me frightened, convinced the angel's warning of the dagger meant she would yet die last night. And she was quick to point out that as my handmaiden, there was nothing immoral about her presence in my room."

That did not seem to appease her brother. "If you took advantage of that—"

"No!" He held up his hands, half-afraid his friend would raise those fists clenched at his sides. "I promise you, Mark. I held her until she fell asleep and then made myself a pallet on the floor." For which she had berated him an hour ago when she awoke. But better her chiding than a full night of fighting off the desire that possessed him, lying beside her on his bed.

Mark studied him from beneath thunderous brows, no doubt marking the shade of red he had flushed and seeing those memories of longing flash through his eyes. But at length he relaxed. A degree. "I know she has always been special to you. But I admit I was surprised when Tamar said you kissed her before my parents, and that she thought she interrupted an embrace when she came in with the dagger. Zipporah...she is nothing like Anna."

"I know. And I did not anticipate this shift in how I look at her, but..." He shrugged and lowered his hands again. "I love her more than I thought I could love anyone, ever. As soon as it is appropriate, when Ben is not so raw, we will make the betrothal official."

Mark nodded, but he did not smile. If anything, he looked more serious than he had a moment earlier. "It will not be easy for you. You know that, do you not? With Anna, the world was curious and willing to forgive you marrying a slave because of her beauty."

But the world could not see that Zipporah was even more beautiful. For whatever reason, the Lord had given her a hidden beauty and so few of them the eyes to see it. But if the world could, they would understand. They would see why she took his breath away. If they could not, though, then he would treasure it all the more, knowing it was a gift kept secret, meant only for those who could love her best.

"I do not care what the world says. I need her."

Another somber nod. "Just tread carefully. Zipporah has never had to deal with these things, with resisting this kind of temptation. She is not accustomed to being the object of desire."

"I know." It made him desire her all the more, somehow. "I will treat her with honor and respect. You have my word."

"I know." Then Mark's gaze went back to Benjamin's door, and he sighed. "What a mess it all is."

"And yet already, blessings have come from it. You have gained a wife, I the promise of one."

"But Ben has lost one." Mark's countenance was tight. "I have never seen him look like this."

"Nor I. But the Lord is not finished here."

"Do you think she will try to harm herself again?"

Samuel tilted his head in consideration. "I pray not. I think she meant her promise—but that is not to say she will not go back on it if she falls into a dark spell. We will have to be attentive every moment of every day."

Mark opened his mouth but then paused, his gaze fastened on the end of the hallway.

Samuel turned too and saw John Mark heading their way, two scrolls in hand and a muted smile beneath his gray beard. Samuel greeted him with a nod as he drew near. "My friend. How goes your work?"

"Finished." In proof, he held up the scrolls. "With the aid of the servants your father lent me as scribes, I have made several copies, both of the good news itself and of the letter Paul sent the church here. I thought to deliver one of each into the hands of your brother." Lines of concern appeared around the man's eyes and mouth. "He can read them to her. Perhaps it will help open her eyes to the truth."

"I know he will appreciate that," Mark said. "Shall I take them in, or would you like to?"

John Mark handed the scrolls over. "You go ahead. I do not want to intrude, though I will continue to pray without ceasing."

Samuel turned with the older man back the way he had come. "And the other copies? Will you send them to others among the brethren?"

"I will take them. It is time I return home." A wistful smile touched his lips. "I look forward to seeing Simon Peter's reaction when he reads the stories he told me."

"How well I understand. You will have to write us and tell us all about it."

"I shall indeed."

They parted ways at the impluvium, and Samuel pointed his feet toward the exit. Then halted. Before he saw Zipporah again, there was one thing he must do. He doubled back down the hallway and went into his own room. Pulled out parchment and ink, a stylus, and got to work.

When he headed for the ilex, it was with the small roll of parchment in hand.

His eyes had to search through the branches to spot Zipporah, but he saw her at last on the limb that Benjamin had once favored, her feet resting on the wall and gaze cast out to the countryside beyond. She had not done that lately, that he had seen—look with longing at the world beyond the villa. She had not even tried to find an excuse to go to Rome after her father promised she could. Yesterday had been her first time over the wall in years.

Did she still long for travel? To see the world? If so, he would give her that. He felt no need to go back into the world himself quite yet, but he would for her. He would do anything for her, to see happiness light her dark eyes. To make her heart-stopping smile bloom on her lips.

"There is my little sparrow, perched in her tree."

She turned, that smile in place. "There is my master, come as he promised."

He ducked under the branch between them and made his way to her. "As promised, yes. Your master, no." He held out the parchment. "Your freedom, sparrow. So long as you promise not to fly too far from me."

"Hmm." She pouted her lip as she took the roll, then set it down and leaned toward him, her arms extended. "I rather liked being yours."

He gripped her waist and pulled her down, let his arms slide around her as hers settled around his neck. "I rather like it too. But not as master and maid-servant. God willing, you will soon call me husband instead."

"Husband." The word sounded like a promise on her tongue. "Yes, I think I will like that even better. How soon, do you think?"

If it were up to him, with no thought to anyone else, he would wed her within the week. But he must consider Benjamin's pain. "I know not. As soon as we can manage it without making Benjamin feel worse." He kissed her, because he could not help himself. And nearly moaned when she pressed up against him, certainly oblivious to the way her nearness chased vows of restraint to the furthest reaches of his mind.

It took him a long moment to remember he should pull away. When he did, it was with a sigh. "Hopefully *very* soon. But I fear it may be a while. He had to promise to divorce her to keep her from injuring herself further."

"Poor Benjamin." Her eyes reflected his trouble. "How can she welcome the disgrace of divorce?"

"He promised to give her money and slaves enough that she could go anywhere she wanted. No one in another city would even know."

Now she sighed and eased away a few more inches. Her eyes shifted, and he got the distinct feeling, as she framed his face in her hands, that she looked beyond his flesh. When her smile came again, it was brighter than ever. "You have embraced forgiveness."

The relief of it sang through him again. He nodded and then motioned with his head toward the wall. "Let us find your necklace, shall we?"

Better to focus on what they *could* find for the moment, rather than wonder at all that had been lost forever.

TAMAR SAT IN THE SAME CHAIR SHE HAD TAKEN FOR THE PAST TWO weeks, filling her mind with a prayer that today, things would go differently. She had been so hopeful at first, when Dara had seemed to open that sliver to Samuel.

But the last words she had spoken were her agreement to stay until she delivered the child, her short thanks to Samuel for bandaging her wound. Since then the mistress had risen, eaten, tended herself. But her eyes were always empty. Her lips were always still. When awake, her hands were at her loom. But if ever she needed something, rather than ask for it she would simply give up her task and return to the bed. She slept, it seemed, half the day away.

Master Benjamin had become nearly as silent, nearly as empty-eyed. Except where Dara's hollowness stretched down forever, his ended in a well of pain that sometimes sprang up. From what Tamar could see, he tried to hold himself together for his family. But the only times he looked like more than a hollow carving was when his siblings all came in together and bombarded him with cheer. Then he managed a smile or two.

Yesterday had revealed a key to his despair, beyond the obvious. Tamar had heard him say to Samuel, in the hall outside the door, "How am I to raise a child alone?"

He would not—that was the simple answer. Samuel had assured him that everyone would help. Tamar had found him last night to assure him *she* would help, would gladly take on the role of nursemaid. But she could see those offers did little to ease him. For starters, the child would need a nurse. No doubt some healthy mother here at Tutelos who would still be nursing a babe at the time and could give that life to the little one.

Perhaps—she flushed at the very thought, and nearly grinned at the memory—perhaps *she* would even be able to take on that role when the mistress's babe was still young. She had no reason to think, of course, that she was with child already. But it had been four days now since the warmth her husband's kisses kindled had finally grown into a flame she could no longer ignore. She had wanted to be sure that when she gave herself to him, she would have no regrets.

She had no regrets. Instead, she had hope. Hope that somehow a child would fill her womb. That this was the time of blessing. And the comfort that even if the Lord did not grant her that, he had given her so much more than she thought she would ever have. A husband who cherished her, one she had so quickly come to desire. A family to love her and welcome her. A Savior whose blood had washed her clean and whose Spirit now filled her.

She could feel him, even as she sat here in the mistress's chamber with its cloak of silence. And he urged her to reach for the scroll sitting on the table. It would not mark the first time she had read to her mistress, but she did not do so daily. Master Benjamin and his parents had been doing so, as had Zipporah—whom they had all tried to convince not to come, but she did anyway. And after a glare from Dara on the first day, her presence had earned no reaction at all.

Tamar unrolled the scroll, her eyes traveling over the Greek words until a few caught her eye. She spoke quietly into the otherwise silent room. "Love should be without hypocrisy. Hate what is evil. Cling to what is good. Be affectionate to one another with the love of a brother, putting each other before yourself—"

"Please stop." Dara's voice sounded more weary than annoyed. Certainly not the hateful, debasing tone she had always used with Tamar before. But still absent any warmth, despite that *please*. Yet the very fact that she spoke for the first time in a fortnight was surely cause for hope. "I tire of hearing this nonsense. It is not so bad when his mother reads the Scriptures to me, but that letter and the account of the carpenter's life are absurd."

Tamar traced a finger over the words. "I would be happy to read to you from the Scriptures if I could, Mistress. But I read only Greek, and they are in Hebrew."

"Then read nothing." Despondency hunched her shoulders as she turned back to her loom. Even her hair lacked luster, though Tamar had been washing it. "No doubt they commanded you to, but you need not obey them. You cannot enjoy those stories and lessons any more than I do."

Something sounded within her like a plucked string on a lyre. The Spirit, she had discovered these last weeks. Resonating.

The time had come to tell Dara of the truth. "Actually, Mistress, I treasure reading them, or hearing them when others read. Each time, I come away with something new to strengthen my faith."

"Your faith." Dara's hands went still and then fell to her lap. She did not look up. "You have been swayed to their side."

"I accepted the sacrifice of the Lamb of God. I have been made over into a new creation." The peace of it spread its wings within her. "For the first time in over a decade, I feel worthy of the air I breathe."

An incredulous breath came from Dara's lips. "To think that Thomas sent you here to strengthen me against them. What would he say if he knew you had turned on all he believes?"

Tamar studied her mistress, an entirely different question settling in her spirit. "In all the seven years I have known you, I have never heard you call him by name. Not until your conversation with your brother two weeks ago."

Dara's hands returned to her loom, though they remained idle. "I...I had no right to call him by name. He is—was—is my master. He is *your* master. You came here by his will, yet you have betrayed him."

It was something more than that. Why else would Dara have immediately begun referring to him by name when the demon left her? But Tamar could not unravel that mystery. She trailed a finger along the edge of the scroll. "Perhaps Thomas sent me. But it was by the will of a greater Master than he. And it is his will I must follow. The Lord brought us here, Mistress. Not so that we could destroy the Christians, but so that we might be saved."

Dara pulled her hands away again and spun on her chair to face Tamar. Confusion rolled in waves over her face. "I do not...I–I hated you. I remember hating you, but it is like the memory of a dream now. As if it were someone else's hatred."

"It *was* someone else's hatred, Mistress. The demon's."

Dara stood and paced to the window. She stared out for a long minute, long enough for that observation to fade away. Then she turned back. "Why did you fear him so? What did he do to you?"

Even now, it made Tamar's throat go tight and dry. "He refused me food. He would give me no water. He would take away my clothing and make me parade before all the other servants. He would force me to beg for a blanket, for a new chamber pot. He locked me in a room with a snake one night. With insects. With whatever I feared. He would tell me I was nothing, nothing but a body created to satisfy him."

Dara's eyes slid shut in the midst of the list. She winced. "Had I known, I...I probably would have laughed over it. Yet now it makes me sick. I never saw that side of him. He always treated me well."

With a sigh, Tamar rolled the scroll back up and set it down. "You never displeased him."

When Dara opened her eyes again, they were bright with a desperate question. "Did he love me? I do not know anymore."

Pain pierced for her, sank deep into Tamar's heart. She stood and made her way to her mistress, dared to reach out and take her hands. "You were special to him. He obviously felt something for you. But I wonder, Mistress, if he knows *how* to love. Love...love is a pure emotion, a holy one. It is patient and kind, which he never knew how to be. Love would not be so selfish, but he always thought first of himself. Love would not take pleasure in causing others pain, in destroying. But destruction is all he knows. If he knew what love was, then he would seek to *know* the truth, not to obliterate it."

"He *does* seek the truth!" Dara gripped her hands fiercely. "That is why he gathered seers to him, prophets—"

"Diviners. Fortune tellers. People who listen to demons whispering in their ears, demons who then follow the customers and make happen what they foretold."

Dara shook her head. "No."

"Yes." Certainty filled her. "Why do you think you could never see accurately when it came to the Christians? Because the demons' effects on them were limited. The Spirit protected them, whispered *real* truth to them, and warnings."

"No." But the word quavered, and Dara's knees buckled. She sagged against the wall and sank to the floor.

Tamar followed her down. She knew not why these things sprang to her tongue—she had not even known Dara's vision had been clouded in regards to the church. "Your powers were great. The demon was strong. But Jesus is greater. The Holy Spirit is stronger. And love, *real* love is what makes them so. Love so great that God would sacrifice his own Son. Love so boundless that the Son would go willingly to death for us. Love so intense that it can turn enemies into leaders of the Way. Love so strong that it can heal all the broken places inside. Mistress...Dara. You need that love. It is the only way to go on from here."

Dara said nothing. Not in response, and not for the remainder of Tamar's hours with her. She just crawled back to her chair, back to her loom, and locked herself away again.

Benjamin took the chair with its familiar wooden seat. Felt the familiar slant of the sun into his eyes. Drew in a breath, as he did every day, and closed his eyes for one more prayer. One more beseeching. *Please, Lord God, let it be today. Let her speak to me today.*

Since the exchange Tamar had told them about a week ago, she had spoken to the others. To his parents, about how Urbanus's family had agreed to come to the wedding. To his siblings, about their work around the villa. Even to Menelaus, about where he and Priscilla would next travel. Only with Zipporah had she clung to silence.

And with Benjamin. He had tried asking her questions. Reading to her. The last few days, he had been telling her stories from his childhood. Thinking, praying, that if she could just know him...

Please, Lord God, let it be today.

"Your cloth is beautiful." He tried a smile, tried to mean it. "What will you do with it?"

She said nothing.

"Perhaps...perhaps you could consider giving some of it to Sarah for her wedding garment. I know she would be honored to wear it. And it is so much finer than anything to be found in the markets. Softer even than the silk."

She said nothing.

"My mother was exclaiming over it yesterday afternoon as well. She said she has never seen the equal of it."

She said nothing.

Benjamin rubbed a hand over his face. "Did I ever tell you of the time I broke one of her necklaces? It was the first gift my abba Jason had given her, a strand of colorful Egyptian beads. I cannot remember now why I even had it out, but Samuel was trying to take it from me, to put it back, and I would not let go.

The string broke, and beads went flying everywhere. I just knew she would be furious. That I would be punished more severely than I ever had been before."

He paused, waiting for some reaction.

She said nothing.

He let his gaze wander to the window, and to the sunlight that promised warmth and comfort. "She was angry, of course. And her frustration got the better of her for a few minutes. But then she paused and took a deep breath, and she crouched down and drew me into her arms. She said, 'That necklace meant a lot to me. But not as much as you do. We will repair it. Together. And as we do, we will remember your father.' Samuel had already gathered the beads together. And so the three of us sat down, and we strung all those tiny beads again. She told me about my father. Samuel piped in with his memories. Father joined us and added his own. By the time we finished, the necklace was whole again. And I had been given the gift of knowing the man I never got to meet."

It took him a moment to realize that the soft sounds of the loom had gone still. He looked over and found Dara watching him, her gaze wary. When her lips parted, his breath fled. When she shook her head, he nearly sagged in resignation.

Then her voice slipped into the hush. "You are blessed to have such a mother."

He tasted fear. He must reply, yet if he spoke wrongly... *Please, God, give me your words.* "I know. She said she told you her story the other day. Of how learning she carried my father's child first seemed a curse to her, how she did not want to be bound to him forever. But how he changed, eventually married her, loved her so deeply. How when she first felt me move within her, love took the place of resentment."

Dara's gaze fell. "I am not like your mother. You ought not to hope I will be."

"I do not—" But he cut the lie off. Of course he did. Of course he hoped she too would come to love their child. And that, when she did, she would not be able to bear the thought of leaving the babe...or him. He looked to the sunlight for strength and tried again. "I cannot help but hope, Dara. I want you to change your mind. I want you to *want* to be my wife, to be a mother to our child. I want a family. A whole one."

She turned away from him again, her fingers back on the shuttle. "I will not change my mind. If you want a wife to care for your child, you will have to find another after I am gone." She darted an arrow of a glance his way. "It ought not to be too difficult for you. You are handsome. Rich. Kind."

The arrow hit its mark. "Yet you cannot love me."

"No. I cannot." She did not even hesitate. Did not falter. "I *will* not."

The three weeks of silence ought to have told him as much. The two months of lies beforehand ought to have proven it. Yet the wound felt new and so raw that he could not sit idly by and let it bleed. He pushed himself to his feet.

But he did his best to smile. "Would you like to take a walk outside?" He had offered it before.

Before, she had ignored him. Today she said, "No."

"Are you certain? The exercise would no doubt do you good." He swallowed. "If it is my presence you object to, I could call for Mother or Sarah or Tamar to accompany you instead."

This time she seemed to give it thought. His mother and Sarah and Tamar would call it progress. He called it another cloud across his hope. "Not today."

He could do nothing but nod and reach for the door. Usually he spent more time than this with her, but he could not right now. Usually Zipporah was the next to come, but she was not yet anywhere within sight when he peered into the hallway.

Deborah was just emerging from her and Jason's chamber though. He called to her, and she seemed happy enough to take his place.

He flew toward the sunlight. Once it warmed his flesh he slowed, soaking it in. And he let his shoulders sag. Then he made himself close his eyes, focus away from himself. *Thank you, Lord. She spoke. I thank you.*

No matter that his heart ached more than ever. God was faithful. God had answered his prayers. God would watch over Dara even when Benjamin could not. When she left him. Left him with a newborn he knew not how to raise nor care for. But whom he knew he wanted. Knew he would give his life for.

His son or daughter. His heir. His future.

"Ben!"

He opened his eyes again and saw Samuel and Zipporah both coming his way, hurrying away from the gate. The looks on their faces warned him that something had happened. His weeping heart prayed it was nothing that would require him right now. "What is it?"

They slowed as they neared, Zipporah's breath quickened but Samuel's normal. Such a short run would not affect him, so it was he who spoke. "Alexander Avitus was just here."

The name should mean something. It did not. "Who?"

The two exchanged a glance. Samuel cleared his throat. "Emperor Nero's friend. The one who...the one we caught her with."

The arrow she had shot into his heart twisted. No doubt his agony showed on his face, but he could not contain it. Not just now. "What did he want?"

"Dara," Zipporah said. She stood so straight in the face of it all. "He demanded we release her to him."

The audacity of it made him straighten. The image of her in that man's arms, still seared into Benjamin's mind, made his hands clench. "You obviously sent him away."

"Yes, but..." She hesitated and looked to Samuel, but he only nodded. Zipporah loosed a quick breath and met Benjamin's gaze again. "There is a demon within him. They are always eager to get within our gates, but this one was in a frenzy, and the man with him. He said he would be back within the week."

Benjamin had to turn partly away and try to gather his strength and his thoughts. He did not want to face the man again—did not trust himself enough. But it should not fall to his brother and friend, to his steward or parents, to turn the senator away.

It should fall to him. "Thank you. I will fast and pray and be ready to meet him when next he comes."

"We will fast and pray with you." Samuel rested a hand on his shoulder, as he always did when he needed to give comfort.

"I know." Benjamin produced a weak smile for his brother and shared it with Zipporah too. Looking at her still hurt. That angry red scar constantly screamed a reminder of all that had happened. Because of him.

But she smiled back brightly, without any resentment. "We will get through this. You are not alone."

"I know." Even if by rights he should be. That was the beauty, though, of faith and love and family. They would not let him carry this burden alone. They would see him through whatever came of the encounter with Alexander Avitus. They would see him through the agonizing months of having Dara close but out of reach. They would see him through raising his child without a mother. They would no doubt pray until a fine, godly wife entered his life.

He did not want to think of another wife. He could not possibly make anyone else happy, as wounded as he was.

Zipporah's eyes went narrow in thought, the cross-shaped scar pulling tight with the action. "What are you doing out here so early? You are always with her still at this hour."

"Deborah took my place. I—Dara spoke to me. It was not exactly encouraging."

"Oh, Benjamin. I am so sorry." She stepped near and took his hand, held it for a moment.

How long had it been since she had done such a thing? Years. Years upon years. Not since she was a child, before her feelings for him changed and he took to avoiding her to spare them both embarrassment.

Yet it did not feel strange to have her hands surrounding his. Neither embarrassing nor uncomfortable. Perhaps because he knew with complete certainty, in that moment, that she had forgiven him for all the many ways he had hurt her.

She increased the pressure on his hand and then released it and stepped way. "I will go relieve Deborah."

Or perhaps...perhaps because he was meant to restore all he damaged. Perhaps...perhaps Samuel had been right all those months ago. Perhaps his future had waited right here all along.

SAMUEL MADE IT A POINT NOT TO WATCH ZIPPORAH WALK AWAY. IF he indulged that desire, Benjamin might notice the longing, and now was not the time for that conversation. Not when his brother looked ready to crack and crumble. Samuel had been waiting, day after day, for some urging from the Spirit that he could broach the subject with him. He had been waiting to see life enter Benjamin's eyes again.

Neither had come. Instead he had felt that hand upon his spirit saying, *Be still.*

Now he held out an arm to indicate they should walk. "Do you want to talk about what she said to you?"

Benjamin's nostrils flared. "It ought not to upset me so—it is nothing she did not say before. That she does not love me, *will* not love me."

"Ben." Heaviness settled in Samuel's chest. No, now was definitely not the time to tell him he had fallen in love again, and that Zipporah loved him in return. That he had lived each day these last three weeks for those few stolen moments they could find under the ilex tree, when he could hold her and kiss her and know that someday she would be his wife. "It has only been a few weeks. Do not despair yet."

"I know. And yet," he said, pausing and turning to face him, "I must plan for what is to come. God willing, I will have a child to think of. For whom I will be responsible. He will need a mother."

The heaviness thudded into his stomach. "You will have no shortage of willing hands to help you, Ben. You know that."

"Just as we had many sets of willing hands to help with us when we were children. All of them special. All of them we love. But no one else could ever be our ima." He looked back to the villa, his gaze conflicted. "I want my child to have a mother. And if Dara insists on divorce, then I have only one choice."

"Remarriage." Why did the word sound like a dirge to Samuel's ears? Why did it bite like fangs? "But how can you be sure you will be ready for that? You are still so raw. And Dara could yet change her mind."

"She could. I pray she will. But if she does not..." Benjamin sighed. "It would have to be somebody who understood all this. Who was willing to be patient with me. Who could love my child as her own, who could teach him the Way. Somebody who...who might be able to find some happiness by my side, even if it takes me a while to mourn Dara's leaving. She would have to be extraordinarily strong. Extraordinarily pure of heart."

He obviously had someone in mind. And the rock in Samuel's stomach told him clearly who that someone must be. "I can think of only one unwed woman who meets that definition." Did his voice sound as choked as it felt?

It must not have. Benjamin did not so much as blink. "Zipporah." He met Samuel's gaze again, his looking so very vulnerable. Laid bare. "Do you think she still loves me, Sam? I know I have hurt her terribly. Through all this, but before too, by ignoring her so long. But she still loved me through those years—do you think she does through this? Or that she could again?"

Benjamin could not know how the questions pummeled him. He could not know how much Samuel wanted to shout *No! No, she does not love you anymore!* He could not know how much he feared the answer was *Yes. She always will.*

He had to look away, though he saw nothing before him. Was this why the Spirit had kept him still? Because had he spoken, Benjamin would not have come to this conclusion—did that mean it was the conclusion he was *meant* to come to?

His brother still waited. Samuel prayed his face gave nothing away. "I dare not answer for her. Not about that."

"I know. And perhaps it would be too much to ask of her, and I should not even think it. She has already given up so much for the brethren, for Tutelos. I do not want to ask anything of her that would require more of a sacrifice. But if it might bring her happiness...if she might *want* to be my wife..."

Why must he look at it so fairly, why could he not make it a selfish suggestion, so that Samuel could dismiss it? He drew in a breath that did nothing to relieve the pressure inside and walked a few more steps. Benjamin kept pace.

He knew not what to say nor what to think. He knew only that he wanted to shout that she was *his*, and that he would not give her up.

But she was not his. She was free. Free to choose who she would love, who she would marry.

And she had loved Benjamin all her life. Why should Samuel think that he had replaced him in her heart? Obviously she said she did not love him any longer when he came back wed to Dara, and with all the ramifications of that. He had been out of reach.

What if that was the root of her feelings for *him*? That, since she could not have Benjamin, she might as well open her heart to Samuel? She loved him, he had no doubt of that. But how much of it was the love of a dear friend? What if she merely submitted to his notions of romance because she wanted him to be happy and thought she had no other options?

He came to a halt again and turned his regard on his brother. For twenty-six years, Samuel had protected him. He had stood at his side. He had done all he could to be friend, guardian, teacher. Because he loved him, this first brother to join his life. And because the hope of the whole church of Rome rested with him.

Samuel loved Benjamin. He loved Zipporah. Did he love them both enough to want them to be happy at his own expense? Could he give her up for him? If that was what the Lord asked him to do?

A shiver swept over him, and in its wake a relief from the turmoil of the questions. If the Lord asked it...then the Lord would have to give him the strength to do it. He gathered up all he could muster right now. "I can speak with her, if you would like, to sound out her feelings before you approach her."

Benjamin looked out toward the wall, toward the wide world Zipporah had always wanted to experience at his side. Would he offer her that, as Samuel had been willing to do? "I would appreciate it. I do not want to anger her or injure her still more with asking this if she would view it as an insult."

Her smile filled Samuel's mind, and her laugh. The way she cooed at her one-legged bird, the ease with which she greeted every trouble that found them. The unwavering determination she showed in standing against what was wrong. In embracing what was right. His warrior queen. "No matter her answer, she will not be angry. Not when you ask from right motives."

Of all the stupid, insufferable, blockheaded suggestions—Zipporah was so furious she could not even move, lest her hand snake out and slap the foolishness out of him. So she stood straight as a rod, her arms at her side, and fumed. "And you said *nothing*?"

Samuel sighed and leaned against the branch of the ilex. "What was I to say?"

"What were you to say? *What were you to say?* You were to say that *you* love me, that we are all but betrothed, that I could not possibly want to marry *him* because I want to marry *you*!"

"Zipporah." Another long sigh. He looked miserable, which ought to have been a clue to this fool of a man that his nobility was ill-placed this time. "I cannot be selfish. Not when it concerns the happiness of two of the people I love most in this world."

She could not slap him. But she was mightily tempted to grip his shoulders and shake some sense into him. "I could not possibly be happy with him! Surely you know that. How on earth could you *not* know that, when your kisses turn my knees to liquid and we have been whispering of our marriage these three weeks?"

He gripped the branch, his knuckles whitening against the bark. "You loved him so long. I know you had given up hope, but now that things have changed... how could you turn him down? You would always regret it. You would always wish I were my brother."

For a moment she just stared at him. How could it be that *he*, the most beautiful man she had ever seen, was insecure about *her* love? By rights, should it not be she who worried that she could never compare to Anna? Should she not even now worry that this was a ploy to back out of their promises?

Except *she* had more sense than that, because *she* knew love when she saw it, and she saw it shining like the sun in his eyes when he looked at her. "You blockhead. You want to see how I could possibly turn him down? Then come."

She spun on her heel, away from the tree and toward the villa.

"Sparrow, wait!" He caught her wrist, which fanned the flames inside higher. "You cannot just charge in there and refuse him. You must consider it."

She pulled her wrist free. "I do not *need* to consider it. I already *know.*"

He reached for her again. "Zipporah—"

"No." She backed away another step, holding up a warning finger. "When you touch me again, Samuel Asinius, it had better be to pull me into your arms, kiss me, and apologize for being such a colossal fool. I imagine I will find your insecurity endearing after it ceases to be so infuriating."

His arm fell to his side. "I just want you to be happy. It may make me miserable, but I must let you go when it is what you need."

She gripped her hair near the roots, but that did nothing to relieve the pressure. "You think I would be happy married to a man I do not love, who does not love me, while the man I *do* love is miserable? Do we not all deserve better than that?"

Torment churned in his green-gold eyes. "He would come to love you quickly, I know he would. How could he not?"

"Because I am not meant for him, I am meant for you!" She surged back across the space between them, gripped his toga, and pulled him against her. Straining up on her toes, she pressed a hard, angry kiss to his mouth that nevertheless made his arms come around her, made him all but lift her from her feet. And then she pulled away with a huff. "Do you mean to tell me you could send me into his arms? You could stand to pass by me in the hall every day and not touch me? You could return to being my brother? Because I cannot. I cannot be your sister again."

For a moment, when his mouth reclaimed hers, when his hands pressed against her back with such fervency, she thought she had gotten through to him.

Then he pulled away with sorrow in his eyes and said, "Pray about it before you answer him."

She growled and stormed toward the villa. She knew no one else the world over who could be so set on selflessness that he could not see how miserable he would make every one of them with it. "Pray about it?" she said to the flock of birds flying overhead. Did Daniel have to pray about whether or not to bow down to the king of Babylon? Did Ruth have to pray about whether to follow Naomi? About the consequences and ramifications, yes.

But not about whether to do what was right when they already knew. And she knew. Knew with everything within her that she was not supposed to be Benjamin's wife, ever. She was never meant to be, she had always known that, and it had become unthinkable when he married Dara.

He *had* a wife. And he could not just give up on her and set his eyes upon when she would leave. If he did, he was as big a fool as his blockheaded brother.

Barely aware of the ground she flew over, she sent an absent wave to Sarah and the children but kept her aim toward the house. Then the hall. Then the chamber that would *not* ever be hers. Tamar would be with her mistress now, and she would not mind an interruption, because *she* was reasonable.

Zipporah entered without knocking, slammed the door shut, and took perhaps a bit too much pleasure from it when Dara started, jumped up, and splayed a hand over her heart.

Apparently she should have tried that tack weeks ago, since it actually spurred the girl to open her mouth. Even if she did just demand, "What is the matter with you?"

"What is the matter with me? Your brother and husband, that is what. Are you aware that those fools have gotten the idiotic notion in their irrational brains that Benjamin should begin planning for when you leave and have a new wife standing in line ready to jump in and raise your babe?"

The surprise of her entrance drained from Dara's face and left it hollow again. "I am the one who suggested it to him. What is it to me?"

"Oh, stop acting like a child!"

Though she had been making to sit again, Dara paused, and her eyes flashed. "Excuse me?"

Perhaps it was an unfair expectation—part of Dara was still likely nine years old, stuck in the age she had been when the creature took her over. But the memories were there, and the maturity that came of them. Zipporah planted her hands on her hips. "I said you need to stop acting like a child. You cannot just run from your husband and baby."

Dara slashed a hand through the air. "They are not *my* husband and baby! *I* did not choose to marry him. *I* did not welcome him to my bed. Why should *I* have to pay the consequences?"

"Did you invite the creature in?"

"What?" Though she had had little color in her cheeks to begin with, now she washed even paler.

Zipporah waved a hand at the window. At the past. "When you were a child. You could not have known what you were doing, I realize that. But when your master prayed over you, did you welcome it? Did you invite it in?"

The quiver of her lip was answer enough.

Zipporah shook her head. "Children do not understand cause and effect, but that does not exempt them from consequences. Do you think when I was thirteen I understood what it meant to see the things of the Spirit? Do you think I understood that within hours of praying for the Lord to show me himself, a man would try to kill me, that I would bear the scar the rest of my life? *No.* But that makes it no less real. No less inescapable."

Dara's hands shook, even after she clenched them. "It is not the same, your story and mine."

"No. It is not. Because at any moment I could have prayed for the Lord to take the gift from me, and he would have. You could not ask the demon to leave and have it happily go. But our actions have consequences." She took a step closer, hands now splayed before her. "You chose to invite it in. So many choose to invite them in without knowing what they do. Without knowing what could happen, without even knowing what they are. Children, especially, are so open that they do not know *how* to refuse when a dark one whispers—that is why their parents must protect them, must always cover them with prayer. Because once a choice is made, it cannot be undone. Once an action is taken, consequences will follow. For you, that means your body seduced a man, welcomed him to your bed. Together you made a baby. A baby that is *yours*."

"No." At least her eyes sparked, if only with anger.

"Denying the truth makes it no less true. If you are not the babe's mother, who is?"

"I do not care who takes it, but I cannot be a mother!"

The fear within Dara all but took her over. Zipporah had little trouble understanding its roots. "You do not want to be *your* mother." She lowered her hands, held the girl's gaze. "So why are you making the same choice she made—to give up her child rather than face what might be a difficult life with him—and expecting different consequences?"

Dara sank onto her chair. "I am not like her. I will not be. It is different."

"Is it?" Zipporah crossed to her and knelt beside her. "The idea of a child makes you panic. That is no doubt how she felt after her first husband died and she had to care for Samuel on her own. So she made the decision that would allow her to be free of that panic—she put him into the care of someone else. She no doubt told herself that he would be better off without her, that the Lord would see to him—and so he did. But what happened to her?"

They all knew the answer. They all knew what she had become, and how easily she had repeated her mistake. Dara squeezed her eyes shut.

Zipporah touched her clenched hands and found them cold. "What will happen to *you* if you abandon your baby? Will you be happy? Or will you be bitter? It will not make you past redemption, Dara—nothing is bigger than God's love for you. But how much more difficult will it be to live with yourself then?"

"But I am not fit to be a mother." A tear made its way from between her eyelids and slid down her cheek. "I do not know how to love. I...I am dead inside."

"How fortunate, then, that we serve a God who quickens the dead. Who breathes life into the lifeless. Do you not think that a God who formed man out of dust can form a new creation in you?"

"New creation." Blinking now against the tears, Dara's gaze went past Zipporah.

A moment later, Tamar settled beside her on the floor and took her mistress's hand too. "That is right. He made one of me. He can make one of you."

Golden curls swayed when she shook her head. "I do not know. About the babe, but...but then there is Benjamin too. I cannot face him for the rest of my life."

"Why not, Mistress? He is a good man. He is kind and noble and virtuous."

"And he is ready to love you." Zipporah had not spoken to him about his marriage, but she knew it was true. "You need only to let him. To show him your true self and be willing to see his. Forgive each other. Decide together to find the good in a situation meant for evil."

Dara sniffed, reclaimed her hands to wipe at her eyes. "I do not understand why you would encourage me to stay with him. If I am out of the way, he may turn to you."

"Not you too!" Zipporah rocked back on her heels with exasperation. "I do not want him to turn to me. I do not love him, I love your blockhead of a brother who can *somehow* follow a kiss that turns me into melted wax with a command to pray about marrying someone else."

Tamar laughed, though she covered it with a hand. Dara just stared at her. Then shook herself. "Samuel? You and Samuel?"

"We have not wanted to say anything to Benjamin while he is so upset, but now Samuel has gotten the addlebrained notion that he was meant not to say anything so that he might make this great sacrifice for his brother." She pushed to her feet so she could pace off the anger that swelled again. "As if I am so inconstant that at the mere mention of Benjamin I will forget my love for Samuel and go running the other direction."

"Why are you telling me this?" Dara's voice sounded shaky and faint. "To pressure *me* into staying with Benjamin so you can marry Samuel?"

"I will not marry Benjamin no matter what you do." Zipporah turned once she got to the window, faced them again. "I am telling you so you understand the situation. And I am telling you because a month ago you would have used it against us all. You would have told Benjamin in such a way that it would drive a wedge between him and Samuel, which would in turn put one between Samuel and me. But I do not think you will do that now. Will you?"

Dara's shoulders rose and fell with the breath she drew in. She shook her head.

"Exactly. I am telling you so that you can see you are not who the demon made you. Nor are you the child who wanted so badly to be loved that she would give her soul to whomever her master bade her. You are someone altogether different now, Dara. And you get to decide who that someone will be."

Emptied of words, Zipporah turned toward the door. Though she got no more than two steps before Dara called her name.

She had stood again, and now she clutched white cloth to her chest. "I do not know who I am. But I know I am sorry. For trying to kill you. For scarring you."

Zipporah's fingers moved of their own will to the new scar, bumpy and raised. But she smiled. "I am not. It is what inspired Samuel to kiss me."

Though she looked about as confident as a baby bird on the edge of the nest for the first time, Dara eased forward and held out the folds of cloth. "Will you take this? It is not much of an apology, but it is all I have that is my own. There is a lot there. Enough for a stola for Sarah, for her wedding. And...one for you, when you wed my brother."

Now Zipporah could find no words at all. She could only meet Dara in the middle of the room and take the impossibly soft cloth from her with a brimming heart. The only thing she could wrap her tongue around felt feeble indeed in the light of someone's first step toward reconciliation. "Thank you."

With a nod, Dara moved backward a step. "Will you visit tomorrow?"

"Of course."

"Then perhaps we could take a walk. Benjamin said I could," she added too quickly. "With him or his mother or sister or Tamar. I am certain he would have included you, too, had I spoken to you yet."

Zipporah nodded. "Dara...I see the walls inside you coming down. Let them. Let them go. Let in the people who want to love you."

Dara made no promises. But neither did she make objections. And her eyes, as Zipporah turned away, were not quite as empty as when she had come.

For today, that counted as a victory.

DARA HAD NOT MEANT TO OBEY ZIPPORAH'S COMMAND. BUT WHEN she tried to raise her protection back into place that evening, she had made the mistake of looking in the mirror. And she had seen her mother staring at her from her own eyes.

Zipporah had been right about that much, at least. She was making her mother's decision. And that could only turn her into the same bitter, conniving woman she had always despised.

Maybe it was better to risk pain than to be empty. Maybe it was better to fail than not to try.

Maybe it was better to live than to die.

For the third day in a row, she strolled outside with Tamar and Zipporah. Sarah had joined them yesterday, but today one of her betrothed's daughters was feeling poorly, and she was sitting with her. Sarah, it seemed, had been born with the knowledge of how to nurture. How to mother. How to love.

Dara was still unconvinced she had the ability. But maybe...maybe she could try. For a while. She could at least hold her baby before she gave it up. Give herself a few days or weeks to see if she would love it. If she would miss it. If its absence would turn her into the stone monster Martha had become.

While Tamar and Zipporah laughed over something, Dara pressed a hand to her abdomen. No one else had mentioned being able to see her condition, but she could. She, who had been so unaware of her body for so long, somehow noticed right away when the fabric began to fall differently over her curves. Soon enough, it would be obvious to all.

It would be obvious to Benjamin. How would he look at her then? Would the dejection always in his eyes fade or increase? Would his stories—all those stories of the life he lived, the life their child could live here—change?

Tamar and Zipporah were right about that too. He was a good man. But she was not a good woman. The things she had done...sometimes it bore down on her in the night and made her reach for the dagger that was not there. It made her want to obliterate herself from the world, remove the stain. The weight had increased as she let those stolen years roll through her mind, as she remembered all the words she had spoken, the pleasure she had taken from hurting people.

Zipporah said she did not have to be that woman. But those were the only memories she had of her growing-up years. Who had she become, if not who the...the demon had made her?

"Stop." Zipporah obeyed her own command and reached out to bring Dara and Tamar to a halt too.

Dara knew that look on her face, though it took a long moment to realize *why* she knew it. It was the look she had used to give Dara, when she looked not *at* her, but *within* her. It was the look she wore when she saw beyond the veil.

Zipporah forced them all back a step. "We must turn around. Now."

Unease flashed over Tamar's face—another echo of what used to be. "What is it?"

"Back to the villa. Now. We must—"

"*Dara!*"

She jolted, and her head jerked toward the road. She had not realized they had walked this direction, but there was the wall. And the gate. And the Roman who was trying to barge his way in, past the servants determined to keep him out.

"Dara!"

She remembered the voice. And the face. And the arms shoving at the steward. She remembered thinking *master* when she looked into his eyes, she remembered leading him to her husband's bed and giving herself to him there.

The memories brought her to her knees and brought her midday meal heaving upward.

Hands smoothed over her hair, either Tamar's or Zipporah's. "Dara, come. Quickly." Zipporah's voice.

His voice. "Let me get to her—she is ill! Can you not see she is ill? She needs me. Dara, come to me! I will take you from these people. It is too dangerous for you now. We will find another way. Come with me."

Another way...another way to destroy them. That was all the master cared about. That was all he *ever* cared about, that and increasing his coffers. But why, why was this Roman spouting the master's words? She spat out the last of the sickness and grappled her way up Tamar's arms so she could stand again.

"Dara." The Roman shoved again at the steward. "Come here, beloved."

Even had Zipporah and Tamar not been holding her fast where she stood, she would not have taken another step toward that man. She shook her head. "I do not know you."

For a second he stood frozen. Then he roared, charged. "What have you done to her? What have you *done*, you fools?"

He broke past the guards. He shouted, but one throat alone could not be responsible for the cacophony that filled her ears. It all echoed, rang, blended together as she tried to turn, tried to run, and tripped over something. Zipporah caught her, but beyond that she could make no sense of the blur of colors and motion.

Until the sound of iron clanging against iron brought her back upright. Until she heard Benjamin, swinging his sword, shout, "Stay away from my wife!"

The Roman must have drawn a sword as well, for one lay in the dirt behind him and his hand still tried to grip it. "She is not yours, dog, she never was. She is mine."

"No." Benjamin struck some stance that looked well practiced and fluid. Sword at the ready, muscles coiled. Limbs perfectly still. "She is not."

The Roman sneered. "Do you know who I am? You do not want to fight me. You will pay and all your precious *church* with you."

Benjamin did not so much as flinch. "I know you are Alexander Avitus, senator and friend of the emperor. I know you have a demon within you. I know you somehow convinced my wife you were her master before we cast the demon from *her*."

He roared again, and Dara shuddered and pressed her face to Zipporah's shoulder. "Who dared to strip her of what she was? Was it you, dog, or your witch? I will kill you both! I will go to the emperor, I will get his weight behind me. We will take this villa from you, we will take *everything* from you, we will crush you beneath our heels like a snake!"

"Stop!" Dara knew not where the will to shout came from, nor why she leapt away from Zipporah and to Benjamin's side. But there she was, gripping her husband's arm with one hand and holding the other up, palm out, toward the Roman. "Please. You have no quarrel with these people. I know I sinned with you, but I do not know *why*. You are not the master I remember. And I—I am not the servant my master made me. I am not that girl anymore. I am someone different now."

His eyes, when he narrowed them, almost looked familiar. But they were a deep brown. Thomas's were hazel. "Come with me, Dara. I can give you back the gift they stripped you of. I can fill you with the power again."

The power. Her eyes yearned for it, yearned for the sight they had grown so accustomed to but were now denied. Her muscles strained for the confidence they had once exuded.

But her stomach clenched. And some other part deep in her chest thudded its *no.* With the power came the hatred and the thirst for destruction that had left her so very empty. She shook her head. "I do not want it."

In a flash, he had reached into the folds of his toga and pulled out a dagger. In the next flash, Benjamin had put himself between her and the Roman.

The senator sneered. "The reach of a dagger is longer, dog, when you throw it." His gaze went to Dara. "I will do it for you, Dara. I will kill for you."

Sorrow surged through her, overtaking the fear and the unexpected courage. She rested a palm against Benjamin's back. He would not budge, she knew that, even if the dagger flew, even if he could not stop it. He would stay right there, between them, so it would not possibly hit her. "But would you die for me? Master?"

His scowl was acidic. "What good would that do either of us?"

"What if it were to save my life?"

Now disgust curled his lip. "I have no time for hypothetical questions, Dara.

Come with me now. Or I will come back with orders from the emperor and this dog and his witch will be executed."

Feeling rushed through her, so intense and unexpected it made her gasp. Too numerous to put names to, too crippling to ignore. She made to step around Benjamin.

He caught her, held her against his back. "No, Dara. Do not."

"I cannot let him kill you, Benjamin, and rip this place apart. If I go—"

"He will come back anyway. You know he will."

"Yes." The Roman shifted, lowered his dagger, pivoted. "I will. You can be sure of that." Fury in every line, he stormed back toward the gate, reclaiming his sword but not brandishing it at any of the guards. He merely mounted his horse and spurred it toward Rome.

Benjamin let his sword fall to the ground and turned, wrapping his arms around her.

She waited for the resistance to come, but it did not. Not now. She wrapped her arms around him too. They knew him, he felt right within them. Not just familiar, but right. "I am sorry. I am so sorry I brought this on you. You must wish you had never met me. I have brought you nothing but trial."

"Dara." One of his hands buried itself in her hair as he had not done in over a month, since before her lips said those terrible things to his mother.

She had missed it. Missed him.

"I am not sorry I met you. We can make it through these trials. We can. The Lord will guide us."

She could not see how. But then...she was not supposed to.

Samuel ran as fast as his legs could move, but still he knew he was too far away to help. Sunlight flashed on blades, people fell and surged up and moved around one another. For a while, no one moved, and he thought maybe he *would* arrive in time to help. In time to toss himself before Zipporah, at least, if a blade yet again tried to find her.

He started down the knoll, his feet on the road.

Alexander Avitus—that was who had pushed his way in, and it struck a note of fear inside Samuel. One that did not ease when the man strode away and then rode away.

Samuel did not slow. Not until he reached her. Then he skidded to a halt and pulled her to him all in one motion, probably crushing the breath out of her.

Though she managed a squeal. And a laugh. And her arms came around him. "I am well, Samuel. I promise. I was not his target."

"Hush." He just had to hold her. Assure himself she was unharmed. Because if she had been taken from him when they had not even spoken in three days, when their last words had been in anger, he would not be able to live with himself.

She chuckled again, nuzzled his cheek, and then nudged his head to the right. "Look."

He looked, and saw Benjamin and Dara also had their arms wrapped around each other.

Zipporah's fingers dug into his side. "I *told* you so!"

He barked out an involuntary laugh and caught her hand. "You did not. You were too angry to be that coherent."

She narrowed those beautiful, fathomless eyes. "Of course I was angry—you were a dolt."

"Of course I was a dolt." He loosed her hand so that he could frame her face. "I was afraid. I *am* afraid. But you were right. I cannot let you go. I cannot go back to being your brother."

She lifted her brows. "I believe I told you what I expected the next time you touched me."

Stubborn Zipporah. His little sparrow. He whispered, "I am sorry." And then he kissed her, mindless of the audience.

At least until Benjamin said, "I believe I missed something."

Dara laughed—actually laughed, the first of those he had heard from her. "My brother is in love with Zipporah."

"Sam!"

Samuel winced at the horror in his brother's voice, knowing full well at what it was aimed.

"You are in love with her, and you said *nothing*?"

Zipporah grinned. "He is a blockhead."

Benjamin snorted. "Apparently he is *your* blockhead."

"All right, all right." Samuel tucked her to his side and turned them both to the others. "I just...I did not want to be selfish. I did not want to be happy at the expense of those I love."

"Sam." Benjamin shook his head. "You have never been selfish a day in your life. But you should have told me. I could have rejoiced with you."

He was not convinced his brother would have been capable of rejoicing, even yesterday. But right this moment, with his arms around Dara, he looked capable indeed. Samuel looked down at his beloved. "We should let everyone rejoice with us."

She smiled right back up at him. "Well then. Why are we standing here in the road?"

He grinned and turned them toward the villa, held her close to his side. But he did not miss the way she glanced over her shoulder at the gate. He could not help but glance back too, and track the plume of dust from the horse speeding to Rome.

They had won a measure of peace and joy today—but he knew well it would not hold for long.

Benjamin punched his pillow and resettled onto his pallet on the floor of his bedroom. It did nothing to make it more comfortable tonight. He had been sleeping here for a month, and other nights the floor did not feel hard.

Tonight, he longed for his bed.

No, he would be honest. He longed for the woman in it. He slid his eyes closed and willed patience into himself. Things had been better this week, since Avitus's threats. Unbelievably better. Dara had been smiling and laughing. She had been talking to him, letting him talk to her. She came to meals with him, sat beside him.

She had been *Dara*. The Dara he had fallen in love with, who she said did not exist. He had begun to believe her about that, but then...this. This young woman who smiled sweetly at him. Who had tried to protect him. Who had chosen him over the man she had betrayed him with.

The woman he loved. He became acquainted with her all over again, as she became acquainted with herself, and he fell in love again. Just as quickly as before. And this time, he laid it before the Lord and felt the wind of the Spirit rush through him. This time, it was right.

But he could not push her. He could not rush her. He certainly could not crawl into bed and pull her to him.

"Benjamin? Are you awake?"

He propped himself up on his elbow and bade his pulse to slow. "Yes. Do you need something?"

In the moonlight from the window, he saw her roll onto her side and dangle her arm off the bed, inches from him. "That passage they read tonight from Paul's letter. He said all things work together to achieve the good thing, for those who love God. But how can you believe that, when you know that man will come back? He could take this all from you."

"He could." But it struck no fear. He sat up the rest of the way. "But this is just a place, Dara. A place I love, yes, that we all work hard for. But just a place. If we are forced from it, then we go elsewhere. And we live, and we spread the good news about Jesus, and more believe. And it will be good."

"But...the next part. That those who love God are called by his purpose. But that he only called those whom he predestined. You all speak as if he wants me, as if your Jesus died for *me*, but how do you know? How do you know he called me, that he predestined me to follow him?"

"Dara." He reached for her hand and wove their fingers together. "Paul said he predestined those whom he foreknew. Who did he foreknow?"

"I do not know. That is the problem."

"But we *do* know." And he smiled, because she was asking. Because she was seeking. "David wrote in his psalms that the Lord knew him before he entered his mother's womb. He knew *all* of us before we were. And so he predestined *all* of us to follow him. To be molded in his image. He calls us, all of us. It is just that we do not all listen to the call."

Dara sighed and rested her chin on her arm. "Tamar has changed so much. I would not recognize her had I not seen the blooming firsthand. I always thought it was ridiculous, those stories about the Nazarene rising from the dead. But that was what he did for Tamar. He breathed life into her, where there had been none." Her fingers curled around his. "Everyone says he will do that for me."

His pulse thudded again. *Dear God, draw her. Draw her into your embrace.* "He will. You have only to ask him. You have only to accept that he made the sacrifice for you already. It is like when serpents came into the camp of Israel—if you were bitten, you died. But God was merciful, and he promised healing to any who would look—just look—at the bronze serpent he told Moses to hold up on his staff. All they had to do was accept the healing. But so many did not. They could not believe. Even so, Jesus offered his salvation freely, and still the masses turn away. Even though their sin is a death sentence, separating them from God."

"I thought I was serving him. That is what Thomas always said. That we were doing the will of Jehovah by stamping out a false religion. But it does not feel false. It feels...like you do. Right."

He swallowed. "I am glad."

She shifted onto her back again, but she did not loose his fingers. Instead, she drew them over and placed them on her stomach. On the gentle slope that had once been flat. "I am not like your mother. But I will not be like mine either. I will be whoever God makes me. And I will be it as your wife, as the mother of your children—if you will still have me."

Yes, this time he felt the wind of the Spirit, and it brought contentment. He spread his hand over her womb. "You know I will."

"Then...you need not sleep on the floor anymore."

He did not need a second invitation. He scrambled up and flopped onto his back beside her on the soft mattress with an exaggerated sigh of pleasure. "Ah. Yes. This is nice."

"Yes. It is," Dara said with a laugh as she cuddled into his side. "I am sorry I was so hateful this last month. I just felt so—"

"Dead inside? I understand that."

"You understand it because of me. And I am sorry for that too."

He ran a hand up her arm, back down to her elbow. "I understand it because I failed to listen to the Spirit, I sinned, and I paid the price for that. But he is faithful. The Lord is always faithful to forgive us and draw us back to him."

"Like you forgive me?"

A smile touched his lips, and he pulled her a little closer. "Like that, but grander. I love you, Dara. But he loves you more. He wants to use all this pain we have suffered for his good—to draw you to himself and pour his saving blood over you. You have only to accept it. To believe Jesus made that sacrifice for you."

She settled a hand on his chest, right above where his heart beat for her. "That is all I must do? Believe?"

"Believe. Be saved. Be willing to let him mold you into whatever vessel he needs you to be."

A moment of moonlight-gilded silence descended, and then she moved the hand over his heart around him and held on. "I believe. I know I sinned so much, and it left me empty, lifeless. But I want him to save me and fill me. I want to live again, like Tamar."

He shifted onto his side and pulled her close, buried his nose in her hair. Stunned, awed by what the Lord had done. He had taken the counterfeit Benjamin had wrongly seized and turned it into pure gold. Taken their sin, cleansed them of it, and made it right. "Thank you, Lord. Thank you."

He prayed it was enough to sustain them through the threats sure to come thundering to their gates again soon.

HE THOUGHT SHE WAS THE MOST BEAUTIFUL WOMAN IN THE WORLD. Zipporah still found that unbelievable, but she saw it so clearly in Samuel's eyes as he gazed at her from across the room. He loved her as she thought no one ever could. And now here they stood, surrounded by the friends and family that mattered most, celebrating their marriage. *Theirs.* Hers and his.

She let her gaze linger on him, this man who had just pledged to be her husband. She would never grow accustomed to his beauty. More, to the beauty of his spirit, his heart. Perhaps the world would look at them—him with his golden curls and perfect face, his muscled figure, and she with her scars and bumped nose—and see a mismatch. But she knew better. Somehow, as the Lord shaped them both through the years, he had molded them to fit each other perfectly. And now they were two halves to the whole. One.

He grinned at her, said something to Cleopas, and came her way. Her heart thrilled at his approach. She held out a hand to him as he drew near, soaking in the memories. The way the summer sun reached under the tent to try to touch him. The way he smiled in that way he reserved just for her.

Her wedding day. A day Zipporah thought she would never see. To a man she had never even hoped to claim until so recently. The man at whose side she had always felt safest, most secure. Loved.

He took her hand, raised it his lips, and stared at her. "Wife."

"Husband." The word made her grin.

"Oh!" Abigail's voice startled her, but she laughed when her new mother's arms closed around them both. She must have come up behind Zipporah. Now she kissed her son's cheek and then turned to her. Smoothed back that curl forever falling over her first scar and kissed her cheek too. "I am so happy to count you as one of my daughters, Zipporah. So proud. And I think Sarah may be convinced to welcome you as a sister too."

Zipporah had to laugh again at that. She had dressed with Sarah and their mothers that morning, had let her dearest friend fuss over her and arrange her hair as Zipporah usually did for her. She had donned the impossibly soft, flowing garment made from layers of Dara's translucent cloth. She had put on her shark's tooth necklace. The wide leather belt. And her mother had lowered the veil over her face, the one that now lay discarded beside her.

"You can consider today practice for Sarah's wedding next month."

Abigail laughed too. "I think I am an expert on them at this point. Although we could do nothing, and she would still be ecstatic, simply because Urbanus's family agreed to come. But today is for you, my precious ones. Enjoy." She kissed them each again and then moved on.

Samuel slipped his arm around Zipporah's waist and looked out over their guests. No curiosity-seekers on this second of his wedding days, just their own. Zipporah pressed tight to his side for a moment and then glanced out into the open when she heard Columba's coo. She grinned up at her husband. "We could slip out for a few minutes. Run away to the ilex tree. No one would miss us."

"You think not?" He lifted a golden brow and chuckled. "I think they will. But I think they will laugh and know exactly where we went. Come."

They slipped out the opening of the tent that had been erected for the wedding feast. A zephyr stirred, swirled around her legs, toyed with the delicate fabric of her stola. She slid her eyes shut and listened to the music of the air, felt it move through her spirit as that soft breath of wind moved over her face.

The music. The music filled her, bright and unworldly. The music bade her open her eyes and see.

"No." Samuel's gaze was already on the distant gate, and on the plume of dust coming toward it. "Not today."

She found his fingers and squeezed them. The music still soared, though she could not see the angel. He must be standing exactly where she did, in his place outside the physical. "Get your father. Get Benjamin."

Samuel leveled a finger at her nose. "Do not move. You do not go near that gate without us, do you hear me?"

"I will not. I promise you."

He vanished from her side. She heard his shout, but it sounded like little more than an echo over the melody in her ears. She heard the resulting tumult within the tent, but even louder were the whispers of prayer that immediately sprang up and outward, filling the air on their way to heaven.

And then the men set off. Titus and Abba and Jacob, Phillip and Menelaus, Samuel and Benjamin and Cleopas and Jason. All of them, all of them running forward to meet the enemy. They would gird themselves with sword and dagger along the way—they would gird themselves with prayer at every step.

The young women flanked her. Dara looped her arm through Zipporah's right, Sarah took her left, Tamar chose her mistress's other side. The older women's voices carried the prayers within the tent.

And the plume grew nearer.

"It is the senator." Dara's whisper shook. "Your wedding will be ruined because of me."

The song passed through her, and the glow of the angel took form before her eyes.

Zipporah sighed. "You cannot ruin this day. It is the day the Lord told us to set aside for this celebration. He knew the senator would come. It is for his good, for his glory."

The angel reached out a hand. *For the Father's glory.*

"What if they try to arrest Benjamin? Hurt him?" Dara let go Zipporah's arm, shook off Tamar's hands. "Maybe I can stop him. Maybe he will listen this time." She took off at a run.

"Dara, no." But she was not listening, and Zipporah had little choice but to obey the beckon. To follow her new sister. She motioned Tamar and Sarah to stay. "I will bring her back. You two stay and pray."

She chased after the blond. Chased after the bright-glowing spirit within her. Faith had ignited strong and true in Dara ten days ago, had increased daily. She greeted the Lord with the enthusiasm of the child so recently set free from her bonds. With that innocent belief in all he could do.

But like a child, she had not learned to listen.

How well Zipporah knew that kind of faith. "Dara! Stop!"

She did not stop. She ran all the faster, her golden curls flying behind her and her white stola snapping in the wind.

Zipporah flew over the familiar ground, up the familiar road. Had a day gone by since her eyes were opened that she had not been called to the gate? But just now she could think only of the first time. When her father and Titus had been ahead of her. When Antonius Merillius had been waiting, a demon within him. She remembered the panic as they drew near to him, the wonder and fear.

Today a great many more were drawing to a halt at their closed gates. Alexander Avitus was at the head, but he had made good on his oath. Behind him was a retinue of soldiers.

Dear Lord! She had no more words, but she knew he heard the groaning of her spirit, the frantic cry within her.

The angel flew ahead and joined the line of his comrades, clustered now around the gate. Zipporah skidded to a halt.

Why were they clustered so? They never clustered. That would leave holes in the hedge, places for the enemy to sneak up behind. They never left their positions, not without others compensating. Not without...

She turned in a circle, her breath tangling within her. They were everywhere. All the times the brethren had prayed, all the times Tutelos had been under attack, but never had she seen so many of the heavenly warriors all at once. Their glow lit up the sky far brighter than the afternoon sun, columns of sparkling light from every part of the wall. From overhead. Surrounding and enclosing.

This, then, was the true battle. The one they had all been training for on their knees.

The Romans came with armor and weapons. A Goliath to their scrawny shepherd boy. But they would meet them with the name of the Lord—a weapon far more powerful than any man's hands could create.

She strode forward, arming herself as she went. Peace upon her feet, taking her forward. Her faith to provide a shield round about her, like the angels around Tutelos. Righteousness to protect her heart and her life, truth to gird and embrace her. Her mind she would protect with the certain knowledge of the salvation Christ had given her, the promise that no matter what, she was his. In her hand she needed no sword—just the Word of God.

Benjamin had caught his wife, mere steps from the gate and the man who would tear it down. Zipporah heard Dara's shout of "No!" aimed at the Romans. Benjamin's response was too soft to reach her ears.

Zipporah's eyes took in what they would not see. The beast within Alexander gnashed and roared, as frantic as it had been every other time he came. Other demons swooped and screeched in the air, bombarding the walls. Bombarding the soldiers.

But the angels fought them off. Not just from the gate, but from the hapless Roman guards who stood ready to obey, but with no personal investment. Not one among them hosted a demon, though a few flinched as one or another got close, hissed, dug at them.

"Yes, Lord, thank you. Protect those men. Strengthen your angels against the attacks. Strengthen us all."

Alexander raised his sword, the dark one jeering. "This is your last chance, dog. Give me what is mine, or I take from you what is yours by the mandate of Caesar. The girl for your family land."

The song again, making Zipporah look to her side and up into the angelic face she knew best.

Behold. He reached out, touched her eyes. *Behold your sister.*

She looked, and she saw what she had been seeing for over a week. Faith, bright and true, young and innocent. But now she saw more. Now she saw a second flame within her, below the first. Brighter. Younger. More innocent. More true.

The babe.

Protect that life, daughter. For the Father's glory. The future of the church depends upon it.

Dara was speaking, but the words made little sense. She heard a refusal, a begging. And though Benjamin did all he could to keep her behind him, she surged around, her arms wide. "You do not want me anyway!" Now the words were clear, crystalline. "You cannot make me anymore into your creation. I am a child of the Most High. Made in *his* image, according to *his* purpose. Not yours!"

At the spark of rage, Zipporah's legs stretched, her feet pounded. Ten feet, five. She shouted a word she did not know, a word that drew the angels to alert. A word that made them move as one. A word that made their swords stretch out and touch the soldiers. A touch, not a strike, but it rendered them immobile, every one.

Alexander, though, lunged away from the angels, off his horse, over the gate. He landed somehow on his feet, his sword over his shoulder and aimed at Benjamin and Dara. "If you are not mine, then you are no one's—you will die!"

"No!" Zipporah's shout joined with everyone else's. She jumped in front of

Dara, facing the Roman, calling to her tongue the next words she needed, the ones to bind and cast out.

He was already lunging, already thrusting. She had no time to speak.

His sword bit. Right above the necklace, in the V created by her wedding garment. She felt it touch, felt it slide in, felt her heart break around it.

The world slowed, and the song filled her ears. Radiant arms came around her. Radiant hands held her as the sword retreated, as she fell. A radiant face appeared over her as her head struck the ground.

It should hurt. She could feel the blood spurting, pooling, clogging her throat. It should hurt, but it did not. She could feel only the light. She could hear only the victory in the shouts of her men as they bound, as they cast out. She could see only heaven in the face of the angel.

For the Father's glory, he said.

She tried to move, but the weight was too great. All she could manage was a flex of her fingers. She expected dirt under them, but instead they found flesh and bone and sinew, and two golden heads, less radiant but no less loving.

"Sparrow!" Samuel's voice broke through the rushing of the wind in her ears, joined the song gaining in volume. "Stay with me. Stay with me, my love. I will get you inside, I will stitch you. I will—"

"No." Did he hear her? Her voice sounded like no more than a wisp to her own ears. She clung to his hand, tried to keep her vision focused on that face she loved so well. "Not this time, Samuel. For the Father's glory."

"No." Pain shone in his eyes, and a stubborn refusal. "You will not die."

Then why did the heavens part? She watched the clouds roll back, saw the light flood down. Felt the weights release. "I am glad." Now her voice sounded as though it belonged to someone else. As if it came from below her. "I am glad I got to love you. For each day we had."

"Sparrow!"

She saw Dara grip her hand too, but she could not feel it. She could not feel the ground beneath her nor the blood choking her. "Do not die, Zipporah. Please. We need you, we all need you."

She could not respond. Her eyes would focus only on that light, her ears filled with that song, so loud now that it drowned out all else. She knew only one word now. *Jesus.*

He stood in the center of the light, the source of the light. So bright she felt she should wince, except that her eyes were no longer bound by human weakness. She saw him in his glory, sorrow and joy mixed on his face, and a hand outstretched.

The print of the nail still darkened it. Proof, eternal proof of his sacrifice.

She put her own hand upon his palm, but the evidence of her work had faded. No more scars on her hand, on her arm. Those had been left with the body that lay in the dirt, soon to return to dirt.

"Well done, faithful servant." But he did not draw her away into eternity yet. He touched her face, where the scar had been, and bade her turn her head. "Behold. For the Father's glory."

She lay lifeless under his hands. Samuel had watched the flame extinguish, had watched her eyes, focused upon the heavens, suddenly go dark. "No." He could lay hold of no other word, no other thought. Because she could not die. That certainty filled him, as surely as guilt had when Anna had died. She could not die. Not yet.

Blood had soaked her wedding garment, turning what was once white to a brilliant crimson. The shark's tooth had not saved her this time, nor the belt. All his shouts had fallen on deaf ears, all his attempts to get to her had failed.

She had not heard him. She had not seen him. When she had skidded to a halt and looked in that way of hers at the gate, he knew she saw the world beyond more than the world that was. The wind had swirled around her, lifting her hair, lifting a layer of her skirt, and she had stood as a queen. A warrior of heaven.

He could not stop her. He knew there was no way he could have, no matter what he might have tried. Because she had been obeying a voice he had not heard. Obeying her call, as she always did.

"No." Dara shook her head, sending her curls dancing over Zipporah, reddening from her blood. Her eyes, green and smoky, met his. "This is not right, Samuel. We can pray for her. Jesus raised that man from the dead, did he not? And did he not say we could do the same, and greater? Pray for her. *Pray for her!*"

Yes. He had tried it once before, in desperation and guilt. Tried to revive a wife no longer of this world. But he felt no desperation now. No guilt. No sorrow. He felt only surety and peace.

The wind blew. The shouts from the others receded. The whisper sounded within him. *Pray for her. For the Father's glory.*

He stretched himself over her. His legs over her legs, his arms over her arms. His face over her face. His heart over her heart, her blood seeping into him.

"You are the Master of life, Lord Jesus," he murmured. "The giver of all. The winds and rains, the seas and the lands obey you. By your blood we are sealed. By your stripes we are healed. By your breath the dead live again."

Heat descended, like it had when the poison had eaten her. But greater, hotter, so intense he could not move, he could not think. He could only let it travel through him, be its road from heaven to her. He let it build as long as he could withstand it, until it filled every bit of him. Until it covered every inch of her.

And then he opened his mouth and let the will of the Lord speak through his tongue. "Zipporah. Arise."

WEIGHT CLOSED OVER HER SOUL—NO GENTLE FLOATING, NO GLID-ing now. With a rush of wind and one last glimpse of that holy light, Zipporah felt her body close around her. She sucked in a breath, so deep and fast it sound-ed like a gasp to her own ears. When she opened her eyes, the world looked faded, compared to glory. Her arms and legs and fingers all felt so small, so ragged, so confining.

But no disappointment pierced, not when she felt the weight of Samuel over her, when he retreated at her breath and looked at her with those eyes she loved so well. He leaped off, up, and held out a hand. Steady. Sure. Zipporah put her fingers in his and let him pull her to her feet, glancing at Dara, who stood with a soft, joyous smile, her fingertips resting on her lips.

Zipporah felt the blood, sticky and wet, covering her torso. But no pain. She splayed a hand over the wound in her chest, finding nothing but a scratch. "Samuel."

He crushed her to his chest.

An animalistic keen pierced the air, made her wince against him as the sound replaced the glory's song in her ears. Her gaze moved beyond her hus-band's arms, to where the senator thrashed against the demon that did not want to let go.

It had no choice. Titus and Benjamin and Abba pounded it with prayers, with the name above all names. The beast screamed again, the man screaming with it as talons slashed one last time before releasing. The dark one shot over the wall—the man looked around him with wide eyes. Shoving Titus and Ben-jamin away, he staggered back, drew his sword.

"No!" Was it she who screamed it? Samuel, Dara? All of them at once? Zip-porah felt the sting of a cry in her throat, but it sounded larger than her own voice to her ears. She lunged forward along with Samuel, even as Titus and Benjamin and Abba jumped back, out of swinging distance.

But the senator's aim was not his liberators. With one last desperate cry, with empty eyes that stared unseeing into the air, he plunged the blade into his stomach.

Zipporah turned her face into Samuel's chest. His toga was stained red and smelled of blood—hers. His hand settled on the back of her head, but he did not press her closer. He bade her turn again.

"The soldiers," he whispered into her hair. "They look like statues, like the stories Father tells of his friends who guarded the tomb of Jesus."

Zipporah looked again at the men who had been touched by the angels' swords, then at the angels who guarded them. She met the golden gaze of one of the warriors. "Release them." She knew that was what she spoke, but the words felt strange to her lips and sounded foreign to her ears. It must have been their tongue she spoke in, for they all moved at once.

And then, so did the men. They gasped much as she had done, splayed hands over chests, looked around dazedly—Stoic discipline forgotten. Their centurion regained himself first and stalked forward.

Titus and Benjamin both met the soldier with nods. "We did not touch him," the elder said, so softly that Zipporah could scarcely hear him.

The soldier nodded in reply. Slowly. "I saw. I saw it all." His gaze drifted toward her and Samuel, incredulity making him linger. Then he edged his shoulders back and crouched down, hefting the still form of the senator over his shoulder. "I will report the truth to the emperor, that he took his own life when the woman would not come with him. But I...I have questions. For myself."

Benjamin's smile looked older, surer than she had seen it before. "We will be here, ready to answer them."

A hard swallow, another nod, and the soldier carried his burden back through the gates.

Zipporah let herself relax against Samuel, let the words mix and babble around her as her family all turned to them. Exclaiming. Gesturing. Wrapping arms around her. Demanding she share what happened.

She had so few words to give them. No language seemed able to express that brilliance, that freedom, that joy. She offered what paltry explanation she could, haltingly, and then did so again as they walked back toward the tent and were met by the women. And then again inside the tent, where the brethren surged around them.

She stood in the center of them all, where she always tried never to be. Everyone took a turn hugging her, touching her face, exclaiming over her.

After a while, she had to let her eyes slide closed. There would be repercussions. There always were. But today, the victory was theirs. Zipporah slid her arm around Samuel's waist and rested her head against him. Her blood had dried in his toga, was drying on her chest too—a sticky mess that she longed to wash clean as soon as they could get away.

Samuel must have read her mind. His arm tightened around her, and he pulled her a step away from the group. "If you all will excuse us, please. My bride still needs tending."

"Of course!" Sarah jumped forward for one more embrace, including them both in it. "If you need help cleaning up, let me know. Or if you just want to retire, you can leave your clothing in the hallway, and we will come and get it, so they can soak."

"As if those stains will ever come out." Dinah scowled, and nudged Sarah out of the way so she could plant a kiss upon Zipporah's forehead. "Go, rest.

And do not rush out to join us in the morning—I will have a breakfast tray delivered."

Their parents all came to bid them farewell too, and then they made their escape. Arm in arm, back toward the villa and their chamber.

"I suppose it was too much to ask," Samuel said as they passed the fountain, a smile in his voice, "that I have a wedding unmarred by violence."

She breathed a laugh and leaned closer to his side. It made walking more difficult but made living so much more worthwhile. "Apparently it is, so long as I am here."

He halted her, cupped her face in his blood-stained hands. "I am so glad you are here. When you jumped in front of her—"

"I had to." She covered his hand with hers. Her fingers were still clean, somehow. "Their babe—the angel said I must protect the baby at all costs."

"I am not chiding you for it." Indeed, his kiss did not taste of a lecture, of disapproval. It tasted only of love. "You obeyed, as you always do. And had death not loosed its hold, you would have died for the Father's glory. But instead, he restored you, so that you might live for his glory a while longer. And those soldiers saw, and they will seek, and perhaps they will believe. Because you were faithful."

"And because you were, to pray when he told you to pray. To believe in the impossible."

He drew her forward again, into the cool, welcoming shade of the villa. Down the familiar hall, into their room. The little wooden sparrow already sat, one-legged, on a shelf. And Columba already chirped a greeting from the window, as if he had been expecting them.

Samuel lifted her, as usual, onto the table. Always the healer, her beloved, set on examining her new wound. But his hands felt different this time as they tenderly touched her chest. He held her gaze, his fingers moving to curl over her shoulders, his thumbs under the gathered straps of her stola. "May I? It seems some thoughtful person delivered hot water. May I wash you of the blood?"

Her heart sped—a miracle in itself. She nodded and watched his face as he slid the soiled cloth from her shoulders. It was stiff where it had once been soft and flowing, and it had dried to a deep, rusted brown in most places. It still stuck to her stomach where it had pooled. But she focused on the love and desire shining in his eyes.

He dampened a cloth in the water and pressed it, warm and soft, to her chest. Rubbed gently at the blood until her skin felt clean again. When he reached the wound, he dabbed instead of rubbing and darted a glance into her eyes. "Does it hurt?"

"As a scratch would. Nothing more."

His breath came out in amazed amusement. "It *looks* like nothing more. Had I not watched him run you through..."

"I know." She slid her eyes shut and leaned back onto her palms, let her head fall back into the sunshine from the window. "We have much to celebrate this day."

"Sparrow." His voice had gone tight and low, and the touch of his fingers changed. He said nothing else.

She needed him to say nothing else. She sat up straight again, loosed the belt from her waist, and went into his arms.

Dara pressed a hand to her stomach, but try as she might, she could not detect from the outside the flutter she had felt within. Abigail had said it was early yet, but she hoped the movement soon grew strong enough. She wanted to be able to share this with Benjamin. The sensation, the certainty of life.

The sun beat down hot and heavy today, making perspiration bead on her brow as she took her daily walk. She lifted her hand from her stomach to her forehead and dabbed at where it trickled from her hairline. Tamar had helped her secure the mass of curls up off her neck. "Perhaps we should move our walks to earlier in the day, or later. It has grown so hot."

Zipporah laughed. She did not look the least bit sweaty, though Dara could not imagine how. "I know well that women further along in their term are always overheated, my sister. But I have never known them to experience it when the babe is still barely a bump beneath their skirts."

"It is *not* just me!" Yet looking at Tamar's grin, and at Zipporah's hair hanging long down her neck, a giggle won out. "Perhaps it is. The point remains."

"We can walk whenever you like, Mistress," Tamar said from the other side of her. "But if it is earlier, you would have to miss visiting with Sarah and the children during their lessons."

"Bother." She did so enjoy hearing Sarah tell the same stories that her father read to them daily. In her telling, they always took on new life as she made them simple and true for the children. Dara's hand went to her stomach again. "Do you think babies can hear us from within the womb? I hope they can. I like to think that this little one will arrive already knowing of his Savior."

Zipporah shrugged, but her smile had not faded. "Perhaps they can. Either way, I think you need not worry overmuch about your child's faith. Just pray for him, instruct him as he grows. Leave the rest to the Lord."

"Her." Tamar leaned around Dara with a mischievous grin. "You mean pray for *her* as *she* grows."

Dara elbowed her friend back into place. "Him."

"Her." Tamar elbowed her back.

The joy bubbled out in another laugh. When had she ever had friends like these, to laugh and jest with? Never. Not until she came home. "I had a dream. It is a boy."

"And *I* had a dream of your daughter playing with mine." Tamar, too, touched her stomach, and happy color bloomed in her cheeks.

"Your dream must have been of our second children. This one is a boy."

With a roll of her eyes, Zipporah tugged Dara to the right and then stepped between them. "Enough. You are both wrong. Dara is having an eagle, and Tamar is having a lion."

They laughed again, kept walking, let it trickle out and fade to nothing. Birds sang in the tree limbs, and from the distant vineyard fields came the sound of many voices lifted in a rhythmic song of praise.

Dara breathed in the hot air with contentment. It mattered not whether her child was a boy or a girl. Whether she was right or wrong. She did not need to know. She did not need to see ahead. Now was quite enough, with the faith that whatever came tomorrow would work for the good of the Lord. Because they loved him.

She found it fulfilling to work beside Samuel. He said she had a gift for healing—she did not quite understand these gifts they spoke of yet, but she knew that when they worked together, she and her brother, they seemed able to do what neither could accomplish alone.

"Ladies."

She looked up at Benjamin's voice, but her smile froze when she saw the look in his eyes. He stood on the road, flanked by Samuel and Mark, and his countenance was in that Stoic mask that meant he held back his emotions. "What is it, my love?"

He held out a hand, and she loosed her hold on Zipporah's arm so she could hurry across the space and put hers in it. "What is it?" she asked again.

He looked from her to Samuel, to Mark, and then to Zipporah and Tamar. "There is a man at the gates. Jewish. He says he has come all the way from Jerusalem to see you, Dara. He says he is your master."

Her blood froze too, and a chill skittered up her spine, belying the heat she had felt moments before. "Thomas?"

Her husband shrugged. "He gave no name."

"In his forties, silver at his temples, hazel eyes?"

Her brother tilted his head as Zipporah joined him. "To the age and hair, yes. But he was not close enough to make out eye color. He is not exactly *at* the gates—he will not come that near."

"We have prayed about it, and we felt you should come." Benjamin gripped her hands, his gaze unblinking. "If you want to."

Want to? If it were Thomas, she did not *want* to face him again.

And yet she must. That certainty settled deep in her spirit, and she nodded. Though then she turned to Tamar. "You do not have to come."

But Tamar looked unaffected as she stood by her husband's side. She even smiled. "I go where you go, Mistress. He has no claim to me any longer—I will not fear him."

"All right then." Indulging in a deep breath, she settled her hand in the crook of Benjamin's elbow and let him lead her toward the gate, the two other couples with them.

"Just remember," her husband whispered into her ear, "to whom you belong. You have only one Master now. And it is not him."

"I know."

The sun glared off the packed dirt of the road, glinted off the iron of the gates, but a cooling breeze swept over her too. Braced her and strengthened her as they walked all the way up to the gate and then stopped. Just inside their walls. A stone's throw from the man who stood glaring at them, a small retinue of familiar slaves behind him.

"There you are! Get your things and come with me at once, Dara. We are going home."

The familiar voice. The familiar face. The familiar tone of authority in his words. But Dara felt no pull. She could scarcely remember the love for him that had once consumed her—more brightly came the memory of how he had appeared to her as a child. A hope. A savior. Someone to take her from Martha, to protect her.

But he never had, had he? He had fed her lies. He had used her for his own purposes. He had led her in opening her spirit to evil, in embracing it and championing it. He taught her only how to destroy.

"Dara." Zipporah moved to her side, her tone breathless and her eyes latched upon Thomas. "The demon he hosts—it is the same one that had been in Alexander."

"What?" Benjamin turned toward their friend, shutting out the image of Thomas. "You are certain? You can tell them apart?"

"Yes. I am certain." She took Dara's hand and squeezed. "That is why you thought him your master. He *was*. The demon within you must have recognized the one within him. It must have left him for a while, then returned."

It answered one question, at least. Though it sent a shudder down her spine.

"Dara! *Now.*"

"No." She stayed safely ensconced at Benjamin's side. Her chin rose. "I will not go back with you, Thomas."

He took a single step nearer, fury snapping in his eyes. "You have no choice, child. You are mine. I paid for you, I own you. You are *mine.*"

"You gave me to Benjamin."

"I did no such thing!"

She gripped her husband's arm tighter. "You told me to marry him. You not only gave permission, you ordered it. I am his."

He spat out words that blistered her ears, turned away, turned back again with a shaking finger pointing her way. "Come. Here."

"You do not want me." She slid her hands down Benjamin's arm so she could grip his hand. "I am not what you made me. I cannot see the future anymore. I am useless to you. Unprofitable."

"You can get it back." He edged another step closer and then seemed to hit an invisible wall. His lips twitched. "I can give the gift to you again. Trust me, beloved. Come with me."

She shook her head. "It would not matter. Even if I came, you could not force a demon inside me again. My soul is not an empty room anymore, waiting for someone to dwell in it. It has been filled with the Holy Spirit. And he is so much stronger than what had been in me before."

Another string of curses fell from his lips, and then he shifted his hateful gaze to Benjamin. "You will at least pay me for my slave, so I can replace her. Which I will do! I will find another seer, a better one. One who can tell me how to destroy you."

Benjamin snorted his opinion of that and pulled out a coin. It flashed in the sun as it flipped through the air and landed in the dust at Thomas's feet.

Her old master sneered. "An assarius?"

A smile pulled at Benjamin's mouth. "It is the current rate for maidservants in these parts. Take it or leave it."

Thomas ground it under his heel. "Keep her. She is worth nothing as she is anyway. Where is Tamar?"

Her friend did not jolt, did not wince. Her fingers in Mark's, she merely stepped forward half a stride. "I am right here. Do you not know me?"

He obviously did not. He jolted, and then a new flood of hatred washed over his face. "You have ruined her too, I see. So be it. I will have to find stronger soldiers to fight this battle against you. But rest assured, find them I will."

He turned back toward his small caravan, sending up puffs of dust with every stomp of his foot.

Zipporah inclined her head. "We will be ready."

They all stood together and watched the band of Jews move off. They all braced together when another plume of dust overtook that first, headed their way. Quickly, too quickly to be anyone on foot or in a wagon.

Horses. An entire group of them, and at their head was a young man not more than a year or two older than Dara. One with fair hair only a shade off from hers and Samuel's.

One with a laurel crown on his head even more golden.

"Lord, help us." Zipporah gripped Samuel's arm on one side while Benjamin transferred Dara's hand to Samuel's other arm.

"Emperor Nero." Benjamin strode forward, dropped to one knee. Confidence and respect, strength and humility. "To what do we owe the honor of your presence?"

"Get up." No graciousness touched the emperor's face. Only command, woven through with barely covered bitterness. "Are you Benjamin Visibullis? Master of this estate?"

Oh, God. God, protect him. Protect my brother. Zipporah gripped Samuel's arm tighter. Dara muttered a prayer nearly identical from his other side. Samuel pulled them both closer.

Benjamin rose. "I am. Can I be of service to you, Caesar?"

For a long moment, the young emperor glared at him, then looked at each of them in turn. His gaze halted on Dara, narrowed. She slid half a step behind her brother.

He turned back to Benjamin. "I know what you did. Not a single one of the soldiers will attest to it, but I know. I know you killed him."

Benjamin's head dipped forward, but his shoulders stayed straight. Strong. Defiant. "Pardon me, Caesar. I realize you must speak of Alexander Avitus, but your soldiers have the right of it. None of us touched him. He fell on his sword."

Silence pulsed, hammered. Nero gripped his horse's reins tighter. "He was my friend."

"I had heard. My condolences for his loss, sir."

"He was my *friend*. I know what you have done, I know what you are. The seer told me. You are Christians."

Benjamin's chin came back up. "To that name we answer proudly. Yes. We are Christians."

The muscle in the emperor's jaw bulged, then relaxed. "You will pay. You, your whore of a wife, your family, your friends. You will *all* pay, any who answer to that name."

Samuel stepped forward, and Zipporah and Dara moved with him. To come up behind Benjamin. To form a wall within the gate.

Benjamin did not move. "You have much power, Caesar. You can take much away. You can exact a great price. But no man has the power to take our faith from us. And so long as we have that, no loss can defeat us."

A sneer curled the handsome lips of the most powerful man in the world. Powerful...but only a man. "I am not a mere man. I am emperor of Rome, the Divine Caesar Nero. I will be patient. But I will see to it. I will be known as the emperor who rid Rome of you vermin. I will be remembered for wiping you out. Mark my words."

"They are marked. But you cannot wipe out the truth. It will spread the faster if you try."

"We shall see. Enjoy your pretty little vineyard while you can, Christian. Before I am through, there will not be one stone left upon another of these walls." With a click to his horse, he spun and galloped off, the other horses and riders with him.

Dara let go her brother and stepped forward to take her husband's hand. Zipporah looked up to meet Samuel's gaze. They had all talked of this incessantly these past weeks. They had reminded themselves that Tutelos was just a place. That if they were forced to flee, God would use it as a means of spreading the good news of salvation.

Even so. It was *their* place, and none of them wanted to leave it by force. Much as Zipporah still hoped to see a bit of the world someday, that was not how she wanted to achieve it.

Dara gripped Benjamin's arm. "One thing I learned, my husband, when the spirit of divination still lived in me. A demon can predict the path a man will take—but he can never anticipate the movement of the Spirit. God will always surprise."

"God will always stand victorious." He squeezed her fingers in return and pivoted them around. Back to face Zipporah and Samuel, Mark and Tamar. Back to face their home. "Come. Let us live the life the Lord gives us, until he sends us a new direction."

And so they walked. A line again, unbroken. A wall against the world.

The wind surged around them. Brilliant, golden light flashed by as Zipporah's warrior friend flew past them and landed a few feet ahead. No message on his lips, no warning in his eyes. Just a nod of approval. A giving of strength.

Dara paused, her head tilted. Question filled her gaze, gone unfocused. "Did you hear something?"

"What?" Benjamin paused too, and looked over his shoulder, back at the gate.

But his wife shook her head. "No, no, not like that. I thought...I thought I heard music. Just a strain of it. But it was the most beautiful sound I have ever heard."

Zipporah met the angel's eyes and smiled.

A NOTE *from the* AUTHOR

A Stray Drop of Blood traveled with me for many years. And after I finished it, I thought, "That's it. It's finished. I'm done." When people started asking me if there was a sequel—and hinting that I left it open for one—I was floored. *More of this story? Seriously??* I had absolutely no intention of doing that. Ever.

Then one day, as I was taking care of my months-old first baby, it came to me. Just a hint, at first, then a trickle, then a rush. Within a day, I had the entire sequel plotted out. I knew Zipporah and Samuel and Benjamin and Dara. I knew the conflict would be between discernment and divination. I frantically wrote pages of notes, then sat back with a sigh. *There.* When I had the time, it would be there.

Fast-forward seven years, and there it still sat, a file of notes but no more. It wasn't until the summer of 2013 that "someday" became "now" for me. That I got clear direction from the Lord that this was the time to finally write that sequel. So I reread *Stray Drop.* I got out my notes. I made some changes. And I got to work.

The most striking thing about this story is, of course, the spiritual aspect. As always when I'm writing something so very much outside my ordinary life, I start out thinking, "I need to research!!" But as always when I'm writing something that is so far outside human understanding, I was unwilling to trust just any sources. So I recalled the teachings of a trusted member of my church association. I prayed. I read my Bible. And I let the story come.

Are there really people who can see into the spiritual world? I believe there are, absolutely. I, however, am not one of them. So do keep in mind that this is largely imagination on my part. But as I wrote Zipporah's experiences, I learned a lot about that world beyond the veil.

But I think what I learned most through the writing of this book is that faith must be deliberate. It must be a way of life, not a circumstance. It must define us, not be a word we use a few times a week. All things I've known, but which struck me anew. Because demons are real, and they're out to get us. Angels are real, but they only do what they're told. We have power to bind and loose, but it's not without limitations. The world, both physical and spiritual, obeys laws. Rules. God's rules.

And we have to play by them too, if we intend to make a difference.

Another concept I introduced in this story is that of being spiritually marked by our past hurts. This is something I'd observed as I read many memoirs of people who suffer an abuse once and then seem to be a magnet for it later, in far different circumstances. Words were finally put to it when I read a book from my publisher called *Listening Prayer: Learning to Hear the Shepherd's Voice* by Joanne Hillman. Joanne, with her years of dedicated service, had observed this too and set out her belief that our spirits bear the marks of our pains, and that the enemy can see it and prey upon us. That matched perfectly with what I'd observed. I also need to credit another WhiteFire author, Gail Kittleson, with the inspiration for Columba. In her *Catching Up with Daylight*, she has a section where she's observing a one-legged bird hop around. I knew as I read her true story that my fictional one needed a bird like that.

Of course, I loved bringing in my old characters from *A Stray Drop of Blood*, introducing some new ones, and explaining Nero's hatred of Christians through my characters. I chose to represent John Mark as being in Rome when he wrote his Gospel, though in fact where he wrote it is debated. He did visit Rome during the span of years in which he's believed to have penned that first Gospel account though, so it's a reasonable guess. It's also believed that he wrote it for the Jewish Christians in Rome, and the window of time in which they're believed to have received it shares an overlapping window with when theologians believe Paul's letter to them would have arrived.

And yes, I know very well I left this one open for another book too. Do I have any ideas yet for that third generation? Um, no. We'll see if one comes to me. And if it does, how many years it might take. In the meantime, my mind is swarming with other ideas for biblical novels.

As always, I love little more than hearing from my readers! I so appreciate each and every one of you. You guys have given me endless support and encouragement through the years, often on the days I need it most. Thank you so much for writing to tell me how much you loved the story of Abigail and Jason and Titus, and for asking me to write this one. Thank you so much for letting me know how God has worked in your lives as you've read my books—you can't know how humbling and amazing it is to see God using my words as I prayed He would.

Please feel free to check out my website at www.RoseannaMWhite.com, and you can e-mail me any time at Roseanna@RoseannaWhite.com or through my website.

discussion questions

1.) In the opening of the book, Zipporah receives an incredible spiritual gift. Do you believe the Spirit can really give such a gift?

2.) In this story we see some of the first "second generation Christians"—those born into families who had followed Jesus when he walked the earth, who were raised in the Way. How do you think their faith may have differed from their parents'? Does it differ from ours?

3.) When you picked up this book, were you expecting the elements of spiritual warfare? How did it settle with you? What questions did it make you ask?

4.) Zipporah mentions in passing a dream she had of demons attacking and the Spirit rushing in after she says Jesus's name. Have you ever experienced a spiritual attack, either waking or sleeping?

5.) The church today often accepts that such miracles as described in *A Soft Breath of Wind* happened in the New Testament days, but are doubtful about how many of them still happen today. Operating on the assumption that humanity doesn't change much, I chose to portray some members of the early church doubting too, and others believing. Where do you stand? Can we today still do miracles through the power of the Spirit? Can we, for instance, raise people from the dead?

6.) What did you expect to happen in the romantic aspects of the book? Were you surprised by how it turned out? Were you happy with it or not?

7.) What was your favorite scene and why? Who were your favorite characters?

8.) If you were a resident of Tutelos, would you have believed Zipporah when Dara arrived? Or would you have trusted Benjamin?

9.) If you were Samuel, how would you have reacted when you came into contact with your birth mother again?

10.) Though this story is purely fiction, I wrote it with a lot of prayer and consideration. And as with every book I write, I prayed the Lord would reveal truth through my fiction. Did he reveal anything new to you while you were reading?

OTHER VISIBULLIS BOOKS

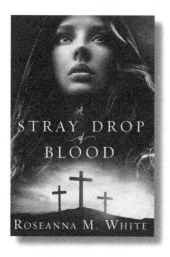

A Stray Drop of Blood

Abigail had resigned herself to a life of slavery...until her master's son changed everything.

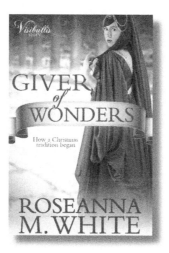

Giver of Wonders

Cyprus Visibullis received a miraculous touch when she was a child... but is even the help of the Wonder Worker enough to save her family now?

ALSO BY ROSEANNA M. WHITE

Jewel of Persia

Kasia is ripped from her family and her dearest friend, Esther, to wed Xerxes. But how is she to love the king of kings without forsaking her Lord?

A Heart's Revolution

In 1783 peace has been declared. And Lark Benton is finally ready to wage a war for her own heart's desire.

Made in the USA
Las Vegas, NV
30 July 2022

52419733R00197